PRAISE FOR MARIA V. SNYDER

"Bestselling author Maria V. Snyder returns to the fantasy world of Ixia with an action-packed adventure filled with magic, danger, and romance. Fans of *Poison Study* will love revisiting the story from Valek's point of view and watching him navigate his conflicted feelings for Yelena and loyalty to the Commander."

— *NEW YORK TIMES* BESTSELLING AUTHOR
JENNIFER ESTEP

"Maria V. Snyder's books are full of magic, adventure and romance. They're impossible to put down!"

— LYNETTE NONI #1 BESTSELLING YA AUTHOR

"This is one of those rare books that will keep readers dreaming long after they've read it."

— *PUBLISHER'S WEEKLY*, STARRED REVIEW OF
POISON STUDY

"This is a book that's hard to put down."

— CHARLAINE HARRIS, *NEW YORK
TIMES* BESTSELLING AUTHOR ON *POISON STUDY*.

ALSO BY MARIA V. SNYDER

Discover more titles by Maria V. Snyder at www.MariaVSnyder.com

THE STUDY OF POISONS

MARIA V. SNYDER

The Study of Poisons / Maria V. Snyder

Cover design by Joy Kenney

Interior Art by Dema Harb

Maps by Martyna Kuklis

Published by Maria V. Snyder

Paperback ISBN 9781946381163

Hardcover ISBN 9781946381187

Digital ISBN 9781946381170

For Joy Kenney my cover designer and graphic artist extraordinaire. Thank you for creating beautiful covers for my stories and for responding to all my last-minute requests for emergency graphics.

In memory of my Uncle Joe and Uncle Louie, you'll both be missed. Also in memory of Trevar Jason McDonald, a lovely young man who left this world too soon to embark on a new adventure.

THE COMMANDER'S CASTLE COMPLEX
Designed by Martyna Kuklis

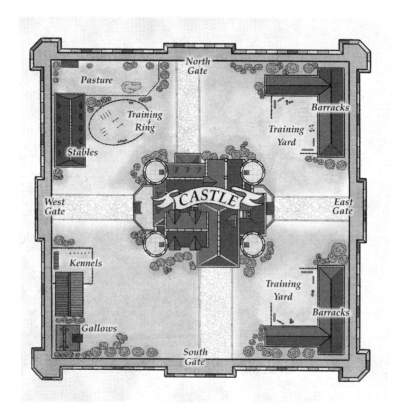

THE TERRITORY OF IXIA & THE CLANS OF SITIA
Designed by Martyna Kuklis

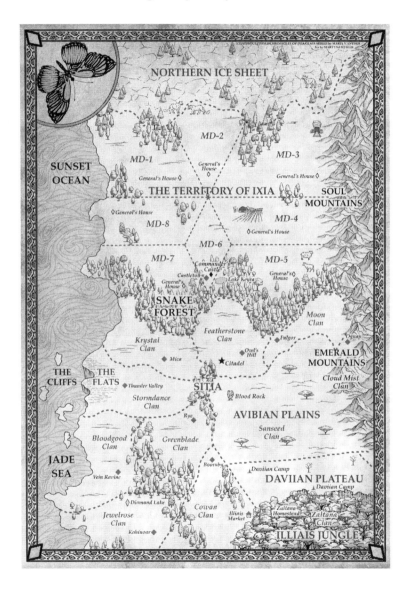

CHAPTER 1

*T*he body hit the floor with a loud thud. After a few more convulsions, the man died with a final breathy exhale. *Good riddance*, Valek thought.

Glancing up, the Commander put the file he'd been reading down. He sighed. "What was wrong with this one, Valek?"

"He'd grown sloppy and lazy. Did you see the way he shoved food into his mouth? He didn't even bother to sniff it. If he had, he would have smelled the poison." Valek stood from his seat in front of the Commander's desk and grabbed the tray. "I'll get you some fresh eggs."

"And you'll need to train a new food taster. In the meantime, you'll have to take over the dangerous job until the next taster is ready."

"It's only risky if you don't know what you're doing." Valek stepped over the body.

"Who is the next person in line for the job?" the Commander asked.

Valek paused. "The next person scheduled for execution is Yelena from MD-5."

"The one who murdered General Brazell's son?" The

1

Commander's voice held a weary indulgence. "You just can't leave her alone, can you?"

"There's more going on with her and I *need* to find out what it is."

"Brazell won't be happy."

"I don't care."

"Just make sure it doesn't affect my meetings with him. We've quite a bit of business to discuss."

"Yes, sir."

"And have someone dispose of Oscar's body."

"It's Oscove...or, it was." Thank fate. Valek had grown tired of the man's schemes.

"Just get it done."

"Yes, sir." Valek left the Commander's office and wove through the maze of desks and officers in the throne room. The actual throne had been dismantled and the gemstones and gold sold long ago. Valek's thoughts, however, remained on the prisoner who was going to be offered the choice between execution and becoming the Commander's new food taster.

Only two people had chosen the noose since the Commander had taken over the Territory of Ixia fifteen years ago. Both had been loyal to the assassinated King of Ixia and chose death over working for the Commander. The rest had hoped to escape and, when they learned it was impossible, turned corrupt or lazy or both. Oscove had been selling secrets to their enemies, which Valek, as the Commander's Chief of Security tolerated until the risks outweighed the benefits.

Valek brought the Commander a clean plate of eggs, then arranged for the removal of Oscove's body before sending an agent to fetch Yelena from death row. Returning to his office, he cleared the files off the extra chair and settled at his desk.

He glanced around the messy room. Piles of books littered the floor. More files, weapons, and maps covered the conference table. He'd accumulated too much stuff over the years—a far cry from when everything he owned fit into one backpack. Valek sighed, missing the simplicity of those days when he worked as an assassin for hire.

A breeze blew from the open window behind him, bringing his thoughts back to the present. Mid-morning sunlight streamed through the glass, warming his back—the one perk of wearing an all-black uniform. That would change in a few weeks, when it was the middle of the hot season, then wearing all black would be bloody hot.

Opening a dossier, he scanned the information on the prisoner. Yelena has been in the dungeon for almost a year. She was eighteen years old when she slit Reyad's throat with a knife, killing him. Valek noted that General Brazell's son had been found on the bed in his room, the sheets soaked with his blood. Yelena admitted to the murder but didn't say why she killed him. Not that it mattered why to the Commander. He didn't tolerate homicide from the citizens of Ixia. Self-defense, accidental, or pre-meditated—they all resulted in the same sentence. Death.

But it irked Valek. He wanted...no, he *needed* an explanation. She had been one of Brazell's orphans. Raised with others who had lost their parents, she was educated and doted on—if he believed the snide comments from the other Ixian generals. Why would she repay Brazell's kindness and generosity by murdering his son? Valek's agents had reported a few strange incidents at Brazell's manor house, indicating there might be something unusual going on with Reyad and perhaps Brazell as well. Valek planned to find out.

Before Yelena arrived, Valek decided to downplay his interests in the circumstances surrounding her incarceration; act as if he didn't care so long as she performed her job.

A light tap on his door announced the arrival of the two dungeon guards and the prisoner. They approached his desk. As Yelena scanned his office, Valek studied the sorry sight in front of him. Coated with muck, bleeding from various scrapes, wearing a tattered prison gown, the poor thing strained to remain upright under the weight of the chains. Her long black hair hung in greasy clumps and an acrid dungeon stench wafted off her, polluting the air. He hadn't expected her to be so... bedraggled and emaciated. She wouldn't survive the first poison-tasting test.

Valek met her green-eyed gaze. An icy calm stared back at him—almost as if challenging him. Interesting. Perhaps he'd been too hasty in his assessment.

"A woman? The next prisoner to be executed is a woman?" He used his most severe tone while pretending to be surprised.

She quivered and guilt panged in his chest over his harsh words. Softening his voice, he said, "I should have taken the time to reread your dossier." Valek discharged the guards with a wave. "You're dismissed." After they left, he motioned for Yelena to sit down on the chair before she fell over.

Her chains jangled when she perched on the edge.

He flipped open her file and feigned reading the information. He'd already memorized it. "Yelena, today may be your lucky day." Valek spotted a brief flare of anger before she bowed her head. She probably thought he referred to her impending execution. He had various reactions to that comment from the other food tasters. Most raged at him, thinking they had nothing left to lose. A couple picked up on the "may be" and allowed a glimmer of hope to show through.

"Well-behaved and respectful. You're starting to look like a good candidate," he said, trying to goad her into a response.

Still avoiding his gaze, she studied the items on his desk instead of reacting to his comment.

He switched tactics. "You've been tried and found guilty of murdering General Brazell's only son, Reyad." Valek paused and stroked his temple as if he'd just made a realization. "That explains why Brazell's here this week, and why he has been unusually interested in the execution schedule." One death row prisoner hanged each season—six souls a year.

Finally, the woman reacted, but not quite as expected. There was fear. However, her body stiffened in determination. Would she try to beg for her life?

"I suppose you're going to protest the conviction. Say you were framed, or you killed out of self-defense." Valek leaned back, waiting for her to plead her case.

"No, sir." Her voice rasped. "I killed him."

Completely surprised, he straightened. He didn't know whether to be impressed or disappointed that she didn't try to explain her actions. Either way, she'd managed to amaze him—something only a few people had ever done. Valek laughed. "This may work out better than I'd planned. Yelena, I'm offering you a choice. You can either be executed, or you can be Commander Ambrose's new food taster. His last taster died recently, and we need to fill the position."

Yelena stared at him in shock. "A fool would refuse the job."

"Well, it's a lifetime position. The training can be lethal. After all, how can you identify poisons in the Commander's food if you don't know what they taste like?" Valek paused and straightened the papers in the folder to let the information sink in and to give her time to ask questions. When she didn't reply, he continued, "You'll get a room in the castle to sleep, but most of the day you'll be with the Commander. No days off. No husband or children. Some prisoners have chosen execution instead. At least then they know exactly when they're going to die, rather than guessing if it's going to come with the next bite." He snapped his teeth together for effect.

Valek knew her thoughts were whirling by the way she trembled.

"Who tastes the Commander's food now?" she asked.

Interesting question. Was she still stunned or was she smarter than he'd thought? "I do. So, I'm anxious to find a replacement. Also, the Code of Behavior states that someone whose life is forfeit must be offered the job."

Yelena stood as if unable to keep still. She dragged the chains behind her as she explored his office. Valek wondered what she was thinking. He hoped she'd take the position.

When she stopped her inspection and faced him, he asked, "What shall I tell the executioner?"

"I am not a fool."

No, she wasn't. Not at all. Valek suppressed a grin. Getting to know her secrets was going to be quite the challenge. And there was nothing he loved more than a challenge.

CHAPTER 2

The first thing Valek needed to do was to ensure his new food taster didn't run away at her first opportunity. He strode to his office door and spoke to the two guards waiting in the hall.

"She's accepted the position. Gunner, go fetch Margg. Zook, please remove her chains," Valek said.

"Yes, sir," Zook and Gunner said in unison.

As the big man unlocked the manacles, Valek returned to his desk. He removed two goblets from his cabinet along with a small glass vial filled with White Fright. Pulling the stopper on the bottle, he poured four white drops into one goblet. Then he glanced at his new food taster. She was still reeling from her sudden change in fate and not paying attention to him. No surprise. A few minutes ago, she'd expected to die.

Valek understood the feeling. He'd been convinced his death was imminent on a number of occasions and the flood of relief after each near miss made his head spin. Giving her some time to settle her emotions, he set the vial on his desk and grabbed a carafe of peach juice, pouring the liquid into the goblets. Then he put the carafe of juice into his cabinet and locked it out of pure habit.

"While we're waiting for Margg, I thought maybe you could use a drink." Valek handed Yelena the goblet laced with White Fright. Raising his, he made a toast. "To Yelena, our newest food taster. May you last longer than your predecessor."

She stared at him in shock.

"Relax, it's a standard toast."

She took a swig and Valek waited. Was she going to throw it up? It was always risky giving a prisoner something other than water, but he had to mask the flavor of the White Fright.

When it appeared she would keep the liquid down, Valek proceeded to teach Yelena her first lesson in poison tasting. Most people thought it was a simple job, that tasters took a bite of food or sipped a drink and waited for the symptoms. Or for death. But assassins who used poison as a weapon knew there were ways around a lazy or stupid food taster, therefore, Valek trained the Commander's tasters so they learned the complex art.

He asked her to identify the ingredients in her drink.

"Peaches sweetened with honey," she said after taking a smaller sip.

"Good. Now take another sip. This time roll the liquid around your tongue before swallowing."

Her dirty face creased as she concentrated. "Orange?"

Erasing that questioning tone would come once she grew confident in her abilities. *If* she survived the tests. "That's right. Now gargle it."

"Gargle?"

Valek nodded. Every food taster he'd trained had asked the same thing with the same startled expression.

She gargled and just about choked on the liquid. "Rotten oranges!"

He laughed at her outraged and slightly indignant cry, happy that she succeeded. Some people just didn't have a suitable sense of taste and would never have picked up the White Fright. Valek handed her his goblet and asked her to repeat the experiment.

Yelena sipped the drink, then hesitated before she squared her shoulders and gargled. Her posture relaxed.

"Better?" He took the now empty cup from her.

"Yes."

He sat down and opened her file. Dipping his quill in ink, he noted her reactions and how quickly she detected the White Fright. However, he wasn't about to tell her what she'd ingested wasn't a poison.

Instead, he said, "You just had your first lesson in food tasting. Your drink was laced with a poison called Butterfly's Dust. Mine wasn't. The only way to detect Butterfly's Dust in a liquid is to gargle it. That rotten-orange flavor you tasted was the poison."

A brief memory of a bright yellow butterfly landing on his hand flashed in his mind. He'd been with his brother Vincent, and they had stared in wonder as the rare creature pulsed its wings. When it flew away, it left behind a light covering of pale-yellow dust on his palm. He'd thought it was an excellent name for a fake poison.

Yelena stood on shaky legs. "Is it lethal?"

"A big enough dose will kill you in two days. The symptoms don't arrive until the second day, but by then it's too late."

"Did I have a lethal dose?"

"Of course. Anything less and you wouldn't have tasted the poison." Valek studied her. Would she faint? Or vomit? Or scream obscenities at him? All three had happened in the past.

Except she did none of those things.

"I warned you the training would be dangerous. But I would hardly give you a poison your body had to fight while you suffered from malnutrition. There is an antidote to Butterfly's

Dust." He picked up the small vial of White Fright from his desk and showed it to her.

She swayed with relief and sank into the chair with a sigh.

"In answer to the question you didn't ask but should have, this—" Valek held up the vial and shook it "—is how we keep the Commander's food taster from escaping."

A little ridge of skin puckered between her dark eyebrows as she stared at him.

"Yelena, you confessed to murder. We would be fools to let you serve the Commander without some guarantees. Guards watch the Commander at all times, and it is doubtful you would be able to reach him with a weapon. For other forms of retaliation, we use Butterfly's Dust." He twirled the vial of White Fright in the sunlight. "You need a daily dose of this to stay alive. The antidote keeps the poison from killing you. As long as you show up each morning in my office, I will give you the antidote. Miss one morning and you'll be dead by the next. Commit a crime or an act of treason and you'll be sent back to the dungeon until the poison takes you. I would avoid that fate if I were you. The poison causes severe stomach cramps and uncontrollable vomiting."

Well, the White Fright would cause those symptoms if she missed a daily dose of it. If she believed the "antidote" would keep her alive, she wouldn't miss a single day. The ruse made his life easier.

As Yelena grappled with the information, the door to Valek's office opened. Margg, his and the Commander's housekeeper, entered. The stout woman would take the new food taster in hand and get her settled. He introduced her to Yelena. Margg shot him an irritated I'm-not-a-babysitter look. Valek ignored it. Margg was perpetually annoyed.

When Margg left, expecting Yelena to follow her, Yelena paused and glanced at the vial on his desk. Too late for questions now. Valek had a busy afternoon scheduled.

"Come to my office tomorrow morning. Margg will direct you."

After a slight hesitation, she followed Margg.

Valek mulled over the encounter. His newest food taster appeared to be intelligent and quick to learn. But would she be able to handle the pressure from multiple sources? The Commander was demanding and intimidating. Margg hated the rule that murderers could avoid the noose by becoming the food taster. And some of the guards agreed with Margg and harassed the taster whenever possible. Brazell would find out about her new position when he attended the execution and a different prisoner was led to the gallows. Would Brazell demand the Commander find another food taster?

Time would tell if Yelena would last more than a season. In the meantime, Valek had plenty of other problems to solve.

THAT AFTERNOON, various members of Valek's spy network, his corps, reported in. He had several operations running concurrently. The black market that sold smuggled goods from Sitia, the country south of Ixia, was almost impossible to stop. Shutting one market down just resulted in another popping up in a different location. It was a constant source of frustration.

And the generals who ruled the eight military districts of Ixia were another cause of exasperation. The eight men constantly bickered and plotted against each other as they tried to gain the Commander's favor. They all wanted to be named his successor. The Commander had already chosen his replacement, but the generals had no idea who it was, so they were ever hopeful that they would impress him enough that it would either reaffirm his decision about them or that he would change his mind.

As if, Valek snorted. The Commander rarely modified his

views. The man was almost as unyielding as the stones Valek carved into statues. Only after hours of grinding and polishing and chipping could Valek transform the dull gray rock into a beautiful black statue that glinted with silver. The same amount of effort was also required to sway the Commander's opinions. Except it didn't always work. And Valek only worked that hard on something worth the effort.

Then there were the Sitian spies sneaking into Ixia. They were harder to find as they used magic to hide. The use of magic was outlawed in Ixia, and it was up to Valek to hunt down the magicians and deal with them. Up to him because he was the only person in Ixia immune to magic.

By the time he finished listening to the reports of his corps, it was time for dinner. Valek hurried to the kitchens to pick up the Commander's meal. Acting as food taster added to his workload, but he was willing to skip a few hours of sleep to figure out the puzzle of Yelena and Brazell.

After getting the tray, he hustled to the Commander's office. The man hated tardiness. When Valek entered, the Commander was still behind his plain wooden desk as if he hadn't moved since this morning. At least Oscove's body had been taken away.

As he crossed the room, Valek noted how completely opposite it was to his own. For one thing, there was no clutter. Everything was neat and organized. Every item had a specific purpose. Nothing personal decorated the space. Well, nothing except the snow cat statue Valek had carved for him. The Commander had a fondness for snow cats.

"What are your thoughts on the new food taster?" the Commander asked as Valek set the tray on his desk.

"A year in the dungeon has taken a physical toll on her." He put a spoonful of the soup into his mouth and rolled it around his tongue before swallowing. Then he inspected and sniffed the beef before sipping the Commander's tea. Tastings had to be done in front of the Commander. The man was too smart to allow it to happen where he couldn't watch. Valek pushed the tray closer. "Your dinner is clean."

The Commander grunted. "Will she survive the tests?"

Valek settled into a chair as he considered. "At this point I'd give her a fifty percent chance."

"That's the same as saying you don't know."

True. "She's young and should be able to recover her strength. But she's small, so I'll have to be careful not to give her too much poison. If I go by the determination in her gaze, then I'd say she'll survive."

"She'll need more than determination."

Also true. Intelligence, quick thinking, and a stubborn will were equally essential.

Between bites of his meal, the Commander asked, "Learn anything interesting this afternoon?"

Valek updated him on what his corps had discovered. "There's another black market operation in Castletown. Sven says he'll have the location pinned down in the next couple of days."

"They are incorrigible. Do I need to start executing the leaders to stop the smuggling?" the Commander asked.

"I think that's too harsh. And it probably won't work. I'd rather put them out of business."

He paused with his spoon halfway to his lips. "How would you do that?"

"We're never going to be able to completely stop the smuggling or the sale of illegal Sitian goods. Instead, we should run them out of business by secretly setting up our own black market with cheaper prices. Eventually the others won't be able to compete."

"That'll be expensive."

"No, it won't. We don't have to bribe the border guards, local officials, or hire lookouts. In fact, we'll make a profit."

"What if they retaliate? Attack our people?" The

Commander loved to play devil's advocate.

Valek gave him a flat look. "My corps won't have any trouble defending themselves."

"But when we shut down our black market, the others will just re-open. Ixians seem to be willing to break the law for luxury goods." The Commander's tone was derisive.

The Commander abhorred decadence and folly and the extravagances of the wealthy. He believed in equality for all. Which was why, when he took control of Ixia, he required everyone in the territory to wear a uniform made of the same fabric. Each Military District was assigned a color to go with black. Valek rather liked the violet and black colors of MD-3's uniforms. Those living in the castle wore red and black—the Commander's colors. Each occupation had a slightly different uniform, so a person knew at a glance if they were talking to a cook or a medic.

"We don't shut down." Valek said. "It'll become a lucrative stream of income."

"I can't sanction that. I'd be breaking my own law."

"Then change the law. If the goods aren't illegal, we can tax them and not have to spend all this bloody time and money on arresting people and shutting them down."

"No. I don't want Sitians in my territory."

"They're already here. It's impossible to keep them out."

"Only a few and you find them quick enough."

"Not all Sitians are magicians. In fact, only a fraction—"

"No. I like the idea of setting up our own black market. But once you run everyone out of business, you'll shut it down."

Another temporary solution, but it could net some useful information. "Yes, sir."

"What else have you learned?"

"I've been keeping an eye on a woman named Star. She calls herself Captain Star and a few of my people are working under-cover in her organization."

"Aside from impersonating an officer, what has this woman done?"

"She's the leader of an information network. She buys and sells secrets, and she runs a gambling den. She also has a few undesirables working for her."

"Undesirables?"

"Assassins on retainer, muscles for hire, thieves, and blackmailers. Basically, she has a hand in every illegal activity in Castletown."

"Is she a threat to me?" the Commander asked.

"No. She's smart enough to keep her activities well away from the castle, but I expect she'll want to expand her operation and will become more dangerous with time."

"And you'll be able to tell when she goes from minor threat to major?"

"Yes. Right now, we're gathering a great deal of useful information and it's worth letting her continue."

"All right. Keep me informed of your progress."

"Yes, sir."

Dismissed, Valek returned to the kitchen for a quick bite before doing his rounds. Although he trusted the guards, he liked to check the security of the castle complex. He stopped in his office to strap on his sword and then headed outside.

The castle sat in the middle of a large square area surrounded by a high wall. There were four entrances, each named after the direction they faced. Valek would have preferred to permanently close the east and west gates to reduce the security risk, but he didn't want to trap those inside should an invading army break through one of the gates.

The sunlight glinted off the stained-glass windows of the four towers at each corner of the castle. It was the only attempt at symmetry in the structure's design. Other than the large rectangle that served as the castle's base, the rest was a haphazard stack of squares, triangles, cylinders, octagons, and he swore there was a rhombus in there somewhere along with a dodecagon. At least it made it easier for Valek to climb the walls. Mostly. Some of those strange angles were treacherous.

According to the history books, three hundred years ago a young prince had been overly fond of his toy blocks and had declared that, when he was king, he'd live in a castle built of colorful blocks and located as far away from the northern ice sheet as possible. Wasted money as far as Valek was concerned, but he had no love for the monarchy. Quite the opposite. His role in the Commander's takeover fifteen years ago had been to assassinate the King and his family.

After checking that all was well at the gates, Valek headed to the training yards to watch the Commander's soldiers. The yards sat in front of the L-shaped barracks that were tucked into the northeast and southeast corners of the complex.

He leaned on the wooden fence and scanned the soldiers. Valek recognized most of them, having sparred with many. The ones that wore green and black were from MD-5, General Brazell's district. The general had arrived with a full retinue of soldiers, advisers, and servants. Interesting how the Commander's people avoided interacting with Brazell's.

At this point in their careers, the Commander's soldiers were all well trained and didn't have a set training schedule, but most worked out each evening and morning to stay in shape and keep their fighting skills sharp. New recruits were sent to the other military districts for basic training. Only the best was assigned to the Commander's castle. And the best of the best was promoted to the Commander's elite unit. Of course, that led to a number of inflated egos. Valek grinned. He enjoyed deflating those egos.

A man spotted Valek and approached. "Fancy a challenge, sir?"

He wore the standard training uniform of a sleeveless tank top and short pants. Wiry and lean, the man sported a goatee and a smirk. A scar ran from his right temple and replaced the lower half of his right ear.

Valek straightened. "It depends."

"On what?"

"Whether or not *you* can offer me a challenge." His gaze slid to the man's companion—a big brute of a guy with short curly blond hair and enough muscles that it'd be difficult to fight the man hand to hand. "Perhaps your friend would prove to be more of a challenge."

"I think I've just been insulted!" The goateed man pressed a hand to his chest.

"You *were* insulted, Janco. Don't think. It's not one of your strengths," the big man said.

Janco shot his friend a glare, before he said to Valek, "In order to defend my honor, I, Lieutenant Janco, challenge you, sir."

"A *challenge* challenge?"

"Yes, sir."

Valek suppressed a sigh. The Commander had been bugging him for years to promote or hire someone as his second-in-command. To appease his boss, Valek had issued a challenge to everyone in Ixia. If any person could beat Valek in a fight, they would become his second. It seemed like a good idea at the time, and he did enjoy getting to know the strengths and weaknesses of the soldiers. But while it kept him in shape, there were times when it was damn inconvenient.

Unbuttoning the top of his adviser's uniform—an all-black shirt with two red diamonds stitched onto the collar—he laid it over the railing. The air had cooled, and it felt good against his bare shoulders. Janco stared at the C-shaped scar in the center of Valek's chest. It was a "gift" from the Commander sixteen years ago when Valek swore his loyalty to the man.

"Weapon?" he asked Janco.

"Swords, sir."

Well, then. This shouldn't take long. Valek pulled his broadsword from its scabbard and hopped over the fence.

He faced his opponent, who held a long, thin rapier. Interesting choice. The weapon certainly matched the physique of the man. At six feet tall, Valek was the same height as Janco, but Valek's build was more athletic than wiry.

The big man acted as referee. "Begin."

Janco moved like lightning, crossing the distance between them in a heartbeat. Valek sidestepped, blocking the thrust of Janco's rapier with the flat of his sword. And then again as Janco quickly parried. Perhaps Valek had been too hasty in thinking the fight wouldn't last long. Staying on the defensive as Janco continued to attack, Valek studied the man's technique. Quick and relentless, Janco knew how to maximize the advantages of his weapon.

The rapier was lighter and longer than a broadsword. And the dangerous part was its sharp tip, which Janco tried to get past Valek's defenses by lunging forward. After a few attempts, the tip slipped through and nicked Valek's torso, drawing first blood. Good thing the challenge ended when there was a clear winner.

"Blood runs even for the infamous. Too bad he now has a C minus," Janco sang as he increased the pace of his lunges.

"Do you have a death wish," Janco's friend hissed at him.

Valek suppressed a smile as he backed up, drawing Janco closer.

"He's on the retreat. Soon he'll be beat," Janco called.

He'd never had an opponent rhyme before. Valek almost wanted to keep fighting just to hear what else the man had to say. Almost. It was time to go on the offensive.

The broadsword was heavy and wide, but both of its edges were sharp. It was a cutting weapon and he had to swing it to strike. Effective for chopping off heads or lopping off arms, the broadsword wasn't the best choice of weapon in a friendly duel.

Or for an extended match—Janco's speedy thrusts kept sneaking past his blocks.

"He might be light on his feet, but soon he'll be tenderized meat," Janco sang.

That was enough. The next time Janco thrust forward, Valek twisted his shoulders and stepped forward. Janco's blade just missed, but Valek's didn't; the edge of his sword cut right through the rapier just before the hilt.

"He has a big mouth, but can he fight without?" Valek asked.

"That doesn't rhyme," Janco said.

Valek rested his blade on the man's shoulder. "Want to try that again?"

"Uh, it's close enough."

"Better. Do you concede?"

He glanced at the remaining stub of his blade and opened his mouth.

"Janco," warned the big man.

Janco closed his mouth, swallowed, and said, "Yes, sir."

"Good." Valek pushed his shoulder-length black hair out of his face. He wished he had a leather tie to keep the annoying ringlets out of his eyes, but he hadn't expected to spar today.

Their fight had drawn a crowd and before any others could issue challenges, Valek turned to the big man and said loud enough for everyone to hear, "I've time for one more match. You in?"

"Yes, sir."

"Your name?"

"Lieutenant Ardenus, sir."

"No one calls him that," Janco said. "Besides, do you know how hard it is to rhyme words with Ardenus while fighting? Almost—"

"Janco." Ardenus just about growled.

"What do people call you, then?" Valek asked.

"Ari, sir."

"All right, Ari. Weapon of choice?"

"Swords, sir."

Valek approved of Ari's broadsword. The question remained if all those muscles and his extra four inches of height would slow Ari down.

"Begin," Janco said.

Unlike his friend, Ari took a defensive stance, preferring to block and counter versus attacking right away. The answer soon became apparent that the man was also flexible and strong. Not as quick as Janco, but Valek doubted anyone was as fast as Janco.

And Ari was smart. Instead of wasting his breath singing out rhymes, he watched and waited for the perfect opportunity to strike.

When Ari went on the offensive, Valek's arm almost went numb from the clash of their swords. Another block knocked him to the ground. The crowd cheered. Valek rolled to his feet before Ari could press his advantage.

The match lengthened. Valek kept his distance and picked up the pace, hoping Ari would tire. He didn't. It was time for Valek to switch to a higher skill level. He liked to give the challenging soldiers a sense that they did well against him. But some people like Ari, were just too good for his more casual fighting style.

Valek drew on his years of experience and changed tactics. Instead of fighting straight on, he sidestepped and dodged. No longer blocking with his sword, he used his flexibility and speed to move in to strike and then dash out of Ari's reach by the time the man countered. Still, it took much longer to get past Ari's defenses than he'd expected.

Ducking under one of Ari's powerful swings, Valek dove to the ground, rolling into a somersault, and then hopped to his feet right behind the big man. In a flash, he tapped Ari's back with the tip of his sword.

"Concede?"

"Yes, sir," Ari said.

The crowd grumbled with disappointment and dispersed.

Valek pulled Ari aside. "Well done, you almost had me."

Sweat streamed down Ari's face, but he wasn't winded. "I don't believe that."

"No?"

"I think you could have ended that match a few moves after it started."

This confirmed Ari's intelligence. "Still, you have the skills. What's your current position?"

"Janco and I are scouts."

Valek's opinion of Ari rose another notch. Big muscular men normally didn't do well creeping through the forest. "You impressed me enough to earn an invitation to become a member of my intelligence network."

"You mean work as a spy?"

"Yes."

"What about Janco?"

"He's good, but not ready for my corps."

Ari's gaze slid to his friend. Janco was gesticulating wildly as he talked to another soldier.

"No, thank you," Ari said.

Ah, they were a package deal. Valek waited. Would Ari offer an explanation?

Ari grinned. "I'm going to train harder and challenge you again. Next time, I'll become your second, sir."

"And Janco?"

"Will be your third."

Valek laughed. "Good luck with that."

He considered the possibility as the big man joined his friend. If Ari and Janco teamed up to fight Valek together, they had a good chance of winning. The combination of Ari's strength and Janco's speed would be very difficult to counter. They'd be a powerful opponent.

They reminded him of his older twin brothers, Victor and Viliam. When they were together there was no stopping them. Ari and Janco might not be brothers, but they had a deep connection. They were power twins. Valek chuckled. Liking the idea of them challenging him together, he decided to aid in their training and assign them to a better unit. Perhaps Parffet's. The captain might have a temper, but the man knew how to train his soldiers.

AFTER HE COOLED DOWN, Valek continued his rounds, looping around the west side of the castle. Since it was close to the beginning of the hot season, the sun set much later. At this time, it hung low, staining the sky pink.

A few horses grazed in the pasture located in the northwest corner of the complex. Their stable was along part of the western wall. The Commander's kennel was also along the wall but further south. The dogs ran out to greet him and he spent a few minutes petting them. They had been very effective in hunting down fugitives and Valek appreciated their help.

When a familiar, yet invisible, sensation brushed his arm, all the dogs raced back to the kennel. Valek met the kennel master's gaze. Did Porter not know Valek could sense when magic was in use? Porter looked away and tended to his charges. Perhaps the kennel master was unaware he was using magic while working with the dogs.

Valek had been on the fence about what to do with the man, who had also worked for the King. Technically he was a magician and, according to the Commander's strict Code of Behavior, he should be executed. Valek kept a close eye on him, but, so far, there was no evidence that he was anything other than a loyal and hardworking man.

A scraping noise cut through the evening air. Valek turned in time to see a set of shutters in the castle open wide. Curious, he stepped into the shadows of the kennel and watched. The window was along the building's rectangular base.

Yelena blocked the sunlight from her eyes as she gazed outside. Valek waited. Typical of Margg to give her a room on the ground floor. She probably hoped Yelena would jump down and run away.

And if she did? Valek would intercept her. She wasn't getting away until she revealed her secrets. When she disappeared inside and closed the shutters, a slight pang of disappointment echoed in his chest, surprising him. Had he been looking forward to the chase? Or to chasing *her*?

CHAPTER 3

*V*alek was awake well before dawn. He needed to clear a space in his office. A task he could have assigned to Margg, but there was a system to his seemingly disheveled piles of files. One that allowed him to find information quickly. Also, one that confused others.

He relocated the various items on his conference table to make an area where he could train Yelena. Right before the sun came up, he went to taste the Commander's breakfast, fetched the supplies he needed for the day's lesson, and returned to his office.

The door opened as he was arranging the food, and he gestured for Yelena to take a seat. Plucking a piece of bacon, he turned his attention to her.

"I hope you're…" Valek's heart squeezed hard—one painful contraction. While bruises and the circles under her eyes remained, the grime and grease had been washed from her face and hair. She was beautiful. Unflinching, she stared back.

"It's amazing what a difference a bath and a uniform can make." Valek feigned disinterest as he chewed the bacon. "I'll have to remember that. It might be useful in the future." He placed two ham omelets in front of her. "Let's get started."

"I'd rather start with the antidote," she said. Her words rushed together as if she couldn't get them out fast enough.

He considered the timing of her last dose. "You shouldn't be feeling any symptoms. They won't arrive until later this afternoon." Still, the mind had a way of overruling the body and she appeared to be worried. He shrugged and unlocked his cabinet of poisons to extract a pipette full of White Fright.

Yelena watched him closely, so after locking the cabinet, he used a slight-of-hand trick he learned to make the key disappear. Valek gave the pipette to her before he settled on the opposite side of the table.

"Drink up so we can start today's lesson."

She squeezed the liquid into her mouth and cringed. White Fright's bitterness made it hard to conceal.

He took the pipette and handed her a blue jar. "Take a sniff."

She held the jar under her nose and inhaled, closing her eyes briefly as if committing the scent to memory. When she glanced at him, he gestured to the food and asked her to find the omelet laced with the poison.

He kept a tight hold on his neutral expression as she sniffed each plate. Finally, she pointed to the correct one.

"Good. Should you pick up that aroma from any of the Commander's food, reject it. The poison is called Tigtus and a single grain of the powder will kill within the hour." Or in Oscove's case, ten grains of the powder had killed him in five minutes. Valek removed the tainted food. "Eat your breakfast." Pointing to the remaining plate, he said, "You'll need your strength."

After she devoured the food, Valek waited to ensure her stomach wouldn't rebel before he had her sniff a number of poisons whose scents were hard to mask. When she put her head in her hands and asked for some paper and writing implements, he realized he'd overwhelmed her with too many. He should have known better.

While angry at himself, her request reminded Valek about how she repaid the kindness Brazell had shown her. He shouldn't forget she was a murderer.

"I don't know why you continue to surprise me. I should have remembered that General Brazell educates his orphans." He found a book, quill, and ink and tossed them in front of her. "Take them back to your room. We've done enough for today."

And he might have to repeat everything because of his mistake. He noticed she was lingering at the threshold. "Now what?"

"I'm not sure where my room is."

He certainly didn't have time to escort her. "Ask the first housekeeper or kitchen maid you find; they're always scurrying about this time of day. Tell them you're in the west servant wing, ground floor. They'll show you."

LATER THAT DAY, Valek was interrupted when Margg arrived to clean his office. She scowled at the mess, but before she could wield her dust mop like a weapon and force Valek to retreat to another room, he called her over to his desk.

Margg wore a housekeeper's uniform which consisted of a long black skirt and black shirt. Her white apron sported two vertical lines of red diamonds and covered her from neck to floor. It was pristine as always and cinched at her wide waist. Everything about Margg was wide and she was a force to be reckoned with. She was also trustworthy and had been loyal to the Commander well before the takeover.

She scowled at him but stood in front of his desk as requested.

"I've a new job for you," he said.

"More babysitting the new rat?"

"Be nice. Yelena might save the Commander's life someday."

Margg harrumphed. "She's more likely to endanger it."

"You say that about all the food tasters."

"Because they're all murderers," she spat. "I've told the Commander a dozen times to change that rule. But he ignores me." Her tone was outraged.

Valek suppressed a smile. Margg could have had any job after the takeover—adviser, spy, general, assistant cook—but she insisted on being the Commander and Valek's personal housekeeper, because she didn't trust anyone else to take care of them the right way. It was like having a very grumpy mother around.

"What's the job?" she asked.

"With Oscove dead, Star is going to be searching for another source of information in the castle. I want you to be that leak."

"Me? I'd never sell secrets!"

"I know, but Star doesn't. And because you're so close to me and the Commander, she will consider you a gift from the sky."

"Or sent to spy on her," Margg said. "I'm well known to be loyal."

"And well known to be disgruntled."

Another harrumph, proving his point. "It's 'cause you boys are always in some sort of danger."

Boys. Valek almost laughed. He was thirty-three years old, and Ambrose was forty.

"And you don't listen to me," she added.

"Then you should have become an adviser and not a housekeeper."

"Not this again." She waved her dust mop at him. "I don't want my advice to backfire, and someone ends up getting killed because of me."

"This should be an easy job for you," Valek said. "You just let the other servants know you're unhappy. That the Commander doesn't pay you enough. Eventually, someone will approach you and ask if you'd like to earn more money."

"But I'm not—"

Valek held up a hand. "You say yes, and I will supply you with the information to sell. Most of it will be accurate, but not that critical. And some of it will be disinformation."

"What if they find out I'm a spy?"

"I've a few others in Star's organization that will alert me if Star is starting to suspect you. In that case, you stop. I won't endanger you."

"If you have others, then why me?"

"They're not in your position. And some aren't supposed to have any connection to the castle. Using them would be too suspicious."

"And the money I earn from selling secrets?"

"Keep it, you've earned it."

"It's dirty money!"

There was no pleasing the woman. "Then give it to me. I'll use it in another operation that catches criminals."

"Well…it's better than babysitting rats." She caught Valek's expression before he could hide it. "You're still going to ask me to do that too, aren't you?"

"Only because I trust you."

Now she pished. "Fine, I'll be your leak. But make sure the Commander knows what I'm doing."

"I will," he promised. "Let me know when you're approached, and we'll figure out what juicy bits of information to sell them."

She grunted in agreement and proceeded to dust and tsk over the state of his office.

◆

OVER THE NEXT TWO WEEKS, Valek trained Yelena in the mornings. He noted her improved health with pleasure as the gauntness dropped from her small frame. Only about five feet four inches tall, she still appeared as if a stiff breeze could knock her over. He had slowed the training schedule to allow her to be fully recovered from her time in the dungeon before starting on the actual tasting the poisons. However, he ensured she learned the five S-steps of food tasting—scan, sniff, sample, stir, sip—that would improve her chances of surviving.

Waiting wasn't something he had done with the others. Was it due to his curiosity about her past, or her quick intelligence, or because of her beautiful tan skin and emerald-green eyes?

He jerked his thoughts from that dangerous speculation. She was fourteen years younger than him. And besides, his loyalty remained with the Commander. No other.

When the Commander reminded him about the execution scheduled for day fifteen of the hot season, Valek decided he would start training Yelena's palate the day before the execution. The first poison should knock her out for a couple days so she wouldn't have to witness the hanging. She also wouldn't accidentally encounter any of General Brazell's people before Valek had a chance to examine Brazell's state of mind over her reprieve.

On the morning of their fourteenth day of training, Yelena arrived with the sun, and he told her it was time to taste poisons.

"I'll start with the deadliest one," he said. "If you don't die from it, the other poisons wouldn't kill you either. I don't want to waste all my time training you only to see you die in the end." He kept his tone neutral, as if her dying would inconvenience him. However, a buzz of anxiety thrummed under his skin as he placed a slender red bottle on his desk.

"It's nasty. Affects the body immediately." It was one of his favorites. "It's called Have a Drink, My Love, or My Love for short because the poison has a history of being used by disheartened wives." He used a pipette to squeeze two drops into a cup of tea. Yelena liked tea and it would dilute the poison a bit. Valek worried that two drops might be too strong for her. "A larger dose would kill you. With a smaller dose, there is a chance you'll survive, but you'll become delusional, paranoid, and completely disoriented for the next few days."

"Valek, why do I have to taste My Love if it has immediate results? Isn't that what a food taster is for? I taste the Commander's food. I keel over, dead. End of the tale." Yelena paced the room. Well, she tried. The number of obstacles must have frustrated her. She kicked over a couple stacks of his books.

He'd thought she would have figured out the reasons for the training on her own during the last two weeks. "A food taster's job is much more complex than that," Valek explained. His hair swung into his face, and he yanked it back in annoyance. It really needed to be cut. "Being able to identify which poison taints the Commander's food can lead me to the poisoner." He handed her the cup of tea. "Even if you only have a split second to shout out 'My Love' before passing out, it will narrow down the list of suspects. There are several assassins who are partial to My Love. The poison is grown in Sitia, the southern lands. It was easy to obtain before the takeover. With the closure of the southern border, only a handful of people have enough money to purchase it illegally."

Valek couldn't resist fixing the knocked over books. "Yelena, your job is very important. That's why I spend so much time training you. A shrewd assassin can watch a taster for several days to discover a pattern." He moved onto the other fallen pile. "For example, the taster might always cut a piece of meat from the left side, or never stir the drink. Some poisons sink to the bottom of the cup. If the taster only sips off the top, then the assassin knows exactly where to place the poison to kill his intended victim." There. Except now, his other piles looked sloppy, and he really should clear a bigger path through his office.

He continued his lecture as he straightened piles. "Once you drink the poison, Margg will help you to your room and take care of you. I'll give her your daily dose of Butterfly's Dust antidote."

Margg entered the office and Valek turned toward Yelena. She stood holding the cup, staring blankly. Valek held his breath. If she refused to drink the poison, he'd have to find a new food taster. And right now, that was the last thing he wanted to do.

Yelena raised the cup in a mock-salute and downed the contents in one gulp. There was no need to perform the S-steps for this test. "Sour apples," she said.

He nodded. She placed the cup on the table and swayed. Valek was next to her in a flash, grabbing her before she tipped over. He lifted her into his arms. She weighed almost nothing.

"Let me have her," Margg said.

"I'll carry her back to her room." He held her closer.

"No, you won't." Margg stared at him. "Do you really want people to see you carrying an unconscious woman?" When he didn't respond, she said, "They're already scared of you. No need to add fuel to the fire."

He really didn't care that most of the castle's citizens were terrified of him. In fact, he encouraged that reputation, but he didn't want anyone to think he cared for the food taster. Because he didn't—tasters never lasted long. Plus, one of his many enemies might think he did and try to use her against him, which would be very tiresome.

Sensing his agreement, Margg reached for Yelena. She moaned and muttered about sprouting flowers and eye sockets. When Margg settled her in her arms, Yelena tried to push her away, but Margg tightened her grip.

"Are you sure you can carry her all the way?" he asked.

"She weighs less than a full chamber pot. I'll take care of her."

Valek opened the door for Margg and watched as she headed to the west side of the castle with her quick, efficient stride. There was nothing Valek could do at this point but wait. Yelena would either survive the poison or not. Her fate was out of his hands. And oh, how he hated that.

HE SPENT the rest of the day preparing for the execution. The gallows needed to be erected. The prisoner needed to be allowed to wash, have a final meal, and sleep in a comfortable bed. Valek arranged for the carpenters to assemble the platform. All the necessary wood and equipment had been stacked in the southwest corner of the castle complex, where the execution would take place.

The Commander wouldn't allow the gallows to remain in place between executions. He'd called it "bully tactics" that were used by weak rulers to instill fear in their people. "Besides, it ceases to be a threat when it becomes part of the background of everyday life," the Commander had said.

Valek re-read the dossier on the man due to be hung. In his mid-thirties and with a history of violence, Horus escalated to murder when he killed his brother, his brother's wife, and his own wife. The brother and wife had tried to stop Horus from killing his wife, but only managed to enrage him further. In this case, Valek agreed with the punishment. There was no redeeming this man and it was a waste of tax money to feed, clothe, and care for him until he died of natural causes. For other cases, he didn't quite agree with the Commander.

Accidents happened. If there wasn't any negligence or ill intent, it was just unfortunate. And a clear case of kill-or-be-killed self-defense was a legitimate reason for death. But the Commander didn't view it that way. He believed accidents could be avoided with enough foresight and a person could defend themselves without resorting to murder.

Valek pulled the files for the next two prisoners on the execution list. Serra was scheduled to be hung during the cooling season. She'd poisoned her husband. Crimes of passion were common. Valek wondered if Yelena had been Reyad's lover before she slit his throat. It would explain why she'd been in his bed. No. Not a lover. Perhaps he tried to rape her, and she defended herself? That would be justified. However, all this speculation was a waste of time. There had to be something else going on with Reyad and he fully intended to uncover the truth.

The prisoner listed for the cold season's execution was named Tentil. He'd killed his three-year-old son with a plow. An accident. Well, that wouldn't do. Good thing Valek had a few months to fix it.

EARLY MORNING SUNLIGHT lit the noose with a rose-colored glow. Random barks from the nearby kennel punctuated the silence and the earthy smell of horses scented the light northerly breeze. Valek stood at the base of the ramp that led up to the platform. Only a handful of people had assembled to witness the execution. The Commander insisted that the hangings not become a spectacle. The victim's families had been invited along with the prisoner's. Horus's parents were in attendance. Living with the nightmare of one son killing the other, they hunched as if shouldering a great weight. Their haggard appearance and lined faces showed their devastation.

General Brazell and his adviser also attended. The general eyed the small group. His sour expression showed no hint of surprise. Short and stocky with graying hair, Brazell leaned closer to his adviser and whispered to him. Adviser Mogkan tipped his head and replied. His words were too low for Valek to discern. Instead, Valek studied Mogkan.

The tall man had pulled his long black hair into a single braid. He wore the standard adviser's uniform, identical to Valek's except the diamond shapes stitched on his collar were green. Mogkan's skin tone was darker than Yelena's, hinting at Sitian blood. But that could be said for most of the citizens living in Military Districts 5, 6, and 7, which were along the Sitian border. Before the takeover, people from both countries used to freely cross, and marriages between Sitians and Ixians had been a normal part of life.

What interested Valek was the fact Brazell hadn't brought Adviser Mogkan to the castle before. New? Or newly promoted? Mogkan's stiff posture also merited scrutiny. He stood with his arms crossed tightly in front of his chest as if trying to hold back his emotions. But which one was he suppressing? Anger? Disgust? Fear?

When Horus was led toward the gallows, Valek's gaze switched to Brazell. The general pressed his lips together and nodded, confirming what Valek suspected. Brazell had found out that Yelena was training to be the new food taster. Now the question remained, would he take advantage of Valek's absence from the castle and her unconscious state and send an assassin? Or would he wait until his business with the Commander was finished? Another possibility occurred to him. Brazell could wait until he returned home. Could wait for months. Revenge had no timeline.

CHAPTER 4

*V*alek considered the risks to Yelena and decided she wasn't in immediate danger. Yet the desire to abandon his post to check on her pulsed in his heart. And the fact he even *considered* leaving worried him. She presented a puzzle and he had spent the last two weeks training her. They had worked well together. She'd asked him intelligent questions and been quick and eager to learn. A refreshing break from the sullen, grudging, and morose temperaments of the other tasters. However, he was smart enough not to get emotionally invested in a food taster.

When Horus reached the platform, the guards removed the manacles around his wrists. The prisoner wore a plain jumpsuit. His craggy face was clean shaven, and his dark brown hair had recently been cut. His feet were bare.

The man rubbed his raw wrists and glanced around.

"Feel free to run. My archers need the practice," Valek said. Not one, but three archers stood on the wall. Their arrows were already notched and ready to fly. The man had a choice between being hanged or skewered with an arrow to the heart.

Horus glared but remained in place. *Smart.*

Valek swept his hand out, indicating the assembled people. "This is your final opportunity to apologize to your family and your victims' families for your actions."

The prisoner faced them. "I'm not sorry."

That makes my job easier. Valek held up a hand, stopping the vitriol Horus's comment produced. Grabbing the man's arm, Valek led him up the ramp to where the Commander waited.

"Horus, you have murdered three people and have been sentenced by me to death by hanging," the Commander said in formal tones.

Valek grabbed the noose and put it around Horus's neck. He braced for resistance, but the man didn't fight and even stepped of his own volition onto the trap door.

"Still not sorry," Horus yelled.

Valek adjusted the knot and tightened the noose, then stepped back. The Commander grabbed the lever. Without preamble, he pulled it. The door dropped open and Horus plunged through. A loud crack sounded just as the rope snapped taut. The dogs in the kennel howled. Porter leaned against the wall, watching the hanging.

Horus's belligerent expression no longer remained on his dead face. A dark stain spread down his legs. To avoid the noxious odor, Valek held his breath as he followed the Commander to the ground.

Valek called for a clean-up crew and gave the carpenters permission to disassemble the gallows. The Commander talked with the family members. Valek scanned the area. Brazell and Mogkan were gone.

Without thought, Valek dashed to the castle, heading straight to Yelena's room. By the time he'd reached the west servant wing, he expected to encounter Brazell's soldiers or Adviser Mogkan with a bloody knife in his hand. Instead, Margg closed Yelena's door behind her as she stepped into the hallway.

"What's wrong?" she asked.

"How's Yelena?" He tightened his grip on the hilt of his sword.

"Still alive." Margg sounded disappointed. "Why do you care?"

"I don't."

Margg waited.

"That's none of your concern." Valek pulled in a calming breath. "Have you seen any of General Brazell's soldiers in this area of the castle?"

"Ah. The old goat knows she's free and you're worried he might be looking for revenge. I'd say it's justified."

"It's not up to you," Valek said in his dangerously flat tone. "The Commander decides. Not anyone else. If he changes his mind, then *he* will pull the lever. Understand?"

She clenched fistfuls of her apron in her hands. Valek had never scolded her before, but her comment about Yelena's death being justified went beyond mere grumpiness.

"Yes." It was almost a growl. Almost.

"And Brazell's people?" he asked.

"I haven't seen anyone."

The pressure in his chest eased.

"Do you really think that old goat would risk upsetting the Commander by killing her before his project is approved?" she asked.

No, he didn't. So why did he... Panic? Yelena was safe. For now.

"Keep a close eye on her," he said. "Let me know if you see any of the old goat's people sniffing around."

"Will do."

As Valek headed to his office, he considered his panicked race to Yelena's room. He blamed his overreaction on the execution. They always set him on edge.

Sven waited for him outside his door. Valek unlocked it and led him to his desk.

"Whiskey?" Valek offered, hoping Sven would give him a reason to have a drink.

"No thanks," Sven said as he settled into the chair opposite.

Sven had dyed his short hair gray and added wrinkles to his face in order to appear to be a man in his late fifties. The shop-keeper's uniform was a nice touch.

"Have you received all your inventory?" Valek asked.

"The last shipment is due tomorrow." Sven laughed. "I found out it's much cheaper to purchase illegal goods on the Sitian side of the border because the risky part, which causes higher prices, is getting them *into* Ixia. Once we open for business, the other black market dealers are not going to know what hit them."

"What about your staff?"

"Hired a bunch of local kids."

"Kids?"

Sven waved a hand. "Young twenty-somethings. Anyone under thirty looks like a kid to me."

"Is using locals wise?"

"Yeah. They're known to the people in town and to the other sellers. And they don't know they're working for us. They think I'm a legitimate illegitimate."

Still. "What do you need them for?"

"I can't advertise that I'm open for business. Those kids are known as 'baiters' and they find customers and bring them to me. Eventually, word will spread, and they'll go from selling to keeping an eye on the authorities. It's also nice to have young backs to lift and move heavy crates." He smoothed his hair. "I have to maintain my cover as an older gentleman recently arrived from MD-4. I'll say it's to take advantage of the warmer weather, but everyone will suspect it's because the authorities were nipping at my heels."

"What happens when you start getting heat from the other dealers? Will the baiters be in harm's way?"

"I've a few of our people on staff for security. They'll handle the heat. As for the kids, they're safe. There's a big group of them and they all work for the various dealers. They all know each other and change bosses multiple times. They're paid by their abilities. Those who can bring in the most customers will fetch the highest prices." Sven chuckled. "I enticed the best of the best away from his current employer by offering to double his fee."

"Who's the best?"

"Kid named Trevar. Good-looking, personable, can charm the most law-abiding citizen into buying illegal goods."

"Is he worth recruiting to the corps?"

"Might be. I'm keeping an eye on him. I'll let you know."

"Good. When are you opening for business?"

"In two days."

"Excellent. Keep me updated."

"You got it." Sven stood and left.

Pleased that the black market op was in good hands, Valek focused on his other major operation. Star. No one had approached Margg yet. Perhaps Star was smarter than he thought and suspected Margg would be working as a double agent. Maybe the castle's gossip network wasn't as efficient as he'd thought. Except, Brazell had found out about Yelena.

It wasn't a secret, and Yelena had been traveling through the castle wearing a food taster's uniform. The servants were bound to notice and talk. If she survived the poison, he'd assign one of his undercover spies to guard her.

If she survived the poison. One day of unconsciousness turned into two and, by the morning of the third day, he dreaded Margg coming to deliver the bad news about his new food taster. *Bad news? Come on, Valek. She's fourteen years younger than you and she's the food taster. A job basically forced upon her. What kind of relationship would come from that? Not a good one.*

～

WEAK MORNING SUNLIGHT brightened his office, signaling sunrise. Not wanting to be late to taste the Commander's breakfast, Valek hurried from his office and almost ran into Yelena.

"Yelena! You made it." Valek smiled, genuinely happy to see her. She appeared healthy with no visible signs of any lingering effects of My Love. "It's been three days. I was beginning to worry." He glanced behind her. "Where's Margg?"

"I haven't seen her."

Odd. "Then you'll need your antidote." Valek returned to his office and filled a pipette with White Fright. Once she drank it, he headed out, but she didn't follow. He gestured for her to come along. Now that she had recovered, she needed to continue her training. "I have to taste the Commander's breakfast." He set a quick pace. "It's time you meet the Commander and watch how food tasting should be done."

Valek led her through the main hallways of the castle. He usually avoided this route, but Yelena needed to see what the Commander had done when he'd taken over Ixia. As they traveled, Valek stole glances at Yelena's expression.

She gawked at the ruined tapestries from the King's era. They remained in their original places despite their soiled and torn appearances. It was a sign to all that the Commander abhorred opulence and wasting money on frivolous things like tapestries. He'd rather the money was spent to aid his people.

When they reached the broken doors that had once barred the entrance into the throne room but now gaped open, Yelena slowed. The impressive archway remained with its beautiful stonework, but the intricately carved wooden doors had been splintered by axes and now hung crookedly on their hinges. They remained in place to remind Ixians that once they had been prevented from having an audience with the King. Now, anyone in Ixia could schedule an audience with the Commander as long as they followed the proper procedures.

Once they crossed the threshold into the throne room, Yelena stopped in surprise. Valek suppressed a chuckle. The jumble of desks and loud buzz of activity that occupied the once grand throne room was overwhelming. The Commander had wanted his advisers and military officers nearby and clearly visible to all. His office was tucked into the back corner. Valek hurried through the maze, leaving Yelena behind. He was already late, and she'd find her way.

The Commander looked up when he entered. "You're late."

"Couldn't be helped. Our new food taster survived My Love and I needed to give her the antidote."

"Survived fully? Or just barely hanging on like that other taster? What's his name? Took him a season to finally die. Poor bastard."

"She appears healthy. I don't know if she'll have nightmares caused by the side effects of the poison or not. Time will tell." And, depending on what happened with Reyad, she might already be experiencing them.

"Make sure she's one hundred percent, Valek. I don't like eating cold sweet cakes."

Valek spotted Yelena hovering on the threshold of the Commander's office. He didn't blame her for hesitating to enter. The man sitting behind the desk held her life in his hands.

"Commander, this is Yelena, your new food taster," Valek said, grabbing her wrist and leading her into the room.

The Commander studied her, focusing all his attention on her. Her stricken expression resembled a rat caught in the jaws of a trap.

He glanced at Valek. "From what Brazell's been hollering about, I expected her to breathe fire."

She stiffened.

"Brazell's a fool," Valek said as he visually assessed the tray of food for foreign objects. "He wanted the drama of a public hanging for his son's killer. I personally would have taken care of her immediately. It would have been within his rights." Valek sipped some tea and sniffed the sweet cakes, seeking odd odors. "Besides, it's clearly written in the Code of Behavior that the next to be hanged gets the job offer. And Brazell was one of the authors." Cutting a piece of one sweet cake from the center and the other from the side, Valek put both pieces in his mouth, chewing slowly. No strange tastes flavored the food. "Here." He handed the plate to the Commander.

"Brazell does have a point," the Commander said. He picked up his tea and stared at the contents. "When does she start? I'm getting tired of cold food."

"A few more days."

"Good," the Commander said to Valek, then turned to Yelena. "You arrive with my food and taste quick. I don't want to be looking for you. Understand?"

"Yes, sir."

"Valek, I'm losing weight because of you. Lunch is in the war room. Don't be late."

"Yes, sir." Dismissed, Valek headed for the door with Yelena right on his heels.

She didn't say a word as they returned to his office, but she lagged whenever he increased his pace. They entered the room and he suppressed a sigh. Margg was dusting, or rather attempting to dust, his stacks of files and books on the table. He wished she wouldn't bother, but he was grateful when she replaced his burnt candles for new ones.

Valek settled behind his desk and studied the food taster. "Yelena, you look exhausted. You make me tired just looking at you. Go rest. Come back after lunch and we'll continue with your training."

She opened her mouth, paused, and nodded before leaving.

Valek waited a few more minutes before asking Margg why Yelena didn't see her this morning.

"Oh, she was up and gone before sunrise," Margg said, waving her feather duster. "I checked the baths just in case she needed help, but when I didn't find her, I figured she'd find her way here."

There was something not quite honest in her reply. Before Valek could question her further, she said, "I've news."

"Oh?"

"I've been approached by Rand. He said that he knows someone who will pay me for information if I am interested."

Rand was the Commander's chief chef. Valek had suspected the man was working with Star. He was both glad and disappointed to learn he had been correct. "And your reply?"

"I grumped at him for even suggesting such a thing. He shrugged and reminded me about my 'caterwauling' over being denied a raise. I countered that I was trying to save for my retirement." Margg huffed. "He made a disparaging remark about how everyone would happily donate to my retirement fund." Another huff of indignation. "I resentfully told him I'd think about it. I thought if I was too eager, he'd suspect."

Smart. "When are you going to agree?"

"In a couple days." She stabbed the duster at the door. "After the news has spread that the rat has survived, and I'm supposed to keep an eye on her. With no additional compensation for the extra work I have to do, it will be the tipping point in my disgruntlement."

A fine plan. Too fine? He knew she held a grudge against the food tasters, but it seemed Yelena irked her more than the others. Or was she really upset about her pay? Only advisers earned more money than Margg. And she'd claimed she wouldn't keep Star's bribes because it was dirty. However, she just demonstrated a sharp mind and a fair bit of acting skills.

Valek suppressed his doubts. The Commander trusted Margg, that was enough for him.

~

VALEK SPENT the rest of the morning reading through the old reports from MD-5. He had assigned spies to every Military District and, if anything strange or unusual happened, they sent him an update. Encrypted, of course, which meant extra time to decipher them. There were two assigned to Brazell's manor house and he'd hoped to find more information on Adviser Mogkan from one of their reports.

Halfway through a boring account of a budget meeting, Valek realized it was time for lunch. If he didn't hurry, he'd be late again. Striding from his office, he raced through the servant's corridors. His thoughts focused on the need to send a request to his spies to discover Mogkan's history.

Yelena suddenly appeared around the corner. Her attention was focused over her shoulder, so she bumped right into him. Her long black hair had sprung from her braid. Cobwebs clung to the strands. Disheveled, dirty, and wild-eyed, she panted for breath as if she'd just run a mile.

"Yelena! What happened to you?" Alarmed, he grabbed her arm to steady her.

She winced in pain, and he immediately let go, noticing the blood-stained tear on her sleeve and the lacerations on her hands.

"I…fell…on some glass."

Fell? Not bloody likely. He waited.

"I'm on my way to get cleaned up." She tried to step past him.

Oh, no you don't. He grasped her shoulder and spun her around. "You need to see a medic."

"Ah…okay." She tried again to slip by him.

"The medic is this way." Valek kept his hand on her shoulder, guiding her back in the direction she had obviously run from. Once they turned the corner, Valek spotted her pursuers. Two of Brazell's guards argued in the middle of the corridor. He cursed under his breath. He should have assigned one of his corps to keep her safe right away.

Valek ignored the men, hoping they'd follow him to a deserted part of the castle. The two guards fell into step behind them. Valek squeezed Yelena's shoulder, silently signaling her not to worry.

When the hallway emptied of people, Valek released his grip and swung around to face Brazell's goons. Yelena wisely moved in closer to him.

"Are you lost?" Valek asked them.

"No, sir," said the goon on the left. He was about a foot taller and much wider than Valek. Armed with a short sword and a knife, the goon eyed Valek.

"Just want to reclaim our prisoner." The goon tried to grab Yelena.

Valek blocked his meaty hand. "*Your* prisoner?" His cold tone held a warning.

The guards glanced at each other before they smirked at him. "Actually, General Brazell's prisoner, sir. Now, if you would..." The goon gestured for Valek to step aside.

They obviously didn't recognize him. "Tell your boss that *Valek* doesn't appreciate having his new food taster chased through the castle. And that I would like her to be left alone."

The guards exchanged another look. Valek suppressed a sigh. *What's the point of having a fearsome reputation if it doesn't work?* Granted, he wore the standard adviser's uniform and didn't look fearsome. He'd forgotten his sword in his haste—a rookie mistake. However, he had plenty of other dangerous weapons tucked away. Too bad they were hidden. Otherwise, the goons would be hesitating instead of shifting into classic fighting stances.

"We have been ordered to bring the *girl* to the General. Not messages," the goon said, pulling his sword from his belt.

His partner also drew his weapon. Valek really didn't have time for a fight. Instead of grabbing his dagger, he palmed a couple of darts that he'd threaded through the cuff of his sleeve. He aimed for their thick necks, throwing a dart into each one. Then he rushed in close, making it difficult for them to swing their swords. Not that he'd given them enough time to react. Ducking under their weapons, he crouched down and spun, sweeping the men's feet out from under them. They crashed to the ground with a curse and a thud. Their weapons clattered to the floor, and all was quiet.

Even though they were motionless, Valek moved away just in case one or both were playing dead. He counted under his breath, giving the sleeping potion time to work its magic. When he reached ten, he bent over the goons and removed his darts. Straightening, he met Yelena's startled gaze.

"It's a dirty way to fight, but I'm late for lunch."

CHAPTER 5

*V*alek stepped over the goons. They'd wake in a couple of hours with headaches. Yelena stood with her arms crossed. He gently took the injured one and inspected the cut near her elbow.

Relieved it wasn't deep, he said, "Not as bad as it looks. You'll live. We'll see the Commander first, then the medic."

He hurried to the Commander's war room. Yelena lagged, but he didn't ease his pace as the Commander was bound to be upset. And, sure enough, the man shot him an annoyed glare when they entered the spacious circular room located in the southeast tower of the castle. Long, thin stained-glass windows that striped three-quarters of the tower let in the afternoon sunlight. A beautiful room except General Brazell sat at the egg-shaped table in the middle of the chamber. The old goat glowered at Yelena, his square face turning red.

The Commander sat at the head, with a tray of untouched food nearby. General Tesso of MD-4 continued eating his lunch, while General Hazal of MD-6 gazed at Yelena and Valek with interest. The group had to have been discussing Brazell's new factory. Any big projects planned within a Military District needed the Commander's approval and he frequently consulted with the generals of the neighboring districts.

"Valek, you're—"

"Late," Valek finished for the Commander. "I know. There was a slight altercation." He pulled Yelena closer.

"Altercation, Valek?" He sighed. "How many dead?"

"None. I couldn't justify the disposal of soldiers merely following General Brazell's orders to hunt down and kill our new food taster. Besides, they weren't very smart. Seems she was on the verge of giving them the slip when she ran into me. Good thing though, or I might not have found out about the incident."

The Commander studied Yelena before he turned to Brazell.

The general jumped to his feet. "She should be dead! I want her dead! She killed my son!"

Valek countered, "But the Code of Behavior—"

"Damn the Code. I'm a general. She killed a *general's* son and here she is…" Emotion choked off Brazell's words.

Valek wondered why the general hadn't been this emotional at the execution. Why save it for now? Was it all an act? If so, it was a good one. The man's fingers curled as if he'd like to strangle Yelena. Valek kept his hand near the hilt of his dagger.

"It's a dishonor to me that she lives," Brazell shouted. "An insult. Train another prisoner. I want her dead!"

With those four words vibrating in the air, Yelena stepped behind Valek. Out of the line of sight and of attack, he approved. It appeared the other generals agreed with Brazell, so her life could very well end in mere moments. A strange protective instinct rose in Valek's chest, and he decided he would fight for her.

"He has a sound argument," the Commander said into the tense silence.

"You have never deviated from what's written in the Code of Behavior," Valek argued. "Start now and you'll begin a trend.

Besides, you'll be killing the brightest food taster we've ever had. She's almost trained." He gestured to the tray of cold food beside the Commander.

Brazell took a step toward the Commander. "She's smart because *I* educated her. I can't believe you're going to listen to this upstart, conniving, sneaky thief—" Brazell stopped.

Valek suppressed a smirk. The old goat had gone too far. Valek's loyalty to the Commander was without fail, and Ambrose trusted his opinion.

"Brazell, leave my food taster alone."

Yelena let out an audible breath. No surprise she'd been holding it in. Valek relaxed as well. He'd won this round, but he knew Brazell wouldn't stop seeking his revenge.

Brazell tried to argue, but the Commander silenced him. "It's an order. Go ahead and build your new factory. Consider your permit approved."

Well played, Old Goat. But are you smart enough to take the carrot?

Silence followed. Brazell gave Yelena a look that promised future pain and death before he strode from the room without another word.

Once he was gone, Tesso and Hazal objected to the speed of the permit approval. They listed their reasons why the decision needed further discussion, but Valek knew they had been looking forward to spending more time at the castle. All the generals wished for one on one time with the Commander to gain his favor and hopefully be assigned as his successor.

Valek ceased to listen to their—what did Margg call it—caterwauling as he tasted the Commander's cold food. Free of poisons, he pushed the plate closer to the Commander, who listened patiently until the generals finished their protestations.

"Your concerns are noted. My order stands," the Commander said. He turned to Valek. "Your food taster had better live up to your endorsements. One slip and you'll be training her replacement prior to your reassignment. You're dismissed."

Valek took Yelena's arm and led her from the chamber. The Commander never made idle threats. While he knew Valek would do anything for him, including washing dishes or shoveling manure, without the need to reassign Valek, the Commander had just linked Yelena's fate with Valek's own. Why?

The Commander probably wanted him to be more invested in her training than Valek had been for the other tasters. Perhaps he thought she'd last longer than the others in that case. He stopped. "Yelena—"

"Don't say anything. Don't threaten or bully or intimidate. I've had enough of that from Brazell. I'll make every effort to be the best taster because I'm getting used to the idea of living. And I don't want to give Brazell the satisfaction of seeing me dead."

She strode down the hallway without waiting for him to reply to her outburst. Then again, she had told him not to say anything. Impressed with her determination, he followed her until it appeared she had no idea where she was going.

He touched her elbow and muttered, "medic," steering her to the left. Valek kept alert for an ambush as they traveled through the corridors. He doubted Brazell had the time to set another one up, but he wouldn't be caught off-guard again.

They reached the infirmary without trouble. Valek's favorite medic was on duty. Channa was efficient and skilled and didn't admonish him when he arrived in need of care. She understood his job was dangerous, saving her nagging for *after* she healed him, usually by insisting he not rush his recovery.

The short-haired woman led Yelena to an empty examination table. Channa wore an all-white uniform with red diamond shapes stitched onto her collar. Spots of bright red blood already stained her sleeve. White was supposed to be better for the patients, but he couldn't help thinking black would hide the blood better.

Yelena stretched out on the table, grunting with pain. Now that the adrenaline had no doubt worn off, she appeared exhausted and vulnerable. Which reminded him that he needed to protect her.

"I'll post some guards outside the door, in case Brazell changes his mind," Valek said. He walked over to where Channa gathered supplies. "She's had a rough afternoon. Can you give her some sleeping pills so she has a good night's sleep?"

Medic Channa nodded and then glanced at Yelena, who was watching them. Valek said good-bye and hurried to find a couple of his corps. Regular castle guards wouldn't help his peace of mind. He needed his specially trained people disguised as regular guards to keep an eye on her.

THE NEXT MORNING, Valek stopped by the kitchen to pick up breakfast for Yelena. The kitchen swarmed with activity. Rand stood amid the chaos, shouting orders as he cooked omelets. A hot fog of steam and grease permeated the air. It smelled delicious. He looped around, counting knives. There were a number of rather large and dangerously sharp ones and he liked to ensure they remained in the kitchen.

Satisfied they were all accounted for, Valek picked up a tray. He filled it with an omelet and a cup of honey tea. On his way out, he stopped one of the servers and requested a special blend of tea. He gave her instructions on how the tea was to be prepared before being delivered to the infirmary.

"Training a new food taster, sir?" she asked.

"Yes."

"And she's already in the infirmary?" Her surprise changed to calculation. "Does she have a weak constitution?"

Ah. She was pumping him for information. The servants liked to gamble on everything, and betting over whether the new food taster would survive the training must be the current obsession.

"Time will tell," he said.

The servant all but growled over his vague reply. He suppressed a grin, thanked her, and left. Stopping by his office to pick up a few things, Valek headed to the infirmary. His corps stood guard outside the entrance. They signaled it had been a quiet night and all was well. Good.

Medic Channa gave him a quick update on Yelena. "She detected the sleeping pills in her tea and wouldn't finish it. She thought someone poisoned it. She didn't eat either but did sleep well. However, something upset her this morning."

He glanced around, seeking trouble. "Do you know who or what?"

"No idea." She left to attend to another patient.

Valek approached Yelena's bed. She stared at the ceiling, but as he drew closer her gaze snapped to her breakfast.

"What's in it?" she demanded. "More sleeping pills? Or another new poison?" Struggling to sit up, she winced and sank back in defeat. "How about giving me something to make me feel good for a change?" She grumped.

No doubt she was in pain from her exertions yesterday. Valek ignored her mood and made a mental note to ask Channa to give her some pain medicine. "How about something to keep you alive?" He tucked the file he carried under his arm and helped her into a sitting position. With a flourish, he offered her the pipette filled with her antidote. Then he placed the tray of food on her lap.

"No need for sleeping pills. The medic told me you picked up on that taste last night." Valek approved. "Taste your breakfast and tell me if you would allow the Commander to eat it."

He watched as she scanned the food, sniffed the omelet,

sampled it, and then stirred the tea before sipping it. She'd picked up on the five S-steps faster than the other food tasters he'd trained.

"Unless the Commander doesn't like honey in his tea, I wouldn't reject this breakfast."

Pride swelled. "Then eat it." Valek kept his tone neutral. How certain was she? A taster needed to be confident.

She hesitated, eyeing him. A little crinkle of skin puckered between her eyebrows. He had the sudden desire to smooth it with his thumb. Yelena ate the entire omelet and then drained the tea.

"Not bad," he said. "No poisons...today."

One of the medics brought another tray to Valek. It held four cups of the special tea he'd ordered. He switched the trays on Yelena's lap. "I want to go over some tasting techniques. Each of these cups contains mint tea. Taste one."

Clasping the closest mug, she took a sip and choked on the strong mint flavor.

Valek grinned. "Taste anything else?"

She took another mouthful. "No."

"All right. Now pinch your nose tight and try again."

After giving him a questioning look, she fumbled with her bandaged arm. Then she pinched her nose and took another sip. "Sweet. No mint." Her voice sounded funny, and she released her nose.

"Correct. Now try the others."

Yelena repeated the test on the other three cups and successfully discovered the hidden tastes. More proof she'd make an excellent taster.

"This technique works for any drink or food. Blocking your sense of smell eliminates all flavors except sweet, sour, bitter, and salt," He lectured. "Some poisons are recognizable by one of those four flavors." Valek paged through his folder. "Here is a complete list of human poisons and their distinct tastes for you to memorize. There are fifty-two known poisons."

She scanned the list and then brandished it in the air. "Why didn't you just give me this list instead of making me sample My Love?"

"What would you learn from a list? Kattsgut tastes sweet. What does that taste like? Honey sweet? Apple sweet? There are different levels of sweetness and the only way to learn them is to taste them yourself. The *only* reason I'm giving you this list is because the Commander wants you working as soon as possible." Valek snapped his folder shut. "Just because you aren't going to taste those poisons now doesn't mean you won't in the future. Memorize that list. Once the medic releases you from the infirmary, I will test your knowledge. If you pass, then you can start work."

"And if I fail?"

Then you'll die, and I'll be...upset. "Then I'll be training a new taster." His voice was flat, monotoned despite his unsettling thoughts. No other taster's death caused him any emotion other than annoyance. He continued. "Brazell will be in the castle for another two weeks. He has more business to attend to. I can't have you guarded all day, so Margg is preparing a room for you in my suite. I'll come back later to see when you'll be discharged."

He left before she could react to the news that she would be staying with him. Before *he* could react to the same news. Valek had fully intended to assign his corps to dress as servants and castle staff and covertly guard her at all times. He didn't want anyone to think he cared about her—because he didn't. But that wasn't what popped out of his mouth. Of course, he could change his mind. He should. Except his apartment had plenty of room and it'd be nice to have some company.

～

VALEK HURRIED to his office to create a schedule to have Yelena followed and protected every time she left his apartment. He resisted taking a shift. Why did he even contemplate it? Not only was he far too busy, but there was absolutely no reason. His corps were more than capable of keeping her safe, and once Brazell and his goons were gone, she could return to her own room. At least, Adviser Mogkan had already left. Brazell wanted him to start construction on the factory right away.

When Valek finished, he tracked down his current spy manager. She had an office on the third floor of the six-story hexagon which housed his corps. Unlike his, hers was neat and sparsely furnished. A good thing, as she kept track of all his corps and assigned them to the various operations that Valek didn't personally oversee. Not quite a second-in-command, but close.

Kenda greeted him with a smile and gestured to the empty seat in front of her desk. Whip smart with a keen memory, she'd worked her way up through the ranks, proving her worth. With her unremarkable appearance, Kenda had the ability to blend into any situation and not leave an impression. He handed her the schedule for Yelena before he sat.

"What type of trouble are you expecting, sir?" Kenda asked.

"An attack or ambush from one or more of General Brazell's people."

"How many more?"

"I doubt he'd send more than two. He doesn't want the Commander to know so they'll be incognito."

She drummed her fingers on the desk as she studied the parchment. "There's no night shift."

Here we go. "Correct. She'll be sleeping in one of the extra rooms in my suite." Both his and the Commander's apartments were only accessible through one entrance that was always guarded.

Kenda was too much of a professional to voice the curiosity dancing in her brown-eyed gaze.

He suppressed a sigh. "It's a tactical decision. Her room is on the ground floor, so we'd need two people to watch her at night and I'm not willing to use up too many of my corps."

"And I know just who to assign. Hildred is back from MD-2 and is already bored. Inrick can take the second shift. They both can handle up to three opponents."

Valek approved. They chatted about the current operations, and he updated her on the black market op. After they finished, he left and searched for Margg. She mopped the floor inside the Commander's war room.

"I need you to clean out one of the extra bedrooms in my suite," he said.

"Why? They're all filled with junk."

An old argument—what was junk to her was treasure to him. "Yelena will be staying there until Brazell leaves the castle."

"Are you insane?" she asked. "She'll kill you in your sleep." She pounded the ground with her mop. It hit with a wet splat, spraying his boots with soapy water.

He raised an eyebrow at her. It'd been over twenty years since anyone got the drop on him while he slept. And only because it'd been an exhausting day while he trained to become an assassin at the School of Night and Shadows. And he'd been thirteen. "Thanks for the vote of confidence."

Margg's grip tightened. "Your suite is filled with weapons. They're hanging on the walls and lying all over the place!"

"I'm aware."

"Are you? One of these days your cockiness is going to get you killed and *I'll* have to scrub your blood off the floor." The mop swept closer.

"I'll apologize now for the inconvenience."

She sighed long and hard. "I don't know why I bother. When do you need the room cleaned?"

"By tomorrow afternoon." And when she opened her mouth, Valek said, "It'll help with your cover. Add to your disgruntlement for Star."

"Oh, aren't you a prince." Her tone implied he was far from princely.

"Happy to oblige." Valek scrambled out of the way as she pushed the mop toward his feet.

VALEK SWUNG by the kitchen later that afternoon, but Rand wasn't overseeing the preparations for the evening meal. Odd. He'd have to come back after the dinner rush. In the meantime, he'd stop at the infirmary.

Medic Channa greeted him at the door. "My shift just finished."

"When is Yelena being discharged?" he asked.

"She can leave at any time."

"Can you keep her until tomorrow morning?"

"Sure." She headed out with a wave.

Valek turned toward Yelena's bed and froze. Rand sat next to her. The cook gestured wildly, and she laughed.

Laughed.

Her smile transformed her face. He'd thought her beautiful before, but now... Valek's heart stuttered to a stop. Then an unfamiliar emotion shocked his heart back into motion with its intensity. It took him a long moment to name it. Jealousy. Margg's words from earlier sounded in his mind. *Are you insane?* Perhaps. Because nothing else explained his illogical reaction.

He drew in a few deep breaths, cleansing the unwelcome emotion from his body. Then he approached Yelena's bed. Rand stopped talking immediately, as if caught gossiping about Valek. He lurched from his chair and made a hasty retreat. Good. Valek watched him limp from the infirmary. Had he come to recruit Yelena? To ask her to spy on the Commander for Star?

Valek faced her. "What was he doing here?" He kept his tone neutral as she told him the cook had come to visit, bringing her a sweet.

"When did you meet him?"

"After I recovered from My Love, I went in search of food and met Rand in the kitchen."

Ah. It was inevitable. They would be working together, and Rand always befriended the food tasters. Which *always* ended badly.

"Watch what you say around him. He's not to be trusted. I would have reassigned him, but the Commander insisted he stay. He *is* a genius in the kitchen. Some kind of protégé. He started cooking for the King at a very young age." Would she take the hint?

Yelena met his warning gaze with one of stubborn refusal. Cold determination radiated from her stiff posture. If he pressed the issue, she would just push back harder. Not worth the effort. Not yet. He looked away, conceding defeat. For now.

"You'll leave the infirmary tomorrow morning." Valek was curt. "Get yourself cleaned up and report to my office to take the test. I won't think you're ready even if you pass, but the Commander ordered me to have you available by lunch." Annoyed, he shook his head. "It's a shortcut. I hate shortcuts."

"Why? You won't have to risk yourself anymore."

Does she really not *see the bigger picture? Or is she goading me?* "In my experience, shortcuts usually lead to death."

"Is that what happened to my predecessor?" she asked.

He wondered what Rand had been telling her. The cook had been grumbling and telling everyone Valek murdered his friend for weeks. He wasn't about to explain his actions or defend them.

"Oscove?" Valek paused. "He didn't have the stomach for it."

CHAPTER 6

$\mathcal{A}$ sharp knock on Valek's door sounded just as he finished clearing the table for Yelena's test. Striding to the door, he opened it wide. Rand pushed in a trolley filled with steaming plates of food, cups of tea, and a handful of fruit drinks. Margg bustled in behind him, her ever-present scowl firmly etched on her face.

Rand and Margg set out the dishes while Valek opened his poison cabinet. Bottles, jars, and vials lined the shelves. Fifty-two poisons, plus White Fright. All various colors. Together, they created a pretty picture—a painting of death. Valek considered his options. Yelena had already smelled the ones known for their distinct scents, and she tasted My Love, so that left... twenty-seven unknowns. It wouldn't be fair to only test her on unfamiliar poisons, so he added twelve of the ones that she knew to the pile.

Margg came over and it took them two trips to carry the poisons to the table, where forty containers waited. He picked up a goblet half full of peach juice and set it on his desk. Then he returned to sort the poisons. Choosing the right poison for each food item to ensure the test was challenging and fair would take some time.

A knock sounded and Hildred poked her head into the room. He joined her in the threshold and lowered his voice. "Report."

"The food taster just left the infirmary with her escort," she said. "When do you want me to start shadowing her?"

"Tomorrow morning."

"Got it." She retreated down the hallway without making a sound.

With not much time to prepare, Valek dismissed Margg and Rand and returned to the table.

"Do you want me to take the trolley, sir?" Rand asked.

"No. Just shove it out of the way. I'll put the dirty dishes on it, and you can have one of your helpers pick it up later."

"Yes, sir." He left.

Valek turned his full attention to the test. Once he decided the best arrangement for lacing the food and drinks, he set to work. Carefully measuring out each dose, he sprinkled, mixed, and stirred until finished. Then he set the untainted peach juice that was on his desk in an inconspicuous location. Expecting Yelena at any moment, Valek raced to return all the poison bottles to the cabinet. Except White Fright. When Yelena passed the test, he'd need it.

When? Was he that confident in her? *Yes.* Working as an assassin for hire, Valek learned how to read and manipulate people. Although it wasn't hard to figure out that Yelena had above average intelligence and was highly motivated.

He returned to his desk to wait for her, filling the time with some paperwork. The estimated time of her arrival came and went. When she was well past due, he considered the implications. In order to pass the test, she had to take it. What would he do if she refused? Or if she ditched her guards and escaped?

The door to his office opened and Yelena burst in.

"Where's your test?" she demanded, tossing her belongings onto the empty chair.

Her gaze flashed with anger and a dusky-red color stained her cheeks. Something or someone had upset her. He glanced at one of her guards. The man signaled all was well. Valek dismissed them with a subtle nod. All his corps learned how to communicate non-verbally. It'd been a life saver during many dangerous operations.

He returned his attention to Yelena, who glared back. Perhaps it was the test that had her so upset. Standing, he swept his arm out with a dramatic flourish, gesturing to the forty items waiting for her. The hot food had cooled, and he hoped the flavor of the poisons hadn't been affected. "Only one item isn't poisoned. Find it. Then eat or drink your selection."

Ignoring him, she methodically applied the five S-steps to every dish, cup, and goblet. He'd provided an empty basin for her to spit into. Watching, he approved her technique and kept his expression neutral throughout. Unlike Yelena, who scowled, grimaced, spat with disgust, and made yuck-faces. It would have been amusing if her life wasn't on the line. When she sipped the peach juice, he held his breath. Her eyebrows drew together, and she crinkled her nose before spitting the mouthful out and moving on to the next item. For the first time, apprehension churned in his gut.

When she finished, she turned to him with fury in her gaze. "You bastard. They're all poisoned."

He'd been called worse things than a bastard. Most of the time, it was well deserved. Not this time. Ice coated his heart at the implication. "Are you sure?"

"Of course. I wouldn't touch anything on that table."

A numbness spread through his body. He moved closer, but he wasn't quite sure why. "I'm sorry, Yelena. You've failed."

She flinched as if struck, then she scanned the table. When her attention returned to him her fury had turned to determination. She demanded Valek prove her wrong.

Brave or stupid? Valek hid his surprise by grabbing the peach juice. "This one is clean."

"Drink it." She challenged.

Or just confident? He hesitated. She'd called him a liar and Valek didn't take orders. He gave them. This was a classic delay tactic. Eventually he would have to... He shied away from that thought. *Might as well humor her.*

Valek sipped the juice. He met her gaze as he rolled the liquid around his tongue. A sharp, bitter taste filled his mouth. He spat.

"Blackberry poison," she said in triumph.

"Yes." Valek examined the cup in his hand. It looked like the one he'd pulled aside earlier. He glanced at the table, seeking another one that might be similar. None of them matched.

"I passed?"

He nodded, but his thoughts remained on the goblet. He returned to his desk and set it down. It had been there the entire time he laced the other dishes. It couldn't have been poisoned... unless it was spiked before coming to his office. No. He choose that cup at random. Which meant either Rand or Margg poisoned it when he was distracted by Hildred.

"I should have known you would try to trick me." Anger filled Yelena's voice.

He met her gaze. "You're all fired up. And it isn't because of the test. Explain yourself."

"Explain? Why do *I* have to explain? Maybe *you* should explain why you read my journal."

"Journal?" Valek looked at her in amazement. That was the last thing he'd expected her to say. "I didn't read anything of yours. But if I had, it would have been within my rights."

"Why?" she demanded.

A few weeks of freedom and she already thinks she has the right to privacy. That she has any rights. Doesn't she understand she's still a prisoner and will always *be one until she dies?* A fact he also needed to remember before he became too attached to her. He quickly squashed the "too late" that popped up in the back of his mind.

Valek opened his mouth, then shut it before he said something he'd regret. When the right words formed, he said, "Yelena, you confessed to murder. You were caught straddling Reyad's body with a bloody knife in your hand. I searched your file for a motive. There was none. Only a report that you refused to answer all questions."

He moved closer. "Since I don't know what motivates you to kill, I can't predict if you'll do it again or what might set you off. I'm bound by the Code of Behavior, so I had to offer you the choice of becoming the new food taster." And then the Commander linked their fates to give him the extra motivation to train her thoroughly, so she not only passed the test but excelled as a food taster. Valek drew a deep breath and continued. "You'll be very close to the Commander on a daily basis. Until I can trust you, I'll be watching you."

The fire in her eyes died. "How do I win your trust?"

Tell me about what happened at Brazell's, about Reyad, and everything about you. He knew she wouldn't confide in him, so he settled on the most pressing question. "Tell me why you killed Reyad."

"You're not ready to believe me."

An interesting response. Was he ready? Valek gazed at the conference table. Someone had poisoned that cup for reasons unknown. At this point, Valek couldn't trust anyone.

"You're right," he said.

"I passed your test. I want my antidote."

At least he'd been right. She not only passed his test, but also survived a murder attempt. He filled a pipette with her "anti-dote" and handed it to her.

"Now what?" she asked.

He glanced out the windows. "Lunch! We're late."

She squeezed the White Fright into her mouth as they hurried from the office. Valek set a quick pace. He hoped the Commander's anger would be tempered by the fact Yelena passed and he no longer had to rely on Valek, who tended to lose track of time.

An argument replaced the usual buzz of voices in the throne room. The Commander leaned against a desk near a knot of advisers and officers. Two obvious factions faced each other, debating a tactical operation. Adviser Tocara and Captain Etta claimed a dog team with a squad of soldiers could find an escaped prisoner in no time, while Adviser Felo and Captain Parffet countered that a highly skilled tracking team didn't need dogs to outsmart a fugitive.

As Valek wove through the desks, he noted the dispute lacked anger. The Commander enjoyed presenting a problem to his team to see what strategies they would use to solve it. In this case, Valek knew the reason for this debate.

He joined the Commander and listened. Yelena hovered behind them. No doubt the discussion of escaping to Sitia would interest her.

For this particular deliberation, the advisers presented their plan, and the captains would, in theory, carry it out. Valek would bet a couple coins on the dog team except Parffet had a number of impressive soldiers in his unit, including his new scouts— Ari and Janco, the power twins.

Valek glanced over his shoulder to ask Yelena her opinion but paused. She was biting down on her knuckle as if in great pain. Then she eased up and inspected her finger. Her teeth had broken the skin and blood welled. That explained the scars on her hands. Anger rose. What had happened to her that she'd needed to suppress her emotions?

She caught him staring and shoved her hands behind her back. He returned his attention to the discussion.

The Commander raised his hand. Quiet descended in an instant. "Excellent points from both sides. We will put your theories to the test. Two teams." Pointing to Captain Etta and Parffet, the Commander ordered, "You'll be the captains. Assemble your teams and organize a plan of attack. Recruit as needed. Valek will supply a fugitive from one of his corps. You have a fortnight to prepare."

Valek and Yelena followed the Commander to his office. Shutting the door, Valek blocked the chaos of voices the Commander's orders had ignited. "Is Marrok's escape to Sitia still bothering you?" he asked.

Marrok was one of the King's loyal men and had protected the royal family. He'd fled to Sitia with a number of his colleagues right after the takeover fifteen years ago but was recently captured in Ixia for spying. Marrok had been scheduled for execution, but unlike the Commander, Valek thought the man would be more useful alive and may have arranged a bit of assistance in the man's escape. Valek had been right. His spies followed Marrok straight back to Sitia and discovered the location of a group of men that might cause trouble for Ixia. They were currently under surveillance.

The Commander frowned. "Yes. Sloppy work, that pursuit. Marrok must have known you were in MD–8. You really need to train a couple of protégés."

Widening his eyes in horror, he joked, "But then I wouldn't be indispensable."

The Commander gave him a rare smile, but it died when he noticed Yelena attempting to blend in with the walls. "Well, Valek, you were right about this one. She survived your test." He turned to her. "Come here."

She approached as if he were a poisonous snake about to strike.

"As my official food taster, you're to report to me with my breakfast. I'll give you my daily itinerary and expect you to be present at each meal. I will not accept tardiness. Understand?"

"Yes, sir."

He glanced at Valek. "She looks fragile. Are you sure she's strong enough?"

"Yes, sir."

The Commander's expression turned inward. Valek braced, mentally preparing examples of Yelena's strength if Ambrose decided she was too much trouble.

"All right. Since I missed lunch, Valek, you will join me for an early dinner. Yelena, you'll start as my food taster tomorrow morning."

Relief coursed through him. "Yes, sir," he said at the same time as Yelena.

They quickly left and returned to Valek's office. She collected her extra uniforms and her journal, which Valek now wished to read. What had she written that just the thought of someone else reading it, would make her so upset?

He led her to the wing of the castle that housed his and the Commander's quarters. Two guards stood next to the large wooden doors that marked the entrance. Valek explained to them that Yelena had permission to enter his residence. They nodded and unlocked the door, revealing a short hallway. On the right side was Valek's apartment and directly across from him was the Commander's suite.

Yelena stopped just inside his living room. Valek glanced around and tried to see it with fresh eyes. The place was as cluttered as his office with books piled everywhere. Dust motes swirled in the shafts of sunlight beaming through the long, thin windows that marked the far wall. The left wall displayed a collection of weapons he no longer used but had wielded in the past. All represented fond memories, especially the knife in the middle. Blood still gleamed on the blade.

She stared at the mounds of rocks on the floor. The gray lumps were streaked with white and not a typical decoration. He wondered if she'd ever connect them to the small black statues of animals and flowers that also littered his apartment. After hours of grinding off the outer surface of those ugly gray stones, they revealed a black interior with glints of silver. It was quite the transformation.

The boxes piled extra high around the first door on the right marked the room Margg must have cleared out for Yelena. Odd that she didn't move them into one of the other two rooms along that wall.

He pointed it out to Yelena. "That room is yours until Brazell leaves the castle. I suggest you get some rest." Then he noticed the books on the end table all discussed various ways to kill someone. They could upset her, or give her ideas, so he picked them up to take to his office. "I'll be back later. Don't go out. I'll bring you dinner." Valek grabbed his key to lock the door but paused. Would she think he was locking her inside? Instead, he caught the door before it could close. "Lock the door behind me. You should be safe here."

Should. He needed to have a conversation with Margg to ensure she would be.

VALEK FOUND Margg waiting for him in his office. The dishes from the test had been cleaned up and the trolley was gone.

"There's no body," she grumped, gesturing to the floor. "I guess the little rat passed."

He gave her a cold, assessing look. "Why do you hate her so much?"

"She's a murderer."

"So am I." He used his deadliest tone. One that had others on their knees, begging for him to spare their lives.

Margg crossed her arms instead. "That's different. She killed the old goat's son. I don't like him, but the old goat fought in the takeover and earned his rank. And losing a child is the worst thing that could *ever* happen to a parent."

He couldn't argue with that logic. "Do you hate her enough to poison her?"

"Poison! Hell no. She should hang for her crimes. That's the Commander's job. Not mine."

He studied her sour expression. "Are you sure?"

"Oh, yes. If the Commander says she can live, then all I can do is make her life miserable."

Classic bully tactics. It would be interesting to see how Yelena handled it. At least he'd eliminated Margg as a suspect. And while he didn't like her bullying Yelena and could easily order Margg to refrain from tormenting her, he needed to keep his distance. His enemies would target Yelena if they knew he cared for her. Besides, there were a few others who felt the same way as Margg, and Yelena needed to learn how to defend herself and how to ignore the comments.

"Were you waiting for me?" he asked Margg.

"Yes. I've a meeting with Star tonight. What information should I sell her?"

"Tell her the new food taster passed the test and detected *all* the poisons."

"All?" Her confusion cleared. "Ah. That's why you asked me about poisoning her." Instead of being offended, she laughed.

It was a hardy guffaw. Valek stared. He'd never heard her laugh before. Or smile.

"You think...I...tried to kill...her," she gasped out between chuckles.

"Glad I could amuse you."

She used a corner of her apron to wipe the tears from her cheeks. "I'm glad my feelings for the new taster are apparent."

"You don't do subtle."

"I'm too old for subtle."

"Can we get back on track? I want you to let Star know that the new food taster is one of the best. And that she's been taken under my wing as I don't have the time or the inclination to train another prisoner. Star's payment for the information will let us know if it's news to her or not."

"A low payment means she knows."

"Right."

"Anything else?"

"No. Hopefully she'll let you know what type of intelligence she's looking for."

"All right." Margg left.

And now Valek had to figure out why Rand would poison Yelena. The cook appeared to enjoy her company. Or had that been a ruse to get information from her? Knowledge, he sold to Star? The only motive Valek could think of was that Star paid Rand to poison Yelena. Although he had no idea why she'd care about the food taster. Yelena could be a good source of intelligence on the Commander.

Valek had already warned Yelena away from Rand and that had only increased her determination to ignore his advice. Valek would need to show her evidence. She wouldn't take him at his word that Rand had both the opportunity and the means —brewing blackberry poison was complicated.

Not at this point. Was he hopeful that she'd trust him at some point in time? Yes. Which meant he'd have to trust her, too.

VALEK JOINED the Commander in the war room for an early dinner. Now that he knew Rand had access to blackberry poison, Valek would have to find it and replace it with a substance that looked the same so Rand would believe he still had the poison but couldn't harm anyone if he decided to try again. Valek could just arrest the cook for possession of an illegal substance, but where was the fun in that? Rand would eventually provide him plenty of information about Star's network.

He updated the Commander on Yelena's test and his theories about Rand and took extra care in tasting his dinner.

"Our new food taster is already causing considerable trouble," the Commander said. "Why don't we just hang her and train the next prisoner on the execution schedule?"

The blood in Valek's veins turned to ice. "That would be Serra. She poisoned her husband."

Ambrose laughed. "She already has the skills and it's a perfect punishment."

Valek wasn't amused. "She has the skills to poison *you*."

"They all do, Valek. Once you train them, they learn how to bypass the standard tasting techniques…what did you call them?"

"S-steps."

"Yes, those. It's bad enough we have to worry about someone assassinating me. To think I might be collateral damage for an assassination attempt on our food taster is just not worth the risk."

"She's worth that risk." Valek held up a hand, stopping the Commander's outburst. "It's a small risk. I doubt they'll try to poison her again. And there's too many questions still unanswered."

"Are the answers that important? Just go in and arrest everyone involved. Problem solved." He waved his fork in the air.

If it were only that easy. "The answers are very important. A mass arrest would be like cutting down a tree. You get the trunk, limbs, and leaves, but the roots remain. Eventually they'll grow new trees in unknown locations, and we'll be back at the beginning."

The Commander chewed for a moment, then he looked at Valek. The golden color and almond-shape of his eyes added to the weight behind his gaze. It pierced Valek's soul.

"You care about her," he said.

It wasn't exactly a question. But there was no way Valek would lie to the Commander. Ever. He might omit certain details or fail to inform Ambrose of all his actions, but when asked a direct question, Valek would always give an honest answer. "Yes."

"How much?"

"I like her. She's intelligent and a survivor. I think she could be an asset to us. All the other food tasters have been...just prisoners, forced to do the job until they died."

"Until you became annoyed with them," he teased.

"Not all of them. There was...one...Firen who was allergic to those strange nuts Tesso brought you. No one knew. Not even Firen."

"Your point?"

"My point is that she has the potential to become a part of our team. To do her job not because she has to, but because she wants to."

"Why would she wish to do such a dangerous job?"

"To protect you." And when the Commander appeared unconvinced, he added, "She's going to learn who you are and what you're trying to do in Ixia. She'll realize on her own just how much better off Ixia is with you in charge. Plus, her sense of taste is keen. The job won't be as risky for her. If she serves you loyally for a few years, she can be promoted."

"Promoted? I don't think that's in the Code of Behavior."

"It isn't, but there's nothing in there that says you *can't* do it."

"True. What would I promote her to?"

"A general or an adviser."

Ambrose laughed. "How about your second-in-command?"

"If she can beat me in a fight, I would agree to that."

"What if she falls in love with me?"

Now Valek laughed despite the strange pang in his chest over the thought. "Even better. Her desire to protect you would only increase."

"What if she falls in love with you? And you fall for her, and you want to get married?"

"That's not going to happen."

The Commander turned serious. "Why not?"

"I'm already married."

"You are?"

"Yes."

"To whom?"

"You." Which meant he was married to his job and to Ixia as well. They were a package deal.

Ambrose pretended to be shocked. "I had no idea."

"Clearly, or we wouldn't have separate apartments."

As intended, the Commander burst out laughing. The man really needed more levity in his life.

"I'm flattered, Valek. But I don't date men."

"Your loss."

"I'm sure," he said dryly. "All right. I'll give Yelena a chance to prove her worth. But if she becomes too troublesome, I expect you to handle it." His tone held no hint of his prior good humor.

"Yes, sir."

VALEK CHANGED into a server's uniform—white pants and shirt with a line of red diamonds down each arm—before stopping in the kitchen. He pulled his hair back into a short ponytail. It wasn't much of a disguise, but it was in the middle of the dinner rush and the kitchen would be chaotic.

As expected, no one gave him a second glance. He moved through the flurry of activity as if he belonged there. Rand's rooms were adjacent to the kitchen and locked. He tried his master key. The cursed thing only worked a fraction of the time, but he was in luck and the door opened. Valek searched for the poison in the two small rooms—a living area and bedroom.

It didn't take long. Rand's possessions could fit into one large box. No bottle, so he left and relocked the door. Grabbing a tray of food to appear busy and to also give to Yelena, he did a circuit of the kitchen, scanning shelves and opening cabinets.

He spotted the blackberry poison sitting on a high shelf in a glass jar. The top of the other containers was coated with dust, which is why that jar caught Valek's attention. Smart of Rand to leave it out in plain sight, yet it was high enough no one would mistakenly use it. There was nothing remarkable about the jar, so it would be an easy switch. Valek would need to come back another time for it.

Returning to his office, he changed back into his adviser's uniform before taking the tray to his apartment. The living room was almost dark and quiet. Yelena must still be asleep in her room. Valek set the tray down and lit the first of the many lanterns hanging on the walls.

With the extra light, Valek spotted Yelena sleeping on the couch. Her journal was resting on her chest, rising and falling with each breath. He paused and took a moment to study her. Relaxed by sleep, she looked her age. When she worked with him, learning new tasting techniques, she seemed years older than nineteen.

The comment about her falling in love with the Commander had caused a strange...emptiness inside Valek. A new sensation. Along with that illogical bout of jealousy when he'd seen her with Rand. What was it about this woman that brought out all these unfamiliar emotions? As if his desire to protect her welled from some primal level deep inside him. Why?

Perhaps it was due to her beauty? Her oval face had lost some of its gauntness. And those eyes—wide and green with sparks of fire when angry. Lean, but not tall at four inches over five feet. Valek had met plenty of beautiful women and none of them ever stirred his soul.

Yelena gave him the impression that below the surface lurked an inner strength. She held her desires and secrets close to her heart and probably wouldn't make friends easily. Perhaps it was the challenge of discovering all those secrets that drew him to her. That once he figured her out, she'd no longer appeal to him. Time would tell.

Valek returned to lighting the lanterns. A book slammed to the ground. He glanced over his shoulder. Yelena's journal was on the floor, and she was sitting up. Letting her get acclimated to the unfamiliar surroundings, he kept working until all the lanterns were lit. The cheery glow might help relax her. He hadn't considered his reputation when he decided to have her stay with him. She might be terrified.

However, when he turned around, she gazed at him with curiosity. "Something wrong with your room?" He picked up the tray of food and handed it to her.

"No. Couldn't sleep."

Valek snorted with amusement. She had a sense of humor. "I see." He gestured toward the tray. "Sorry your dinner is cold. I was detained."

She automatically performed the five S-steps and then glanced at him. Probably to gauge his reaction at her obvious distrust. But he was glad and hoped he'd instilled in her a life-long and life-saving habit. Eating as if she'd been starving, she asked him who else had a key to his suite.

"Just the Commander and Margg. Will that help you sleep better?"

She ignored his question, and asked, "Is Margg your personal housekeeper?"

Ah. The real reason for the worry. "Mine and the Commander's. We wanted someone we could trust. Someone instantly recognizable. She was with us before the takeover, so her loyalty is beyond doubt."

He hoped his explanation would allay her fears, and he sat at his writing desk with the intention of getting some work done. But he couldn't resist giving her a lesson even though it had nothing to do with poison tasting. He swiveled to face her. "Remember when you were in the war room?"

Her eyebrows crinkled with confusion, but she nodded.

"There were three generals in the room. Brazell, you knew, but can you identify the other two?"

"Tesso and Hazal," she answered promptly.

"Can you describe them? Hair color? Eyes?"

She hesitated; her gaze grew distant before she shook her head. "I think General Tesso had a beard."

"You identified them by their uniforms and didn't look at their faces. Correct?"

"Yes."

"That's what I thought. That's the problem with the uniform requirement. It makes a person lazy. A guard will see a housekeeping uniform and just assume that person belongs in the castle. It's too easy for someone to sneak about, which is why I keep the Commander always surrounded by loyal people. And why Margg is the only housekeeper permitted to clean the Commander's and my suites and offices."

"Why not dismiss all the servants in the castle and use your own people?"

"Soldiers make up the majority of our army. Civilians who joined prior to the takeover were made advisers or given other prominent positions. Some of the King's servants were already on our payroll, and the others we paid double what they earned working for the King. Well-paid servants are happy servants."

"Does the entire castle's staff get paid?"

"Yes."

"Including the food taster?"

The conversation had taken an interesting turn. "No."

"Why not?"

"The food taster is paid in advance. How much is your life worth?"

CHAPTER 7

*S*he stared at him in shock. The reality of her current life had hit her harder than Valek intended. He swiveled back to his desk. It would be rather stupid to pay the food taster. If they somehow figured out the Butterfly's Dust ruse, they could save up their funds and escape. A slight chance, since only Valek knew about the fake poison. It might make more sense to pay them. Then the temptation to sell secrets wouldn't be as strong. Which made him wonder...

He turned back to her. "What would you buy with the money?"

"A hairbrush, nightclothes, and I'd spend some at the festival." Her answer came out all in one breath.

Her list didn't have anything that he'd expected, like luxuries or sweets. Except for the festival, she wanted practical things. The fire festival was an annual pain in Valek's ass. Crime always spiked, people became drunk and disorderly, and there was always trouble. Always. It was due to start in eleven days. Yelena was better off staying in the castle.

"You can get some nightclothes from the seamstress, Dilana.

She should have included them with your uniforms. As to the rest, you'll have to make do with what you can find."

Her disappointment tightened around his heart like barbed wire. Valek turned away before he could grab a bag of coins and press them into her hands just to see her smile. *Gah, what's gotten into you?*

OVER THE NEXT FEW DAYS, Yelena settled into her job as the Commander's food taster while Valek focused on his various operations. Sven had been in business for five days and Valek wanted to see how the newest black market dealer was doing.

He changed into the kitchen server's uniform again. This time he rubbed some oil into his hair, making it look unwashed and greasy from working in the kitchen. Using some flesh-colored putty, he sculpted a softer nose for his face. Then he applied makeup to darken his skin a few shades, so he matched most of the people living in Castletown. Valek had grown up near the Northern Ice Pack in what was now MD-1. The sun hardly shone there, and he had the pale skin to prove it. Adding some coal soot to his clothes and chin helped the impression of being one of the people assigned to keep the ovens hot. He finished his disguise with a pair of spectacles. The lenses were just glass, but it was surprisingly effective.

Valek left the castle complex via the west gate and headed straight southwest. He crossed the grass field that spread from the castle's stone buttress for a quarter of a mile in all directions. No buildings or trees were allowed in that area. Nothing that an army or an assassin could use to hide behind or to climb over the wall.

He strode on the path toward Castletown, an unimaginative name courtesy of the Commander. Frankly, Valek preferred Jeweltown, its old name. Not because it was named in honor of

Queen Jewel, but because the city had been laid out like the facets of a jewel. The symmetry of the place soothed him. It was a break from the castle's haphazard shapes.

The sun warmed him, and a slight breeze blew the scent of living green and sunflowers toward him. He kept an eye on his surroundings but didn't expect trouble as he neared the town. The tents for the fire festival would be set up in the fields directly west of Castletown. A few others walked on the path. Travel between the town and the castle flowed all day long. Workers arrived for their shifts or left to go home. Soldiers frequently visited town on their days off.

The main market was located near the center of town and Valek stopped there first. His cover as a kitchen server helped him fit right in. He approached a stand selling herbs and spices.

The merchant's smile widened. "I have everything you need, sir. All fresh and grown in my own backyard, tended by my lovely wife and children."

"And I'm sure your prices reflect all that love and care."

"Oh no. You're my friend, I'll give you a good deal. The best deal for the best herbs in town."

Valek enjoyed haggling and soon purchased a bag full of crushed anise for a decent price. The spice resembled and smelled just like blackberry poison. Then he wandered around the stalls as if shopping, but he scanned the other shoppers. A number of young people wove through the crowd. They chatted with various shoppers and sometimes led them away from the market. No doubt they were the baiters for the black market dealers.

Stopping in front of a stall selling farm tools, Valek glanced at the collection. He picked up a scythe. It was rusted and dull. There were a few ancient butcher knives, small hammers, and chisels, but nothing that could be used as a proper weapon.

"Can I help you, sir?" the seller asked.

"Do you have anything…sharper? Longer? Newer?"

The man raised his eyebrows. "I'm not sure what—"

"Something I could…" Valek made a stabbing motion.

"Oh no, sir. That would be a weapon and they are illegal to sell and to own in Ixia."

And yet Valek had confiscated plenty of them during the fire festival last year. He thanked the man and went in search of another dealer.

He didn't get far before a man sidled up to Valek and said, "I know where you can buy some weapons."

Valek studied him. Not as young as the others—maybe early thirties, he wore a worn merchant's uniform. If he was a legitimate seller, he'd be paying taxes and be able to get new uniforms for free.

"I've no interest in wooden replicas or anything manufactured with cheap steel," Valek said.

"I guarantee they're all made with genuine Sitian metal. All high-quality goods."

"And all illegal."

"Not at all, sir. They're leftovers from before the takeover."

Valek allowed the man to lead him to a narrow alley. A cliché, but they were out of sight of the other sellers and Castletown's guards, who were also referred to as the watch as they kept a close eye on the town's citizens.

The man removed a long, thin knife from his cloak. "This is a Sitian blade made from ore mined from the Emerald Mountains. And if you don't give me your pouch full of coins, I'm going to ram it straight into your heart." His tone turned menacing.

Not a baiter, but a thief. Unexpected, but not unwelcome. The man faced him with his feet close together and the weapon held out in his right hand. A rookie. And considering the punishment for murder was death, the threat was empty. However, it was probably effective, as most people would see the sharp blade and hand over their money in fear.

"You can't drive it straight into my heart, mate," Valek corrected. "The sternum is a rather thick bone, and you don't have the proper stance to generate the amount of thrust you'd need to pierce it with that weapon."

"How about straight into your balls then?" He lowered the point.

"That's a much better threat."

"Come on, *mate*, hand it over."

"And then what? I report you to the watch and they find and arrest you."

A sneer. "You're trying to purchase *illegal* goods. You rat me out and I rat you out. Consider your coins a bribe to keep me quiet."

That was rather smart. "I'll pass."

"You'll what?"

"Pass. I'm not giving you a single coin. What are you going to do now?" Valek was genuinely curious.

"I'm—"

"Hey!" a shout echoed through the alley.

The would-be thief glanced to his right. It was too good of a distraction for Valek to pass up. He grabbed the man's wrist and twisted hard. Yanking the knife from the man's now nerveless fingers, Valek swept the thief's feet out from under him. He followed him to the ground and poked the tip of the weapon into the man's abdomen. The thief froze.

"To stab a person in the heart, you have to angle the blade up underneath the sternum," Valek instructed. "And I'm the *only* person in Ixia that can get away with murder." The poor sap gaped at him in horror. Fun.

A young man with sandy-blond hair ran up beside them. "Are you okay?" he puffed. "I saw…"

Valek raised an eyebrow.

"Oh. Guess you don't need help."

"No, but thanks for the distraction. Was it planned?"

"Planned?"

"Yes, your timely arrival. Was it planned?"

"No! I saw he had a knife out."

"Yeah right, Trevar," the thief spat. "You came here to steal him away for your new boss."

"You're no longer a baiter, Brent. None of the dealers will hire you because you scare away potential customers by robbing them!"

"If the dealers paid me better I—"

"Enough," Valek ordered. It was obvious these two weren't working together. "Trevar, please fetch the watch."

The young man's bright blue eyes almost popped out of his head. "Really?"

"Really."

"Uh, okay." He dashed off.

"You can't," Brent said, "I'll tell them about you."

"Tell them what? I took this knife from you. And I've a witness who saw you threatening me."

Trevar came back with two officers. Brent immediately cried foul, claiming he was the victim and Valek had been the one offering to sell the black market goods. Valek handed the knife to one of the officers and explained. With Trevar backing him up, the watch arrested Brent and hauled him away.

"What's going to happen to him?" Trevar asked.

"Don't you know? It's listed in the Code of Behavior."

"Well, it's been a long time since school…"

Doubtful, he appeared in his early twenties. "Armed robbery is four years of incarceration and hard work in a correctional facility." The Commander ensured the prisoners earned the cost of keeping them in the facility. "And he won't be chasing off your customers for a while."

Trevar glanced around. But the small crowd that had gawked at the arrest had dispersed. No one ever really lingered in Castletown. A person without a reason for hanging around drew too much attention. The bulk of the Commander's army had been assigned to work in the towns and cities of Ixia as guards to keep the peace and ensure everyone followed the Code of Behavior. They also meted out justice in accordance with its guidelines when they didn't.

"Did you come to steal me away from Brent?" Valek asked.

"Not exactly."

Valek waited.

"I knew you were looking for black market goods—everyone did due to your performance in the market." He smiled, flashing a set of dimples. "But when I spotted Brent leading you away..." He shrugged.

Sven was right about this one. He had lots of potential and even picked up that Valek had been acting. "You came to help me."

"I waited outside the alley, thinking Brent would grab your money and run. Then I'd trip him and get your pouch back for you." Another brilliant smile. "I figured you'd be so grateful that you'd spend lots of coins in my boss' shop." Then he sobered. "But he was taking so long, I worried Brent was really going to stab you so..." Another shrug.

"Thank you for the help."

Trevar cocked his head to the side. "I don't think you really needed my help."

Ah yes, he was perceptive. "Well, I work in a kitchen, so I'm used to handling sharp knives. And I'm a bit of a collector, so..."

The bright smile returned. "What a coincidence. My boss has a vast inventory of unique and unusual blades. Would you be interested in meeting him?"

"Lead the way."

Valek followed Trevar to a small shop on a narrow side street. There was nothing remarkable about the area or the building that housed the store. The goods arranged in the window were all legal kitchen wares. A bell dinged when they entered and Valek scanned the tables, chairs, napkins, dishes, cutlery, and bread boxes on display. A decent selection.

Trevar ducked behind the counter and went through a dark curtain. Valek shopped. He admired a set of chairs that had flowers carved into the wooden backrest. Running a finger over the grooves, he considered carving wood versus stone. The softer material would be much easier to work with. Perhaps when he retired. He huffed. Doubtful he'd live to retire.

Sven stepped from the back room and Trevar shot Valek a big smile before dashing out to round up more customers.

Turning on the charm, Sven said, "My young assistant says you're a connoisseur of kitchen knives."

"Connoisseur?" Valek laughed. "I doubt young Trevar knows what that word means."

"And he failed to see through your disguise," Sven said with a wry smile.

"To be fair, so did you."

"Until you spoke."

"And if I used an accent?"

"Then I'd recognize you by your eyes."

"Aww." Valek batted his eyelashes at Sven.

He shook his head. "While I'm happy to see you, is there a reason for your visit?"

"I wanted to see your shop."

"I could have given you the address."

"You could, but where's the fun in that?"

"Oh, I don't know, maybe saving some time might be fun." Sven gestured to the black curtain. "This way."

They went into the back room, which was almost a mirror image of the front room. "Down here." Sven led him to a metal staircase that wound into the darkness. The man lit a lantern and descended. "At least you found Trevar."

"He found me."

"Oh?"

Valek explained the attempted robbery. "Catching a thief was fun."

"The baiters will be happy. Brent's been giving them a bad reputation." At the bottom of the steps, Sven pulled back another dark curtain, revealing a big space filled with crates and lit by several lanterns. "Welcome to my lair."

Laughing, Valek ducked inside. "Ah. Nice."

"This is where the real money is made."

"How's business?"

"Booming." Sven gestured to a stack of empty crates. "I've already sold out of Greenblade cigars."

"That popular?"

"When you sell them for two silvers instead of five silvers, word spreads."

"And we're still making a profit?"

"Yes. They cost us five coppers each. We're earning five coppers and a silver on each sale—a hundred and fifty percent markup."

"Nice."

"It's a shame we'll have to shut down some day. We could fund dozens of operations with the proceeds."

"I'm working on it. You know the Commander…"

"The word stubborn doesn't quite work for him. He's beyond that."

Valek agreed. "How's the competition?"

"Grumpy. They still have their loyal customer base, but it's a matter of time before those people start demanding to buy goods at my prices, which they can't do, so those shoppers will come to me."

"And then?"

"I expect anger, accusations, and verbal threats."

"Accusations?"

"For being a sting operation. When none of my buyers are arrested, I'll get another surge of customers along with thugs sent by the other dealers to warn me off. When that doesn't work, they'll resort to violence." Sven held up a hand. "By then, I'll have enough of our corps in place to stop them and make them 'disappear.' I'll be a legend."

"Now who's having fun?" Valek teased.

Sven continued with his tour, lifting lids and showing Valek the contents of the various crates—silk, perfume, whiskey, and jewelry.

"Do you have any Sitian weapons?" Valek asked.

"Of course. I just received a shipment of cloud-kissed daggers from Delip." He removed a footlong knife from a small box. It had a metal sheath decorated with black swirls. Sven handed it to Valek.

It was surprisingly light. "Cloud-kissed isn't an impressive name." Valek pulled the knife free. Engravings that matched the design on the sheath decorated the double-edged blade.

"It was manufactured by the Cloudmist Clan in Sitia. They're known for their high-quality blades forged from local ore. Each of their daggers have been 'kissed' with their seal of authenticity." Sven pointed to a glyph on the top of dagger's pommel. "Only their weapons are marked with that seal."

Valek peered closer. "It resembles a mountain peak above some clouds. It looks easy to copy."

"The design is, but the entire hilt is misted with...I'm not quite sure what the material is, but it's...grippy. And no one has been able to replicate it, so fakes are easy to spot. Try it."

Tiny soft bumps coated the hilt. He grasped it as he would during a fight. It fit perfectly in his hand as if custom made. The material stuck to his skin, but not in an unpleasant way. It *was* grippy. "This would be great for those with sweaty palms, or for fighting in the rain or when you have blood on your hands." He practiced a few lunges. It weighed nothing compared to his other knives. He was in love.

"It'll give anyone an advantage," Sven agreed.

Including his enemies. If Brent had a cloud-kissed dagger, it would have been harder for Valek to yank it from his grasp.

"How many of these have you sold?"

"None so far. They're too expensive for the average black market buyer. But I suspect once word gets around to the collectors, I'll sell a few."

"I need to take this one along."

"To help with your cover as a connoisseur of knives?"

"Sure, let's go with that."

Sven laughed. "Will I ever see it again?"

"Only if you anger me."

THE FIRE FESTIVAL drew closer and Valek still hadn't decided on who would be the fugitive for the Commander's exercise. Two days before he needed to inform Ambrose of his pick, Valek stopped in Kenda's office and settled in the extra chair.

"Come to check on your food taster?" she asked.

No, but... "Any news?"

"Nope. According to Hildred, it's been as boring as watching dust collect. No attacks, no ambushes, and no illicit activities. She's been doing her job and, other than the cook, she doesn't talk to anyone."

Good. His interactions with Yelena had been limited. Each morning he gave her a dose of White Fright and then he didn't see her again until the evening. He made sure to be there after dinner instead of working late in his office. He didn't know why it was important. It just was. They only shared a few hours together in his suite before she went to sleep, and he joined the Commander for drinks. A couple times they talked, but she was just as comfortable reading on the couch or writing in her journal while he worked.

It was...nice.

"Is there something else?" Kenda asked, breaking the silence.

"Yes. I need to assign someone to play fugitive. Do you have any suggestions?"

"No. Our corps have been trained to avoid capture. They'll run circles around the grunts."

"Tell me something I don't know. Are there any new recruits?"

"No. You'll need to pick one of the grunts who is smarter than average. Has anyone challenged you recently who had potential?"

Valek considered Lieutenant Ari. The big man had shown some creativity while he'd fought Valek. However, Ari had been assigned to Captain Parffet's team and would be hunting the fugitive. Valek would rather see how Ari and his partner, Janco, handled the search.

"I don't know," he said. "Using a grunt as a fugitive means they'll have the same training as their pursuers. They'll be able to predict each other's moves. Unless one of the soldiers can break out of the military mindset and be imaginative. I'll go have a look. Thanks." He left.

VALEK SCANNED the groups of soldiers inside the training yards. Some worked on basic moves, others sparred, and a few performed strengthening and conditioning exercises. He hoped someone would stand out. If he lingered long enough, one of them might gather the courage to challenge him. Plus, he needed to find a fugitive, so he waited.

"I challenge you, sir!"

Valek turned. A tall, skinny boy pointed a sword at him. Valek hid his amusement. The boy...young man was clearly terrified and hadn't learned how to control his emotions before a fight.

"Don't you think you should have a few more seasons of practice before challenging me?" Valek asked even though there was no limit on the number of challenges a person could request.

"I'm twenty-four, sir."

Oops.

"All right, then. Let's see what you got." Valek removed his shirt and hopped the fence.

Turned out the boy didn't have much. Valek disarmed him in three moves. Neither did the next four contenders. Wiping sweat off his face in disgust, he decided he'd had enough and headed to the baths.

That night, Valek sat at his writing desk and focused all his attention on finding the right person. Not his corps and no military personnel, so who did that leave? Advisers. A smart group in general. The Commander had over a dozen of them, including Valek. Not all of them kept in shape, but a prisoner would be malnourished. Valek considered each of them and wrote down two names as potentials.

Next up, servants. A mixed group. No names popped into his head except Margg's. She'd never agree to run around in the woods. Rand was clever, but Valek didn't trust him to return to the castle, and the Commander would be upset to lose his favorite chef.

Then there was the medical staff. Medic Channa met most of the requirements. Intelligent, resourceful, and energetic, she'd give the grunts a good chase. He wrote her name down.

Who else? He could use a real prisoner. They'd be desperate enough to be a challenge to recapture. But they also might escape and that wouldn't be good for anyone, including Valek.

The door to his suite opened and Yelena entered. Returning from the baths, she smelled of lavender soap. He was about to ask her opinion on who would make a good fugitive when inspiration struck.

Yelena. She would be perfect. He circled her name.

⁓

THE NEXT DAY, Valek visited the Commander, hoping Yelena would still be tasting his lunch.

"Have you found a fugitive for the exercise?" the Commander asked Valek as soon as he entered.

Yelena stood by the sideboard, tasting his drink.

"Yes. I know the perfect person for the job." Valek settled into the chair facing the Commander.

"Who?"

"Yelena."

"What!" Yelena exclaimed.

"Explain," the Commander ordered.

Valek smiled at their predictable responses. "My people are trained to avoid capture. Assigning one of them wouldn't be fair to the search party. Therefore, we need a person not skilled in the art of evasion, but who is intelligent enough to bring some challenge to the exercise."

The need to move propelled him to his feet. "The fugitive needs an incentive for a good chase yet must return to the castle. I can't use a real prisoner. None of the servants have any imagination. I briefly considered the medic, but she's needed here in case of emergencies. I was about to assign one of your soldiers when I thought of Yelena."

Valek gestured toward her. "She's smart." He counted with his fingers to emphasize his words. "She'll have an incentive to perform well, and an incentive to return."

"Incentives?" A frown creased the Commander's face.

Time for the hook. "The food taster receives no wages. But for this extra job, and others like it in the future, she can be paid. The longer she evades capture, the higher the payment. As for the incentive to return, that should be obvious." They both believed she needed that daily antidote to Butterfly's Dust to stay alive.

"And if I refuse?" she asked.

"I'll recruit one of the soldiers. But I'll be disappointed. I thought you would appreciate the challenge." He really hoped she wouldn't refuse.

"Maybe I don't—"

"Enough." The Commander's voice was curt. "It's preposterous, Valek."

"That's the whole point. A soldier would make predictable moves. She's an unknown."

"*You* might outguess our fugitive, but the people I've assigned to the exercise aren't that quick. I'm hoping to find someone who can be trained as your assistant. I understand what you're waiting for, but I don't believe it'll happen anytime soon. We need someone now." The Commander sighed. "Valek, why do you constantly undermine my orders to instruct an assistant?"

"Because so far, I have disagreed with your choices. When the suitable candidate appears, then all efforts to train them will be fully endorsed."

The Commander took the tray from Yelena's hands and asked her to fetch him some hot tea. She bolted from the office in obvious relief.

"Why didn't you mention this to me last night?" Ambrose asked him.

Valek settled back in the chair. "I knew you wouldn't like it, and our late-night meetings are for..." He turned his palms up, trying to find the right words. "Winding down and good news. Not for arguments."

"So, you decided to give me this news in front of Yelena?"

"Two birds...one stone," he tried.

Ambrose gave him an icy glare.

"I wanted to see her reaction and I think if she knows you support the decision, she'll be more inclined to accept."

"She'll be at risk. Brazell is still here. Once the news spreads—"

"It won't. Only the three of us will know. Yelena's too smart and too much of a survivor to risk Brazell finding out."

The Commander leaned back in his chair and crossed his arms. Not a good sign. "And that offer to pay her?"

"This isn't part of her food tasting duties. Besides, if she earns some coins, then she won't be as tempted to sell our secrets to Star and others."

"As tempted?"

"That'll depend on how greedy she is." Although from the list of items she had desired, Valek doubted it.

"And other future jobs? Does that link back to your desire to have her become a member of our team?"

"Yes. These opportunities will give her a chance to see what we're doing. Who we are."

"That's important to you." The Commander said more to himself than Valek. He relaxed a bit.

Sensing he might have convinced him, Valek kept quiet.

"How much will you pay her?" he asked.

"A couple golds."

"I hope this works out, Valek. The exercise is for training and if she's captured easily—"

"She won't be."

The Commander smiled. "Care to bet on it?"

"Of course. Our standard bet?"

"Of course."

Yelena returned with the hot tea. Valek told her they'd pay her two golds to be the fugitive.

"The exercise is scheduled to take place during the fire festival. A busy time for the soldiers. Should we postpone it until after?" Valek asked the Commander.

"No. The added commotion will increase the level of difficulty for our pursuers."

"Well, Yelena, that gives you only a few days to prepare. Fair enough, since some prisoners plan an escape route, while others see an opportunity and bolt. Are you interested in the challenge?" Valek asked. He held his breath.

"Yes." The word burst from her as if she'd been trying to suppress it. "On the condition that Brazell not be informed of my participation."

His mood soured. Did she think he was an idiot? "Isn't having a room in my personal suite an indication that I'm properly concerned with your well-being?"

They glared at each other.

"Speaking of Brazell," the Commander interrupted. "He gave me a gift. A new dessert that his chef invented. He thought I might like it."

Commander Ambrose set a wooden box onto his desk and opened it. Inside were towers of brown squares. Odd. Valek picked up a piece and sniffed it. It gave off a nutty scent. "I hope you didn't try any." The shiny and smooth cube was about the size of a fingernail. It had rough edges that shed brown flakes.

"It's too blatant, even for Brazell, to be poisoned. But, no, I didn't."

Valek handed Yelena the container. "Yelena, take some pieces at random and taste them."

She sorted through the box and picked out four pieces. Inspecting each, she sniffed then hesitated before putting one into her mouth. Valek watched as her expression changed from thoughtful to...he wasn't quite sure. Dreamy? The Commander stood up as she shoved the rest of the brown cubes into her mouth. Did he think she'd pass out? Was the dessert some type of drug?

"Unbelievable! What is it?" Yelena asked. Her green eyes flashed with delight.

Valek and the Commander exchanged puzzled looks.

The Commander said, "Brazell called it Criollo. Why? Is there poison in it?"

"No. No poisons. It's just…" She gestured. "Try it."

Valek tossed a piece into his mouth. As the dessert melted on his tongue, the nutty aroma was enhanced. Both sweet and bitter flavors coated his mouth.

The Commander's eyes widened in surprise after he popped a cube into his mouth. Then his tongue dashed along his lips and teeth, sucking all the remaining flavor from them. He immediately grabbed another piece.

Unsettled by the Commander's reaction, Valek said, "It's sweet. Different. But I don't taste anything unbelievable about it." He wiped the brown flakes from his hands.

Now Yelena exchanged a look with the Commander. Valek suspected he'd missed something important. Perhaps this dessert didn't have the same effect on him. He'd have to keep a closer eye on them to see if this Criollo was addictive.

VALEK DRESSED in his kitchen server's uniform and pocketed a glass jar filled with the fake blackberry poison. He headed to the kitchen. Dinner had just finished, but there was always the bustling clean-up activity after each meal.

He spotted Margg and an animated group huddled around Rand. It wasn't the best time to look inconspicuous. About to leave, Valek stopped when Margg's voice cut through the din.

"I'll bet that little rat won't last an hour," she said. "I'll give fifty to one to anyone stupid enough to think the rat will last the day. And one hundred to one to the sucker who thinks she won't be caught." The room erupted with the sounds of betting.

The voices pounded against Valek as he grappled with the realization that Yelena had told Rand about being the fugitive for the exercise. Margg had to be talking about her, since she only referred to Yelena as a rat. Granted, he hadn't told Yelena to keep it a secret, but he didn't think he *needed* to. She'd been so concerned about Brazell finding out.

Fury replaced shock, and he cursed long and hard.

"I'll bet a month's wages that Yelena stays free all day," Rand's voice boomed out. Silence followed.

Then Margg laughed. "You've been in the kitchen too long, Rand. The heat's cooked your brain to mush. I think you're starting to like the little rat. Better lock up your knives when she's here or she may—"

"All right, that's enough," Rand said. "Dinner's over. Everyone out of my kitchen."

Valek shuffled out with the rest of them. He seethed with anger and walked the hallways without a destination in mind. His thoughts sizzled and for the first time in decades, he had no idea what to do.

Eventually, he looped back to the kitchen. As he neared, Rand's voice reached him. "...Sammy, Liza and maybe Dilana. Why?"

"When are you leaving?" Yelena asked.

Valek pressed his hands against the wall to keep from running into the kitchen and doing something they'd regret.

"After dinner," Rand said. "It's the only time everyone is free. The Commander always orders an easy meal for the first night of the festival so the kitchen staff can leave early. If you want to come, just meet us here tomorrow."

The fire festival. Rand had invited her to join them. At least she didn't immediately agree. Although the fact she was considering it showed just how wrong he'd been about her intelligence. Needing to move, Valek strode through the hallways. The Commander would gloat about being right if he wasn't angry at Valek for defending her so many times.

Years later, or so it seemed, Valek was back at the now dark and empty kitchen. He swapped out the blackberry poison. And that just increased his rage. Rand had tried to poison her and now they were friends. Perhaps he should warn her.

No.

The Commander's orders sounded in his head, *if she becomes too troublesome, I expect you to handle it.*

Time to handle it. Valek returned to his office and changed back into his adviser's uniform. Grimly, he tucked his new cloud-kissed dagger into his belt. He hadn't thought he'd need to use it so soon.

With an icy determination crusting over all his emotions, he headed to his apartment. Yelena had lit the lanterns, but she wasn't on the couch. Her door was closed but not locked. He allowed a moment of annoyance. *Did the woman have any self-preservation instincts?*

Light spilled in behind him as Valek entered and paused, letting his eyes adjust to the darkness.

Yelena slept curled up on her side. He fingered the hilt, but decided she needed to know why she was about to die. Approaching the bed, he grabbed her shoulders, yanked her from the blankets, and slammed her into the wall.

She stared at him in horror. Her loose hair framed her oval face. Yelena weighed almost nothing. He shifted his hold, freeing a hand so he could draw his dagger.

"Valek?"

CHAPTER 8

*I*f she becomes too troublesome, I expect you to handle it, the Commander had ordered.

But the terror trembling in her voice, and her confused and surprised gaze cracked through his icy defenses. Suddenly, he couldn't do it. Troublesome? Yes. Too troublesome? Not yet. Her indiscretion would end up killing her eventually.

"Valek, what's wrong?" she asked in barely a whisper.

He dropped her and returned to the living area. Standing next to his desk, he stared at nothing.

"If this is about the books…" she said behind him.

Valek turned. "Books? You think this is about books?" How could she *not* know? "I've been a fool. All this time I admired your survival instincts and intelligence. But now…" He paused as words failed him. "I overheard some servants discussing you as the fugitive. They were placing wagers. How could you be so stupid, so indiscreet? I considered killing you now to save myself the trouble of hunting for your dead body later."

"I didn't tell a soul." Her words came out sharp with anger. "How can you think I would jeopardize my own life?"

"Why should I believe you? The only other person who

knew was the Commander."

"Well, Valek, you're the spymaster. Couldn't someone have overheard the conversation? Who else has access to this room? You left your notes in full view on your desk." Before he could glance at his notes, she hurried on. "They were conspicuous. If I noticed them with just a quick glance, then they begged for inspection by someone seeking information."

"What are you saying? Who are you accusing?" But he knew who had access to his rooms. And who was leading the betting in the kitchen. Margg. He shouldn't have trusted her, and he'd almost killed Yelena because of his mistake. Nausea swirled in his stomach.

"I have my suspicions," she said. "But I'll accuse nobody without proof. It's unfair, and who would believe me?"

"No one." Valek snatched a gray rock from his desk and hurled it toward the wall. It exploded with a satisfying crack, raining debris, and taking the rest of his anger with it. Yelena wouldn't accuse Margg, but she was smart enough to figure out the housekeeper had leaked the information, unlike him. And if he'd really thought about it, there was the possibility of another person overhearing his and the Commander's conversation. He should apologize.

Valek decided to play dumb instead. Shouldn't be hard considering he'd leapt to the wrong conclusion about Yelena with almost disastrous results. This way he could explore the possibility of a leak and see if she suspected anyone else.

"Except me." He sank into his chair. "Either I'm addicted to risk or you're starting to make sense and we have a leak. An informer, a gossip, a mole. Whoever he is, we need to find him." Hmmm. He might have laid it on too thick.

"Or her."

Valek frowned. He needed to have a conversation with Margg. "Do we play it safe and find another fugitive? Or cancel the exercise? Or continue as planned and make you both fugitive and bait? Enticing our spy to reveal himself." He grimaced. Had Margg told Star about the exercise? "Or herself."

"You don't think Brazell will come after me?"

Now that Valek wasn't stupid with rage, he considered Brazell's response to the news. If the old goat ruined the exercise, the Commander would rescind his permission to build his factory. "No. It's too soon. I don't expect Brazell to try to kill you before his factory is up and running. Once he gets what he wants, then it's going to get interesting around here."

"Oh good. I can barely stay awake now from all the boredom."

He appreciated the sarcasm, but he kept his expression neutral. "It's your choice, Yelena."

She considered. He wouldn't blame her if she decided not to play fugitive. By attacking her, Valek had demonstrated that he didn't trust her. Why should she trust him? Yet, he desired her trust. Ah, hell. These strange and fickle emotions needed to be squashed. He imagined stuffing them all into a glass jar and shoving on the lid.

"Okay. I'll dangle on the hook to see what fish swims out. But who's going to hold the net?" she asked.

"I will." And the lid popped off, releasing a strong protective instinct. "Don't alter your plans. I'll take care of everything." Valek picked up the paper with her name on it and dipped the corner of it into a lantern, setting it on fire. "I should probably follow you to the fire festival tomorrow night. Unless logic has made you decide to turn down Rand's offer and stay in the castle." He let the burning paper float to the stone floor.

"How did you—"

Valek waited.

She huffed. "I'm going. It's a risk. So what? I take a risk every time I sip the Commander's tea. At least this time I might get a chance to enjoy myself."

Despite his attack, she didn't scare easily. Good. "It's hard to have fun at the festival without money." Valek crushed the dying embers of the paper under his boot.

"I'll manage."

He needed to apologize to her. "Would you like an advance on your wage as the fugitive?"

"No. I'll earn the money."

Really needed to apologize. "Suit yourself but let me know if you change your mind. And don't concern yourself about the books. Read all the books you want."

She headed back to her room but paused with her hand resting on the doorknob.

"Thanks," she said to the door, unwilling to look at Valek.

"For the books?"

"No. The offer."

And now it was time to say he was sorry. "You're welcome."

Valek hunted down Margg in the morning, ambushing her as she left the dining room. "We need to talk."

She frowned. "Now?"

"Now."

"Here?"

"No. My office."

From the number of sighs she released as she followed him, he knew she was annoyed. Too bad.

When they entered his office, he shut the door and rounded on her. "The entire kitchen staff is gossiping about Yelena being the fugitive. Who else did you tell besides Rand and his team?" When she opened her mouth, he added, "Don't you dare lie to me. Did you tell Star as well?"

Margg pursed her lips at his icy tone. Then she huffed. "Yes. Star pays double for any information about that rat. You left that note out about her, so I figured you wanted me to tell Star."

That would teach him not to think information was safe in his apartment. "What else have you told Star about Yelena?"

She glanced at her boots and then out the window.

This would be bad. Valek braced. "Out with it."

"I told Star that Yelena would be at the fire festival tonight."

Nothing surprising, and it reaffirmed that he needed to assign more of his corps at the festival to help keep Yelena safe. "Do you know why Star wants Yelena dead?"

"No." Margg peered at him. "Why do you care? She's disposable."

A wave of fury rushed through his veins, but he kept his stone mask on tight. "I don't care about her. I *care* about my operation with Star. There's a reason behind the information I ask you to relay to her. You can't give Star any additional information without checking with me first."

"Then you should have said so."

Valek fingered his new dagger. Just how upset would Ambrose be if he killed the housekeeper? "I shouldn't have to. But, fine, I'm saying it now. What else have you told her?"

She squirmed under his scrutiny. He gave his flat stare in warning.

Finally, she blurted, "No one was approaching me about selling secrets, so I...wanted to gain Star's attention. I...told the old goat about Yelena being out of commission for a few days and where to find her."

Valek growled.

Margg rushed on. "I also told Rand, and that very night, he asked me if I wanted to sell secrets. So, it worked!"

He'd made a mistake involving Margg in this operation. "From now on, you are not allowed to deviate from the script. Understand?"

"Yes."

"I also want the keys to my office and suite." He held out his hand.

"You what?"

"Keys. Now. You're no longer my housekeeper." Ambrose was too paranoid to keep any sensitive information where Margg could find it. Or anyone. A valuable lesson Valek should have learned. He'd become way too complacent these last ten years.

"Fine." She pulled out her keys. An impressive amount. Margg threaded two from the ring and gave them to him. "When you're sick of living in your own filth, don't come crawling to me." With that she spun on her heels and left his office.

VALEK SPENT the rest of the day getting ready for the fire festival. After a brief meeting with Hildred and Inrick, Yelena's shadows, and another with Kenda regarding assigning two more corps to Yelena's detail for that evening, he worked on his disguise.

This time he used putty to soften his angular features and to add wrinkles, aging his face by ten years. Covering his skin and the putty with makeup, he then rubbed some soft wax into his hair, giving it a slightly wild look. The beauty of the wax was he could smooth his hair or make it messier, depending on the circumstances.

Of his collection of uniforms, he chose the simple blue tunic and pants that farmers wore. Officially Castletown and the Commander's castle were in MD-6, General Hazal's district, but the residents of both wore the Commander's color of red and black. The farmers who worked the fields around the city wore Hazal's colors of blue and black.

Valek tucked various weapons into his clothing. Everything needed to be hidden or he'd draw attention. Pity he couldn't take his new cloud-kissed blade, but the switchblade strapped to his thigh would do in a pinch—the right pocket of every single pair of pants he owned had a hole big enough for him to draw the weapon. Finally, he clipped a leather pouch and his pewter mug onto his belt to help with his farmer cover. The pouch was supposedly to carry his purchases, and the mug to taste all the ales for sale.

A low-level anxiety simmered in his chest. Another unfamiliar experience. Valek had complete confidence in his team of shadows and in himself to keep Yelena safe, but she was the wild card. Young and inexperienced in this type of work, her reactions and body language tonight could warn off those who sought to harm her. Not that he wished her harm, but he needed to discover who was after her, and why.

Satisfied with his disguise, he left the castle complex through the west gate. The thick air still held the day's heat, but the cloudless sky promised for a cool night. A wash of pink and indigo colored the western horizon and transformed the sun into a bloated blood orange.

He spotted the bright flags flying above the massive pavilions that had been erected earlier in the day. Streaked with candy colors, the dozen canvas tents hosted the main attractions, while their smaller cousins held various competitions and displayed award-winning crafts. Market stands, food vendors, and entertainers were scattered everywhere, wedged into every space between tents.

Valek marveled that the festival workers had set it all up in a day. A few people rushed from tent to tent, attending to last minute details. Sunset marked the official opening, but he'd wanted to scope it out before dark and before Yelena arrived.

As he wove through the festival, Valek noted hiding spots, narrow gaps, and hidden entrances to the pavilions. On his second circuit, he created a mental map. The layout remained basically the same each year. Only the denizens changed. Attendees arrived as the sun sank and the festival workers lit the torches lining the walkways. The aroma of cooked beef, fried vegetables, and baked goods laced the cooling air. Valek's stomach grumbled in response.

On his last loop, Valek stopped at a stand selling kitchen wares. Sure enough, Sven crouched under the table, sorting through a box.

When he straightened, he smiled. "Did you come to steal another dagger?"

"It's not stealing when *I'm* funding the operation. Speaking of which, don't tell me you're selling black market goods at the festival?"

"Selling? No. Taking orders for goods delivered later? Yes."

"Enough to cover the cost of the stand fee?"

"Oh, yes. This is the most profitable time of the year." He swept a hand out, indicating the thickening crowd. "People are having fun, they're drinking, they're splurging on luxury items, and souvenirs."

"Souvenirs?"

Sven picked up a short and wide tumbler and handed it to him. Orange, yellow, and red flames decorated the thick glass as if someone had rolled up a stained-glass window.

"These were specially made for the fire festival," Sven said with pride.

"In Ixia?"

"Hell no. Nobody has that type of creativity here. But the glass artists in Sitia are very talented. Especially in the city of Booruby."

Valek stared at the rows of glasses. "You said you weren't selling any illegal goods."

Sven pished. "There's no way to prove they were manufactured in Sitia. If I didn't tell you, you wouldn't have looked twice at them."

True. "I think you're enjoying your new role entirely too much."

"Just doing my job. And if I happen to make a pile of money for the Commander and he agrees to keep me in business..." He shrugged.

Valek laughed and waved good-bye. Most of Valek's operations were difficult, requiring his corps to make sacrifices and be constantly vigilant about being discovered. It was a nice change of pace when an agent enjoyed the operation.

At a barbecue pit, he bought a shank of beef and paid to fill his mug with his favorite barley ale. Carrying his dinner to a place where he could watch for Yelena, he settled in. The sun had set, but the blazing bonfires and torches kept the central thoroughfares brightly lit. He had found a deep shadow near the main entrance in which to wait for her.

Her group was easy to spot when they came into view an hour later. Sammy, Rand's fetch boy, raced ahead. Porter walked with the pantler, Liza, while Rand limped next to Yelena. She had braided colorful ribbons in her hair. They suited her, just like the wide smile she flashed at Rand. The cook gestured wildly, and she laughed. Valek curled his fingers into fists.

As they neared, Yelena's gaze was captured by the fire festival. By this point in the evening, it was no longer an inanimate collection of tents. The people moved through it like blood through veins. Voices, music, singing, and merchants hawking their wares mixed together and transformed into a physical excitement that drummed through the air like a heartbeat.

It lived.

Yelena's expression turned to wonder as she followed Rand, who hurried through the crowds to the baking competition tent. Not surprised that the cook needed to check the results and get his ego stroked, Valek followed. He didn't search for Hildred, Inrick or the others in the mass of people surrounding them. He trusted his corps to be in position and to appear if there was any trouble. Yelena also seemed to be following his instructions on how to spot a tail. They'd only had time for a brief lesson, but it appeared she had listened to him. Good. Would she notice him? Like so many others, he carried his mug of ale. Unlike them, he scanned faces over the lip, and assessed body language for threats.

When Rand exited the tent, he wore a jubilant expression. *Must have won again. That should make him less sullen for a few weeks.* Rand bought everyone a glass of wine and they celebrated as they continued to explore. The flow of people moved like a river and swept them along toward a massive tent with red and white stripes.

Inside the pavilion, the qualifying round of the acrobatic competition had started. A bunch of brightly costumed acrobats jumped on trampolines, walked on tight ropes high above the spectators, and performed tumbling routines on the floor mats. Feet thudded, chalk billowed, and the crowd murmured in awe. The earthy odor of sweat mixed with the dry musk of the piles of straw used to break the entrants' falls.

Yelena, Rand, and the others sat on the bleachers to view the competition. Valek remained close enough to reach her if something happened. Instead of viewing the displays of physical prowess in the main arena, he kept his attention focused on Yelena and those around her.

She watched the acrobats with a rapt expression, but then Rand leaned toward her and broke the spell. Rand gloated about something before facing forward again. After that, Yelena's gaze grew distant and then troubled.

Had she recognized someone in the crowd? Valek examined the rows of people, seeking soldiers wearing green and black uniforms. No one. But they could also be in disguise.

Yelena hunched over and bit her knuckle. Alarmed, Valek reached for his switchblade, but she appeared to be in no danger. Rand finally noticed and put his arm around her shoulders. Valek fingered the hilt, but Rand only roused her from... What? Why did she suddenly become so...frightened?

Rand handed her a meat pie. Pride swelled in Valek's chest when she performed the five S-steps. But she didn't eat much as she talked to the cook. When they stood to leave, Valek hurried out. Perhaps she was afraid he wasn't guarding her like he promised. She might need confirmation that he was nearby.

Valek took a couple big gulps of his ale and spilled the rest down his tunic. Ugh. When he spotted Yelena and Rand arm in arm, he had to crush the desire to yank Rand into some dark corner.

Acting and smelling drunk, Valek bumped into Yelena, causing her to stumble.

When she glanced at him, he mumbled, "Pardon me," and saluted her with his mug. No recognition touched her face, so he bowed, pretended to lose his balance, and landed at her feet, hoping she would help him stand and he could tell her that he had her back.

Except a loud pulsing rhythm surged through the crowd and shook the ground. Drawn by the commotion, Yelena stepped over him.

At least his disguise worked. Valek stood and brushed the dust off his uniform. He looked at the crowd in front of him but didn't see Yelena. Not panicking, he scanned the press of people entering the entertainment tent.

Hildred appeared beside him. "Where did she go?" Her voice was tight with tension.

Then Inrick and the two other shadows were next to him.

"She must be at the entrance of the tent with Rand," Inrick said. "I can see his head. Not hers, she's too short."

No. She'd disappeared too quickly. "Fan out with your teammate," Valek ordered. "She couldn't have gone far."

He took the right side, searching. It was the unnatural lurching stride of the four big men that caught his attention at first. That and how close they stood to each other as if—

Ribbons flashed between shoulders. Yelena.

Valek whistled to his corps and hurried after the goons. They dragged her away from the crowd and disappeared between two medium-sized tents. He remembered there was an empty area behind the pavilions with three ways to get in.

His team caught up. Valek sent each pair to the other sides of the tents. "Don't let them pass you."

"What about you?" Hildred asked.

"I'm taking this one."

"But—"

"Noooo—" the scream cut off.

Yelena. Every particle of his being cried out with one primal directive: *She. Can't. Die.*

"Go! Now!" Valek ran through the narrow gap and broke through a sticky substance as if he'd just run through a spider web.

Magic. He cursed.

When he reached the area, he paused for a second to analyze the scene and let his eyes adjust to the semi-darkness. Three big men held Yelena, while another strangled her with a garrote. A woman stood nearby watching.

"Hurry up! She's starting to project," the woman said.

Oh no. Not tonight. Not ever. Valek stepped forward and held out his mug. "Excuse me, sirs, do you know where I can get a refill?" He slurred his words.

As expected, they turned their attention to Valek. The man with the garrote let go and pulled a knife. Thank fate. But when Yelena went limp, fury sent a surge of energy through him.

The man lunged. Valek turned his mug. The blade stabbed into the mug instead of his heart. Nice. He twisted the mug with a hard jerk. The knife flew through the air. Not wasting time, Valek slammed the pewter mug into the man's temple. He crumbled just as his three companions rushed Valek. They didn't waste any time. Two grabbed his upper arms and shoulders, holding him in place while the third managed to punch Valek in the face. Twice.

Pain shot through his jaw and cheek; he tasted the metallic tang of blood. Then magic surrounded him, pushing against his skin, weighing him down, slowing his movements. No way this would be a fair fight. Valek changed tactics. He needed to end this. Now.

Since the two men already supported his weight, he lifted his legs and wrapped his left one around the third guy's neck, Using the heel of his right boot to apply pressure, he snapped the man's neck. The two idiots holding him stared in shock. They hadn't bothered to secure his wrists, so he swung his mug into the right man's groin, when the goon doubled over, Valek slammed it into his face. Yelping, the man released his hold on Valek as his blood gushed.

With one arm free, he turned to the last goon and smashed the mug into his nose before striking him on the temple. The man collapsed. It took mere seconds, but because of the magic around him Valek gasped for breath as if he'd run for miles. The magic intensified and he met the magician's gaze. By the incredible force of her power, he suspected she was a master magician.

He wondered what she was trying to do with her power. Kill him? Knock him unconscious? She wore a hawk mistress' uniform, and her hair was pulled back into a severe bun. Her bronze skin tone was similar to those who lived in southern Sitia. Probably a member of the Bloodgood or Jewelrose Clans.

Yelena stood and wobbled. He almost cheered out loud until the movement drew the southern magician's attention. Valek swayed as the magic around him disappeared. But then Yelena sank back to the ground with a tired smile.

Oh no.

Panic soon gripped Yelena's face and she thrashed, clawing at her face. He might be immune to magic, but Yelena wasn't. The magician was going to kill her.

CHAPTER 9

*V*alek was next to Yelena in a heartbeat. He tried to block the magician's power with his body while he shook Yelena's shoulders. The magician must have control of her mind, and there was only one way to break the spell.

"Recite poisons in your mind!" he shouted in her ear.

She calmed and went limp, giving up. Not a good sign.

"Recite! Now! That's an order!"

Come on, come on, he silently chanted.

Scrunching her face, her gaze sought his. Then she gasped for air and Valek wanted to jump for joy. He'd analyze the strength of that emotion later. Much later.

"Keep reciting," he urged, glancing around.

The southern magician had disappeared and so had most of Valek's energy. He stood and helped Yelena to her feet. She swayed and he steadied her, placing his hand on her shoulder. Yelena covered his hand with hers. A warm buzz emanated from the touch. For a second, he thought she'd rush into his arms. And he longed for the contact, would welcome it, but she straightened and stepped away.

He returned to the four men. Turning one man over, he

cursed. "Southerners." Then he checked their pulses. "Two alive. I'll have them taken to the castle for questioning." And just where were his back-ups?

"What about the woman?" she asked with a rasp.

She'd have a sore throat for a couple days. "Gone."

"Will you search for her?"

The magician knew the risks of being caught in Ixia. She was probably halfway to Sitia by now and, if not, she had enough power to disappear in Ixia. Frankly, Valek didn't have the energy. "Yelena, she's a southern magician. I took my eyes off her, so there's no way I can find her now."

Trembling, Yelena stared at the men on the ground. Not wanting to upset her further, he took her by the arm and led her back toward the festival.

"Magician?" she asked. "I thought they were banished from Ixia."

"Although very unwelcome, some visit Ixia anyway." And were killed when captured.

"But I thought—"

"Not now. I'll explain later. Right now, I want you to catch up with Rand and his friends. Pretend nothing has happened. I doubt she'll try again tonight." He escorted her through the shadows and kept an eye out for his corps, the magician, and Rand.

Rand was easy to find. The tall cook had returned to the acrobatics tent and was yelling Yelena's name. By the way he staggered, the man was probably drunk. Or feeling guilty? Hmmm, he'd have to investigate the possibility Rand had set her up.

She moved toward her friend. The torchlight illuminated the black strap around her throat.

"Yelena, wait," Valek said, gesturing her closer. He reached for the garrote, but she stepped back. Ah. Even after he'd saved her life, she still didn't trust him. Yet, she braced and waited.

Progress. Valek tried again and pulled the strap from her neck and handed it to her, showing her what had almost killed her.

She shivered and flung it to the ground before joining Rand. Valek picked it up. Lavender scented the leather. The weapon might come in handy someday. Perhaps he'd wrap it around the southern magician's neck. One could hope.

Hildred and Inrick appeared next to him.

"Where have you been?" he demanded.

"We couldn't get to you," Hildred said.

"Did you get lost?"

"No. We encountered some type of invisible barrier."

The magic spiderweb he'd broken through. Valek should have known.

"I know it sounds crazy," Inrick said. "But eventually the barrier disappeared, and we rushed in to find the bodies and no sign of you or Yelena. What happened?"

Valek would explain later. "Where are the others?"

"Back with the bodies just in case you returned."

"Go tell them you found us," he said to Inrick. "Then fetch a clean-up crew. Take the two still breathing to the infirmary. As soon as they're conscious, interrogate them."

"Yes, sir." Inrick dashed off.

"And me?" Hildred asked.

"You're with me. We're staying with Yelena until she's safe inside my suite."

"Yes, sir."

THE BRUISES on Valek's jaw ached and all he desired was a long hot soak followed by collapsing into his bed. Instead, he took a quick bath, changed into a clean uniform, and reported to the Commander for their nightly meeting—a tradition that had started soon after the takeover. The only time they didn't meet was when either of them was out of town, or when Valek was working undercover.

Resisting the temptation to check on Yelena, Valek knocked on the Commander's door. It was well after midnight and Ambrose may have gone to bed. In which case, he wouldn't answer. But the door swung open. The Commander eyed Valek's face and then stepped back, allowing him in.

His suite was a mirror image of Valek's with the same L-shaped living area, same number of rooms on two floors. Except Ambrose's place was pristine. Not a book out of place. No clutter. And no personality. Not that Valek was brave enough to point that out.

"Sit," the Commander gestured to the couches. Two of them faced each other with a low table between them.

A tumbler, half full of an amber liquid, and a report rested on the table. Valek sank into the cushions while Ambrose poured him a drink. He handed the glass to Valek before settling opposite him. The strong scent of peach brandy stung his nose. Valek refrained from downing the alcohol in one gulp.

"The fire festival is already causing trouble," Ambrose said, jabbing a finger at the report. "Merchants fighting over their tent locations, entertainers demanding more money, and crime rates doubling, why do I fund this…this…unnecessary and expensive frivolity every year?"

This argument was as old as the festival. And Valek knew this was just the opening salvo and not a legitimate question. He sipped his drink.

"And if those bruises are any indication, I'm sure you're about to report more trouble. Who came after our food taster this time? Brazell? Star?"

"Neither fish took our bait."

"No?"

"No. Instead, we lured a big, dangerous shark." He drained his drink. The Commander did the same. Valek took both glasses, refilled them, and returned to his seat before recounting the evening's events.

Ambrose listened without interruption. At the end, he asked, "Why does a southern magician wish my food taster dead?"

"No idea." Although Valek was happy to note Ambrose's use of *my*.

"I'd say this qualifies as Yelena being too troublesome, but it goes well beyond that."

"It does. And if she dies, then any chance to solve this mystery will die with her."

"Then I trust you to find out *exactly* what is going on and stop it."

"Yes, sir."

AFTER HIS MEETING with the Commander, Valek headed to the infirmary. Inrick guarded the two unconscious goons. Medic Channa guessed it would be a couple more hours before they woke.

"Did you have to hit them so hard?" she asked, annoyed. "One has a cracked skull and may have brain damage."

"Four against one, Channa. I'm lucky it wasn't me who had to be carried in here."

Her expression softened. "How's the jaw?" She fingered the bruises. "Do you need any pain medicine? Or have you already self-medicated?" She sniffed. "Peach?"

"Yes, to both questions. The Commander always has the good stuff." The brandy had dulled the throb.

Channa handed him some smelling salts. "For your…guests. Wave these under their noses every thirty minutes or so. You might be able to wake one of them up sooner."

"Thanks."

Valek joined Inrick. They discussed the evening's events as they waited, comparing notes.

"Did you see these guys at the festival?" Valek asked.

"Not together. And I only noticed the blacksmith earlier in the crowd because half his beard was singed off. You'd think he would have shaved the rest."

"Unless that's part of his disguise."

"Could be." He shrugged. "Truthfully, I wasn't looking for the obvious goons. I thought General Brazell would send an assassin, or his soldiers would be wearing civilian clothes."

Inrick made an interesting point. Had Star or Brazell hired the southern magician to kill Yelena? Would a master-level magician be working for hire? Unlikely. No. There had to be something else going on.

After multiple attempts, they finally roused one of the goons. Unfortunately, he had been a grunt for hire and his job was to aid in the kidnapping. All he knew was that the man with the knife had hired him and the woman acted like his boss.

Discouraged, Valek left the infirmary and returned to his apartment. He blinked at the sudden brightness. All the lanterns blazed and, sitting on the couch wide awake and obviously waiting for him, was Yelena. He glanced longingly at the stairs up to his bedroom, bit back a sigh, and studied her.

"Haven't you slept?" he asked.

"No. But neither have you," she said, sounding like a little kid.

"I can sleep all day. You need to taste the Commander's breakfast in an hour."

"What *I* need are answers."

"To what questions?" Valek started extinguishing the lanterns.

"Why is a southern magician trying to kill me?"

"A good question. The very same one I was going to ask you."

"How should I know?" She threw her hands up in frustration. "Brazell's guards I could understand. But magicians! It's not like I've been going around making southern magicians angry."

"Ahhh...that's a shame. Since you have a real talent for angering people." Valek sunk into the chair by his desk and rested his throbbing head in his hands. "A southern magician, Yelena, a master-level southern *magician.* Do you know that there are only four master magicians in Sitia? Four. And since the takeover, they've stayed in Sitia. On occasion they send a minion or two with minor magical abilities into the Territory to see what we're up to. So far, each spy has been intercepted and dealt with. Commander Ambrose will not tolerate magic in Ixia."

And it was damned inconvenient for Valek. Needing to move, he stood up and snatched a gray rock from his desk. Carving helped focus his thoughts, perhaps just holding a stone would help as well. He paced around the living room. Yelena pulled her legs underneath her.

"For the southerners to risk one of their master magicians, the reason has to be..." Valek squeezed the stone in his hand as he searched for the right descriptor. She needed to know the danger. "Momentous. So why are they after you?" He sighed and sank down on the couch next to her. "Well, let's try to reason this out. You obviously have some southern blood in your heritage."

"What?"

Why was she surprised? Had she not noticed her skin tone? Or were the other children in Brazell's orphanage similar in coloring?

"Your coloring is a bit darker than the typical northerner," he explained. "Your features have a southern quality. Green eyes are very rare in the Territory but are more common in Sitia."

She stared at him in shock. Did she believe these qualities were bad? In his opinion, they enhanced her beauty.

"It's nothing to be ashamed of," he reassured her. "When the King was in power, the border to Sitia was open to commerce and trade. People moved freely between the regions, and marriages were inevitable. I would guess you were left behind right after the takeover, when people panicked and fled south before we closed the border. It was complete mayhem. I don't know what they were expecting when the Commander came to power. Mass killings? All we did was give everyone a uniform and a job."

Her frozen expression remained, and he regretted having implied her parents had left her behind. What a terrible comment. He didn't mean to imply that. She was probably an orphan before the takeover and the people in charge of her care left her behind. No, that didn't sound nice either. The silence lengthened.

"Well, anyway, I digress." Valek stood and resumed his pacing. "I doubt it was missing family members. They wouldn't want to kill you. Is there anything else, besides murdering Reyad, that you did in the past? Witnessed a crime? Overheard plans for a rebellion? Anything at all?"

"No. Nothing."

Valek tapped the rock against his forehead. Why had he said, 'other than murdering Reyad?' He really needed to stop talking and go to sleep before he wrecked their tenuous relationship. "Then let's assume this has to do with Reyad. Perhaps he was in league with some southerners and your killing him ruined their plans. Maybe they're scheming to retake Ixia. Or they think you know something about this plot. But I've heard nothing about Sitia attacking us. And why would they? Sitia knows the Commander is content to stay in the north and vice versa." Valek rubbed a hand over his face. The bruises ached.

Ignoring the pain, he continued, "Perhaps Brazell has gotten creative in his old age and hired southerners to kill you; thereby accomplishing his desire to see you dead without implicating himself. No. That doesn't make sense. Brazell would have hired thugs, no need for a magician. Unless he has connections I'm not aware of, which is highly doubtful." Valek looked around the room as if the answer lurked in a shadowy corner. Instead, he noticed the sky had lightened, signaling the sun's arrival. Setting the rock down, he finished extinguishing the lanterns, but his thoughts kept burning.

What else would be important enough for Sitia to risk a master-level magician? There were currently no Sitians in the dungeon awaiting execution, so no one to rescue. People born with magical abilities were rare, and only four people presently had master-level powers. He froze as a thought occurred to him. He gazed at Yelena. Could *she* be a magician?

"What?" she asked in alarm.

"Magicians will come north to smuggle one of their own kind to safety," Valek said. But he had sensed no magic from Yelena. "Then why kill you? Unless you're a Soulfinder, they wouldn't want you dead." Sitians feared Soulfinders, who were rumored to be extremely powerful and dangerous magicians who ignored the Ethical Code that governed the magicians. But there hadn't been any Soulfinders in a century. Regardless, nothing about the attack made sense. Valek yawned and the ache in his jaw flared to life. "I'm too tired to think straight. I'm going to bed." He walked to the stairs.

"Valek."

He paused with his foot on the first step, hoping it wasn't important.

"My antidote."

"Of course." Normally, he would wake up at dawn, draw a dose of White Fright for her, and bring it downstairs.

Valek trudged up the steps. No footprints disturbed the powder he'd sprinkled in front of his bedroom doors. And the thin paper he'd wedged between the door and the ceiling remained in place. When he'd worked as an assassin, he frequently laid in wait in his victim's bedroom, and he took cautions to ensure that didn't happen to him. It was a pain in the ass to reset his safeguards every day, but well worth the effort.

Even with his precautions, he checked for intruders before unlocking his cabinet. With piles of rocks and books heaped on top, nothing about his poison chest stood out from the rest of the furniture crammed in his room. However, a searcher would find it in no time. And that lock would easily be bypassed by removing the pins in the hinges. Or a sharp ax would work as well.

As he filled a pipette with Yelena's "antidote," he wondered if she had explored upstairs. Did she spot the powder and avoid his bedroom? There were plenty of other rooms to investigate.

By the time he returned downstairs, the sunlight had strengthened and illuminated the nasty black and blue bruise that ringed Yelena's neck. Anger surged through him. That master magician wouldn't survive another encounter with Valek.

"You might want to wear your hair down today," he said, handing her the pipette.

"Why?" She ran her long fingers through her hair. They caught in the once bright ribbons that were now dull and torn.

"To cover the marks on your neck." Not that the Commander cared, but anyone who encountered Yelena today would notice and wonder what happened. Valek enjoyed having a ruthless reputation—it made his life easier at times—but the thought of anyone believing he could strangle or harm Yelena— a person he was actively protecting, a person he had to admit he'd grown to care for—upset him very much.

◇

VALEK FINISHED PAINTING his face with the colors of the forest. He adjusted the tight hood on his head, tucking a few stray hairs underneath the fabric. Except for the blue of his eyes, his entire body was covered in green camouflage.

The one-piece outfit clung to his skin, revealing his muscles and almost everything else. Thank fate Dilana had sown extra material to cover his groin and overlapped the fabric so there was…er…access when nature called. She'd also added a number of pockets for his smaller weapons. Today's exercise involved traveling through the thick woods. Loose clothing and big weapons like a sword would only impede his movements.

Satisfied with his camouflage, Valek headed out the south gate and jogged to the Snake Forest. It formed a natural border with Sitia, extending from the Soul Mountains in the east all the way to the Sunset Ocean in the west. As an added precaution, the Commander had the forest cleared an extra hundred feet on the Ixian side to make it easier for the border guards to spot anyone trying to leave Ixia or Sitians trying to illegally sneak into the country.

The predawn air was cool and crisp. Dew had condensed onto the grass. Valek looked back. There was just enough light to illuminate his boot prints across the damp field. He wondered if Yelena would notice them on her way into the forest.

As the fugitive, Yelena would naturally head to Sitia, which was why he found a comfortable spot among the underbrush directly south of the castle to await her arrival. It was warmer among the trees. Their leaves trapped the day's heat and the air cooled slower than out on the grassy plain. The scent of pine, moist earth, and living green filled the air. Night insects buzzed. Valek enjoyed the peace.

It didn't take long for shafts of sunlight to pierce the tree canopy. Sunrise marked the beginning of the exercise. Yelena would have one hour's head start before the two teams began their hunt. Captain Etta's dog team would include Porter, the kennel master. Lieutenants Ari and Janco would be a part of Captain Parffet's team. From what he'd learned about Yelena, Valek believed she'd outwit the humans, but wouldn't be able to lose the dogs. Time would tell.

Yelena's arrival in the forest fifteen minutes later was far from stealthy. Disappointed, Valek amended his earlier predictions about her abilities. Her heavy footsteps thudded. Branches snapped. Bushes shook. Leaves crunched.

He followed the obvious trail she created without an attempt at furtiveness. Any noise he caused was drowned out by all her commotion. After three quarters of an hour, the ruckus stopped suddenly. Valek slowed. The gurgle of water filled the silence. He eased around a bend and froze. Yelena knelt next to the stream.

Moving deeper into the brush, Valek crept closer. She dipped her hands into the water, pulling out handfuls of mud. He had a couple seconds to wonder what she planned, when she smeared the brown goo on her face, ears, and the back of her neck. Ah. That explained why she'd twisted her hair into a tight bun. But what of her bright red uniform shirt? Would she cover that in mud as well?

No. Instead, she stood and stamped a couple of boot prints into the stream's bank and then retraced her earlier route. That was unexpected. He'd thought she'd walk into the stream in order to trick the dogs. It wouldn't work for Porter's dogs, they followed both air and ground scents, but she probably wasn't aware of their unusual dual training.

Intrigued, Valek inched through the bushes and spotted her red tunic in the middle of her trail. Crouched over her backpack, she removed a few items. Too far to discern the objects, Valek waited. Soon enough, she tossed something up into the tree canopy only to catch it on the way down. He moved closer. She tried again. On her third attempt, Valek realized what she'd been doing. He pumped a fist, silently celebrating with her as her grappling hook snagged the branch of a Velvatt tree. A rope tied to the hook hung down from the thick limb.

Then he watched with growing admiration as she grabbed the cord and climbed about fifteen feet onto the branch with a lithe grace. He'd been far too quick to judge her this morning. The trail she had laid was a decoy for both teams. No one would suspect she had climbed into the trees. Because she used a rope, there would be no marks on the Velvatt's smooth trunk. Smart. Very smart.

But what of her red uniform? Valek remained on the forest floor as she turned downwind and navigated through the tree-tops. He tracked her by the noise and by the flashes of red between the leaves. Yelena still had a head start so the rustling branches shouldn't give her away, but it was only a matter of time before the others caught up.

After about a half hour, she stopped. Perched high above in a Cheketo tree, she was very hard to spot due to the large green circular-shaped leaves. About eight inches wide and spotted with brown, the leaves created an effective cover. All remained quiet and he approved of her hiding place. He would have liked her to be farther from the castle, but her current location would be hard to find unless the dogs managed to pick up her scent. Valek scanned the area. He'd need a comfortable spot to wait.

A ripping sound from above punctured the silence. Valek shifted to get a better view. Yelena stripped the big Cheketo leaves. Why would she expose her position? Confused, he watched.

As the reason for her actions became clear, his heart confirmed what the confusing emotions he'd been experiencing since the night of the fire festival meant. Confirmed what he'd been pushing away and denying. Confirmed that there was someone else besides the Commander that he would gladly die for. That a world without Yelena would be a world not worth living in. That he'd fallen in love with her.

Of course, he couldn't confess to her any of his emotions. Loving her would only make her more of a target to his enemies, and he knew she didn't feel the same way about him. Besides, she was too smart to fall for him. She'd just camouflaged her bright red uniform shirt with Cheketo leaves. Amazing.

Then she set off through the trees, heading east. This time, she moved slowly, keeping the noise to a minimum. Valek remained on the forest floor, tracking her. She spent the rest of the morning climbing from tree to tree. At times, she used her grappling hook to bring branches closer together. Others, she swung from tree to tree. Whenever he spotted her through the leaves, a wide smile always lit her face. Good for her. It made him happy to see her enjoying the exercise.

By lunch time, she reached a well-used road and stopped to eat. The east-west trail was one of the trading routes between Ixia and Sitia before the takeover. It should have grown over by now, but, by the recent ruts and broken branches, smugglers and black market dealers had been using it. Valek sighed. It never stopped. Never. He'd have to dispatch a team to lay in wait and arrest the caravans.

Valek munched on a piece of jerky as he considered the logistics of stopping the illegal activity. A subtle rustling noise sounded to his left, followed by a faint rasp. After a few more quiet swishes, Valek suspected Parffet's trackers had caught up to Yelena. He waited.

"See anything?" a man asked.

Valek recognized the voice—Lieutenant Ari. Nice.

"No. All clear," Janco said, sounding annoyed.

Both were closer to Valek than he'd suspected. Impressive skills, but not good enough to figure out their quarry sat just above their heads.

Eventually, they broke cover and stood in the middle of the road.

"Stupid idea, coming east. She's probably at the southern border by now," Janco grumbled.

"That's what the dog boys figured, even though the hounds lost her scent," Ari said.

Pride swelled in Valek's chest. She'd confused the dogs.

"I don't know if I follow the logic of going east," Janco said.

Ari sighed. "You're not supposed to follow the logic. The captain ordered us east; we go east. He seems to think she'll head deeper into MD–5. Familiar territory for her."

"Well, what if she doesn't come back? Another stupid idea, using the food taster," Janco complained. "She's a criminal."

"That's not our concern. That's Valek's problem. I'm sure if she got away, he would take care of her."

Valek considered. Would he chase after Yelena? Or let her escape? An interesting dilemma.

"Let's go. We're supposed to rendezvous with the captain at the lake. Oh, and try to keep the noise down. You sound like a panicked moose crashing through the woods," Ari chided.

"Oh yeah. Like you could hear me over your specially trained 'woodland-animal footsteps,'" Janco countered. "It was like listening to two deer humping each other."

The men laughed and disappeared into the underbrush, one on each side of the path. Yelena remained in place. Probably waiting until the two trackers moved further east. Then she once again proved her intelligence and changed course, heading south.

About to follow, Valek paused. A hundred yards down the trail, Ari and Janco stepped from the underbrush. He froze.

"Told you I heard something rustle the trees," Janco gloated.

"And our prey bought the 'need to rendezvous east' comment. She's probably heading south," Ari said.

Valek had to admire their abilities. But did they know Yelena watched them from the trees or did they only suspect she was nearby? Either way, he would have some fun and test them.

Moving west, Valek crackled the bushes.

"She's going west," Ari whispered.

"Toward the dog team." Janco groaned.

"Not if we find her first." Ari gestured and the two men melted into the woods.

Valek grinned. Game on. He led them on a merry chase through the forest, looping back and making figure eights. He didn't want to get too far from Yelena. No doubt his path frustrated the men as he stayed just out of reach. They could have broken cover and split, trapping Valek between them, but that was against orders. The Commander's soldiers all stayed in pairs no matter the circumstances. You never left your partner. Never.

Which reminded Valek, he needed to end this chase and find Yelena. Doubling back, he was about to give them the slip when a strong and familiar magic brushed his skin. The southern magician lurked in the forest and Yelena was alone.

CHAPTER 10

A cold wave of fear washed over Valek. He rocked back on his heels, then clamped the panic down hard. No time for emotions. Time for action. He broke cover and hunted the southern magician by sensing her magic. The desire to hurry pulsed in his veins, urging him to move faster. Tracking a person by the touch of their magic was tricky at the best of times, but it was all Valek had.

Ari and Janco also lost all pretense of stealth. They crashed through the brush behind him. Valek hoped they'd catch up, as he'd need the back up. How many goons did she hire this time? Was Yelena already dead?

He stumbled at that thought. Then he ruthlessly dismissed it, focusing on the task at hand. Find the magician. Kill the magician. He picked up his pace. Find the magician. Kill the magician.

After a few minutes, her magic swelled. The air around him thickened like honey, slowing him down. Cursing, he pushed through it, but she must have been sending out her full power. And damn. The strength of a master magician was extraordinary.

The noises behind him ceased and he hoped she hadn't killed Ari and Janco. Regardless, Valek was now on his own.

He fought for every step.

Find the magician. Kill the magician.

Two more steps. Breathe in. Three steps. Exhale. Two.

Find the magician. Kill the magician.

Her magic suddenly disappeared and Valek fell forward, crashing to the ground. He scrambled to his feet. Without the magic, he had no way to track her. Scanning the forest, Valek spotted a brighter area to the south that might indicate a clearing. He jumped over roots and bushes, not caring about the noise, but some sense prevailed, and he slowed before he could burst into the open area and probably right into an ambush.

Valek eased closer. Yelena sat in the middle of the clearing, rooting through her backpack. Not only alive, but she also appeared unharmed. The power of his relief knocked him to his knees. It took him a moment to regain his composure and another dozen heartbeats to suppress the overwhelming desire to run to her, sweep her into his arms, hug her tight, and never let her go. He huffed a laugh over what he imagined would be her response. A slap to the face if he was lucky, a kick to the groin if he wasn't.

He pulled it together and scanned the clearing, searching for the magician and her goons. Gone. But how far? And which direction? Valek looped to the south. A few broken branches dripped sap, indicating someone had recently passed through. He followed the trail for a few minutes. But he grew uneasy when the distance between him and Yelena increased. No matter how much he wished to thrust his knife into the magician's heart, he would not leave Yelena unprotected again.

Turning back, he paused when the branches shook above him. Yelena had returned to the tree canopy and was heading in the same direction as the magician. South. Did Yelena have a death wish?

To make matters worse, Ari and Janco had resumed the hunt. So much for not leaving Yelena unprotected. She'd already survived two encounters with the magician, he hoped she'd stay safe for another half an hour or so. That was about how long it would take to lead the trackers away from her.

But then an odd and unwelcome thought popped into his head. Perhaps the magician hadn't ambushed Yelena. Perhaps this was a prearranged meeting. That the attack and attempt to kill her at the fire festival had all been an act, and Yelena was spying for the Sitians. The implications… Valek shoved those thoughts to the back of his mind. He'd consider it later. Right now, he needed to deal with Ari and Janco.

The lieutenants picked up his clues and followed him. Valek traveled south-west until he reached another well-used road in the forest. Lovely. Just how many paths did the smugglers use? Valek would worry about that later. For now, he would take advantage of it. He crossed over and left signs of his passage to the south, then backtracked to the road and jogged east.

It took him a bit of time to find Yelena. She sat on a branch high above the path, but with a clear view. Smart. Valek summoned his remaining energy and climbed a nearby tree. Keeping to the sturdier limbs, he scrambled higher than Yelena in order to find a way to cross over to her perch. His opinion of her skills increased. She had made traveling through the tree canopy look easy.

Not wanting to scare her, Valek rustled the branch over her head before joining her. She scanned his skin-tight suit and then glanced at her ad hoc camouflage, which was torn and frayed in places.

Oh no, he won't let her feel inferior or self-conscious. "You're unbelievable." And he meant it.

"Is that good or bad?" she asked.

"Good. I assumed you would give the soldiers a good chase, and you did. But I never expected this." Valek pointed at her camouflage and gestured toward the surrounding tree canopy. "And to top it all off, you encountered the magician and somehow managed to survive." He used an accusatory tone to see if it would provoke any signs of guilt or duplicity.

"I don't know what exactly happened. I found myself tearing through the woods until I reached a clearing, where she was waiting. The only thing she told me was that I had ruined her plans by killing Reyad, and then pain slammed into my skull."

Genuine horror filled her eyes. The primal urge to comfort her swelled inside him. Valek tightened his control, keeping his arms at his sides and not around her.

"I started reciting poisons," she continued. "I tried to push the pain away. Then the attack stopped, and she said you were getting too close. When I opened my eyes, she had disappeared."

That was plausible. "Why didn't you wait for me in the clearing?"

"I didn't know where she had gone. I felt safer in the trees, knowing you'd be able to find me."

And that was smart. Yet the thought that she might be working with the magician wouldn't quite disappear. Yelena claimed she ruined the magician's plans by murdering Reyad, which fit with one of his theories.

Yelena sorted through her backpack, avoiding eye contact. Valek knew she held many secrets in her heart. She was still afraid of him. He hoped she'd trust him and accusing her of not telling him the whole truth wouldn't help with that goal. He could be very patient.

Instead, he focused on the positive. Grinning, he said, "We certainly proved the Commander wrong. He thought you'd be caught by midmorning." And he owed Valek a gold coin. Bonus.

She smiled back at him and Valek almost fell off the branch. He'd do just about anything to keep her smiling at him.

"Why does the Commander hate magicians so much?" she asked.

His good humor faded. It was natural she'd be curious about magicians after one had attacked her twice, but was she really pumping him for information? No way to tell, so he answered her. "He has many reasons. They were the King's colleagues. Aberrations of nature, who used their power for purely selfish and greedy reasons. They amassed wealth and jewels, curing the sick only if the dying's family could pay their exorbitant fee. The King's magicians played mind games with everyone, taking delight in causing havoc. The Commander wants nothing to do with them."

"What about using them for his purposes?" she asked.

"He thinks magicians are not to be trusted, but I'm of two minds about that." He glanced at the path below. "I understand the Commander's concern, killing all the King's magicians was a good strategy, but I think the younger generation born with power could be recruited for our intelligence network. We disagree on this issue, and despite my arguments the Commander has—" Valek stopped, he didn't want to scare her.

"Has what?" she prompted.

He shouldn't sugar coat anything. Yelena would learn everything about the Commander eventually. Might as well be truthful. "Ordered that those born with even the slightest amount of magical power be killed immediately."

She gasped in horror. "Those poor children."

Great. Now she thought he killed babies. "It's brutal, but not that brutal." Valek hated that part of his job. "The ability to connect with the power source doesn't occur until after puberty, which is around age sixteen. It usually takes another year for someone other than their family to notice and report them. Then, they either escape to Sitia, or I find them." And helped them escape, but only a couple people knew about that, and it had to remain a secret or the Commander would write an order for *Valek's* execution.

He watched as Yelena gazed into the distance. No doubt

imagining him hunting down and assassinating teenagers. So much for building trust. Valek searched for a topic to change the subject, but voices drifted on the wind. The trackers? Or the dog team? He wasn't sure, but he grabbed Yelena's arm, and signaled her to be quiet.

Soon the voices grew louder, and the sounds of hoofbeats reached him. It didn't take long for a caravan to appear on the road. Valek scanned the wagons, seeking threats. Two mules and one driver for each of the six wagons. No visible weapons on the men, who wore ill-fitting brown trader uniforms. The brown color due to the nomadic nature of their occupation. Traders didn't live in one Military District, so they wore all the colors mixed together.

However, no legitimate traders would travel through the Snake Forest when there were perfectly smooth roads connecting all the cities in Ixia.

Five of the wagons transported indistinguishable burlap sacks. They probably contained black market goods. Yellow oval-shaped pods filled the last wagon. Odd. What were they? And where were they going with that strange cargo?

Once they were out of sight, Valek decided he'd swipe a few samples. "Don't move, I'll be back," he whispered to Yelena before dropping down to the path.

Valek jogged to catch up. It was easy to follow the caravan. The men talked and laughed as the wooden wheels rattled over the stones. Small saplings and bushes thwacked the sides, adding to the din and masking his footsteps. All that noise meant they'd either bribed the border patrol guards or knew this section of the forest had been cleared of guards for the exercise.

Or it could be a shipment for Sven, which would explain their ease. However, the caravan was too far east to be for his agent. Valek guessed they were headed to MD-5. Almost all the major cities of Ixia had black markets, so that wasn't a surprise.

The merchant's ease also aided him, since the men didn't bother scanning the surrounding forest for border guards. Nor did they glance behind them. Perhaps they had scouts, checking the route ahead. In that case, the scouts hadn't seen Yelena and Valek in the trees. Then again, Valek hadn't detected them either.

Regardless of why, Valek jogged up to the last wagon filled with those strange yellow pods. He plucked one from the moving wagon and examined it. It was roughly oval shaped, like an egg that had been elongated. Bigger than an egg, it was about eight inches long and four inches thick in the middle, with the ends tapering down to one inch. Valek hefted it—solid. It weighed about a pound.

He set it on the side of the road and hurried to pick four more, placing them along the route. Looking inside the burlap sacks would be trickier. Valek kept pace with the caravan until they stopped to water the mules. Fortunately, the drivers took buckets to a nearby stream. While they crashed through the bush, Valek cut open one of the sacks.

Brown rocks spilled out. Odd. He picked one up. It was a... bean? Perhaps a root vegetable. Only about the size of the top of his thumb, they smelled earthy and slightly acidic. Valek checked a bunch of the bags in the wagons. All carried the same thing. He found an empty sack and quickly scooped a handful of the mystery beans before the men returned.

Then he picked up the pods on his way back to Yelena, dropping them into the bag. He'd have to figure out what the items were and their purpose. And he needed to follow the caravan to learn their destination.

Yelena waited for him in the tree. He waved her down. As she descended, he noted her earlier grace had fled, and, when she dropped beside him with a thud, it confirmed her physical state. After spending almost an entire day climbing, the woman must be exhausted. She'd need to hold on a little longer.

He handed her the sack. She opened it, peered inside, and removed a pod to inspect it.

"How did you get these?" she asked, sounding a bit amazed.

"Trade secret." Valek grinned, enjoying that he'd impressed her. "Getting the pods was easy, but I had to wait for the men to water their mules to look in the burlap sacks."

She returned the pod to the bag and then dug deeper, drawing out a handful of the beans. "What's this?"

"They're from the sacks," he explained. "I want you to take these back to Commander Ambrose. Tell him I don't know what they are or where they came from, and I'm following the caravan to see where they're going."

"Are they doing something illegal?" she asked.

"I'm not sure. If these pods and beans are from Sitia, then yes. It's illegal to trade with the south. One thing I do know, those men aren't traders." He waited to see if she'd ask how he'd known.

Her brows crinkled in that adorable way before they smoothed. "Their uniforms don't fit. Borrowed maybe? Or stolen?"

Smart. "Most likely stolen. If you're going to borrow a uniform, I would think you'd find one that fits." Valek considered. The sun would soon set, and just the thought of Yelena alone in the forest at night sent a finger of dread down his spine. Then he remembered Ari and Janco. They should be nearby.

"Yelena, I want you to find those two men you saw this afternoon and have them escort you back to the castle. I don't want you alone. If the magician plans on attacking you again, she'll have to deal with two more, and I doubt she'd have the energy. Don't tell anyone about your tree climbing, the magician, or the caravan. But give a complete report about everything to the Commander."

"What about my antidote?"

He thought she'd be more interested in where the lieutenants were, but, then again, she was thinking further ahead, and perhaps she already knew their location. "The Commander keeps a supply handy. He'll give it to you. And don't worry about your incentive. You've earned every coin. When I get back, I'll make sure you get it. Now, I need to keep moving or I'll spend the rest of the night catching up to the caravan." Although, he doubted he'd get any sleep. He turned to go.

"Valek, wait," she said. "How do I find the others?"

Ah, there it was. "Just follow this path." He pointed in the direction the wagons had come from. "I managed to shake them off my tail before I caught up with you. The soldiers were heading south-west; they're probably staking out this trail. Technically, that's the best strategy."

Valek jogged away, but, once he was out of sight, he just couldn't go further until he knew Yelena was safe. He looped back around and melted into the forest. With all the noise she made stamping on the gravel, he didn't worry about his own. He closed the distance just as Janco shouted, broke cover, and tackled her.

"Got you!" Janco said.

Valek took a deep breath. The desire to chastise the lieutenant for being too rough, preferably with a smack to the back of the man's head, pulsed in his heart.

"Isn't that a bit much, Janco?" Ari asked.

Relieved Ari would be kinder, and that Yelena was safe, Valek retreated. He had to catch up with the caravan before it left the trail. Yet another puzzle to solve.

Valek finally reached the wagons late into the night. They had pulled off the road and stopped in a clearing. The six men sat around a campfire, talking. A campfire, which *should* draw the attention of the border patrols. Even with scouts, that was a bold move.

Using Yelena's trick, Valek climbed a nearby tree and

found a sturdy branch to sit on while he watched. He calculated the distance he'd traveled—roughly eight miles—and determined they were just far enough east to be out of the exercise zone.

As the night grew colder and the fire died, the men fell asleep wrapped in blankets. Valek chewed on half a piece of jerky and wished he'd brought more food and clothing along. At one point in his life, he'd carried everything he needed and owned in his pack. Ah, how times had changed. He hadn't expected the exercise to take all day, let alone lead to an overnight mission, but that was no excuse for not being prepared.

He'd grown…soft? Perhaps. Or used to assigning his corps to do the leg work—the boring and tedious labor that consisted of the bulk of a spy's job.

Valek dozed on and off throughout the chilly night. The men woke at sunrise, and, after a quick breakfast, continued east on the trail. Valek finished the other half of the jerky, stretched his stiff muscles, and jogged after the caravan. Not the worst night of his life and certainly similar to other nights he'd spent on missions. When his stomach rumbled, he remembered the time he stalked the King's brother. The man had gone on an extensive hunting trip with a dozen guards. By the time Valek had the opportunity to assassinate the man, Valek had run out of food and hadn't eaten for three days.

The good old days? No. Life was better after the takeover. And now…life had gotten even more interesting with the arrival of Yelena.

Late on the second day of the trip, the caravan was finally ambushed by a border patrol. They appeared on the road, blocking the wagons, while the rest of the unit came from the sides of the path, encircling the back of the caravan and effectively trapping it.

Valek had been far enough behind to avoid the unit. Blending in with the bushes, he moved deeper into the woods and crept closer to listen to the conversation.

"...be here?" the captain of the unit asked. A striking and tall woman, who had pulled her hair back into a knot.

"Of course," the lead driver responded. He pulled a scroll from his pack and handed it to the captain. "Permission from General Brazell."

The captain raised a slender eyebrow before unrolling and scanning the document. If the caravan wished to keep a low profile, forging papers from the general wouldn't be the way to go.

After reading through, the captain asked, "Why are you traveling on a forest road and not on an approved trading route?"

The driver gestured to the contents of the wagons. "These are some of the ingredients for the general's new feed mill. They grow in the forest."

Still skeptical, the captain glanced into the wagons and opened one of the bags, exposing the beans. "What are these?"

"I dunno." The driver shrugged. "I'm hired to transport them."

Either he was a good actor, or he'd no clue. Valek leaned toward the latter.

The captain looked at her second.

"I don't recognize them. They're not on the list of illegal goods and substances," he said.

"A new drug?" she asked him. "Or used to make alcohol?"

He stepped closer and grabbed a handful of the beans. Sniffing them, he took a bite and spat it out. "Unlikely. Is the signature forged?"

"Unlikely."

He gave her a wry smile. "Then I'm of the opinion these are legit."

Valek held his breath, would the captain agree? Or had she noticed the trader's ill-fitting uniforms.

"Then you won't mind escorting the caravan and ensuring it arrives safely at its destination."

Nice. Valek approved.

"Yes, sir."

"Take Rodgers and Elithia with you. You can catch up with us at the barracks," the captain ordered.

"Yes, sir."

The driver shrugged, appearing unconcerned by his new escorts. "Suit yourselves." He clicked at the mules. They lurched forward.

The trio of guards followed in the caravan's wake. The captain watched the wagons as they disappeared around a bend.

"Something wrong, Cap?" one of the guards asked.

"Maybe. They had all the right answers, but...it just seemed odd." Then she grinned. "I'm sure if it's a wild goose chase, Lieutenant Mell will let me know multiple times."

They all chuckled until Valek broke cover. Then they grabbed the hilts of their swords, suddenly all very serious.

Valek raised his hands, showing he was unarmed. "Nice work, Captain."

"Thanks. Who the hell are you?"

"Adviser Valek."

The guards laughed, but the captain stared at him. "Where's your identification papers?"

He spread his arms wide. "Sorry, no *pockets*."

"Stand down," she told her unit, recognizing the code word. "Are you trailing that caravan, sir?"

"I was."

She pressed a hand to her forehead. "Did I just ruin your operation? Or fail some test?"

"No, to both. You helped, Captain..."

"Unice, sir."

He explained to Captain Unice, "If you hadn't stopped them, I would have stayed with them until the end of their journey. Now that I know their destination and alleged cargo, I can go back to the castle. But I'll need you to send me a report on what your Lieutenant Mell discovers right away."

"Yes, sir."

"Thank you."

To save time, Valek took a direct path, cutting northwest through the Snake Forest until he reached the main east-west road from Castletown to MD-5. The underbrush wasn't as thick along this route due to the diligent efforts of the Commander's landscape crew.

Anxious to return and check on Yelena, Valek only stopped for a few hours to rest. When he neared Castletown, he spotted a large group of people on the road, heading toward him. He stepped into the forest when he recognized the green and black colors of their uniforms.

Valek leaned next to a tree as Brazell's procession passed. Thank fate, the old goat was leaving the castle. One less worry. Then a pang gripped his chest. Would Yelena insist on returning to her room in the servants' wing? The strength of his reaction shouldn't have surprised him. He'd been enjoying sharing his apartment with her even though he knew he should keep his distance. But the thought of her unprotected... No. She would remain with him. Unless she wished to return to her own room. He wouldn't order her to stay.

He increased his pace, reaching the castle in the afternoon. It'd been four days since they parted in the forest, and, as much as he wanted to find Yelena, he needed food, a bath, and a nap.

But he stopped in Kenda's office to ensure Yelena had returned from the fugitive exercise and was in good health.

"Everything's fine," Kenda assured him. "Do you want Hildred and Inrick to stop trailing her now that Brazell and his goons are gone?"

Did he? No. Not really. Not ever. But the danger with Brazell was gone, and she was smart enough to avoid trouble. Plus, it was an invasion of her privacy and, if he wanted her to trust him and become part of his team, it had to stop. "Yes. But not until tomorrow."

"Got it."

He asked her to assign a couple agents to find out more about Brazell's new factory and to stake out that route in the woods to see who else was using it.

"On it," she said.

Satisfied, he left. The hot water of his bath drained his remaining energy. Good thing he'd eaten before the long soak, or he wouldn't have had the energy to chew. He fell into his bed with a sigh.

WHEN HE WOKE, it was dark. He worried he'd slept through his nightly meeting with the Commander, but he'd only been asleep a few hours. He opened his door, grabbed the top of the door-frame, and swung over the powder on the floor, landing lightly. The lanterns downstairs had been lit. He crept down the steps and spotted Yelena on the couch reading. The part of him that needed to see her whole and hale with his own eyes relaxed. Another part chided him. *She's resourceful*, it said.

But just how resourceful, Valek wondered. What would she do if someone had snuck into their apartment to ambush her? Why not test her? He retreated to the big sitting room at the opposite end of the hall from his bedroom. The upper floor was almost identical to the lower level. In the fifteen years Valek lived here, he'd managed to fill up both with books, rocks, and oddities. He picked up a heavy tome and slammed it on the floor approximately over Yelena's location. Then he found a dark corner to wait.

It wasn't long before she arrived at the top of the steps with a lantern in one hand and a kitchen knife in the other. That was a surprise. And the lantern would make it harder for him to remain hidden. She was methodical, checking the sitting room slow enough for him to keep out of the lantern's light. Except when something scared her, and she yipped. He ducked as she spun around. After a few moments, she resumed her search, opening the doors to the three rooms off the sitting room and peeking inside. All filled with junk. He really needed to clean everything out.

When she went down the hall to his bedroom, Valek stayed at the top of the stairs. Would she go in? Did he want her to? She shone the light along the floor, revealing the white powder. Yelena must have figured out what the undisturbed powder meant because she turned back to check the rooms along the hallway. There were three and only one of them contained anything personal.

Sure enough, when she opened *that* door, instead of shining the light inside and retreating, she stepped inside. Her boots crunched on the layer of rock dust. Valek moved to the threshold of his carving room. The only place in the apartment that was clear of clutter, and where the gray rocks from MD-1 had been sorted into their various sizes. His sanctuary.

Yelena reached the back table and examined his carving tools—a grinding wheel, metal files, and various sized chisels. Would she make the connection between the ugly gray rocks with white streaks and the black statues with silver highlights? Since he'd stopped working as an assassin for hire, his carvings were now inspired by nature, animals, and insects.

She set the lantern down and picked up the one figurine among a dozen that meant the most to him. It was one of his most recent pieces. And his current favorite. Fate must be playing a cruel joke. Yelena examined the butterfly and a strange sensation twisted in his heart as if she peered into his soul.

Uncomfortable with being so exposed, he decided to see how she'd react to an ambush. He scuffed his boot as he rushed her. She whirled in time to spot him, raising her knife too late as Valek unarmed her in an instant.

He pressed the knife to her neck, and she stilled, staring at him in fear. He waited for her to recognize him and relax, but she had frozen instead.

"Snooping?" he asked, stepping back to show her he didn't intend to harm her. Valek needed to remember she wasn't one of his corps. That he shouldn't be testing her. Not yet.

She broke her freeze and said, "I heard a noise. I came to—"

"Investigate." Valek finished. "Searching for an intruder is different from examining statues." He pointed to the butterfly clutched in her hand. "You were snooping."

"Yes."

"Good. Curiosity is a commendable trait. I wondered when you would explore up here. Find anything interesting?" He kept his tone light.

She held up the butterfly. "It's beautiful."

He shrugged, downplaying her compliment as if his heart hadn't swelled with pleasure. "Carving focuses my mind."

Yelena set the statue back on the table, but her hand lingered for a moment. Did she know what that butterfly meant to him? That he'd carved it after that stressful night of the Fire Festival, when he'd almost lost her, when his thoughts about her had spun as fast as the grinding wheel?

Not wanting to see her expression, Valek headed to the door. She grabbed the lantern and followed.

"I really did hear a noise," she said.

"I know. I knocked a book over to see what you would do. I didn't expect a knife, though. Is it the one missing from the kitchen?"

"Did Rand report it?"

"No. It just makes sense to keep track of large kitchen knives, so when one goes missing, you're not surprised when someone attacks you with it." Valek handed the knife to her. "You should return it. Knives won't help you against the caliber of people after you."

They went downstairs. Yelena picked up a book from the couch. From the title, it appeared to be about trees, which reminded him about their encounter in the forest. "What does the Commander think of the pods?"

"He thinks they're from Sitia. He returned them to me so I could discover what they are. I've been doing research in the library." Yelena handed him the book.

Valek suppressed a grin. Ambrose had finally accepted the idea of Yelena doing more than tasting his food. He flipped through the pages of the book. It was about fruit trees. "Find anything?"

"Not yet."

"Your actions as our fugitive must have impressed the Commander. Normally, he would have assigned this sort of thing to one of his science advisers."

She squirmed at the compliment, averting her gaze. "Where did the caravan go?"

Valek paused. He didn't have all the information, but if he wished for her to be part of the team, he should keep her informed. "Brazell's new factory."

"What's the product?"

"It's supposed to be a feed mill." Valek returned the book. "And I don't know why he would need those pods and beans." He considered and then mused aloud, "Maybe they're a secret ingredient. Maybe they're added to the feed to enhance the cow's milk supply. Then every farmer would buy Brazell's feed instead of growing their own. Or something along that line. Or maybe not. I'm not an expert." Valek pulled at his hair as if he could pull the answers from his mind. "I'll have to study his permit to see what I'm missing. Either way, I assigned some of my corps to stake out the route and infiltrate the factory. At this point I need more information."

"Brazell left the castle this afternoon."

"I passed his retinue on my way back. Good. One less thing to worry about." Valek crossed to his desk. He needed to catch up on some work before his meeting with Ambrose.

"Should I return to my old room now that Brazell's gone?" Yelena asked tentatively.

Valek analyzed not only her tone, but her word choice, and determined she didn't really want to leave. Or was that just wishful thinking? "No. You're still in danger. The magician hasn't been dealt with yet." Which was true. He returned to work and waited for her reaction.

After a few long minutes, she asked, "Exactly how do you deal with a magician?"

He twisted in his seat and met her gaze. Didn't she remember their earlier conversation? "I've told you before."

"But their powers…"

Ah, she was worried he couldn't protect her. "Have no effect on me. When I get close, I can feel their power pressing and vibrating on my skin and moving toward them is like walking through thick syrup. It takes effort, but I always win in the end. Always."

"How close?"

It depended on the strength of the magician. But was she looking for comfort or information she could relay to the southern magician? He hedged. "I have to be in the same room."

She relaxed as if reassured. "Why didn't you kill the southern magician at the festival?"

Because he was more worried about Yelena at the time. "Yelena, I'm not invincible. Fighting four men while she threw every ounce of her power at me was exhausting. Chasing her down would have been a fruitless endeavor."

She mulled over his explanation. "Is being resistant to magic a form of magic?"

Not this again. Every single one of his adversaries had tried to use that logic to persuade the Commander that Valek should be executed as a magician. "No."

"What about the knife?" She gestured to the weapon.

It hung on the wall in the center of his collection. Bright red blood stained the blade. Still wet after fifteen years.

Understanding her logic, Valek laughed. "That was the knife I used to kill the King. *He* was a magician. When his magic couldn't stop me from plunging that knife into his heart, he cursed me with his dying breath. It was rather melodramatic. He willed that I should be plagued with guilt over his murder and have his blood stain my hands forever. With my peculiar immunity to magic, the curse attached to the knife instead of me." Valek remembered the King's desperate bribes for his life. He'd offered his daughter, money, and power. But he couldn't give Valek his heart's desire—his three older brothers alive and well. "It was a shame to lose my favorite blade, but it does make for a nice trophy."

CHAPTER 11

That night, Valek joined the Commander in his suite. As Valek sat on the couch, he noticed a bowl filled with those brown squares…Criollo. Odd. Ambrose never ate this late at night. And he rarely indulged in sweets.

Ambrose noticed the direction of his gaze. "Don't worry. Yelena has checked them." He handed Valek a tumbler. "I discovered they pair well with alcohol." To prove it, he ate a few before taking a sip.

Valek tasted the amber liquid in his glass. "Whiskey?"

"I figured you'd had a rough couple of days." Ambrose settled across from him.

Ah, nice. And, even nicer… "You owe me a gold coin."

"I do," he said dryly. "Your confidence in Yelena's abilities wasn't misplaced. She certainly gave the two teams quite the challenge, outsmarting both." Ambrose raised his glass to his lips but paused. "Clearly, more training is necessary."

"I agree, but you should know there were two lieutenants who were tracking Yelena."

"Ari and Ganko? I already promoted them to captains."

"It's Janco, and that's good. They deserve it. They would have captured her in the early afternoon, but I may have...interfered."

Ambrose sighed. "May have?"

"Consider it an additional test of their tracking abilities. Besides, Yelena had shown a great deal of ingenuity up to that point, I wanted to see what else she would do." He swallowed a mouthful of whiskey. The smooth, smoky flavor burned all the way down. "And if the exercise had ended then, we wouldn't have encountered that caravan."

"What did you learn about it?"

Valek explained what he'd found out regarding the shipment. "I'm hoping I'll hear from Captain Unice about where the traders ended their journey."

"Those pods and beans are not grown in Ixia," Ambrose said. "Not even in the Snake Forest. They must be from Sitia." He drummed his fingers on his glass. "I've asked Yelena to investigate their origins."

Valek lifted an eyebrow, inviting Ambrose to continue.

"Yes. You are right. She's an asset to our team."

"Wow." Valek pressed a hand to his chest in mock astonishment. Well, not really mock as it *was* the first time Valek could remember Ambrose uttering those words to him. "See? Admitting I'm right didn't kill you. Maybe now you'll do it more often."

"Doubtful." He covered his grin by draining his whiskey.

Valek studied him. He appeared more...relaxed? No. More... agreeable? Not quite. More...open? That was it.

Ambrose's good mood didn't last. "It doesn't make sense for Brazell to break the law for a feed factory. Something else must be going on."

Valek considered the reasons people resorted to criminal activity. "It's not for money, Brazell has plenty. Power? He's at the highest rank possible. If he's aiming for your job, I doubt a feed factory would change your mind about your successor."

"How do you know Brazell isn't my successor?"

"Because I'm your successor."

No emotion creased Ambrose's face, but an intensity lit his golden eyes. "You're not supposed to know that."

And you would never have given it away that easily. Something was wrong.

"I didn't. I guessed. And from your reaction, I guessed right. And for the record, I don't want your job. Never did. I'll only step in if you die of natural causes or of extreme old age. If someone assassinates you, I've failed my duty and will follow you to the fire world." The C-shaped scar on his chest burned with his promise.

"And spend the rest of eternity arguing?"

"We could play poker. I've a killer poker face."

Ambrose laughed and relaxed back into his seat. "Guessing about Brazell's motives at this point is a waste of time."

And guessing about Ambrose's strange mood would also be a waste of time. Unless… He eyed the now empty bowl of Criollo. Everything else about their nightly meeting remained the same. Was the Criollo some type of new drug?

"True," Valek said. "And it might be another person in his district that is spearheading the illegal activities. Brazell might not know."

"He signed his name to the permission paper."

"You're the only person in Ixia who reads every single word on every single document before you sign it." Valek held up a hand. "Not a criticism, but everyone else scans and signs and moves on to the next sheet."

Ambrose's huff of annoyance lacked oomph. "All right, we'll wait until we have all the facts." He stood and refilled their glasses. "Do you have more insight into why that southern magician is after Yelena? I'm not sure I believe she'd make two attempts on Yelena's life just for revenge."

He made a good point. "No, but I'm working on it."

"Good."

The topic turned to routine issues as they finished their drinks. By the time Valek returned to his suite, Yelena had gone to bed. She'd left a few lanterns burning. The soft yellow glow illuminated the cleared space around her end of the couch. Her books and notes were stacked on the end table. His had been pushed into a corner. Instead of annoyance, a warmth spread like the whisky had earlier. She'd carved out a space for herself not only in his living room, but in his heart.

Taking one lantern in hand, he extinguished the others. Despite the fatigue dragging at his limbs, he entered his carving room. Valek picked up the butterfly and his thoughts turned to Yelena and the master magician.

He doubted Yelena was a Sitian spy. She wouldn't go to such lengths to end up in the dungeon and hope to be the next in line for execution when a new food taster was needed. No, there were too many variables. It was more likely that she'd overheard something or seen something between a magician and Reyad, or the old goat. Something incriminating that Yelena had no idea was important. Not the feed factory because that started after Yelena was sentenced to death.

It had to be important. The woman tried to kill her twice. Yelena's explanation of her escape from the second attempt didn't match what he knew of the magician's abilities. She had plenty of time to finish the job before Valek arrived.

Would Yelena make a deal with the woman in the woods in order to save her life? Did she promise Yelena she'd stop her attacks in exchange for information about the Commander? And if she did, could Valek blame her?

VALEK WOKE early to give Yelena her daily dose of White Fright and then returned to bed. He slept well into the morning—a rare indulgence. To make up for it, he headed to the training yard in the afternoon. He wore a sleeveless tunic and comfortable pants made with that same stretchy fabric that Dilana had used for his camouflage suit.

Valek watched the soldiers train and waited for a brave soul to work up their nerve. Soon enough he was challenged, and he hopped the fence. The sergeant chose a sword and the first of many sparring matches began. Fun.

In his experience, sparring was the best way to stay in shape. Push-ups and sit-ups all helped build muscle, and running built endurance, but fighting an opponent was key to success. Each person was an unknown. Each had a different skill level. And each chose the weapon. All these factors forced Valek to be adaptable. To not get stuck using predictable techniques, and to become proficient with all weapons. And, on occasion, Valek learned a new move.

Experience was another reason to spar multiple people. The more times you fought, the more confidence you gained, which helped manage your emotions.

Valek remembered his first teacher's, Hedda, advice on fighting. "Lose the anger," she had said. "Then lose all those other annoying emotions while you're at it." So easy to say, so hard to do, but Valek had learned to control them. Emotions were still useful at times.

He disarmed his opponent, and another stepped into his place. The matches blurred together as the audience grew. Most of the soldiers approached with swords, but one challenger held a knife.

Valek grinned and drew his cloud-kissed dagger. Time to test his new baby out. He loved knife fighting. Something about being close to his opponent, punching and blocking. It was similar to hand-to-hand combat but with an added degree of danger. The sharp blade acted as an extension of his hand. Or hands if anyone picked two blades for the challenge. So far, no one ever had. Pity.

The man had no idea how to fight with a knife. Valek unarmed him in two moves. He glanced around at the crowd and spotted Yelena watching. She stood next to Ari and Janco. And for some reason, he straightened.

He called for one final challenger and a tall woman with long blond hair twisted into a braid, stepped up. She held a bo staff. An unusual weapon. The five-foot-long staff of wood was an inch in diameter and slightly tapered at each end. It wasn't usually a killing weapon, but rather used to knock an opponent down or unconscious. But it could kill if the wielder knew what they were doing.

Valek picked up one of the bo staffs used for training. He rubbed his hands along the grain, then held it in the ready position in front of his body. The blond attacked with a hard and fast swing toward his temple, he blocked and countered. She ducked and executed a series of strikes to his ribs, each one faster than the last. He kept pace, admiring her skills.

She had what Hedda had claimed were not emotions—determination, persistence, concentration, focus, and drive.

The match lengthened and Valek tested her techniques. She moved the bo with accuracy and power but kept repeating the same attack combinations. And appeared a bit flustered when he mixed up his volleys. When he poured on the speed, she back peddled, holding her bo parallel to the ground—a basic defensive move and not effective. The bo was also too far away from her body when she tried to create more space between them.

Valek swung his bo around in an unconventional move and slammed the tip of it right on the mid-point of hers. The force of the blow cracked her bo in two pieces. Match over.

The soldier stared at her broken bo a moment before conceding the fight. She shook his hand. "Thank you for the opportunity."

"You have potential, Lieutenant…"

"Maren, sir."

"Are you hoping to be invited to my corps?"

"No, sir."

"Looking to become my second, then?"

"No, sir."

Now she had his full attention. "Then why challenge me?"

"Bragging rights, sir."

He laughed. "Keep training, put in the work, and you might be the best fighter with the bo staff in Ixia."

"May I speak frankly, sir?"

"Of course."

"You have it wrong. It's not that I *might* be, but that I *will* be the best bo fighter in Ixia."

"I stand corrected."

VALEK'S MUSCLES ached after the seven...nine matches. He was about to return to the castle when he noticed Yelena was still with Ari and Janco. They stood together in the training yard. It didn't take him long to figure out they were teaching her basic punches and kicks.

Curious, he leaned on the fence and watched. Compared to the two men, she resembled a delicate flower growing between two thick sunflowers. Yet she moved with an athletic grace and obvious strength as her punches into the training bag rocked Janco back on his heels. Of course, she couldn't move Ari. Not even with her kicks. Valek doubted he could move Ari. A horse might even have a difficult time knocking the man off his solid fighting stance.

When they finished the session, Yelena headed toward the castle. Wishing to talk to her, Valek hurried to catch up.

"See you in the morning," Janco called, sounding gleeful.

She turned and froze when she saw Valek.

"Your punches are slow," he said, breaking the sudden awkwardness. He took her hand and ignored the flutter in his chest as he examined her knuckles. They were bruised in the correct places. "At least your technique is good. If you hold weights in your hands while you train, your punches will be much quicker without them."

"I can continue?" she asked. Her tone was full of disbelief as she stared at him.

Even though Valek and the Commander wished to make her a part of the team, she still considered herself a prisoner. Because a prisoner would never be allowed to learn how to fight. He hoped allowing her to train would help her realize what they were trying to do.

Reluctant to let go of her hand, he said, "I think it's an excellent idea. How did you get the power twins to agree to teach you?"

"Power twins?"

"Combine Ari's strength with Janco's speed, and they would be unbeatable. But, so far, I haven't had to test my theory since they haven't tried to fight me together. No one said I couldn't have more than one second-in-command. You're not going to give me away, are you?"

"No."

Valek squeezed her hand and released his grip. "Good. They're probably the best instructors at the castle. How did you meet them?" he asked, feigning ignorance.

"They were the men who found me in the forest. The Commander promoted them, and I took advantage of their gratitude." She absently rubbed her hand.

"Opportunistic and underhanded, I love it." Valek laughed despite worrying that he'd upset her by holding her hand too long.

As they walked toward the castle, he noticed a few hostile

glares aimed at Yelena. When they reached the entrance, he stopped. "There's one problem."

"What?"

"You shouldn't train so visibly. Word spreads quickly. If Brazell finds out and makes a fuss, the Commander will order you to stop. And it'll make the Commander suspicious." More like paranoid. The man had just agreed to consider Yelena a team member. To find out she was training already...too much too soon.

They entered the castle, and it gave Valek an idea.

"Why don't you make use of all those empty storerooms in the lower level of the castle? You can still run laps in the morning for exercise," Valek said, guessing Ari and Janco would include it as part of her training.

Her wince confirmed he'd guessed right. He hid his grin. Not many people enjoyed running, but they appreciated it later when they found they had the stamina to fight an opponent. Or outrun a pursuer.

They walked through the castle in companionable silence. Valek remembered why he'd rushed to catch up to her. "Mentioning Brazell reminds me that I've been wanting to ask you about that Criollo that the Commander enjoys. Do you like the taste of it?"

"Yes, it's an excellent dessert."

"If you stopped eating it, how would you feel?"

"Well..." She hesitated. No doubt wondering about the strange direction of their conversation.

"Truthfully, I would be disappointed. I look forward to eating a piece every morning," she said.

That was significant. "Have you ever craved the Criollo?" Valek inquired.

"Like an addiction?"

Impressed she made the connection so fast, he nodded.

"I don't think so, but..."

"But what?"

"I only eat it once a day. The Commander has a piece after every meal, including his evening snack. Why this sudden concern?" she asked.

"Just a feeling. It might be nothing." Valek hoped.

They entered the Commander's office in time for Yelena to taste his dinner.

"Well, Valek, any new promotions?" the Commander asked.

How did he know? Then Valek realized he still wore his training uniform. "No. But Maren shows promise. Unfortunately, she doesn't want to be in my corps or even be my second. She just wants to beat me." Valek grinned, delighted by the challenge.

"And can she?" the Commander inquired.

"With time and the proper training. She's deadly with her bo; it's just her tactics that need work."

"Then what do we do with her?"

"Promote her to a general and retire some of those old windbags. We could use some fresh blood in the upper ranks," Valek said.

"Valek, you never had a good grasp of military structure."

"Then promote her to lieutenant today, captain tomorrow, major the next day, colonel the day after, and general the day after that." What he never had a good grasp on was why it took so bloody long for a talented soldier to climb through the ranks.

"I'll take it under advisement." The Commander flashed Yelena an annoyed glance. "Anything else?" he asked Valek.

Yelena had finished tasting, Valek grabbed her arm before she could leave. "I'd like to try an experiment. I want Yelena to taste the Criollo every time you do for a week, then the next week I'll taste it for you. I want to see if anything happens to her when she stops eating the dessert."

"No." The Commander raised a hand when Valek started to argue. "I recognize your concern, but I think it's misplaced."

"Humor me."

"We can try your experiment once Rand duplicates the recipe from General Brazell. Acceptable?"

No, but it was progress. "Yes, sir."

"Good. I want you to join me in a meeting with General Kitvivan. We're just starting the cooling season, and he's already worried about snow cats." The Commander turned. "Yelena, you're dismissed."

"Yes, sir," she said, rushing from the room.

"What the hell was that about, Valek?" The Commander demanded once she was gone.

"I'm just being cautious."

"You practically accused me of being addicted to Criollo in front of Yelena. It couldn't wait until tonight?"

"She's eating it, too. And I thought having another perspective might help. And she might pick up—"

"And you call me paranoid. It's just a dessert, Valek. I'm experiencing no ill effects. If I do, I'll stop eating it. Let it go for now."

"Yes, sir."

"Good. The meeting with Kitvivan starts in an hour."

Valek had just enough time to bathe and change before joining the Commander in the war room. General Kitvivan entered with his retinue. The meeting started, but Valek soon grew bored, and his thoughts turned to the puzzles he needed to solve. He created a mental to-do list.

The Commander's sharp tone caught his attention. "You will *not* set traps for the snow cats. Do you understand?"

"Yes, sir," General Kitvivan said through clenched teeth.

"Just leave them alone and they'll leave your district alone."

"But they don't. They kill a dozen cattle a year."

"And storms kill another dozen. It's all part of living near the Northern Ice Pack. If you can't handle it, then I will assign another to take your place."

Valek studied the Commander. Normally, he wouldn't be so...passionate about the snow cats in public. It was well known that the Commander was the only person in Ixia to successfully hunt and kill one of the big wily cats. What wasn't public knowledge was the Commander's high regard for the creatures.

"I can handle it," Kitvivan said tightly.

"Good. Now do you have any *real* business left to discuss?" the Commander asked in a dangerous tone. One that warned the general not to waste anymore of his time. Kitvivan wisely ended the meeting and made a quick exit.

The Commander caught Valek's eye. "What?"

"Do you want me to assign an agent to ensure the general doesn't set traps?" Valek asked.

"You don't think he'll follow my orders?" His tone rumbled dangerously.

Valek chose his words with care. "I think MD-1 is far enough from here that word probably won't get back to us if he sets the traps. Those cats can be a menace in the middle of the cold season when they're hungry." *And you're not quite yourself.* But Valek was smart enough not to say that aloud.

"All right, assign an agent."

"Yes, sir."

"You're dismissed."

After he left the war room, Valek rubbed his chest. He had the odd impression that he'd just dodged a lethal blow.

A COUPLE DAYS after the meeting with Kitvivan, Valek received the report from Captain Unice. Her lieutenant had escorted the caravan to a building site. The main structure was still under construction, but there were four completed silos. From the various roasting and sifting equipment on the site, Lieutenant

Mell determined that the site would eventually become a "big ass" feed factory and was legitimate.

At the end of the official report was a note from Unice, *Please tell me that something, anything about this factory is illegal so I can get Mell to stop saying* I told you so *in a hundred different and not so subtle ways.*

Valek laughed. He'd have liked to oblige her, but he'd have to wait for the report from his corps staking out the path in the Snake Forest to prove the beans and pods were from Sitia. Yelena's research had yet to find an official designation for them, which almost verified they weren't grown in Ixia. Even though the Commander claimed they were of southern origin, he required Valek to obtain hard evidence before he could arrest or accuse anyone. And there was a slim chance there could be a section of the forest that had been cultivated to grow them.

He received confirmation about the beans and pods three days later. The report from his field agents stated that the empty wagons from MD-5 had crossed into Sitia through a hidden pathway. And they also spotted another caravan full of those beans, heading east toward MD-5.

Considering that the factory wasn't even in operation, Valek wondered just how much they needed to begin manufacturing. It sounded as if they were stock piling the beans.

When Valek joined the Commander for a drink that evening, he explained what he'd learned about the beans and pods.

"Should I stop the caravans and see if General Brazell squawks?" Valek asked. He sipped the blackberry brandy carefully. It wasn't his favorite because it tasted like blackberry poison. Since the near poisoning miss with Yelena, the flavor of the liquor turned his stomach. He set it on the table next to Ambrose's bowl of Criollo, whose presence had become as routine as their meetings.

"No. Let's wait."

"*You* want to wait?" Valek tried to hide his surprise.

"Isn't that what you're always nagging me to do? I thought I'd skip the argument and save time."

"Except this time, I think we should shut it all down until we know exactly what Brazell's producing." They had completely switched roles and Valek didn't know if he should be amused or concerned.

Ambrose waved away the suggestion. "We don't even know if Brazell is aware of where the beans are coming from. One of his advisers could be in charge of ordering the ingredients." He sat up straighter. "Besides, we haven't confirmed their purpose. Maybe they plan to plant the beans and grow a crop in Ixia. Then it won't be illegal anymore." Ambrose gave him a smug smile.

Valek could argue the legality of that last comment, but all the other points were valid. Yet his gut warned it was a bad idea.

"Keep working on the investigation, Valek."

"Yes, sir."

Valek needed to decide if he would infiltrate the factory or reassign the two agents already working at Brazell's manor house. He hadn't been on a long assignment in a while, and he rather enjoyed the challenge. But the thought of leaving Yelena for an extended time made him physically ill.

He realized he'd been enjoying her company in the evenings far too much. Which was a surprise since it was all rather... domestic. They chatted about their day. Yelena discussed the progress on her research, and she asked him questions about fighting and self-defense. He sought her advice on a few personnel problems and minor investigations. How had that become the highlight of his day? This love stuff was strange.

In the end, he sent a message to the two agents to switch to working undercover in the feed factory. Another two agents were sent to follow the wagons all the way to the very source of the beans and pods. Now it was just a waiting game.

In the meantime, he kept tabs on Yelena's training, visiting the storeroom where she worked with the power twins and Maren. He highly approved of the addition of the lieutenant. The four of them together would be a formidable team once Yelena's skills caught up to the rest of them. And Valek fully intended for them all to become a part of his corps. But not in the traditional way. They would stay together and would work directly with him instead of reporting to Kenda. He looked forward to that day.

For the first time, he'd found his team. The Commander kept harping on him to find a second, well, he'd found four seconds. They just didn't know it yet.

Whenever he observed their training sessions, he tried to stay out of the way. However, he couldn't resist commenting or making a suggestion or two. And on occasion they'd ask him to spar, which he enjoyed. Very much.

TWO DAYS before the beginning of the cooling season, Valek was working in his office when Kenda entered. Sweat soaked her uniform and her hair had spung from its leather tie.

"What's wrong?" he asked.

"Bit of a commotion at the east gate," she said. "A young man insisted he needed to see you. He was quite agitated and had fresh blood on his uniform. He tried to muscle past security, but they stopped him. They notified me and it took a bunch of us to subdue him."

A growing unease swirled in his stomach. "What's his name?"

"He didn't say, just kept screaming that Sven sent him to find you."

Trevar. Valek went cold. There was only one reason for Sven to send his best baiter. His agent was in trouble.

CHAPTER 12

*V*alek shoved his fear and worry for Sven down deep inside him and stood. "Where is he?" he asked Kenda.

"In one of the holding cells."

"Let's go."

He followed her down to the level right above the dungeon. The half dozen cells in this area were for temporary inmates. It was a place for them to wait until they were either sent to a correctional facility or the Commander's dungeon.

In the last cell on the right, Trevar sat hunched over with his elbows on his knees, holding his head in his hands. Blood soaked his merchant uniform. Too much.

"Are you injured?" Valek asked.

Trevar straightened and hopped to his feet. "No." He stopped right in front of Valek on the other side of the bars, then glared at Kenda. "I asked to speak with *Valek*, not some cook."

"You *demanded*. Maybe if you'd *asked*, I'd—"

"What happened to Sven?" Valek asked, cutting her off.

His gaze returned. And Valek waited as the young man made the necessary connections.

"They attacked him," Trevar said in a low voice.

No doubt *they* were the other black market dealers. "What about Sven's helpers?"

"Them, too. It happened sometime last night. I found them this morning. Sven was…"

And now Trevar was here, which meant Sven was still alive and hopefully the others as well. "Kenda, go get Medic Channa and her team. Meet me at the west gate."

"No. He's…he's…" Trevar took a shaky breath. "He's dead. They all are. I think Sven was waiting for me." A half sob. "I'm always the first to arrive and…and he grabbed my hand and… told me to find you to tell you…" Another sob.

"Tell me what?" Valek urged gently despite the grief pulsing in his chest.

"That he…underestimated the others. That greed was a monster he couldn't slay." Trevar wiped his eyes.

"Who's greed?"

Trevar stared at him. "It's their greed. He took all their business. Instead of finding something else to do, the dealers attacked him."

"And?"

"What the hell? I just told you he *died* and you're playing twenty questions? Don't you care?"

"I care very much. Enough that Sven knew if things got too hot, he could contact me, and I'd send reinforcements or we'd just shut the entire operation down. It wasn't worth his life."

"But…" Trevar sighed. "Sven was greedy, too. He enjoyed his role too much and ignored the signs that it was getting hot."

"Exactly."

Trevar rubbed his face. "I tried to warn him."

"And?"

He dropped his arms. "He thanked me. Said he could handle it. But he didn't *feel* the change."

"The change?"

"Yeah. You know…" He tapped his chest. "A vibe. The city normally hums, but the pitch changed. Weird, I know." Then he grabbed the bars in sudden terror. "It's not magic! I swear!"

"Relax. I know. It's your intuition. You know the city and the people so well; your unconscious picks up when things change."

Trevar slumped against the bars. "Whew."

And now Valek needed to assess the extent of the damage. "After Sven died, did you come straight here?"

"No. Sven said to take the back alleys." He gestured to his blood-soaked uniform. "I doubt I would have gotten far looking like this."

True. "Did anyone follow you?"

"I don't know."

Valek had to assume the black market dealers left a watcher to see Trevar's reaction, which meant they knew he headed for the castle.

"No, wait. Someone followed me right after I left Sven's store. I thought it was one of the attackers, so I ditched them as soon as I could."

That gave Valek a few more options. "What happens to the baiters when a black market dealer is shut down?"

"We're hired by the other dealers. Well, the good ones are."

"I want you to return to the city and see if anyone will hire you."

"But they might think I'm working for you!"

"And if they do?"

"They won't hire me, and the other baiters will ignore me."

"In that case, return here."

"Why?"

"I'll hire you as a spy. You'll be trained and sent to other cities on missions."

"Why me?"

"Sven vouched for you. Said you have the chops."

"He…" Trevar took a deep breath. "He taught me some cool

162

stuff. Like stuff about body language. I knew a little, I'd always get a certain…sense about a shopper, but, wow, once he explained it, my success rate doubled."

"Spy training will include more cool stuff," Valek said with a wry grin.

"But what if I am hired and my friends don't shun me?"

"Then your spy training will have to wait a few weeks." Valek explained what he needed Trevar to do.

VALEK ACCOMPANIED the six-person clean up team to Sven's shop. To avoid drawing unwanted attention, they waited until deep into the night. Lanterns hanging on the lamp posts remained lit until dawn and the streets were empty of all but a watch patrol. The people on duty took one look at Valek and his team and decided to find another street to check. Smart. He was in no mood to deal with them.

The team lit their handheld lanterns right outside Sven's shop. Glass shards crunched under Valek's boots as he entered. The door had been smashed open and it hung crookedly on its hinges. The displays of the legal kitchen goods lay on their sides. Pieces of broken crockery littered the ground. He scanned the shelves, noting the absence of most of the merchandise—probably stolen.

The damage to the back room matched the front, but it also included broken floorboards and large holes in the walls. Valek wrapped his emotions in cold determination as the team found the stairs. He followed them down.

Splintered wood covered the floor and two bloodied bodies. Sven lay half under a broken crate with red staining the planks. Valek knelt next to his friend and closed Sven's eyes. He bent his head a moment, silently cursing the man for underestimating the danger. For not assigning more colleagues for protection—

Kenda had confirmed that only two other agents worked with Sven. Then Valek went to his other agents and closed their eyes as well. The three of them had served Valek and the Commander loyally and would be honored as heroes.

The clean-up crew went to work, packing the bodies into bags with handles. Valek searched through the wreckage. All the black market items were gone as well. No doubt they now graced the shelves of the other dealers' showrooms.

Valek grabbed one of the lanterns and returned to the back room. He inspected the holes in the walls and floor. It appeared as if the attackers searched for something hidden. Sven might have misread the danger, but the man wouldn't have stashed his profits in such obvious hiding places. Back behind a privacy screen, Valek found a chamber pot. Holding his breath, he picked it up and undid the false bottom. A large pouch thudded to the ground with a loud clank. He replaced the bottom and set the pot down before scooping up the heavy leather bag.

Dozens of gold coins shone from inside the purse. One thing Sven hadn't underestimated was the profits from the operation. Valek sighed. He'd rather have Sven and his two agents alive than a pouch full of gold. All of his corps understood the dangers of their job. All knew it could be fatal. All had heard the stories of other missions that ended badly. What they didn't know was how much their deaths weighed on Valek. How much he grieved for each one.

After the team carried the bodies toward the castle, Valek lingered in Castletown. He considered his other operation. From her clandestine meetings with Star, Margg had located the woman's main place of business. No longer content with his agents just watching the building, Valek wanted one of his spies in the upper echelons of Star's organization. Except that wouldn't happen any time soon because gaining trust and climbing the ranks took seasons. He wouldn't make Sven's mistake and underestimate his enemy. A wait-and-see approach wasn't enough, Valek needed to know Star's plans *before* she implemented them.

Valek studied Star's building. Wedged between its neighbors, the four-story wooden structure matched all the others in the row. Nothing about it stood out or showed any indication of the illegal dealings within its walls. He noted the addresses of the two residences bookending Star's. Then he looped around to the alley behind the row. It was dark. No doubt Star had watchers lurking in the shadows to warn her in case of a raid.

Not wishing to sound an alarm, Valek returned to the castle. The next day he sent an agent to Castletown's government office to find out who lived in the buildings on either side of Star's.

"WHICH DAY DO you want to schedule this season's execution?" Valek asked the Commander. He sipped the peach brandy. It was too sweet for his taste, but Ambrose was determined to find the perfect drink to compliment his evening Criollo. "Horus was on the fifteenth and the one before him was on the twentieth." They were a week into the cooling season and Valek needed time to contact family members and prepare the prisoner.

"It doesn't matter, just pick one." Ambrose relaxed back on the couch in his suite. He'd unbuttoned the top two buttons on his uniform. Unprecedented.

Valek checked his response before the words could escape his lips. It *always* mattered to the Commander. He eyed the half-filled bowl of Criollo. Brazell's chef had sent a large shipment of the confection without the promised recipe. The Commander had taken it in stride. Considering how much the man ate on a daily basis, Valek had expected anger or, at least, annoyance over the missing recipe.

"How about the nineteenth?" Valek asked.

"Fine. Take care of it."

"I normally do," Valek said slowly.

"I meant *all* of it." He yanked an imaginary lever.

Valek had killed for the Commander many times before and would do it again—all part of his job. Yet, the Commander strongly believed in personally executing the prisoners.

Unable to keep silent, Valek said, "You always—"

"I'm not a slave to routine."

Actually, he was. Once again, Valek bit back his reply. He'd been doing that quite a lot lately.

"I've recently decided to delegate more," continued the Commander. "There are so many details to attend to with running a country, I no longer wish to do everything. You should be happy. You've been telling me to hire more staff for years."

He should. And overseeing the executions would make doing things like switching out prisoners much easier. But the timing of the decision was...off.

The Commander changed the subject and the tension between them dissipated as they discussed more mundane topics.

After the meeting, Valek returned to his apartment. Yelena had gone to bed, and he fought the urge to wake her. Instead, he paced. Which didn't help. At all. He needed to talk through the problem. Except, he had no one to talk to. And, if he did, would they think he was overreacting? Was he?

The Commander's change in personality nagged at him. No. Not a change, but a...relaxation. Which should be a good thing. Yet, it alarmed him even though the Commander was being reasonable. It made sense for the man to slow down after decades of hard work and delegate his more onerous tasks. Yet, it didn't.

It had started after that damn Criollo showed up. Could

Valek really blame a dessert? Besides, he had no proof. Nothing except knowing the Commander better than anyone else in Ixia. He paused outside Yelena's door. The desire to discuss his concerns with her pulsed in his chest. In the past couple months, he'd learned to trust her opinion. And she'd been—

Another thought occurred to him. Yelena became the official food taster around the same time Brazell gifted the Criollo to the Commander. Could she be the reason for his...mellowing? Could Ambrose be in love with her?

A truly staggering thought, Valek backed away from her door as if it were on fire. In all the years they'd worked together, the Commander hadn't shown the slightest interest in anyone. Well, not to Valek. Ambrose always kept his personal thoughts private, but Valek had learned to read the very subtle—practically nonexistent—cues that reflected his friend's concealed emotions.

But now? The cues were no longer elusive. They shouted in comparison. However, the Commander had exhibited more passion for the snow cats than Yelena.

Valek sank onto the couch as a tidal wave of relief left him shaky. He thought he had a firm grip on his own emotions regarding Yelena. Obviously not. They'd been living in this domestic bubble, but she'd never indicated any interest in him other than a professional one. Which was exactly as it should be. They worked together and it would ruin their relationship if he professed his love and she ran away horrified.

With that thought, he gathered the messy octopus of his emotions, wrangled it into a box, and shoved it deep enough inside him to ignore. He would be content with having her close and with being able to solve puzzles together.

Of course, he was in utter denial, but wishing for something out of his reach or control was a waste of time and energy.

∾

Two weeks into the cooling season, Valek waited until Yelena left the training room to go taste the Commander's lunch before he entered. Ari, Janco, and Maren were putting away the practice weapons and chatting. The air was hot and stuffy and fogged with the distinct odor of sweat.

It said quite a bit about their relationship with Valek when they didn't snap to attention once they spotted him. Part pleased and part annoyed, he didn't waste time with pleasantries.

"I've a mission for you," he said.

That straightened their spines.

Janco's gaze brightened with glee. "Finally! I'm so bored with all this training. We're supposed to be scouting for the Commander's elite guard, but he never goes *anywhere*!"

"Careful what you wish for," Maren muttered.

Ari shot his partner a warning look, but it was ignored as usual. "Do you need us to scout for you?" he asked.

"No. I already know you can scout. I'd like to determine if you can each lead a small team on a smash and grab mission."

Janco rubbed his hands together. "Ho boy! Can't wait."

Maren cocked her hip. "We'll need to clear it with our commanding officers."

Raising a single brow, Valek waited.

"Oh. You outrank our commanding officers."

"I outrank everyone except the Commander." Not a boast, but a reminder.

Scratching his ear, Janco asked, "How does that work? You don't have a military rank."

"Neither does the Commander," Valek said.

Janco opened his mouth and then closed it. A crinkle of confusion popped between his eyebrows.

"It's *his* army," Ari said. "He *chose* his title."

"And appointed me his second-in-command."

"Why don't I know this?" Janco asked.

"Because it's *ancient* history," Maren snarked.

"Nice." Valek appreciated the well-timed dig at his age. Even though, at thirty-three, he was about seven years older than Maren and Janco, and five years older than Ari. *And fourteen years older than Yelena.*

Janco continued to complain. "They should teach it to all the soldiers."

"They do, you dolt. You probably slept through all the required military classes," Ari said.

"What did they expect me to do? They scheduled them in the mornings."

Ari turned to Valek. "What about Yelena? Is she going to be part of this mission."

"No," Maren said. "Otherwise, he would have arrived before she left."

"Do you think she's capable of participating?" Valek asked Ari.

"Not yet."

Interesting. Valek thought she might be inherently too hesitant for the intensity needed in a smash and grab. "Yet?"

"She has a fierce side," Ari said.

Good to know.

"When is this mission?" Maren asked.

"In two days. Meet at the west gate an hour before sunrise."

Janco groaned.

"You'd rather sit this one out?"

"No, sir. I just don't like mornings. I don't know why everything has to happen in the morning. What's wrong with evenings? What about an hour *after* sunset?"

"When you're in charge, you can set the time."

Janco puffed out his chest. "Did you hear that? *When*! Not *if*!"

Now it was Ari and Maren's turn to groan.

"Please don't encourage him, sir," Ari said. "It has the same effect of giving a toddler sugar."

"Hey!" Janco protested.

Everyone ignored him.

"Should we dress for night ops?" Ari asked Valek.

"No. Wear your uniforms. There's going to be a show."

Excitement shone from Janco's dark-brown eyes. "A smash and grab and a show? You really know how to spoil a guy."

VALEK LEANED against the building across from Trevar's apartment. The lanterns flickering along the street caused the shadows to dance. Insects buzzed. Except for the occasional soldier on patrol, no one else was in sight. With no clouds covering the sky, the night air held a bite of frost. Valek tucked his cold hands inside the pockets of his heavy pants. Cloaks impeded his motions, so to keep from freezing during the colder seasons, Valek wore Dilana's special heavy clothing. Her words, not his. She sewed an extra flannel layer in the plain clothes, making them thicker and warmer and him very grateful.

Two hours before sunrise, Trevar exited through the front door. He wore a short cape and carried a knapsack. Trevar paused and glanced around then ducked down an alley. Classic behavior for someone who was up to no good. Valek waited for a beat. When no one else appeared, Valek followed the young man.

Trevar's circuitous route eventually led to the castle. Despite checking for a tail, Trevar failed to spot Valek. Not a big concern, as Valek ensured no one else had taken the slightest interest in Trevar.

Light blazed from the western gate. The guards led Trevar to the gate house. Valek did a sweep of the area just in case someone hid in the shadows before he went inside. If anyone had seen Trevar enter the complex, Valek would have had to cancel the mission.

The night officer in charge of the gate stood and relinquished his desk when Valek entered the small office. Trevar stood on the opposite side. The captain nodded and left, leaving them alone.

"Any problems?" Valek asked Trevar.

"It was rough at first," he said. "None of the dealers were sure if they could trust me. But I convinced them that I was just working as Sven's baiter and not involved with his business. And I *didn't* steal his profits."

"How did you convince them?"

"Even when no one would hire me, I still brought in customers. For free. But I spread them out to all the dealers. Eventually, one hired me, so I'd bring my customers just to him."

"And the profits?"

He patted his stomach. "Hard to buy food when working for free. The other baiters also vouched that I'd been going hungry."

Smart. "Did you get the information I needed?"

Trevar's grin was sharp and a bit feral. "Yes, and more. Do you have a map of Castletown?"

Valek gestured to the top of the desk. He'd left a map there earlier. Handing Trevar a piece of charcoal, he stepped back.

Trevar marked various buildings and warehouses with a black X. He circled one of them and tapped it with the charcoal. "This dealer's name is Bunton, and he's the one who killed Sven."

Valek stilled. "Him personally? Or did he order the hit?"

"Personally."

"Do you have proof?"

"He bragged about it. Wanted me to spread the word to the other black market dealers. To warn them not to undercut everyone. To not be another Sven. Or they'd end up just like him."

That seemed too good to be true. "Are you sure he wasn't lying?"

"He had Sven's merchandise and his dagger."

Cold fury burned in his heart. That knife had been a gift from Valek. "Good work, Trevar. Sven would be proud of you."

The young man nodded.

A knock sounded. The captain poked his head into the room. "Your team leaders are here, sir."

"Send them in."

"What are you going to do now?" Trevar asked.

"We're going shopping."

"THAT'S TECHNICALLY A RAID," Janco said after Valek explained the mission to his six team leaders. They crowded around the small desk, studying the map. "A smash and grab involves more property damage and—"

"Janco," Ari warned.

"Feel free to make a mess," Valek said. "That's part of the show."

"Ah." Janco grinned.

Valek assigned the location of one X to each leader. "Memorize the address."

"What about this one?" Maren asked, pointing to the circled X.

"That's mine," he said. "You'll each have an eight-person squad. Six will be the Commander's soldiers, and two from the town watch. I don't care how you smash," he glanced at Janco, "as long as you wait until sunrise." Valek gave the leaders a few more instructions on the op.

"Can I be on your team?" Trevar asked Valek when he'd

finished. The young man had been standing to the side, probably hoping no one noticed him.

"No. You're not trained."

Trevar opened his mouth. "But I'm the one who—"

"No. Any questions?" Valek asked the rest of them. Aside from Ari, Janco, and Maren, the other three were members of his corps and all professionals. No one responded, so he continued, "All right, go brief your squads."

They filed out.

"What about me?" Trevar asked Valek.

"Follow me."

They went outside. Valek approached Kenda, who had been organizing the soldiers and the members of the watch patrol who would be assisting.

"Seven teams?" she asked.

"Yes, our intel on the number of dealers was correct."

"I'll update the stand-bys." She eyed Trevar. "Are you ready to start your training?"

"I...think so," he said.

"It's either yes or no, boy." She snapped.

Trevar straightened. "Yes."

"Good. Just one bag?"

"Everything I own."

"Good. In our business, we travel light. We don't get attached to stuff." She shot Valek a look. She didn't approve of the clutter in his office and took every opportunity to let him know. "If you're on an undercover mission and have to leave everything behind, then it's not a big deal."

Before she could go on, Valek cut in. "You'll learn many more survival skills, Trevar. Go with Kenda. She'll oversee your training." He clasped the young man on the shoulder. "Thank you for your help."

Trevar nodded and Valek joined his squad. They had half an hour to get into position. The deep black of the sky had lightened a hue. Valek briefed them on their mission and assigned tasks before they headed out the west gate.

～

VALEK'S SQUAD waited in the shadows around Bunton's warehouse. According to Trevar, the black market dealer and his staff lived on the second floor. Normally, Valek would case the building, mark all the exits, and find out exactly how many people he'd encounter inside. He'd go in silently with his corps and the neighbors wouldn't see or hear a thing.

But a smash and grab was a noisy, public affair.

At dawn, they busted in the front doors, startling the two guards in the main bay where Bunton's legitimate business operated. Rolls of fabric filled oversized shelves, and clothing in various stages of completion hung from hangers. Sewing tables with spools of colorful thread lined the open space.

"Drop your weapons!" his team yelled at the guards.

"Hands up!"

"Down on the ground!"

Valek sprinted up the steps with four soldiers behind him. At the top, a man still in his pajamas brandished a short sword. Valek ducked under the blade and tackled the guy. As they hit the floor, Valek yanked the weapon from his hands. Then he rolled to his feet and kept on going, leaving the now unarmed man for his team to secure.

He raced through the various rooms. The key to a successful attack were surprise, speed, and intensity. Disoriented after being rudely woken, most of the people he encountered offered no resistance. However, the element of surprise had faded by the time he reached a large opulent office. A man in a merchant uniform stood on the far side. His right hand grasped the knob of another door—probably an exit. Four guards armed with long daggers made a wall between Valek and the man.

"Are you Bunton?" Valek asked the man.

"And if I am?" the man asked.

"Then you're under arrest," Valek said.

Bunton paused. "For what?"

"Murder, and the buying and selling of illegal goods."

"That's quite the list. Aren't you forgetting something?" Bunton's gaze slid past Valek's shoulder. "Or is it just you here to arrest me?"

What was the point of being the most feared man in Ixia if no one recognized him? Perhaps Valek should wear a name tag. "They're on the way."

"Thanks for the warning." Bunton opened the door.

Two of his squad members rushed in. They pounced on Bunton, taking him down and cuffing his wrists. Valek took advantage of the distraction to hit a couple of the goons with darts laced with sleeping potion. Then he yanked two more darts from his sleeve and lunged at the closest guard. Too bad the office wasn't large enough for a proper fight. Valek jabbed him with a dart, then spun away to prick the last goon. As he waited for the potion to kick in, he dodged and wove and avoided most of the men's clumsy strikes. A few of them slipped past his defenses, but the heavy fabric of his uniform kept the blades from cutting his skin. Eventually they all slowed and tottered and collapsed to the floor.

His team yanked Bunton to his feet, bookending the black market dealer.

"You can't prove anything," Bunton said. "I'm a legitimate businessman."

Valek plucked Sven's dagger from Bunton's belt and pulled the weapon from its scabbard. The black metal shone in the weak morning sunlight. The unique etchings on the blade were clearly visible. His grip on the hilt tightened as the desire to stab the knife into Bunton's heart shot through him. He raised his eyebrows at Bunton instead of killing him.

"I bought it from someone else. I'd no idea it was stolen."

A loud crash sounded from below. Followed by the crack of splitting wood and the ring of shattered glass hitting the floor. Ah, the smashing had begun.

"Do you want to tell me again how you're legitimate?" Valek asked.

"They won't find any contraband and you'll have to pay for all that damage."

"Take him down with the others," he said to his squad. Then he did a sweep of the rooms, ensuring everyone had been either knocked out or escorted downstairs.

Bunton seemed rather confident about the contraband, so Valek searched for hidden storerooms. Nothing. There could be an underground storage area, but that would be rather obvious. Before he joined his squad, Valek scanned the ceiling, checking for spiders. Or in this case, a concealed entrance.

He found it in the fifth room he entered. The panel blended with the wooden beams supporting the roof and he almost missed it except for a strange knot in the wood which ended up being the latch.

When Valek pulled the panel down, a set of stairs unfolded, reaching the floor. Nice. He climbed up and poked his head into the building's attic. Beams of sunlight pierced the small holes in the walls of the vast space, revealing stacks of crates and piles of illegal merchandise. Gotcha.

Valek joined his team in the main bay. They had made a proper mess of Bunton's equipment and supplies. Bunton and his employees all stood along one wall with their wrists manacled.

One of his soldiers came up to him. "Sorry, sir, we were unable to find any incriminating evidence."

Bunton smirked.

"Then it's a good thing I found plenty," Valek said. "It's all in the attic."

The dealer's good mood disappeared, but his confidence remained. "You still can't prove murder."

Valek'd had enough. He strode to the man and leaned close. "Who said I *have to* prove it?"

For the first time, Bunton appeared uncertain. His gaze swept Valek, probably noting the lack of a uniform and military insignia. "The Commander requires a full hearing for all those accused of causing the death of another person," he said.

"If that's what you need to tell yourself to get through the next couple of months, then go right ahead," Valek said. He gestured to his squad. "Take the workers and family members to the watch building for questioning. Bunton and his goons are going to the castle for interrogation."

They paraded their captives through the streets of Castletown. Neighbors and the curious lined the streets to watch the show. The squad members loudly proclaimed they'd arrested all the black market dealers as a warning to any others who might be considering going into the business. The show would work. At least, temporarily. Eventually a new group of people would fill in the gaps despite the danger. Greed never died.

Ari's and Janco's squads joined the parade. Ari scowled at everyone, playing the part, while Janco waved at the onlookers. A slice along Janco's upper arm bled, otherwise he appeared uninjured.

"Trouble?" he asked Janco, nodding at his arm.

"I fell for the old damsel-in-distress trick," he said in disgust.

"Oh?" Valek hadn't heard that one.

"You know," he gestured. "Young woman, huddled in a corner, scared, and crying. I tried to calm her down and reached out to help her up. She pulled a knife on *me*. And then *I* get called a brute for defending myself." He huffed.

"Any other problems with the smash and grab?" Valek asked them both.

"No," Ari said.

"Nope. It was fun, although I think it was more of a raid," Janco said. Then asked, "What's going to happen to all that loot? One place had boxes filled to the brim with Greenblade cigars."

"It will all get confiscated and destroyed."

"Too bad we can't do something with all that stuff," Janco said.

"What would you do?"

"Me? The weapons would go into the armory, the cigars could be used as...incentives...no, gifts to the soldiers for a job well done. Or we could use it for bribes."

"Bribes?"

"Yeah, to get people to talk."

"What can we give *you* to stop talking?" Maren asked Janco as she joined them. "I heard you and your squad two streets over."

Unaffected by her comments, Janco said, "Just following orders."

After they dropped off the workers and family members to be processed at the watch building, the dealers were taken to the castle along with Bunton and his men. Valek would soon discover which of them helped Bunton kill Sven and his agents.

As for Bunton, if he put a farmer's uniform on the man, Bunton would be a perfect body double for Tentil, the prisoner scheduled for the cold season's execution.

"STAR WANTS to get the little rat on her payroll," Margg said to Valek.

It was three weeks before the beginning of the cold season and he'd been working in his office when she'd arrived with the news.

"In what capacity?" Valek asked, annoyed. He didn't like Margg referring to Yelena as a little rat, but he couldn't risk letting the housekeeper know it bothered him. Not until Yelena became an official part of his team.

"Providing information that supposedly the rat is privy to that I'm not. And I'm supposed to be the go between, which is good for us because *I* won't tell Star anything important."

"Yelena won't agree to sell secrets to Star."

"I think she will." When Valek didn't respond, she added, "Star's been pressuring me to ask, so let me ask. If the little rat says no, then it's a no."

There'd be no harm in letting Margg ask. Although he did wonder if Yelena would tell him about Margg's offer. "All right, but I want to be nearby when you ask her."

"Are you *that* sure she'll say no?"

"Yes."

"Want to bet on it?"

"You sound like Rand."

"You and the Commander make bets all the time."

True. "All right. How much?"

"A gold."

"Deal."

Margg left in a better mood than she'd arrived. Valek considered Star's operation. He had moved four of his agents into the building next to Star's and they'd drilled tiny holes in the walls to listen to her plans. They reported to him on a regular basis or when they learned something important, but Margg, who didn't know about the agents next door, still updated him about her meetings.

He wondered if Star had really been pressuring her, or if it was Margg's idea to approach Yelena to get her into trouble. He'd have to find out.

~

A FEW DAYS LATER, Valek and Margg waited for Yelena near the entrance of the baths. The corridors in this area were dimly lit so there were plenty of shadows. Just to be safe, Valek stayed on the far side. If Yelena kept to her routine, she'd pass Margg on her way to get washed up after training.

It didn't take long before Valek spotted Yelena walking toward them. She moved stiffly and her hand rested on her ribs as if she'd been injured. He had to clamp down on the sudden irrational desire to find her training partners and trounce them.

When Yelena drew closer, Margg stepped into view, blocking her.

Surprised, Yelena immediately backed up and assumed a fight stance. Pride at her reaction warmed his heart.

"What do you want?" Yelena asked after a beat. She sounded annoyed and on edge at the same time. "Are you running another errand for your master like a good doggie?"

Nice dig.

"Better than being a rat caught in a trap," Margg said.

Yelena brushed past the larger woman.

"Would the rat like some cheese?" Margg asked.

Yelena stopped and turned. "What?"

"Cheese. Money. Gold. I bet you're the kind of rat that would do anything for a piece of cheese."

"What would I have to do to get a piece of cheese?" Yelena asked.

"I have a source that pays well for information. It's the perfect setup for a little rat," Margg said.

"What kind of information?"

"Anything you might overhear while you're scurrying around the Commander's office or Valek's apartment. My contact pays on a sliding scale; the juicier the news, the bigger the chunk of cheese."

Even though he knew Yelena would refuse, Valek held his breath.

"How does it work?"

Just wait. Don't *jump to conclusions.*

"You give me the information," she said, "and I pass it along. I collect the money, and give it to you, minus a fifteen percent fee."

"And I'm supposed to believe that you'd stick to a fifteen percent cut of a total I'd be unaware of?"

Wait. Just...wait. She's...just being... He wasn't sure.

Margg shrugged. "It's either that or nothing. I'd think that a half-starved rat like you would pounce on any morsel, no matter how small." Margg stepped away as if she was about to leave.

Good. Go. Go.

"What if we went to your source together?" Yelena asked, stopping her. "Then you'd still receive your fee."

CHAPTER 13

*S*tunned, Valek gaped at Yelena as if she'd just transformed into another person. He'd been so sure of her response that he had no other reaction than total and complete disbelief.

Margg took the acceptance in stride, but she seemed uncertain about the unexpected request. "I'll have to check," Margg said before continuing down the hallway. She swept past Valek without glancing at him—all part of the plan, but a triumphant expression lit her face.

Yelena stared after Margg for a while. Then, instead of going into the baths, she followed the housekeeper. Valek pressed back into the shadows, but she hurried by without spotting him. And then he realized she was skipping her bath to go taste the Commander's dinner.

Valek had to get there first and warn the Commander not to say *anything* to her. Not until Valek could process everything and…he'd no idea. As soon as she was out of sight, he ran. She might have discovered some of the shortcuts in the castle, but he'd been living there for the last fifteen years.

She hadn't reached the throne room yet when Valek burst into the office. He had only a few minutes.

The Commander looked up. "Is there a problem?"

"Yes, and I'll explain later. But for now, please don't tell Yelena anything."

"I don't normally."

"Also hide any important information on your desk."

The Commander slammed a fist on his desk. "You vouched for her. And now you're telling me she's a traitor."

"She's not. Well, not yet. It's complicated and she'll be here soon."

"And you came running to tell me not to blab. To hide classified information. What the hell, Valek? Do I look like a complete moron to you?"

Any other time, Valek would have apologized, backed down, and tried to smooth things over. But he'd been blindsided by Yelena's betrayal and the Commander's change in personality. He'd had enough. Anger ignited in his chest.

"You're not being *you*," Valek said.

"What?"

"You're acting different. I didn't want you thinking you could trust Yelena and tell her—"

"Tell her what? Something like I changed my successor?"

"You didn't. You wouldn't."

"I did."

The hits just kept coming. "Whatever possessed you to change your successor?" Valek demanded.

"You really do want to be in charge," the Commander said in a low, flat tone. "And now you want me to tell you my new successor so you can go assassinate him?"

The conversation had spiraled out of control and gone into the realm of ridiculous. Valek reigned in his temper and tried reason. "In the sixteen years I've known you, you've *never* reversed a decision. This isn't a ploy to discover your successor. I just want to know why you changed your mind. Why now?"

"That is absolutely none of your business. You've pledged your loyalty to me, that means I give the orders and you obey *without question*. Do you understand?"

He understood that either the Commander and Yelena had been both acting out of character, or he had completely misread them. But as the Commander so callously reminded him, he'd sworn his allegiance, which meant following his orders.

"Always, sir," he said in a clipped tone, suppressing the fury burning inside him.

Needing to leave before he did or said something he'd regret —or get hanged for—Valek jerked the door open. Yelena stumbled into the office and some of his anger escaped his efforts to control it. "Yelena, where the hell have you been? The Commander's waiting for his dinner." On the edge of exploding, Valek strode through the throne room. The other officers and advisers took one look at his expression and wisely moved from his path.

Valek had no memory of the trip back to his apartment. Once there, he released his hold on his emotions. Red hot rage, the sick knot of betrayal, and the uncertainty and fear about the Commander's behavior rolled through his body with such strength, Valek had to move, or risk being crushed by the force of them.

This—

He paced around the living room, but the amount of energy expanded wasn't near enough. Valek picked up his gray rocks and hurled them at the walls. The explosion caused by each impact matched the roar of his blood and gave him a tiny bit of relief.

This was why—

He heaved rock after rock until his arms ached. And it still wasn't enough. It'd never be enough.

This was why I shouldn't—

Prowling, he clutched two rocks in his fists, digging his fingernails into the hard surface.

This was why I shouldn't have fallen—

Valek smashed the rocks together. Pain pierced his hands and shot up his forearms.

This was why I shouldn't have fallen in love—

Stomping on a rock, he crushed it under his boot. Going over to a pile of rocks, he proceeded to turn them into rubble.

This was why I shouldn't have fallen in love with Yelena.

He kicked over the piles of books, making a mess and enough noise to cover Yelena's entrance. Valek wondered how long she stood there gaping at him in shock.

"What do you want?" he snarled.

"Nothing." She fled to her room.

Good.

He stared at her closed door. It wasn't her fault he'd fallen for her. Yelena had kept him at a distance from the beginning as, being an intelligent woman, she should.

Oh no. This was *all* his fault. He'd gotten carried away, thinking she'd be part of his team. Thinking that she'd be as loyal to the Commander as he was. He'd let his emotions overrule logic and plain good sense. And now he was paying the price.

After all those months, years, really, of suppressing his feelings, Valek indulged in a three-day vent. Or perhaps he should refer to it as a three-day sulk? Either way, it was three days of ill humor and having to interact with Yelena without letting her know that he no longer viewed her as an ally but as an enemy.

Three days to purge everything from his soul in order to prepare for the day when he'd have to kill Yelena. Because that was inevitable. She'd sell secrets to Star and scheme to escape and eventually...

Pure ice filled the emptiness inside him. He welcomed the

crisp, clarity it lent to his thoughts and the hard edge it gave him. Valek focused on work with a renewed determination.

Sitting at his desk in his apartment, he read through the reports from the agents listening in on Star. She traded and bartered for information, which she sold to clients. Star also acted as a middleman for clients needing to hire goons or find people willing to break the law. Gambling was mentioned often in her conversations, but no indication she operated a parlor. However, one name jumped out at him in connection to the gambling. Figured. Valek shut the report in disgust.

He turned his attention to the next problem. Brazell had finally sent the Criollo recipe, which meant Rand would make enough for everyone to eat. Would the castle residents change? Would they all become more relaxed like the Commander? What would be the consequences? Unknown at this point. In any case, Valek needed to determine the effects of Criollo.

Reading through the list of ingredients in the Criollo recipe that he had surreptitiously copied, he paused when the door of his suite opened and clicked closed. Yelena. She'd been hiding in her bedroom the last three nights. Perhaps it was time for her to move out.

Instead of fleeing, she said, "I may have discovered what those beans are."

Mildly surprised that she had kept working on Brazell's factory beans, he swiveled to face her. "Really?" He used his coldest and flattest tone of voice. Could he really trust anything she said?

She met his gaze and stepped back. "I…" She swallowed. "I was talking to Rand, and he mentioned missing coffee. Do you remember coffee? A southern drink."

"No." Of course, he remembered coffee. Of all the Sitian goods that had been banned after the takeover, coffee had caused the loudest and longest outcry from the Ixians. Though he didn't know coffee started out as beans.

"I think our beans might be coffee. If you don't know what coffee is, perhaps I should show them to Rand. If that's alright with you?"

All right? She'd already talked to the cook. And just like Rand, she'd sell the Commander out for a handful of coins. Anger cracked through the ice around his heart. "Go ahead; share your ideas with Rand. Your buddy, your best friend. You're just like him."

She blinked at him. "What?"

"Do as you like. I don't care." Valek turned his back to her. Obviously from his heated reaction, he needed to work harder at *not* caring. At least his comments chased her away. But this time, her lock snapped in place.

Ah. He'd scared her. Good. She should be scared.

He turned his thoughts to the beans. If they were coffee beans, then why would Brazell wish to produce an outlawed southern drink? Everyone would know immediately as the smell would give it away. Unless Brazell hoped to grow the beans in Ixia? That would solve the legal issues and Ixians would buy coffee in bulk, making the general a richer man.

Valek would have to research how and where coffee was grown. His agents still hadn't returned from following those wagons into Sitia. It'd been over sixty days since they'd left. If the beans were grown in the Illiais Jungle in the far south, then the length of time matched. He'd give them another week before sending scouts to locate them.

Pulling out the most recent report from his agents at the factory site, Valek read it. They said all the equipment had been installed and the next step would be to send test batches through. He'd have to wait for more updates from the factory and hope his agents didn't get caught in Sitia.

～

A WEEK after asking Yelena to spy, Margg had a morning meeting with Star. Not quite trusting the housekeeper, Valek followed her through the streets of Castletown. It had been a difficult few days. The Commander had demanded an explanation about Yelena and insisted Valek catch her in the act of treason as soon as possible.

Margg headed straight to Star's building and was admitted. Valek looped around back and entered the house to the left. Star only posted a watcher in the alley at night. The person was easy to bypass, as they tended to sleep slouched in the doorway to her residence.

The narrow home had been abandoned a few years ago. The previous occupants had left nothing behind. Valek climbed to the third level where Inrick sat against a wall, jotting down notes. On the other side of that wall was Star's study. He nodded at Valek but didn't say anything because voices could be clearly heard on both sides of the wall through the holes.

Valek sat next to Inrick and listened.

"…were right. She agreed to sell information," Margg said.

"Of course, I was right," a female voice with a slight nasal tang said. "I've had the last four food tasters on my payroll."

Four? No. Only the last two. The woman was lying to make herself seem more accomplished.

"Did she tell you anything of value?" Star asked.

"No. She wants to meet with you." Margg's tone was heavy with disgust. "The little rat doesn't trust me."

"Smart. In this business, trusting is a weakness."

Valek agreed with that sentiment. Yet, it didn't quite work in real life. You *had* to trust some people, or you couldn't call it living. He trusted the Commander and his agents. And, yes, it was difficult to rely on them, especially when an agent turned out to be untrustworthy. In that case, all he could do was damage control, move on, and hope he learned a new way to detect those who might turn on him in the future.

"You trust me," Margg said.

"For now. Your information has been accurate. Although, I would have liked some warning about the black market raid. My clients count on me to warn them."

Star earned the bulk of her money from selling intelligence and she had quite the network of informers. Nice to know none of his agents tipped her off about the smash and grab.

Margg huffed. "I wasn't privy to that information."

"Do you think the little rat would have known?"

"I've no idea, but she has access to Valek's suite—"

"She's still living there? Even though Brazell is gone?"

"Yes."

"Why?"

"I don't know."

"Do you have anything new for me?" Star asked, sounding annoyed.

"Valek's been in a foul mood since he argued with the Commander. I don't know what that's about."

"Maybe one of his missions isn't going well. Perhaps the food taster will know."

"Maybe. When do you want to meet her?" Margg asked.

"Tomorrow night."

AFTER FOLLOWING Margg back to the castle, Valek was unable to focus on work. After a fruitless afternoon, he gave up and returned to his apartment. Lighting a lantern, he carried it up to his carving studio. He sorted through various shapes and sizes of rocks before one "spoke" to him. It sounded crazy, but he'd learned to let his subconscious pick his next project.

This time, the rock that had called was roughly circular and a bit flat. *A good skipping stone.* Hidden inside lurked another shape. One that he needed to free. One that would be revealed as he chiseled, chipped, and grinded away the surplus.

As he worked, his thoughts churned through his various problems. Valek wondered what news Yelena would sell to Star. Would she mention the Commander's addiction to Criollo? Or about the change in his successor? She'd been right outside the door and had to have overheard their argument. Valek hadn't raised his voice to Ambrose in a very long time. And since then, the Commander had been distant and cold to Valek. No surprise, as Valek had completely misjudged Yelena and put the Commander at risk. At least he'd learned about her before he included her in his team and she could sell damaging information. Should he set out some false data in various places to test if she snooped through his desk, or office, or the Commander's office? Perhaps he'd include a few true tidbits, just to give her some credibility with Star. Might as well determine the holes in his security before arresting her. And he should—was that a knock?

He stopped grinding as Yelena opened the door. "What is it?" he asked.

She stood in the entrance. "I've had an offer. Someone wants to pay me for information about the Commander."

He faced her. Was she confessing? With her tense posture and the crease of uncertainty on her face, she appeared ready to bolt. "Why tell me?"

"I thought you might want to follow along. This might be the one who has been leaking information about me." It took him a moment to switch gears and for all her words to make sense. Before he could comment, she continued, "Espionage is illegal. You might want to make an arrest, or maybe even feed this leak some misinformation. You know, spy stuff. Remember? Or have you become bored with that, too?" Her question was sharp with anger.

It finally sunk in. She'd agreed to sell information to Star in order to help him and the Commander. Not *betray* them. The ice inside him melted in one gushing torrent, leaving him light-headed. Yelena peered at him, waiting for his answer.

Valek pulled it together. "Who?" he asked. "And when?"

"Margg approached me, and she mentioned a contact. We're meeting tomorrow night."

"All right, proceed as planned. I'll tail you to the rendezvous and see who we're dealing with. We'll start by feeding this contact some accurate information to make you look reliable. Perhaps the Commander's change of successor would work. It's harmless information that will be made public anyway. Then we'll go from there."

As they discussed the details of the mission, Valek kept his emotions in check, despite the relief and chagrin over jumping to conclusions and the horror of contemplating ending her life that twirled inside him like his grinding wheel. After they finished planning, she headed out the door.

He'd been wrong about her and he wanted to fix that mistake, to show he trusted her, believed in her. "Yelena."

She halted in the threshold, looking back over her shoulder.

"You once said I wasn't ready to believe your reason for killing Reyad. I'll believe you now."

"But I'm not ready to tell you," she said and left.

It wasn't a complete rejection. Not ready meant she might be able to confide in him in the future. And no wonder she didn't trust him. He'd just spent the last week either in a rage or freezing her out.

Valek fidgeted with the rock he'd been working on as another thought occurred to him. What if she never let down her guard around him? Could she still be a member of his team? No. Until she trusted him, she'd just be a well-trained food taster.

He glanced at the almost finished carving in his hand. It was a Cheketo leaf. Smiling, Valek remembered Yelena had glued the big round leaves to camouflage her red uniform when she'd acted as a fugitive. Considering the southern magician's interest in her and a few other puzzles, Yelena was still camouflaged.

Tonight, he had learned he couldn't rush her. That she'd either eventually trust him or not. But he was determined to work at earning that trust. Even if it meant peeling off one Cheketo leaf at a time.

∾

"TRUST her or don't trust her, which one is it, Valek?" the Commander asked in exasperation.

"Trust her. Yelena proved her loyalty last night. *I'm* the one who overreacted."

"You? Overreact? Is this the same man who pushed me down a flight of stairs when General Rasmussen sneezed?"

At the Commander's teasing tone, Valek relaxed back into the chair. They were in his office, and all was apparently forgiven. "In my defense, that sneeze sounded like the twang of a bow string. I thought an assassin had targeted you. Better a sprained knee than an arrow in the heart."

"A sprained *ankle*."

"You're not going to let me live that one down, are you?"

"No."

"Good to know. And I also wanted to let you know those factory beans of Brazell's are grown in Sitia. My agents arrived early this morning. They followed the wagons all the way to the Illiais Jungle. Seems the pods grow on the trunks of short jungle trees. I still don't know what the beans are used for. It's not coffee. I found out those beans are shaped differently."

"Valek, that's enough. Leave Brazell's feed mill alone. He obtained the proper permits, there's no need to investigate further."

Where did this come from? "But he's buying illegal goods."

"No. He's not. He's *stealing* them so he can grow those pods in Ixia."

"How do you know?"

"He sent me an update about the factory. Those beans help the cows produce more milk and increase a steer's weight."

"No matter how they're obtained, the beans are still illegal," Valek said because it appeared the Commander had lost all reason.

"In this case, he has my approval."

Valek had no response. Getting angry or questioning the Commander's decision would be pointless. "Yes, sir."

"Good, because you're going to be busy over the next couple weeks. The generals will be here for the annual brandy meeting, and a Sitian delegation is coming to visit us."

Valek laughed, but no humor touched the Commander's gaze. "You're serious?"

"Yes." He indicated a piece of parchment on his desk. "The Sitian Council has requested a meeting and I've agreed."

It took every bit of Valek's willpower not to react. "When are they coming?"

"In a week. I expect them to be treated as guests and not enemies. Understand?"

"Yes, sir."

Valek left the office in a daze. As soon as he entered a deserted hallway, he leaned against the wall. His thoughts spun. The Commander was not himself. That was now a fact.

Considering the typical reasons for a person acting strangely, Valek ruled out blackmail and love right away. That left magic and addiction. Valek would have sensed if magic was in use, but he wasn't with the Commander all day. As for addiction, that fit the facts better. Up until recently, the only source of Criollo was from Brazell. The general could have found out about Valek's investigation of his factory and implied he'd stop sending the dessert if Valek didn't stop. Then why send the recipe? Brazell would lose his advantage. Unless…Criollo somehow made a person more open to suggestions? Perhaps Brazell had an aide or adviser in the castle who had been talking to the Commander.

Valek needed to figure out just how the Criollo worked. After stopping by Kenda's office to arrange for one of his agents to steal some Criollo from the kitchen, he headed to the training room. Yelena and the others should be just finishing their workout for the day. Sure enough, when he entered, they sat on the bench chatting.

Maren took one look at his expression and jumped to her feet. But she wasn't who he needed to talk to, and he asked her and the power twins to leave. Once they were gone, he paced, trying to find the right words to explain without sounding like an idiot.

"What's wrong?" Yelena asked. "Is it about tonight?"

"No," he rushed to assure her. "We're all set for tonight. This is about the Commander." He paused.

"What about him?"

"Has he been meeting with anyone strange this week?"

"Strange?"

"Someone you don't know or an adviser from another Military District?"

"Not that I've seen. Why?"

Valek paused again, not sure how to describe what'd been going on. "Commander Ambrose has agreed to admit a Sitian delegation."

"That's bad?" she asked, confused.

Unable to hold in his emotions any longer, he said, "He hates southerners! They've requested a meeting with him every year since the takeover. And for the last fifteen years, the Commander has replied with a single word: no. Now they're due to arrive in a week." Valek's pacing increased. "Ever since you became the food taster and that Criollo showed up, the

Commander has been acting different. I couldn't put my finger on it before, it was just a nagging feeling, but now I have two particular incidents."

"The change in his successor and now the southern delegation?"

"Exactly." He took a deep breath. "I've misdirected some Criollo to our suite. I want you to eat a piece whenever he does. But you're not to tell anyone, not even the Commander. That's an order."

"Yes, sir."

"Keep your meeting with Margg tonight. I'll be there."

"Should I tell Margg's contact about the southern delegation?"

"No. Use the change of the Commander's successor. It's already floating around as a rumor, so you'll just confirm it." Happy that he had a plan to test the Criollo, Valek strode from the room.

A part of him didn't like not telling Yelena that the substance might be addictive or make a person susceptible to suggestions, but he wouldn't get an honest reaction from her if she suspected or fought the effects. On the other hand, telling her about it afterwards would ruin any progress he might have made on earning her trust. He needed to think of a better solution.

He returned to his office. Soon after, Kenda arrived.

"I put a box of that Criollo you wanted in your suite," she said.

"Was Hildred busy?"

"No." She shrugged. "I thought it'd be easier to steal it than explain what I needed to Hildred. It wasn't."

"You should have waited for the dinner rush."

"That wasn't it. The stuff was locked in Rand's rooms. Seems the recipe was either wrong or the chef couldn't get it to work and what's left of the Criollo is considered valuable."

Smart of Brazell to send a fake recipe. That would put the

blame on Rand, and Brazell would be able to continue supplying it to the Commander.

The door to his office flew open. One of the medical staff rushed in. Valek jumped to his feet. "What's wrong?"

"Medic Channa…" she puffed. "Sent me… Yelena…"

His world slowed to a stop.

"Yelena's…been injured."

CHAPTER 14

The world snapped into motion. Valek raced to the infirmary while his thoughts spiraled with a litany of dire injuries. Half convinced she was near death, Valek burst through the doors. Yelena lay on an examination table, but she was conscious. Thank fate!

"What happened?" Valek demanded when he arrived at her side.

Yelena frowned at Channa. The medic took Yelena's right hand. Blood dripped from a deep cut across her palm. A similar wound bled from her left hand. Both defensive injuries. Valek bit back a curse as he scanned her body for other gashes.

Channa said, "Broken glass leaves jagged lacerations. These clean slices are obviously from a knife. I'm required to report it."

True. Valek wished to be informed about any knife fights.

Yelena turned her attention to him. "I was attacked."

"By who?" He'd kill them.

She glanced at the medic, signaling a need for privacy.

"Could you excuse us for a minute?" he asked Channa.

Clearly unhappy about his request, she hesitated. "Five minutes," she ordered, and walked to her desk.

"Who?" Valek repeated.

"Nix, a guard in Parffet's unit. Said he worked for Brazell and warned me to stop training."

"I'll kill him."

"No, you won't," she said as if scolding a toddler. "You'll use him. He's a link to Brazell."

He met her gaze. She was right, using Nix was a smart idea. Yet the fire in his veins demanded the man pay for hurting her. He tamped down the bloodlust; he could always kill Nix later. "Where did he attack you?"

"A storeroom about four or five doors up from our training room."

"He's probably long gone by now. I'll send someone to the barracks." Because he didn't trust himself not to kill the man on sight.

"He won't be there."

"Why not?" Valek waited.

"If he's not in the storeroom, he won't have gotten far. You might want to send a couple of men."

"I see." Valek paused. Ari had said she'd a fierce side. And she'd been learning self-defense from the best soldiers in the Commander's army. "So, your training has been progressing to your satisfaction?"

"Better than expected."

No kidding. Impressed and proud, Valek hurried from the infirmary and almost bumped into Kenda, who'd been waiting in the hallway.

"Everything okay?" she asked.

"She's fine. I'll explain on the way."

He led her to the empty training room, and then counted storerooms. A weak, yellow glow shone through the half open door of the fourth one on the left. Curses and murmurs emanated, indicating Nix was conscious. Valek drew his knife and slowly pushed the door wider.

An almost bald man sat on the floor cradling his right arm to his chest. He wore a lieutenant's uniform. The air stank of sweat and blood ran from his nose. His left knee appeared swollen. Noting the empty sheath at Nix's waist, Valek scanned the area for the missing weapon, ensuring it wasn't within Nix's reach.

"Wow," Kenda whispered. "She did a number on him. Go her."

Nix spotted them in the doorway. "Figures the bitch squealed."

A cold fury welled. Valek returned his weapon to its holder before he could gut the man and strangle him with his own intestines. "We'll need a few more agents to help carry him out," he said to Kenda.

"But it looks like he can walk?"

Valek gave her a tight smile. "Not for long."

"Oh. Okay, I'll be back." Kenda left.

As Valek approached, Nix said, "The bitch attacked me."

Valek grabbed his injured arm and Nix screamed. Ah, she'd broken his elbow. Good. He released it just as fast and snatched up Nix's uninjured arm. "Tell me why you attacked my food taster, or I'll snap this one in half."

"Orders from General Brazell." Nix spat. "Shouldn't be a surprise."

"Orders to kill or scare her?"

"Scare. Harass. Humiliate. Anything to make her life miserable."

"Why not kill?"

"He wants that pleasure—argh!"

Twisting Nix's arm, Valek asked, "When?"

"I don't know. Ahhh!"

The clear snap of the man's shoulder dislocating momentarily appeased Valek. "What is he planning?"

"Don't know!"

Valek pressed his foot on Nix's injured knee. "Who else is working for him?"

"Don't know that either!"

Valek stomped on the knee. Nix screamed in agony before fainting. Too bad. He had more questions for the man. Yelena must have shattered his kneecap. Smart. She'd prevented Nix from chasing after her or running away.

Kenda returned with Inrick and two agents. "Did you kill him?" she asked.

"Not yet. Take him to the infirmary. Once he regains consciousness, I'll question him again." If Channa allowed it. Perhaps he'd wait until Nix healed to do another round of interrogation.

"Yes, sir."

Kenda and the others picked Nix up. Rousing briefly, he groaned in pain. Valek was about to follow them to check on Yelena when he realized it was almost time for the Commander's dinner. He changed direction and hurried to the Commander's office.

"Something wrong with Yelena?" the Commander asked when Valek tasted his dinner.

"I gave her the night off."

"Oh?"

The Commander had enough time to get used to the idea of Yelena being a part of their team. Time to update him on her status. "She's been training with Ari and Janco. She just started knife defense and was cut." It was a perfectly truthful response. Anyone who trained with knives or swords collected an assortment of scars in the process. The Commander didn't need to know about Nix. Not yet.

"All part of the fun."

"Isn't that my line?" Valek asked, setting the tray on the desk as he let out a breath, glad the Commander had taken the news about Yelena's training in stride.

"You're not the only one who enjoys a good knife fight. In fact, we should schedule some time to spar. I'd like to keep my skills sharp."

"Funny. You would also enjoy reminding me that I still can't beat you."

"There's that."

Valek left the office and encountered Yelena in the throne room. "I've taken care of dinner." He guided her back through the maze of desks. "Find Margg and cancel tonight's meeting, then go back to our suite and get some rest."

"Cancel? What for? It would look suspicious. I'll wear gloves to cover the bandages. It's cold enough at night; nobody will notice."

Not the bandages, but they'd see the wild shine in her eyes, the small cut on her neck and the high color in her cheeks.

"I'm fine," she said.

He smiled. "You should take a look at yourself in a mirror." He was more worried about her nerves. If she was too jumpy— no, being nervous could go in her favor. "All right. We'll proceed as planned."

They stopped at Valek's office. "I have some work to finish. Rest and don't worry. I'll be close by tonight." He inserted his key.

"Valek?"

"Yes."

"What will happen to Nix?"

"We'll patch him up, threaten him with years in the dungeon if he doesn't cooperate, and, when he's done helping us, I'll reassign him to MD–1. Good enough? Or should I kill him?" He hoped she'd chose that option because he'd happily kill Nix for her.

She gave him a wicked grin. "No. Reassignment's good. If I had wanted him dead, I would have done it myself."

He straightened in surprise. Would she really have killed

him? Then she shot him a smirk worthy of Janco and headed down the hall. Ah. He loved seeing that confidence and humor in her. Especially so soon after being attacked.

VALEK WATCHED from the shadows as two figures exited the west gate of the castle complex. In the bright moonlight, he easily recognized them as Yelena and Margg. They headed to Castletown as planned. He followed them, keeping his distance.

Full moons could either be a boon or a curse, depending on the mission. In this case, it was early enough in the evening that their presence on the streets wouldn't raise suspicion. Plus, Margg walked with the determined stride of a person who knew exactly where she was going. The watch would hardly give her a second glance. They'd been trained to notice those who looked over their shoulders or hesitated at road crossings or darted into shadows.

Margg and Yelena arrived at Star's house without trouble. Valek caught a quick glance of the sharp-nosed woman who answered the door. The red head wore an innkeeper's uniform. Was that Star? They were admitted inside. Valek looped around to the alley, entered the house next door, and took the steps two at a time to the third floor.

A single candle lit the room where Inrick sat against the wall. Black curtains hung over the windows. Valek signaled that everything had proceeded as planned before sitting next to him. Although the holes were hidden behind a large piece of furniture in Star's office, faint lantern light from that side illuminated them.

Multiple footsteps and the squeak of wooden floorboards sounded, warning them of activity.

"The food taster," Star said with a satisfied purr. "I knew it was only a matter of time before I had you in my employ."

"Who are you?" Yelena asked in a dismissive tone, letting Star know she wasn't going to play around.

"You can call me Captain Star."

No response from Yelena.

"I'm not part of Ambrose's military," Star explained. And Valek guessed Yelena must have appeared dubious about her captain title. "I have my own. Has Margg explained how I work?"

"Yes."

"Good. This will be a simple exchange. This isn't a social call; I don't want gossip or hearsay. And don't inquire about my business or about me. All you need to know is my name. Agreed?"

"Agreed."

"Good. What do you got?" Star asked. A chair creaked.

"The Commander has changed his successor," Yelena said.

"How do you know?" Star asked.

"I overheard the Commander and Valek talking."

"Ah, yes. Valek." Star paused. "Why are you living in his apartment?"

"None of your business," Yelena replied in a firm tone.

Valek approved of Yelena's no-nonsense demeanor. It worked well for this situation.

"So why should I trust you?" Star asked.

"Because Valek would kill me if he knew I was here. You know it as well as I do. How much is my information worth?"

Another smart and accurate comment. A faint jingle of coins sounded.

"Your fifteen percent," Star said. A pause, and then, "Anything else?" Star asked.

"Not at this time," Yelena replied.

"When you have something for me, tell Margg. She'll arrange another meeting."

Footsteps and more squeaks sounded before Star asked her staff what they thought about the food taster.

Valek tapped on the notebook, letting Inrick know to keep taking notes while Valek hurried to meet with Margg and Yelena. He reached the alley just as they turned the corner. He took Yelena's arm and guided her into the house, pulling her into a room on the first floor. Margg followed. The moonlight poured through the windows, illuminating them. Yelena peered at him in confusion.

"I was right, Valek," Margg said. "She sold the Commander out for a gold coin. Check her pocket."

"Actually, Yelena came to me before the meeting. She believed she was going to expose *you*," Valek said to Margg.

Her gloating grin disappeared. "Why didn't you tell me?" she demanded.

"No time."

"Margg's not the leak?" Yelena asked, still confused.

"No. Margg works for me. We've been feeding Star some rather unique information and hoping to find out who her other clients are. Star's been pestering Margg to get you involved, and I thought it would be a good opportunity to test your loyalty."

Margg shot him a that's-not-quite-the-truth look, but she said, "I had hoped to send this rat back to the dungeon where she belongs. Now she'll still be scurrying around. Still a threat." Annoyed, Margg poked Yelena's arm with a meaty finger.

Yelena moved. In a heartbeat, she had Margg's arm twisted up behind her back. Margg yelped as Yelena raised her hand up high, forcing the housekeeper to bend forward. Curious to see how this played out, Valek waited.

"I am *not* a rat," Yelena said through clenched teeth. "I've proved my loyalty. You *will* get off my back. No more nasty messages in the dust. No more prying into my things. Or the next time, I'll break your arm." Yelena shoved her hard as she released her grip.

Margg stumbled and landed on the ground in a heap. Pink-faced, she lurched to her feet. As she opened her mouth to protest, Valek stopped her with a glance.

"Well said, Yelena. Margg, you're dismissed," Valek ordered.

Margg's mouth snapped closed as she spun on her heel and left the room.

"She's not friendly," Yelena said.

And you handled her perfectly. "No. That is precisely why I like her." Or rather why he *had* liked her. He avoided Yelena's gaze for a moment, reluctant to tell her the real reason he brought her inside instead of meeting back at their suite. Finally, he said, "Yelena, I'm going to show you something you're not going to like, but I think it's important that you know."

"Oh yeah? Like I enjoyed your test of faith?" Her words dripped with sarcasm.

"I warned you that I tested the food taster from time to time." Before she could respond, he stopped her. "Be quiet and stay close behind me."

He led her back around to the street and found a good place in the shadows to witness Star's next visitor.

"The person who has been leaking information to Star is due to arrive soon," Valek whispered in her ear. His lips lightly brushed her cheek and a spike of heat hit him dead center. She smelled like lavender. He moved back before he did something incredibly stupid, like press a kiss to her temple.

After a few tense minutes, a lone figure with an uneven gait walked down the street. Yelena sucked in a breath as she recognized her friend. Her only friend, who also sold secrets to Star, including information about the food taster. Valek knew she wouldn't have believed him. That she'd have to see Rand knock on Star's door and be admitted.

"Another test?" she asked Valek after the chef disappeared inside. She sounded desperate. "Is he working for you?"

He shook his head and wanted to apologize. To hold her tight and comfort her. Instead, he motioned for her to follow him back around to the alley, inside the house, and up the stairs. This was going to be hard enough on Yelena, so Valek signaled Inrick to give them some privacy. He took the notebook and the agent's place on the floor.

Yelena crouched next to him and peered through the small holes, then she rested her forehead against the wall and closed her eyes. Valek resisted pulling her into his arms.

"Generals are coming to town this week," Rand said. "That's nothing new, but the Commander ordered a feast, so something's up. Something significant. But I haven't been able to figure out what."

"Let me know as soon as possible," Star replied. Then she paused. "Maybe Yelena knows what's going on."

Yelena stiffened.

"I doubt it. She was surprised when I mentioned the feast, so I didn't ask her. She might know more later this week. I'll try again."

"Don't bother. I'll ask her myself." The sleek tone of Star's voice indicated she'd enjoyed dropping this news on Rand.

"Yelena?" Rand sputtered. "Working for you? Impossible. That's not her style."

"Are you suggesting she's working for Valek?" Alarm tightened her voice.

Yelena glanced at Valek in panic. He shook his head, waving his hand in a "don't worry" gesture.

"No. She wouldn't." Rand had recovered. "I'm just surprised, but I shouldn't be. She could use the money, and who am I to think any less of her for it?"

"Well, you shouldn't be thinking of her at all. As I see it, she's disposable. The only concern I'll have when she dies is," who's going to replace her and how quickly can I bribe them?"

"Star, once again you've shown me in the most repulsive way that the sooner I pay off my debt to you the better. How much credit do I get for tonight's information?"

"Two silvers. I'll mark it in my book, but it won't make much difference."

"What do you mean?"

"Haven't you figured it out by now? You'll never pay off your debt. As soon as you get close, you always gamble yourself right down another hole. You're too weak, Rand. Too swayed by your own emotions. Easily addicted and lacking in willpower."

"Oh, that's right. You claim to be a magician. Have you read my mind, Captain? 'Captain Star'—what a laugh! If you really had magic, Valek would have taken care of you long ago. I know you're not as smart as you claim." Rand's uneven gait rasped on the floorboards.

If the woman had magic, Valek hadn't detected it. Then again, he hadn't spent any time in her company. And he wasn't sure if he could sense magic through a wall.

"I don't need to read your mind," Star called. "All I have to do is review your history, Rand. It's all there."

Valek waited a few heartbeats before he stood and helped Yelena to her feet. Not that she needed help, but she held her body as if afraid she'd break.

Inrick returned and Valek gave him the notebook. Then led Yelena down the stairs and through the quiet streets. He kept to the shadows, but once they left the city, he relaxed and walked next to her.

"I'm sorry," Valek said, breaking the silence. "I know Rand was your friend."

"How long have you known?" she asked.

"I've suspected for the last three months, but only procured the hard evidence this month."

"What tipped you off?"

"Rand and his staff helped me with that poison test I gave you. He stayed while I laced the food with poison. I left that goblet of peach juice on my desk to keep it clean. It *was* a fair test. Blackberry poison was in that cup, but I didn't put it there." Valek paused, letting the information sink in.

When she didn't react, he continued. "An interesting property of blackberries is that only when they're prepared in a special solution of grain alcohol and yeast and cooked with extreme care to the proper temperature are they poisonous. Most cooks, and certainly not their assistants, don't possess the skills or the knowledge to achieve that result."

She stumbled as the realization hit her that Rand had tried to kill her. Yelena dashed to the side of the road and vomited. Valek followed and supported her while her body convulsed, wishing he had a cool rag for her forehead.

"Thanks," she said, grabbing some leaves to wipe her mouth.

Her legs were trembling, so Valek kept an arm around her as they headed through the south gate and toward the castle. Yelena pressed against him, fitting in so perfectly that he wanted to savor the moment. Yet the circumstances were far from ideal.

"There's more. Do you want to hear it?" Valek asked.

"No."

They continued without speaking.

"Did Rand set me up at the fire festival?" she asked.

"In a way."

"That's not an answer."

"The goons that nabbed you waited for you near the baking tent, so I suspected that Rand had told Star you would be there. But then he wouldn't let you out of his sight. It was as if he was protecting you. Remember how upset he was when he couldn't find you? How relieved he was when he spotted you alive and whole?"

"I thought he was drunk," she said.

"I suspect Rand is an unwilling participant. At the time of the poison test, he hardly knew you, but as your friendship grew, I imagine he finds himself in a difficult situation. He doesn't want to hurt you, but he needs to pay off his gambling debt. Star has an extensive organization, with plenty more thugs to replace the ones I took care of, thugs who would be willing to break a few bones for their boss. Does that make you feel any better?"

"No."

Valek had tried, but she'd taken the news hard. He wasn't sure what else he could say. He was more a man of action. Would she feel better if he offered to assassinate Rand? Or to arrest him? Probably not.

When they reached the castle's entrance, she stopped. "Anything else you want to tell me?" she asked. "Did Ari and Janco set me up for Nix's attack? Do you have another test of loyalty for me up your sleeve? Maybe the next time, I'll actually fail. A prospect that seems appealing!" Yelena pushed away his arm. "When you warned me that you would test me from time to time, I thought you meant spiking my food. But it seems there is more than one way to poison a person's heart, and it doesn't even require a meal."

Did she blame him for Rand's deceptions? Or was she just upset that he had hidden the betrayal from her? While Rand's actions were bad, being deceived certainly wasn't the worst thing a person had to deal with in life.

"Everyone makes choices in life. Some bad, some good. It's called living, and if you want to bow out, then go right ahead. But don't do it halfway. Don't linger in whiner's limbo," Valek said, his voice gruff. "I don't know what horrors you faced prior to your arrival in our dungeon. If I had to guess, I would think they were worse than what you have discovered tonight.

Perhaps that will put things into perspective." Without waiting for an answer, he strode into the castle.

GENERALS and their retinues swarmed the castle over the next couple days. Valek spent the bulk of his time putting out proverbial fires caused by the inflated egos of the generals and their staff members, who expected to be treated like royalty and were outraged when no one capitulated. It happened every year and Valek had long ago ceased to be surprised by their apparent memory loss.

The barracks also filled with soldiers from all the Military Districts of Ixia. They used the annual meeting as a chance to spar new opponents, swap stories, catch-up with friends, and drink, which led to drunken boasts, fights, and trips to the infirmary. If Sitia wished to attack the castle, any evening during this week would be the best time. However small the chances of that happening, Valek still sent his agents to keep watch on the Sitian border and a handful of others to act as bouncers and listeners in the barracks. Drunken soldiers tended to blab.

In the afternoons, Valek needed to be available to fight challengers. Many soldiers in the generals' security forces had been promoted because they were the best in their districts. They arrived each year eager to prove it by beating Valek. At least those opponents managed to give him a few decent matches.

And some, like his current challenger, made it fun. The sergeant from MD-4 had chosen rapiers. While lightweight, the long, thin, triangular sword was Valek's least favorite weapon. Blocking and parrying was all done with a twist of the wrist. And the shuffling back and forth and lunging was limiting. He'd rather chop an attacker's head off with his broadsword than poke someone full of holes with the tip of a rapier. It was a great weapon when fighting in a narrow hallway, but out in the open... Meh.

However, the sergeant kept up a fast pace of attack and she took advantage of the wide training yard. He countered one quick set of lunges, reposed, and stabbed air. She'd sidestepped out of range. Nice. She grinned and jabbed at Valek's unprotected side. He blocked just in time, turning a puncture into a surface scratch. Then she poured on the speed.

Blocking, Valek backed up as her sword sliced through the air around him. Metal clinked against metal in a steady beat. Cheers from the onlookers encouraged her. Valek stayed on the defensive to learn what else she could do. The sergeant had an impressive range of attacks and a few unique moves that almost slipped past his blocks.

Her speed reminded him of Janco, and, with that thought, Valek discovered her weakness. Instead of ending the match, he switched to the offensive to test her. She countered with ease. Counting beats in his head until he had her internal rhythm, he altered the beat. Lunge. Lunge. Pause. Block. Pause. Duck. Lunge. Duck. Tackle.

Her rapier flew from her hand as she hit the ground. She conceded the match and allowed Valek to help her to her feet.

Once she caught her breath, she said, "That's not a legal move."

"Am I disqualified?"

She opened her mouth and hesitated. "Point taken. Does that mean there are no rules when fighting you?"

"Yes."

"And I can break them as well?"

"If there are no rules, then there's nothing to break."

She grinned. "Then I'll see you next year."

"I look forward to it, Sergeant…"

"Pasha, sir."

They shook hands and parted. Pasha was his last match of

the day. Valek glanced at the dispersing crowd, looking for Janco. A sword fight between Pasha and Janco would be good practice for them both. Instead, Valek spotted Maren having fun fighting one of the visiting soldiers with her bo staff. She'd improved a great deal while training with Yelena and the power twins. He'd thought Ari and Janco would also take advantage of new blood, but he hadn't seen them in the yard since the generals arrived.

And now that he was paying attention, it seemed there were far more of Brazell's soldiers than any other Military District. A matter of timing, or did the old goat bring extra? Valek would have to ask his agents for a head count.

His unease grew as he encountered a few of Brazell's soldiers in the hallways of the castle. Not that they were banned, the main dining hall served everyone living in the complex. Yet it was a few hours until dinner. Their presence made him very glad Yelena had been remaining in their suite during her off hours since the generals had arrived. Smart move. She avoided both her ex-friend Rand and Brazell's people. It had been four days since she'd learned of his treachery and she'd been quiet, withdrawn, and brittle.

The only thing she appeared to enjoy was eating the stolen Criollo, which caused Valek to worry she'd become addicted, or her personality would change. So far, nothing seemed amiss. Yet.

They had discussed what to do about Rand, and she'd agreed to pretend they were still friends so Valek could continue observing Star.

Valek washed up and headed to his office. The generals' brandy meeting was tomorrow evening, and he had a few things to do to prepare. While there, Inrick arrived to give his report in person.

This can't be good.

"Star knows about the southern delegation," Inrick said as soon as he closed the door behind him.

That was fast. "From Rand?"

"No. An unknown client."

That was unexpected and a bit alarming because it meant the Commander had told someone. With the generals and their staff in constant meetings with him, it could be any one of them who sold the information to Star. "Unknown or new?"

"New. Arrogant bastard, too. Star never said his name. When he left, I tried to get eyes on him, but he had on a cloak and his hood was pulled low over his face."

"Did he tell her anything else important?"

"No, but he wanted to hire her to cause trouble with the delegation."

This kept getting better and better. "What kind of trouble?"

"Big enough to ruin a relationship between Ixia and Sitia. Big enough to stop any peace treaties or trading agreements. He told her to use her imagination."

Valek cursed.

"Yeah," Inrick agreed. "Star said she had just the thing. Except she never explained what the thing is to him or anyone else, and I've been listening for hours."

"Did you update your replacement?"

"Yeah, Hildred knows what's going on."

Hopefully they would discover Star's plans before the delegation arrived. "I want eyes on Star's front and back doors around the clock. Keep track of everyone who comes and goes. Follow anyone new or suspicious and find out who they are."

"Yes, sir." Inrick snapped a salute and left.

Valek sat behind his desk and rubbed his face. If they didn't discover what Star planned, he'd have to prepare for every single contingency. Considering he could think of a large number of ways to disrupt the meeting, Valek would need to bring in all his agents in order to stop the trouble before it began. However, that was his next problem to solve. Right now, the generals were his priority.

Rummaging through the boxes underneath the conference table, Valek located the one containing eight bottles of brandy. Each general brought a bottle of their signature brandy to the meeting to share. A tradition, and one that Yelena was unfamiliar with. She would need to taste the Commander's pour—all eight of them—for poisons.

Strong alcohol made it difficult for a food taster to pick up other flavors unless they were accustomed to the taste of the liquor. Yelena needed to become familiar with each brandy.

Valek hefted the box. Darkness pressed against the windows, indicating he'd missed dinner. Before he reached the door, it opened, and Kenda poked her head in. Her sour expression meant more bad news.

"Trouble?" he asked.

"Not sure. Some of Brazell's soldiers are boasting about a bounty being offered for the person who, and I quote, 'bags the food taster.'"

That would explain the extra soldiers in the castle. Worry for Yelena swirled, but he kept it in check. "Drunk boasting?"

"Mostly. But there are a few serious ones. Enough that she needs to be extra careful. I could also assign a few agents to watch her."

Except Kenda didn't sound enthusiastic about the suggestion. No surprise, as they needed all their agents for other tasks.

"No need. I'll warn her and I'll keep an eye out. She's already been laying low."

"Good. I'll let you know if there's an imminent threat."

"Thanks."

She held the door open for him and spotted the brandy bottles as he walked past. "Rough day?" she teased.

"You've no idea."

"Oh? Something up?"

He explained about Star as they walked through the castle.

"Couldn't we just arrest her now?" Kenda asked in exasperation.

"We could, but then the rest of her network disappears and her client hires someone else to disrupt the Sitian's visit. This way, we might find out who he is and what they're planning beforehand."

"And if we don't?"

"Then we'll just have to be smarter than they are."

"Easier said than done." She waved goodbye as she headed toward her office.

Valek's arms ached by the time he reached his apartment. He shifted the heavy box to one arm as he opened the door. No light shone from inside. Not quite panicking, he entered, set the box down, and lit a lantern.

Perhaps Yelena was taking a nap.

Her room was empty.

He kept a firm grip on his emotions as he searched the castle for her. She wasn't in the training room. Or the kitchen. Or the library. Or the Commander's office, but she had tasted his dinner. Did Brazell's goons nab her on her way back to their suite? Was Valek too late?

CHAPTER 15

*V*alek refused to panic. Yelena had shown she could defend herself. Besides, he couldn't tear the complex apart looking for her. It would draw too much attention and let everyone know how much he cared for her. A food taster wasn't considered missing until they failed to show up for a scheduled meal. At that point, he could search the entire area, and everyone would believe she'd escaped.

Despite his hammering heart, Valek returned to their apartment to wait. He lit the lanterns and tried to focus on work. The next execution was scheduled for after the Sitian delegation and Valek needed to get the paperwork for Tentil finalized.

When a key rasped in the lock, Valek just about jumped out of his skin. *Yelena. Thank fate.* He drew in a deep breath and released it along with all his pent-up fear. Then he replaced it with a neutral expression before he turned to her.

"Where have you been?" he asked a bit harsher than he'd planned.

"With Janco," she said.

A sudden image of the two of them kissing in some abandoned storeroom flashed in his mind. "Doing what?" Valek demanded, hopping to his feet.

"Discussing fighting tactics."

"Oh." Valek relaxed. *Bloody hell, get a grip, man.* "Well, that's all right. But from now on, I need to know where you are at all times, and I suggest you stay in the castle and keep a low profile for a while. General Brazell's guards have set a bounty on your head."

"A bounty?" Alarm filled her eyes and she paled.

He hadn't meant to scare her. "It could be a rumor or just drunken soldiers' talk. But until they leave, I want you protected." Valek's tone was firm. *Too firm?* "I don't want to train another taster," he added.

"I'll be careful."

"No. You'll be paranoid. You'll move in a crowd, keep to well-lit areas and you'll make certain to have an escort with you whenever you're walking down empty hallways late at night. Understood?" *That was over the top. Apparently, his emotions had decided to stop taking orders.*

"Yes, sir."

"Good." *Time to change the subject before he revealed just how much he cared for her.* "The generals' brandy meeting is scheduled for tomorrow evening. Each general will bring a bottle of his finest brandy to share as they discuss Ixian business late into the night. You will be needed to taste the Commander's drinks." Valek lifted the box of brandy bottles from the floor and set it on the table. He pulled out a small drinking glass that had been nestled inside. "I want you to sample each brandy once tonight and at least twice tomorrow, so you know how each one tastes clean of poisons." He handed Yelena the glass. "Each bottle is labeled according to the type of brandy, and which general brings it."

Yelena grabbed one of the bottles. It was General Dinno's cherry brandy. She poured a mouthful, performed the five S-steps, and swallowed. Her eyebrows shot up in surprise as a ruddy flush spread on her cheeks. Adorable.

"I suggest you use the 'slurp and spit' method, so you don't get drunk," Valek said, keeping a straight face.

"Good point." She found another glass in the box and picked up a different bottle.

Valek returned to his work. He tried concentrating on the forms before him, but he kept stealing glances at Yelena. She dutifully worked on tasting the various brandies. Her face creased in distaste over a few of the stronger flavors. After spitting out General Rasmussen's peach brandy, Yelena licked her lips. All of Valek's attention suddenly focused on them as he imagined kissing her and tasting the sweet liquor. Fire burned in his core.

He wrenched his thoughts from going further down that dangerous path. Forms. Needed. To be. Filled out. Valek worked on them as if his life depended on it.

THE DAY OF THE GENERALS' meeting, Valek received nothing but bad news. Still no insight into what Star planned. And his agents had discovered ten of Brazell's soldiers passed out in the barracks. They reeked of alcohol, but also sported bloody noses, black eyes, cuts, and bruises. They'd been on the losing side of a fight, but none of the other soldiers could recall who else had been involved or when it happened.

Valek spotted Ari in the training yard after his afternoon bouts. He called the big man over.

"Sir?" Ari asked. Despite the cold air, he wore a sleeveless tunic and short pants.

"Seems several soldiers from MD-5 were attacked last night. Do you know anything about it?"

"I know they were drunk. I know they were obnoxious. I

know they said things about our food taster that they really shouldn't have in mixed company," Ari said.

Valek suspected that might have been the case. "Mixed?"

"Soldiers from all over Ixia." Ari swept a hand out, indicating the people around them who wore different colored training uniforms. Purple bruises stained his thick knuckles; he'd either been punching the heavy bag or another person recently. Perhaps more than one person.

"Ah. Anything else?"

"Yes, 'attacked' is a strong word, sir."

"Oh? What word would you suggest?"

"Disciplined. They learned a valuable lesson and it was a good example for the other soldiers."

"Would Janco agree with this...word?"

"Most definitely."

"Anyone else?"

"Lieutenant Maren likes that word as well. According to Janco, she's 'very particular with her vernacular.'"

Valek laughed. "I stand corrected. I'll consider this matter settled."

"It is."

"And future incidents?"

"Will be handled." Ari flexed his arm muscles.

"Good." A bit of weight lifted from his shoulders knowing the three of them would protect Yelena from drunken soldiers. Now he needed to keep her safe around drunken generals and their advisers.

Valek said goodbye. He hurried to the castle. The brandy meeting would start after dinner and last late into the night. It was best to attend with a full stomach.

∾

His dress uniform hung between his sneak suit and his camouflage outfit. Valek yanked it out and tossed it on his bed. No need to worry that the damn thing might wrinkle. The thick, itchy fabric refused to bend. Not to mention it was almost impossible to pierce. A good quality during a knife fight, but the uncomfortable and tight cut of the black uniform made fighting in it difficult.

Valek buttoned up the jacket. Pain pricked his chest. One of the medals had lost its back. He longed to rip them all out. The Commander insisted on giving him them over the years. Six obnoxious rows of them plus the red braids hanging off his shoulders, given to him for bravery or something like that. If he were truly brave, he'd attend the meeting in his regular uniform.

He yanked the offending medal out and moved another to its place. Surely the Commander would be too busy to notice. Except that was *exactly* the thing he would notice. Sighing, Valek searched for the missing back.

By the time he finished dressing, Valek wanted to tear his clothes off. It would be a long night. He descended to the living room where Yelena waited. She took one look at him, covered her mouth, and laughed at his ridiculous uniform.

He didn't blame her. "Enough. I have to wear this damn thing once a year and, as far as I'm concerned, it's one time too many." Valek tugged at the tight collar. "Ready?"

She joined him at the door. Her gaze swept over him, and he expected her to burst into giggles again.

"You look stunning," she said.

"Really?" Valek glanced down at his clothes in surprise. Stunning? Valek straightened and stopped yanking on his collar.

"Yes. You do," she said.

Warmth spread. He'd heard about women liking a man in uniform, but he'd never experienced it before. Despite hating everything about it, Valek would wear his dress uniform everyday just to keep Yelena smiling at him.

~

THE COMMANDER'S war room bustled with activity. Valek scanned the room, counting generals and their advisers. Only two advisers per general were permitted to attend the meeting. Valek recognized most of them. Servants set out platters of food and drink, and then lit the lanterns that hung between the long, thin, stained-glass windows. The colors muted due to the setting sun.

General Brazell glared at Yelena. But instead of stepping behind Valek and hiding like she'd done seasons ago; she stood her ground. Good for her. Adviser Mogkan, though, gazed at her with a cunning appraisal. Valek fought the urge to slap the man upside his head.

The Commander sat at the top of the egg-shaped table, which signaled everyone to be seated. Valek claimed the empty chair to the Commander's right. Mostly out of sight, Yelena perched on the stool behind them. At least she had a wall to lean on when the discussion dragged. This annual get together allowed the generals to report on what each of them had accomplished over the course of the year. Also, to decide on certain issues or brainstorm solutions to problems. They all had a vote, but the Commander's decision was final and not always aligned with the majority.

Pounding a wooden gavel on the table, the Commander signaled the official start of the meeting. Silence fell.

"Before we launch into the scheduled topics," the Commander said, indicating the detailed agenda which had been distributed earlier, "I have an important announcement. I have appointed a new successor."

Valek studied expressions and body language as the generals absorbed the news. Shock at first, and then a few showed anger, a couple appeared concerned, but most were confused. Brazell fought to keep a straight face. His brown eyes sparkled with delight as the edges of his mouth curled up. An odd reaction, unless he knew he'd been chosen.

Murmurs buzzed and tension fogged the air as the Commander handed each of the generals a sealed envelope. Inside was an encoded piece of a puzzle. Only when all eight pieces were together, and then deciphered from a key that Valek held, would it reveal the name of the new successor. The generals tucked them into their briefcases.

Ignoring the unsettled atmosphere, the Commander started the meeting with a call to General Kitvivan of MD-1 to proceed with business. A bottle of Kitvivan's highest quality white brandy slid around the table. Each general poured a couple fingers worth of alcohol into their glasses. Valek served the Commander before splashing a mouthful into his own. Yelena sipped from the Commander's tumbler. Protocol dictated that she swallowed just in case she missed an off flavor or foreign scent.

Valek spent too much time staring at her lips as she tasted the liquor. She handed it back and the Commander took a drink, signaling to everyone that it was safe. If anyone wished to assassinate all the generals, this meeting would be the perfect opportunity. So, they were *all* counting on Yelena. Even him. And, for the first time, he'd no doubts about the food taster's abilities.

Kitvivan talked about the problems his district was having with mining and the frequency of the blizzards blowing from the Northern Ice Pack. It didn't take long, though, for him to start whining about his favorite subject—snow cats.

"Come on, Kit. Enough about the cats. Just feed them up on the pack ice like we do, and they won't bother you," General Chenzo of MD-2 said in exasperation.

"Feed them so they'll get healthy and fat and start breeding like rabbits? We'll go broke supplying the meat," Kitvivan shot back.

Valek stopped listening. Instead, he considered the eight generals. Or, rather, the eight old men. Even the youngest, General Franis of MD-3, had to be close to sixty years old. Set in their ways, quarrelsome, and unpleasant, they all needed to retire. Ixia was stagnating under their leadership. The younger generation was restless and bored. Even this meeting's agenda could be from any of the brandy meetings in the last six years. The same issues with no creative solutions. The same old, same old.

Perhaps Valek could encourage them to retire. Or just assassinate them. No one would be missed. Except by the Commander. Which was the problem. Ambrose had grown up in Military District 3. His family worked a large and deep diamond mine at the base of the Soul Mountains and so did many of these generals. They'd been supervisors who had worked decades in dangerous mine shafts and had barely been paid a living wage.

When Ambrose had started preaching about the injustices of the monarchy, these men were his early supporters. With their leadership abilities, they helped build a following that eventually turned into an army. They acted as bodyguards when the King of Ixia sent assassins, Valek had been one of them. He hadn't known his client was of royal blood. Good thing the generals also taught Ambrose how to fight. Otherwise Valek would have killed Ambrose. Instead, the Commander bested Valek and claimed his loyalty by carving a C onto Valek's chest.

These old men had been pivotal in the successful takeover. Valek appreciated their efforts and service, but they should retire and enjoy the rest of their lives instead of arguing about how many sheep could graze in the plains before stressing the native grasses.

The Commander would never suggest they move on. He respected them and would be forever loyal to them. Unless they undermined the Commander's leadership or plotted another takeover. Or failed to follow the Code of Behavior, which Valek knew Brazell was doing. Too bad, he didn't have any proof except those beans, which the Commander had decided to ignore.

General Brazell caused quite a stir when it was his turn to discuss MD-5. He sent a silver tray with brown lumps around the table, instead of a bottle of brandy. At least it was something new. By the mutters, it wasn't being embraced. No surprise. For the first time, Valek agreed with the generals. The lumps turned out to be Criollo. If Brazell managed to get them all addicted to it, he'd be able to get them to vote in his favor and would have more influence than any of them. Was that his plan?

Brazell explained about the Criollo and invited everyone to take a bite without waiting for Yelena's all clear. She moaned and Valek whipped around ready to catch her before she hit her head on the stone floor. But she gave the all-clear sign and closed her eyes as she consumed the rest of the Criollo. She licked her lips and fingertips, cleaning off every bit of the dessert. Heat flushed through him, and he was tempted to offer his portion to her. Instead, he bit into the lump. The inside had been filled with the General's famous strawberry brandy. Wow. No wonder Yelena moaned. The mixture of the sweet alcohol and Criollo exploded on his tongue. He'd eaten nothing like it before. Nor, he suspected, had the other generals. They eyed the leftovers.

Brazell then launched into his report. The construction of his new feed factory had been completed, but he didn't offer any more details. Valek hadn't heard from his agents assigned to watch the factory in a while. Had they been discovered? Or was there nothing to report? Valek made a note to follow up.

The meeting continued. Yelena appeared a bit glassy-eyed after sipping the sixth glass of brandy. It wasn't long before she relaxed back and nodded off. Valek grinned. He'd let her sleep it off and would taste the two remaining brandies.

Sometime during General Tesso's presentation, a strangeness pressed. At first, Valek couldn't pin it down. A smell? None of the lanterns had gone out. The half-eaten food wasn't rotting. Nothing but alcohol fumes. A breeze? All the windows were closed. A noise? Yelena's light snoring sounded behind him. Then an invisible spider web brushed his left cheek. Magic. Very light. Very faint.

He straightened in alarm and scanned the room. Most everyone focused on Tesso. A few took notes or looked bored out of their minds. One adviser had rested his chin on his hand and his eyes were closed. Sleeping or using magic? This had never happened during a brandy meeting before. It had to be one of the new advisers. Valek studied each of them but couldn't pinpoint where the magic originated. Mogkan stared at Yelena. A smug smile twisted his lips. The adviser had been paying more attention to her than to the proceedings.

Valek glanced at the Commander. He gazed into the distance, obviously not listening to Tesso, which was odd. Valek leaned closer and the magic pressed harder. The magician had targeted the Commander.

Valek bumped Ambrose's arm, hoping to break the spell. "What's going on?" he whispered. "Where were you?"

"Just remembering a time long ago," the Commander said, sounding wistful and not at all like himself. "More enjoyable than listening to General Tesso's excruciatingly detailed report on the corn harvest in MD–4."

Normally, the Commander loved those details. A bountiful corn harvest meant plenty of food for his people. At least Valek succeeded in stopping the magic. And it didn't reappear during the rest of the meeting.

At the end of the meeting, the Commander pounded his gavel. "Last item, gentlemen," the Commander said. "A Sitian delegation has requested a meeting."

The generals launched into all the familiar arguments that

Valek could recite by heart. And just like the fifteen times before, the northern generals—Kitvivian, Chenzo, Franis, Dinno—voted against it, and the southern ones—Brazell, Hazel, Tesso, Rasmussen—voted in favor of a conference.

The Commander ended the discussions. "I acknowledge your opinions about Sitia, but the southerners would rather trade with us than attack us. We have more men and metal. A fact they are well aware of. To attack Sitia we would expend many lives and large sums of money. And for what? Their luxury items aren't worth the cost. I'm content with Ixia. We have cured the land of the King's disease. Perhaps my successor will want more. You'll have to wait until then."

A murmur of surprise raced through the war room. Brazell nodded in agreement. His smile had an edge, as if he'd known about the Commander's change in heart all along.

"I have already agreed to meet with the southern contingent," the Commander continued. "They're due to arrive in four days. You have until then to express your specific concerns to me before departing for your home districts. Meeting adjourned." The bang from the Commander's gavel echoed throughout the dead silent room.

The Commander rose and Valek gestured for Yelena to join them. The generals were bound to make angry accusations at each other, and it was best to go. Yelena wobbled slightly but caught her balance. A lightweight, she probably never drank so much alcohol at one time.

The war room erupted into loud arguments as soon as they left.

"That should stir things up a bit," the Commander said dryly.

"I would advise against vacationing in MD-8 this year," Valek said. His tone dripped with sarcasm. "The way Dinno reacted to your announcement about the southern delegation, I would expect him to pepper your beach house with sand spiders." Valek shivered. About the size of a cat, their bite was venomous. "A horribly painful way to die."

They walked, or in Yelena's case, staggered back to their apartments in silence. When they reached the Commander's suite, Valek said, "I'd watch out for Rasmussen too. He didn't take the news of the change in your successor well."

"I watch out for everyone, Valek. You know that," the Commander said.

Except, Valek feared that the Commander's vigilance hadn't been enough this time. Ambrose closed the door behind him, signaling he was too tired for their nightcap.

He and Yelena entered their suite, but Valek was far from sleepy. He ripped off the jacket of his damn dress uniform and tossed it onto the couch. Pointing to a chair, he said, "Sit. We need to talk." Well, he *needed* to discuss what happened in the brandy meeting.

She sprawled on the chair and looped a leg over the arm.

He paced the length of the living room. "Two things were very wrong tonight."

"Oh, come on. I just dozed for a minute," she said a bit too loud.

He stopped and looked at her. "No, no. You did fine. I meant about the meeting; the generals." He continued to pace. "First, Brazell seemed unusually happy about the change in successor and the Sitian delegation. He's always wanted a trade treaty, but he typically exercises a more cautious approach. And second, there was a magician in the room."

"What?" Surprised, she sat up straighter.

"Magic. Very subtle, from a trained professional. I only felt it once, a brief touch, but I couldn't pinpoint the source. But the magician had to be in the room, or I wouldn't have felt it."

"When?"

"During Tesso's long-winded dissertation about corn." Valek relaxed a bit. It had only been that one time during the six-hour meeting. "About the same time your snoring could be heard halfway across the room."

"Ha," she snorted. "You were so stiff at that meeting I thought rigor mortis had set in."

Nice retort. "I doubt you could have looked any better sitting in that uncomfortable dress uniform all night. I imagine Dilana sprayed on extra starch with malicious glee." Then he sobered. "Do you know Adviser Mogkan? He eyed you most of the evening."

"I know of him. He was Reyad's primary adviser. They also hunted together."

"What's he like?" Valek asked.

"Same kind of vermin as Reyad and Nix," she said with searing anger. Then she slapped both hands over her mouth as if she'd just given away a secret.

That was the most emotion he'd seen from her regarding Reyad. Was it the alcohol talking or was she finally trusting him? "There were a number of new advisers at the meeting. I guess I'll have to check them out one by one. It seems we have a new southern spy with magic abilities." He sighed. "It never ends." Suddenly tired, he perched on the edge of the couch.

"If it did, you'd be out of a job." She climbed onto the couch behind him and grabbed his shoulders.

If she planned to strangle him, he doubted he could stop her because he'd frozen in complete shock. She kneaded the tight muscles along his back and neck, and he realized she was giving him a massage. He relaxed and enjoyed it. It'd probably never happen again.

"What would you do," she asked, "if suddenly the world was perfect, and you had no one to spy on?"

"I'd be bored," Valek said. *Unless you were with me, love.*

"Come on, seriously. A change in profession." She dug her thumbs into the muscles at the base of his neck.

He almost groaned out loud.

"A fire dancer?" she asked.

Doubtful. "No. An arms teacher?" Valek countered.

"No. It's a perfect world. No weapons allowed." She moved her hands lower.

No one had touched him like this since... Ever.

"How about a scholar?" she asked. "You've read all these books lying around, haven't you? Or are they just to make it difficult for someone to sneak in?"

He had indeed. "Books serve me in so many ways. But I doubt your perfect society would need a scholar on murder."

The massage stopped. Did he just ruin the mood by mentioning murder? He'd been talking about himself, but perhaps it reminded her of Reyad?

"No. Definitely not," she said.

He moved on. "A sculptor? I could carve extravagant statues. We could redecorate the castle and liven things up. How about you?" he asked as she pressed her fingers into the small of his back. "What would you do?"

"Acrobatics."

"An acrobat! Well, that explains a lot." No wonder she had glided through the trees with such ease and learned how to fight so quickly.

Her hands reached around to his stomach. His confusion over her change in direction burned away into sudden desire as she fumbled to unbutton his pants.

CHAPTER 16

*R*ed hot desire raced through him, igniting his blood and setting fire to his heart. He'd been waiting for some sign of her affection, and he'd love nothing better than to be with her, but not this way. Not when she'd regret it in the morning. Not when he didn't know if it was her or the alcohol fueling her actions.

He grabbed her wrists, stopping her. "Yelena, you're drunk." His voice was hoarse. Releasing her, he stood, and swept her into his arms. Fighting the urgent need to kiss her and draw her tight against his chest, he carried her to her bedroom and laid her on the bed. "Get some sleep, Yelena," Valek whispered. All he could manage when the rest of his body was staging a revolt.

Fleeing before he could change his mind and join her under the covers, he rushed to the balcony outside the suite and sucked in big gulps of cold night air. To extinguish the burning inside him, he chugged icy water from the pitcher he kept there. Leaving her had to be the hardest thing he'd ever done.

Valek had lain with several different people as part of his undercover assignments. No one like Yelena. No one who stirred his passion. No one who he admired. No one who was as smart. In all his years, he'd never met *anyone* like her. And he'd been perfectly fine with that. He didn't need this complication in his life. But what were the odds that he'd meet another like her? Slim to none. Even so, he decided to admire from afar unless she made the next move when sober.

With his emotions back under control, Valek changed into his all-black sneak suit—his favorite. Pulling the hood over his head, he donned a pair of dark glasses. There were a few hours until the sun rose, and his curiosity needed to be sated. He stopped by his desk to pick up a few supplies. Tucking them into various hidden pockets, he returned to the balcony. Then he found hand holds and toe holds among the stones of the wall and climbed.

The unusual shape of the castle made climbing easy. Navigating was another matter. Just as the maze of hallways and rooms on the inside confused many new people, it was easy to get just as lost on the outside. However, after all the years of practice, Valek knew the quickest and simplest way to the guest suites.

Practice also allowed him to open the shutters without a sound, drop into the room, and perform a search. There was enough moonlight coming from the windows to avoid bumping into the furniture.

Valek started with General Brazell's suite. He crept on silent feet, but, by the loud snoring emanating from the bedroom, he doubted a slammed door would wake the general.

Brazell's briefcase was lying on the desk in the receiving room. Valek removed the envelope with the puzzle piece. Pulling out a small knife, he lit a lantern and heated the blade in the flame for a minute. Then he slid it under the wax seal that secured the flap. The technique allowed him to open the envelope without breaking the seal.

He removed the puzzle piece and copied the letters and numbers onto a piece of paper he'd brought along. Valek would have loved to read through the other documents in Brazell's briefcase, but he had seven more visits to make before dawn. He heated the knife again to melt the wax and reseal the envelope. Then he headed to Dinno's suite.

It took him a couple hours to find and copy the rest of the puzzle pieces—eight sets of numbers and letters. It was an hour or so before the sun rose when Valek returned to his suite. Movement on the balcony drew his attention. He fingered his knife but recognized Yelena clutching the water pitcher. Ah. Probably hungover. He landed lightly just in case she had a headache as well as a dry mouth.

"Valek?" she whispered, uncertain.

He smiled then removed the dark glasses.

"What are you doing?" she asked.

"Reconnaissance. The generals tend to stay up late after the Commander leaves the brandy meeting. So, I had to wait until everyone had gone to bed." Valek went inside and pulled off his hood. Lighting the lantern on his desk, he took the paper from his pocket.

"I hate a mystery. I would have let the identity of the Commander's successor remain a secret, as I have for fifteen years, but tonight's opportunity was too tempting. With eight drunken generals sleeping it off, I could have danced on their beds without waking them. Not one among them has any imagination. I watched all the generals put their envelopes from the Commander right into their briefcases." Valek motioned her closer. "Here, help me decipher this." He handed her the paper.

She hesitated. Would she mention the incident earlier or pretend it didn't happen? Perhaps she didn't remember because of the alcohol. Either way, he'd treat her as a professional and a part of his team. But he was inordinately glad when she pulled up a chair to help.

"How did you break the wax seal?" she asked.

"Rookie trick. All you need is a sharp knife and a tiny flame. Now read me the first set of letters." He wrote them down: G, E, S, E, I. They didn't form a word, so he moved the letters into different combinations until they made the word *siege*. He opened a book of symbols leftover from the monarchy and flipped pages until he reached the one that matched the word—a large blue star-shaped symbol centered in the middle of three circles.

"What's that?" Yelena asked.

"The old battle symbol for *siege*. The dead King used these markings to communicate with his captains during times of war. They were originally created hundreds of years ago by a great strategist. Read me the next set. They should be numbers."

She told him twenty-seven and ten. He counted the lines of text until he reached line twenty-seven and then counted the letters and spaces in that line. The tenth character was A. On a clean piece of paper, he wrote A. Then he asked her for the next set of letters and numbers and repeated the process. He ended up with the letters: A, E, L, B, L, SPACE, Z, R, which was easy to rearrange into: BRAZELL. Not a surprise, and another clue that the general was influencing the Commander. Because normally, Brazell wasn't a favorite and he'd make a horrible Commander.

"Who is it?" Yelena asked.

"Guess," he said.

She glanced at him with bloodshot eyes.

"I'll give you a hint. Who was the happiest about the change? Whose name keeps popping up during the most bizarre situations?"

He studied her expression and saw the horror fill her gaze as she figured it out. She would be the first person executed under the new regime.

Nodding, he said, "Right. Brazell." *And I won't let him harm you, love.* Valek would switch out the puzzle pieces tomorrow night and name a new successor. After all, if the Commander was dead no one would know. And if he was caught and hung as a traitor, it'd still be worth it to save Yelena.

AFTER LEARNING nothing new about the trouble Star planned for the Sitian delegation, Valek held a meeting in his office with Kenda and a few of his agents. He also invited Ari, Janco, and Maren. They brainstormed ways a person or persons could ruin relations between the two countries.

"An archer in the trees of the Snake Forest," Ari said. "Most of the leaves are down, so they could kill a few Sitian officials before the delegation even reaches the castle."

"Do we know which route through the forest the Sitians are going to use?" asked Inrick.

"The main north-south route is the most direct from the Sitian Citadel to the castle," Valek said.

"In that case, Ari and I can scout ahead of the delegation and clean out any nasties lying in wait." Janco's eyes lit with glee.

"Can they?" Kenda asked Valek.

Offended, Janco said, "Of course. We're the only ones who found Yelena during the fugitive exercise."

"What if there is more than one…er…nasty?" she asked.

"No problemo, puppy dog. We can handle multiple nasties."

But Kenda raised a good point. Star would probably have some backups just in case the first archer missed.

"I can go along and babysit," Maren snarked.

Janco snorted. "Can you be quiet in the woods?"

"Can *you*?" she shot back. "With all the prattling you do when you fight, I'd—"

"I don't—"

"Janco," Ari warned.

"It's a good idea to have two teams of two," Valek said. "Ari, can you recruit a fourth scout?"

"Yes, sir."

"Good. That covers the delegation's trip to the castle and their trip home. Once inside, they'll be assigned to the guest wing, where we can guard and protect them."

"*And* keep an eye on them," Kenda said. "For all we know they could be assassins after the Commander."

"True. Kenda, you're in charge of the schedule and ensuring the delegation is safe within the castle."

"Yes, sir. What about during the meetings with the Commander?"

"I'll be there," Valek said. "And during the feast or any other public event, we'll have plenty of our people in position."

"What about their food?" Ari asked. "Will their meals be sent up to their quarters?"

"No," Valek said, wondering if Ari would have thought of targeting their food prior to becoming friends with Yelena. "They'll eat in the dining hall along with everyone else. Star won't risk poisoning them and the Commander's entire staff."

"Why not?" Janco asked. "That would ruin any chance of a relationship with Sitia."

"No, it wouldn't," Ari said. "It would unite the Sitians and Ixians against a common enemy."

"Ah. But what if the Sitians *want* to poison everyone?"

Glad he'd invited the power twins, he said, "We'll have an undercover agent in the kitchen during their visit."

"What about during the feast when everyone is served individually?" Ari asked.

"We have Yelena to check for poisons." Although he hoped nothing happened to her during the feast. Huh. That was the first time he thought of the food taster over the Commander. Not good.

They continued to discuss ways to counter any potential attack. Just knowing there would be an attempt to ruin the relationship between Sitia and Ixia gave his people an advantage. They'd taken away the element of surprise, which would allow his people to react faster. Valek's anxiety eased by the end of the meeting.

~

HE STOPPED in Kenda's office early the next morning for a quick update on the generals. Valek planned to report to the Commander later about the measures he was taking to ensure the meeting with the Sitians went as smoothly as possible.

"They're mostly behaving. For a bunch of so-called gentlemen, they squabble like children," she said.

"What are they arguing about? The new successor or the Sitian delegation?"

"You'd think it would be one of them, but no. Right now, it's all about who has the most time with the Commander. They've been whining that General Brazell is taking up too much of his time."

"Is he?"

Kenda flipped through a stack of papers on her desk. "Actually, yeah. He's scheduled for more time slots than any other. And for longer. He's due to be with the Commander for three hours this morning. That's after having two meetings in the last two days. What could they possibly have to talk about?"

A very good question. And it was more alarming that the Commander had set the schedule. "Then I'd better get to his office before Brazell does."

Valek left her office at a quick clip, hurrying through the castle. When he entered the throne room, he spotted Yelena waiting outside the Commander's door. Oh no.

"What are you doing out here?" Valek asked. "Haven't you tasted his breakfast yet?"

"I was ordered to wait. He's with Brazell and Mogkan."

Already? What were they doing? Valek pushed past Yelena and barged into the office. Magic slammed into him. Adviser Mogkan stood behind the Commander with his fingertips on the Commander's temples. Ambrose stared into the distance much like he had at the brandy meeting. Valek reached for his dagger. Mogkan had to be the magician. Because it would have been almost impossible for Brazell to keep his magic a secret from Valek for all these years.

Mogkan stepped away, and said, "You can definitely feel, sir, that this is an excellent way to ease a headache."

The magic stopped and the Commander blinked as if just waking up. "Thank you, Mogkan," he said. Then he glared at Valek. "What's so important?"

"Disturbing news, sir." Valek said. Not a lie as discovering Mogkan touching the Commander was rather disturbing. He needed to get rid of Brazell and Mogkan so he could warn the Commander and get a signed arrest warrant. "I would like to discuss it in private." Valek held his breath. *Come on, Ambrose.* And released it when the Commander rescheduled the meeting and dismissed them.

"Yelena, taste the Commander's breakfast now," Valek ordered.

"Yes, sir."

Valek worried they may have poisoned the food. Not a smart move, considering the Commander just changed his successor to Brazell, but still, watching Yelena taste the food troubled him. She checked it twice and then set the tray on the Commander's desk. Whew.

"Yelena, if I have to eat cold food again, I'll have you whipped. Understand?" the Commander asked.

"Yes, sir," she said.

Smart. It would have been useless to argue.

"You're dismissed," he ordered. And when the door closed behind her, he said, "Valek, what the hell is going on?"

"Mogkan was using magic on you, sir. I had to get him away from you before he could do any more damage."

"Adviser Mogkan, a magician? Nonsense."

"I felt it when I entered your office."

"Either it's your imagination, or Yelena's been very good at keeping a secret."

Valek took a step back as if he'd been punched in the gut. His imagination! Where the bloody hell was this coming from?

The Commander took his silence as agreement. "It would explain why that southern magician is interested in my food taster. Perhaps she tried to recruit her."

"It's not Yelena. I've been living with her for seasons, I would have felt her using magic by now. Why was Mogkan touching your head?"

"I had a terrible migraine and he massaged it away. If that's magic, then he's welcome to continue healing headaches."

His comment just further confirmed the Commander wasn't acting like himself, yet Valek couldn't help saying, "Mogkan might have been implanting thoughts into your head."

"That's utter nonsense, Valek."

"Is it? You've been spending more time with Brazell than the other generals."

"We have business to discuss."

"What business?"

"That's none of your concern. You will leave General Brazell and Adviser Mogkan alone. Understand?"

He understood that somehow Brazell and Mogkan had influenced the Commander. "Yes, sir."

"Good. You're dismissed."

Valek left and stood outside the door. For the first time since becoming the chief of security, he'd no idea how to proceed.

How to fix the problem. He couldn't assassinate Brazell or Mogkan. Not without any proof of wrong doing. That was the biggest problem. He had no real evidence. Nothing.

Frustrated and angry, Valek stalked away, heading in no particular direction. His thoughts churned, but no brilliant insight sparked. He'd have to wait until Brazell and Mogkan left the castle, and then somehow stop the Commander from eating Criollo. If Criollo was significant. If not, then it might have been magic all along. But why didn't he—

Valek stopped.

Had he just imagined a brush of magic against his skin? No.

Turning, Valek tracked the press of magic. He took a few wrong turns, but then he made a left and halted in surprise. Mogkan leaned over Yelena. Lying prone on the floor, she held his hand. It appeared like a romantic encounter, but he remembered Yelena had called the adviser vermin. When her lips turned blue and magic ballooned around them, Valek broke from his startlement and lunged at the adviser, knocking him flat.

Wrapping his hands around the man's neck, Valek squeezed. He kept his gaze on Yelena. If she was harmed, he'd happily strangle Mogkan. She gasped for breath and blinked then focused on him.

Valek stood and yanked Mogkan to his feet. He now had evidence and a witness. "I hope you're aware of the penalty for being a magician in Ixia," Valek said. "If not, I'd be delighted to enlighten you."

Mogkan smoothed his rumpled tunic and fixed his braid. "Some would say your ability to resist magic makes *you* a magician, Valek."

"The Commander thinks otherwise. You're under arrest."

"Then you're in for a big surprise. I suggest you discuss these false accusations with the Commander before you do anything drastic," Mogkan said.

Wrong thing to say. "How about I kill you right now?" Valek moved closer.

Magic surged. Yelena yelled and curled into a tight ball. He stepped forward. She screamed again.

"Any closer, and she'll be a corpse," Mogkan said.

CHAPTER 17

alek froze. Could he kill Mogkan before he killed Yelena? Probably. Maybe. He shifted his weight, preparing to lunge. No. *Nothing* was worth risking her life.

"Well, now. That's interesting. The old Valek really wouldn't have cared if I killed his food taster. Yelena, my child, I just realized how incredibly useful you are." Mogkan grinned.

As the magician walked away, another wave of magic swept through the hallway. Yelena fainted. Valek rushed to feel for a pulse. A steady throb met his fingertips. Her breathing appeared normal.

Next time, Valek vowed. Next time, Mogkan didn't get to walk away.

Valek scooped Yelena up and held her close enough that he could smell her lavender soap. He debated if he should take her to the infirmary or not. The thought of leaving her there alone and unprotected… He hugged her tighter. No. Not happening. Instead, he carried her to their suite. She either had a concussion or had passed out due to the lack of air.

The two soldiers, who guarded the entrance to their suites,

straightened but said nothing even though they both eyed Yelena.

"Millicent, go fetch the medic. Dagon, go find Captains Ari and Janco and have them report to me A-sap."

"We're not allowed to leave our positions, sir," Dagon said.

"*I'm* giving you permission."

"Is this a test?" Millicent asked.

He'd trained them too well. "No. Go. Hurry, please."

"Yes, sir," they snapped and headed in two different directions.

He continued into his suite and gently laid Yelena down on her bed. Pulling the blanket up to her chin, he tucked her in before he dampened a cloth with water and placed it over her forehead in case she woke with a headache.

Valek strode out to the entrance and acted as guard until the soldiers returned. He doubted anyone tried to get in during the few minutes it was unprotected, but he'd check the Commander's apartment just to be sure.

Medic Channa arrived first. She carried her medical kit. "Something wrong?"

"This way." He left Millicent to resume her position. Once they were inside his suite, he explained to Channa he'd found Yelena on the ground unconscious.

The medic asked him to wait in the living room while she examined Yelena. Unable to stay still, he paced, hating that he couldn't do anything to help, wishing for the first time in his life that he possessed magical healing abilities. However, if she had a brain injury, the Sitian healers couldn't fix her either. Valek had learned quite a bit about magical abilities while stalking the late King of Ixia.

Channa finally finished and closed the door behind her.

"Well?" he asked.

She set her bag on the couch and dug inside. "She doesn't have a concussion. From the contusions around her throat, I'd say she was strangled, but there's no pattern. The bruising doesn't look like fingers, or a rope, had wrapped around her neck. My best guess is she fainted after something blocked her windpipe temporarily." Channa handed him a packet filled with a yellow powder. "When she wakes, mix this in water and have her drink it all. It should help with any pain or dizziness."

"Thank you."

"Are you going to tell me why you brought her here instead of the infirmary?"

"No."

"All righty. If she doesn't wake in the next couple of hours, let me know."

"I will."

The medic left and he continued his pacing. He needed to protect the Commander from Mogkan, but he couldn't leave Yelena although he knew she was safe inside their suite. Or was she? Mogkan could kill the guards outside. Why would he? He could influence the Commander, who could order her execution. Overwhelmed with so many possibilities, Valek sank onto the couch. All he could do at this point was hope that when Mogkan said Yelena was incredibly useful, it meant he wouldn't try to kill her again.

WHEN ARI AND JANCO ARRIVED, they stood awkwardly in the living room. Janco gawked at Valek's wall full of weapons and Ari switched between standing at attention and at ease. Since he conducted all his business in his office, only the Commander, Margg, and Yelena had ever seen his apartment. Until today.

"Sit down," Valek said, indicating the couch.

They perched on the edge.

"I've a new assignment for you both," he said.

"Another smash and grab?" Janco asked with excitement. "Or an ambush?"

"No. I need you to guard Yelena while the generals are here."

Ari leaned forward. "We've been keeping an eye out for her since she gave that favorable report to the Commander about us. Still are even though she's now quite capable of protecting herself against an opponent. So, something big must have happened recently. Can we ask what?"

Valek considered how much to tell them. If they knew the nature of the threat, they'd be better able to handle a problem. But could he trust them to keep it secret?

Janco turned serious. "Yelena's our friend and colleague. We'd never do anything to endanger her." He had correctly interpreted Valek's hesitation.

Valek explained what happened. "It shouldn't be a surprise that Brazell's still after her."

"It isn't," Ari said.

"Hiring a magician is beyond hard core," Janco said. "Magic's illegal. And creepy." He shuddered.

"You let me worry about that. Your job is to protect Yelena. She should be safe here, but outside these rooms, don't let her out of your sight."

"Yes, sir," they said in unison.

"If you start having strange thoughts, or Yelena acts out of character, or if anything seems off, bring her to me right away. I might be able to block the magic."

"Define strange thoughts," Janco said.

"I'll explain it to him later," Ari said.

"It's a legitimate question!"

"I need to get back to the Commander," Valek said. "Can you stay here until she wakes?"

"Yes, sir," Ari said. "And we'll coordinate with her regarding her schedule."

"Thanks. I'll tell the guards you have permission to enter my suite. They always have a key." Valek remembered the medicine for Yelena. He poured a glass of water and mixed in the powder. "I'll put this on her nightstand. Make sure she drinks it all."

"Yes, sir."

Valek eased Yelena's door open. Mid-morning sunlight flowed in behind him, illuminating the room. As he set the glass down, she jerked and struggled to sit up.

"It's all right," Valek said, pressing her shoulder down so she didn't fall off the bed. The tight knot that had been wrapped around his heart relaxed its grip.

Yelena reached for her head and grabbed the cloth. He picked up the cup. She blinked at him and scanned the room.

"Drink this." Valek handed her the glass.

She cringed at the flavor, but he insisted she finish and then set the cup on the table. Lines of exhaustion marked her face, and, while he wanted to ask her about the attack, he'd wait until later.

"Rest," he ordered. He turned to leave.

"Valek," she said. "Why didn't you kill Mogkan?"

He longed to tell her the truth. *Because I love you.* But that wouldn't be wise. "A tactical maneuver. Mogkan would have killed you before I could finish him. You're the key to too many puzzles. I need you." He strode to the door and grabbed the knob but paused at the threshold. "I've reported Mogkan to the Commander, but he was…" Valek squeezed until the metal under his fingers cracked. "Unconcerned, so I'll be guarding the Commander until Brazell and Mogkan leave. I've reassigned Ari and Janco as your personal bodyguards. Don't leave this suite without them. And stop eating Criollo. I'll taste the Commander's Criollo. I want to see if anything happens to you." He left.

He never should have allowed her to eat the extra Criollo. If Brazell and Mogkan were using the substance to influence the Commander, it might have made Yelena more susceptible to

Mogkan's magic. If. Maybe. Might. How he hated those three words.

"She's awake, but I ordered her to rest," Valek said to Ari and Janco. "If she listens, she'll stay in her room until it's time to taste the Commander's lunch."

"Who wants to bet she comes out right after Valek leaves?" Janco asked.

Apparently, no one.

AFTER CHECKING the Commander's suite and ensuring no one hid inside, Valek stopped by Kenda's to make a copy of the generals' meeting schedule before he arrived at the Commander's office.

"What are you doing here, Valek? I've an appointment—"

"In ten minutes." He waved the sheet of paper. "I know. I'm going to attend all your remaining meetings with the generals."

The Commander studied him. "Does this have to do with your ridiculous claim about Adviser Mogkan?"

Valek wanted to point out the Commander had never thought his claims ridiculous before. "Does it matter? I'm your Chief of Security and I've determined that you need extra security."

"Then post more guards outside my door."

"That would be ineffective, sir."

"It's a waste of your time."

"I disagree, sir."

"What about the security measures for the Sitian delegation?"

"Covered."

"And this season's execution?"

"Taken care of." Mostly.

"I can order you to leave."

He could. "Humor me, please. I promise to stay out of the way and not offer my opinion on anything unless asked."

The Commander sighed. "I'm not happy about it."

"Clearly."

"But you've earned the right to be paranoid. Didn't I give you a medal for that once?"

"You did." A rare event where Valek had been more suspicious than the Commander and had saved him from an assassin. Back in the early days, right after the takeover.

The Commander grinned evilly. "All right, you can stay, but you'll have to wear your dress uniform when the delegation arrives and again during the feast."

Nasty. "An honor." Valek's tone indicated the opposite.

"That's the spirit."

Valek had won the round but standing behind the Commander as he conducted meeting after meeting with the various generals and their advisers didn't feel like winning. The discussions were bloody boring. And annoying, he had no idea how the Commander endured such banality. There was so much talking over minor concerns that had easy solutions if everyone just put their egos aside.

After two and a half days of it, Valek decided he'd rather be tortured. At least, no one used magic and Brazell and Mogkan canceled their last meeting with the Commander, giving them both a break. The generals were due to leave in the morning, thank fate, and Valek had his own work to do.

He escorted the Commander to his suite for an early night.

"No need for our nightcap, Valek. I'm too tired." He headed inside.

Glad to have the extra time, Valek turned to go, but Millicent stopped him.

"The food taster left a little while ago, sir," she reported. "She didn't have the captains with her, so I thought I should let you know."

"Good call. Do you know where she was going?" Why would she leave and risk getting killed?

"No. But she went that way." She pointed to the left.

Not helpful and Valek didn't have time to track Yelena down. He'd have to trust she could protect herself and hope she didn't run into Mogkan. At least she now had a switchblade thanks to Janco—not that it had helped her when Mogkan attacked.

"Thanks," he said and hurried away.

As he jogged to his office, he contemplated various reasons Yelena would leave without an escort. Perhaps she planned to meet up with Ari and Janco for another training session. Or she grew bored and wanted some exercise. Valek should bring an extra set of weapons to their suite so she could practice without leaving. His inner caveman agreed.

Valek paused before he unlocked his door. The sliver of black wood that he'd inserted into the jam had fallen to the floor. Someone had picked the locks. Either a person with a death wish, or an assassin lying in wait? Or a thief that was long gone?

He pulled his dagger and inserted his key. Swinging the door wide, he braced for an attack. No one stood inside, but someone could still be hiding. There were certainly plenty of places. Ready to defend himself, he crossed to his desk. Then he smelled the lovely scent of lavender and relaxed. Valek had found his intruder. Yelena. Janco had said she was quick to learn how to pick locks. The captain had cleared teaching her the technique and gifting her the knife with Valek, who thought both were a good idea.

Impressed by her ability to pick his three complicated locks, he sat in his chair and glanced around. Another sliver of wood lay on the floor underneath his poison cabinet. Ah, she wished to learn the recipe to her antidote. He applauded her efforts. Valek would do the same in her position. Scanning the piles of books and boxes, he guessed she hid behind the conference table. Fun.

A knock sounded.

"Come," said Valek.

"Your, ah...package has arrived, sir," Inrick said.

"Bring him in." Valek stood.

Inrick escorted a tall man with wide shoulders and a big bushy beard. Now gaunt, Tentil had probably been muscled and robust before his stay in the Commander's dungeon. The chains around his wrists and ankles clanked as he approached Valek's desk. The foul stench of excrement and body odor chased away the lavender aroma.

"You're dismissed," Valek said to Inrick. No need to get another agent in trouble if the Commander found out.

Valek studied the man and resumed his seat. "Well, Tentil. Are you aware that you're next in line for the noose?"

"Yes, sir," he whispered, gazing at the floor.

Valek pretended to read his dossier like he'd done with Yelena. "You're here because you killed your three-year-old son with a plow, claiming it was an accident. Is that correct?" he asked.

"Yes, sir. My wife had just died. I was unable to afford a nanny. I didn't know he had climbed under." The man's voice was pinched with pain.

"Tentil, there are no excuses in Ixia," Valek chided.

"Yes, sir. I know, sir. I want to die, sir. The guilt is too hard to bear."

"Then dying wouldn't be adequate punishment, would it?"

Tentil glanced up at him in surprise.

"Living would be a harsher sentence. In fact, I know of a profitable farmstead in MD–4 that has tragically lost both the farmer and his wife, leaving behind three sons under the age of six. Tentil will hang tomorrow, or so everyone shall believe, but you will be escorted to MD–4 to take over the operation of a corn plantation and the job of raising those three boys. I suggest your first order of business should be to hire a nanny. Understand?"

"But…" Tentil gawked at him.

"The Code of Behavior has been excellent at ridding Ixia of undesirables, but it is somewhat lacking in basic human compassion. Despite my arguments, the Commander fails to grasp this point, so I occasionally take matters into my own hands. Keep your mouth shut, and you will live. One of my associates will check on you from time to time."

The man swayed and Valek worried he might faint. Another knock sounded.

"Come," Valek said. "Perfect timing as always, Wing. Did you bring the documents?"

Wing handed Valek a stack of papers—all expertly forged and official.

"Your new identity," Valek said to Tentil. "I believe our business is concluded. Wing will escort you to MD–4."

Wing unlocked the chains and they clanked to the floor.

"You're dismissed," Valek said to them both.

"Yes, sir." Tentil's voice cracked as tears streaked down his dirty face. Dazed, he followed Wing.

It had been a hell of a bad week but helping Tentil was a bright spot in the darkness. Valek pushed his chair back and rested his feet on the desk. He yawned loudly. The next part would be another cherished memory.

"So, Yelena, did you find our conversation interesting?" he called.

No response.

"I know you're behind the table."

She popped up and glared at him. "How did you—"

"You favor lavender-scented soap, and I wouldn't be alive today if I couldn't determine when someone had picked my locks. Assassins love to ambush, leaving dead bodies behind mysteriously locked doors. Fun stuff." Valek yawned again. It'd been an exhausting week, and it wasn't over yet.

"You're not angry?" she asked in surprise.

"No, relieved actually. I wondered when you would search my office for the recipe to the antidote."

"Relieved?" she spat in anger. "That I might try to escape? That I rifled through your papers? You're that confident that I won't succeed?"

Oh no, that hadn't been what he meant at all. "I'm relieved that you're following the standard steps of escaping, and *not* inventing a unique plan. If I know what you're doing, then I can anticipate your next move. If not, I might miss something. Learning how to pick locks naturally leads to this." Valek gestured around the room. "But, since the formula has not been written down and only I know it, I'm confident you won't find it."

She set her jaw and balled her hands into fists. "Okay, so there's no chance for escape. How about this? You gave Tentil a new life, why not me?"

Ah. Good question. "How do you know I haven't already?" Valek dropped his feet and leaned forward. "Why do you think you were in the dungeon for almost a year? Was it only luck that you happened to be the next in line when Oscove died? Perhaps I was merely acting at our first meeting when I seemed so surprised that you were a woman."

She crinkled her brow. "What do you want, Valek?" she demanded. "Do you want me to give up trying? Be content with this poisoned life?"

"Do you really want to know?" Valek asked with intensity. *Do you want to know I've fallen in love with you? Or would that scare you more than dying from Butterfly's Dust?* He stood and walked over to her.

"Yes."

"I want you…" Too much. "Not as an unwilling servant, but

as a loyal staff member. You're intelligent, quick-thinking, and becoming a decent fighter. I want you to be as dedicated as I am at keeping the Commander safe. Yes, it's a dangerous job, but, on the other hand, one miscalculated somersault on the tightrope could break your neck. That's what I want. Will you be able to give it to me?" Valek met her gaze, seeking an answer. "Besides, where would you go? You belong here." *With me, love.*

CHAPTER 18

The wait for her answer stretched to infinity. Each second an epoch of uncertainty and doubt.

"I don't know," she finally said. "There's too much…"

"That you haven't told me?" He guessed. She still hadn't confided in him about Reyad and what really happened in the Snake Forest with the Sitian master magician.

She nodded.

"Trusting is hard. Knowing who to trust, even harder," Valek said. He certainly had plenty of experience.

"And my track record has been rather horrendous. A weakness of mine."

"No, a strength. Look at Ari and Janco. They appointed themselves your protectors long before I assigned them. All because you stood up for them to the Commander when their own captain wouldn't. Think about what you have right now before you give me an answer. You have gained the Commander's and Maren's respect, and Ari's and Janco's loyalty."

"What have I earned from you, Valek? Loyalty? Respect? Trust?"

You have my heart. But that wasn't what she needed to hear.

"You have my attention. But give me what I want, and you can have everything." He promised.

She met his gaze, then turned and left his office. She needed time. He knew that. He'd give her all the time she needed. Deep inside, he sensed that it'd be worth the wait. That, if...no, when she committed and trusted him, revealing her true self, she'd knock him off his feet.

$\sim$

THE GENERALS and their retinues assembled to leave the next morning. Valek had five minutes to breathe a sigh of relief before sending Ari, Janco, Maren, and a soldier named Annika to ensure the safe passage of the Sitian delegation, who was due to arrive late the next afternoon.

In the meantime, he had a black market dealer to hang. It was the third day of the cold season, and he hadn't wanted the spectacle of a hanging when the generals and all those soldiers were in residence. Nor did he wish for the Sitians to witness it, so today was the day.

The carpenters had already constructed the gallows. Bunton stood between two guards. He wore a standard prison jumpsuit and had shaved. His swagger from his arrest was long gone. During questioning, he had confessed to murdering Sven, waiving his right to a trial—the first bit of good news for Valek. The second bit was learning Bunton's son, Loman had killed one of Valek's agents. Valek had given Bunton the option to pretend to be Tentil, including wearing a fake nose and makeup, to save his son's life. Because Bunton agreed, Loman would spend ten years in prison and be released.

Aware of this deal, Bunton's wife stood with the small group of witnesses along with Loman and his guards, Tentil's sister and mother. Once Tentil settled into his new life, Valek would arrange for his mother and sister's family to move to MD-4, where they'd learn of Tentil's real fate. Valek's family had been destroyed by murder and he didn't wish for anyone else's family to suffer unduly.

Also in attendance was Adrik, Sven's son; and Trevar, both new members of Valek's corps and still in training.

Bunton was led over to where Valek waited. The guards removed his manacles.

"This is your final opportunity to apologize to your family and your victims' families for your actions," Valek said.

The prisoner turned to the small crowd. "I'm sorry. I made a mistake."

Short and sincere, just the way Valek liked it. He took Bunton's arm and led him up the ramp. Then he looped the noose around his neck. The Commander usually announced the prisoner's crime, but Valek thought it was unnecessary. When he yanked the lever, he met Loman's gaze. The man flinched when his father's body jerked to a stop. Then he looked at Adrik. Sven's son was grim, but he nodded when he met Valek's gaze.

Afterwards, Valek talked to Adrik and Trevar. "This job is very dangerous," he said. "And you don't always get justice. Some missions go sideways, and you barely escape with your life. You can be severely injured. It's hard to have a family when you're gone on missions for months, maybe years."

"Are you trying to scare us?" Trevar asked.

"No. I want you to know all the risks involved when you become an agent. They outweigh the rewards."

"What are the rewards?"

"Saving a life, preventing a crime, outsmarting the bad guys, keeping people safe."

"How does hanging a murderer keep people safe?" Adrik asked. "The person they killed is still dead."

"It makes another potential murderer stop to consider the consequences before they act. *If* they can think. Sometimes, it's a crime of passion and there's no logic. And sometimes they believe they're smart enough to get away with it. Very few are, most are caught. Since the takeover, the number of murders has gone down significantly."

"I'll take those risks," Trevar said. "If I prevent one crime, it'd be worth it."

"My dad didn't spend a lot of time with me when I was growing up, but he made up for it during those long breaks he had between missions," Adrik said. "He believed in you and the Commander, and I do, too."

Valek was glad they were dedicated, but a part of him worried about them. So many of his agents had died and he tried to keep his distance from his corps. Tried to not get emotionally attached. Yet they were his family. Like all the members of his corps, he would be there when Adrik and Trevar graduated from training. He'd give them each a special gift and a small piece of his heart.

THE SITIAN DELEGATION arrived at the castle without trouble. Ari and Janco reported that the two teams had encountered no one, which meant the danger from Star remained.

Valek stood in the war room with the Commander and several high-ranking officials and advisers. A nervous excitement flowed through everyone, along with a simmering nervousness. Dressed in his formal uniform, Valek resisted tugging at the collar. He glanced at Yelena standing behind him. Did she still think he was stunning? Her gaze was firmly fixed on the entrance. The Sitians had arrived.

They wore colorful silk robes with animal figures embroidered on the fabric. The floor-length garments could be hiding any number of weapons. He counted five of them, all wearing animal-shaped masks that covered their faces. Exotic feathers and fur trimmed the masks. A status symbol or an intimidation tactic? Not being able to see their expressions or read their body language unnerved him. Was that the point of their clothing? To hide as much from the Ixians as possible?

The Sitians stopped three feet before the Commander. They fanned out into a V pattern like birds flying south during the cooling season. Fittingly, the lead bird wore a mask fashioned into a hawk.

"We bring you greetings and salutations from your southern neighbors," the leader said formally. "We hope this meeting will bring our two lands closer together. To show our commitment to this endeavor, we have come prepared to reveal ourselves to you." The hawk and her four companions removed their masks at the same time.

Valek recognized the woman who stood too close to the Commander—the southern master magician. The most dangerous person in the room by far. Valek braced for a magical attack, but nothing happened. Not yet. She had the power to reach the Commander anywhere in the castle complex. He met Yelena's gaze. Her horrified expression said it all—this was the worst possible situation.

"Ixia welcomes you to our land, and hopes to make a fresh start," the Commander said.

The magician replied with more formal words, but Valek ceased to listen. Instead, he formulated a plan of attack if she used her magic. He signaled his agents disguised as officials to be ready to subdue the other four Sitians while he stopped the leader. Unless the Sitians were all magicians, then all bets were off.

Valek considered. Knowing the Commander's views on magic, would the Sitians risk so many of them? Even in Sitia, magicians were rare and considered a valuable resource. If he had to guess, the master magician was probably the only person with power.

Despite his misgivings, everyone behaved, and the official greeting ceremony finished. The southerners were led to their quarters to rest and get ready for the feast. Valek would have to warn Kenda. Their agents would be no match for a master magician. And this situation was exactly the reason Valek had championed for the Commander to have a magician on his staff.

Valek stopped Yelena before she could join the others leaving the war room. They needed to warn the Commander.

"Okay, Valek, let's hear it. Some dire warning, I presume?" the Commander asked, sighing.

"The Sitian leader is a master magician," Valek said. He was getting tired of being sighed at like he was some drama king, making a big deal out of everything.

"That's to be expected. How else could they know we're sincere about creating a trade treaty? We could have ambushed them instead. It's a logical move." The Commander moved to leave.

"She doesn't trouble you?" Valek asked. "She's tried to kill Yelena."

The Commander looked at her. "It would be unwise to kill my food taster. Such an act could be misinterpreted as an assassination attempt and halt negotiations. Yelena is safe…for now." He shrugged, unconcerned, and left the war room.

Valek stared after the Commander. Or rather his body. Ambrose was no longer there. Or no longer in control. "Damn."

"Now what?" Yelena asked.

Frustrated, he kicked one of the chairs. "I anticipated a magician with the southern delegation, but not *her*." This complicated everything. "I'll leave the power twins assigned to you while she's here. Although, if she's determined to get you, there's nothing they or I can do. I lucked out with Mogkan because I was just around the corner when I felt his power surge. Let's hope she behaves while she's a guest in our land."

Valek pushed the chair back in place with a bang. "At least I know where all the magicians are. Mogkan was the one I felt during the generals' brandy meeting. And the southern master is now in the castle. Unless any more decide to show up, we should be safe."

"What about Captain Star?" she asked.

"Star's a charlatan. Her claims of being a magician are just a tactic for scaring her informers, so they don't double-cross her." Valek sighed. "Generals, Sitians, and feasts increase my workload. Which reminds me, you need to stay for the entire feast tonight. A tiresome chore, but at least the food should be good. I've heard Rand wanted to use the Criollo for a new dessert, but the Commander refused his request. Another puzzle, since Brazell has been sending the stuff by the wagonload and has promised to ship the dessert to all the other generals. They were clamoring after it like it was gold."

He needed to find the source of that Criollo and shut it down before Brazell could influence everyone. Which reminded him. "Any unusual symptoms, feelings, or appetites since you stopped eating the Criollo?"

"A mild craving," she said. "But nothing like an addiction. I find myself thinking about it from time to time, wishing for a piece."

Valek frowned. "It might be too soon. The Criollo could still be in your bloodstream. You'll inform me if something happens?"

"Yes."

"Good. I'll see you tonight." Valek hurried to Kenda's office to warn her of what their agents needed to guard against—if they could. Then he rushed to make the final preparations for the feast.

DECKED OUT FOR THE FEAST, the dining room blazed with light. Gold and crimson-colored ribbons looped from the ceiling. His corps had hung them while they checked the ceiling for spiders. The twelve-piece band's instruments had also been inspected for weapons and darts. Valek imagined a trumpet player with good aim would make an effective assassin. The band played boring music in the corner.

His agents, dressed in all black, stood between the seams of the heavy black curtains that covered the walls. Even with the light, they blended in with the fabric. Red curtains alternated with the black, creating stripes.

Valek sat at the head table with the Commander and the Sitians. Their table was set on top of a dais for several reasons. The extra height gave Valek a better view of the room, which had round tables filled with high-ranking officers, advisers, and more of his corps. He also ensured that the black curtains behind them were hung two feet from the wall so if the Commander needed to evacuate, there was not only a gap for him to run, but he'd be hidden from view. The dais also hid Yelena from everyone on the main floor. She perched on a low stool right behind Valek.

Ari and Janco had been assigned seats near the door in case anyone tried to attack during the feast. Their fighting skills had drastically improved since they'd been training with Maren and Valek, making them qualified to guard the entrance. They also had an open path to the dais in case Yelena needed them.

Valek scanned the room for trouble as he enjoyed his meal. Rand had exceeded expectations—the roasted meat melted in his mouth. The best part, neither he, nor Yelena, detected anything foreign in the food.

When the meal was finished, half the lanterns were extinguished. Valek leaned forward and grasped the hilt of his sword. He noted that his agents by the curtains also prepared for action. The next event ran the highest risk for Star's interference.

The band increased their tempo and volume until a pulsing beat filled the room, signaling the entrance of the troupe of fire dancers the Commander had hired to perform for the Sitians despite Valek's objections.

Carrying blazing staffs of wood, they raced into the cleared area in the middle of the room. At least they didn't rush to ignite the curtains. Well, not yet. Valek watched closely as they performed a complex dance routine. They whirled and somersaulted and flipped while twirling their flaming staffs. An impressive display of coordination, timing, and athleticism.

He remembered Yelena's comment about him becoming a fire dancer. Leaning back, he said, "I don't think I would have made it past the audition, Yelena. I probably would have set my hair on fire by this point."

"What's a singed head for the sake of art?" she teased.

Laughing, he returned his attention to the dancers. At the end of their routine, they earned a standing ovation. The crowd chanted for more and the troupe obliged. Twice. Coated with a sheen of sweat, they blew kisses to the crowd before leaving the room.

Once the applause died down, the master magician stood. She held a bottle of Sitia's famous cognac. Opening it, she poured an amber colored liquor into three tumblers. Touched that she'd included him, Valek handed the Commander's glass to Yelena to taste.

Yelena performed the first three S-steps, but after swirling the liquid around her mouth, she spat it out with force. She gagged and sputtered and finally choked out, "My Love."

Bloody hell. Valek knocked the other glasses over as Yelena toppled from her stool and sprawled on the floor. He ducked down and pushed her off the dais and behind the curtain, hoping she didn't hit her head too hard. Then he spun, grabbed the bottle of Sitian cognac hidden under the table, that he'd bought earlier just in case, and stood.

"I'm so sorry. I tripped on the tablecloth," he said to everyone. He mopped clumsily at the spilled cognac, making wild gestures with his right hand while swapping his new bottle for the magician's. "Guess I'm not used to such fine dining." A few people laughed and Valek spotted Ari and Janco edging toward the back of the dais. Good.

A servant brought three new glasses and Valek poured the cognac. He sipped from one glass, ensuring it was indeed clean and handed it to the Commander, who frowned. The third glass he gave to the magician. She stared at him in surprise tinged with fear.

"Just go with it," he whispered to them both.

The master magician held out her drink and said, "My name is Irys Jewelrose and I'm here on behalf of the Sitian Council. The Council is honored to be invited to Ixia, and we hope this visit will include reaching an agreement with you in the sharing of our knowledge and goods. We also hope that this will be the start of a long friendship between our two countries." She raised the glass higher. "To Ixia and Sitia!"

The Commander raised his tumbler and clinked it with hers before drinking. Valek downed his cognac in one gulp. He needed its warmth, as he'd have to endure the inevitable questions while worrying about Yelena. Did she swallow a lethal dose? At least, Ari and Janco had noticed what happened and had come to her aid.

The toast signaled the end of the feast. The band returned to playing boring songs as people milled about talking and laughing. The feast was a success. Pity the Commander didn't have more of them. It would boost morale.

"My office, now," the Commander ordered him and Irys.

They glanced at each other before following the Commander. Valek checked behind the curtain to make sure Yelena was gone. He grabbed both bottles of cognac—his had a small black dot on the label—and joined them. No one said a word during the trip to the office.

The Commander sat on the edge of his desk. "Explain what just happened."

"The Sitian cognac was laced with a lethal poison called, Have a Drink, My Love," Valek said.

Irys sucked in a breath. "Poisoned? Are you sure?"

"Yes. Did you not notice our food taster passing out?"

"I… But we drank…"

He held up his cognac. "We drank from an untainted bottle." Then he set them down on the desk.

It didn't take long for the magician to understand. Horror replaced her confusion. Irys turned to the Commander. "We did *not* poison the cognac. I swear, we would *never* try to ruin this meeting. It's too important."

"We know." The Commander looked at Valek, inviting him to continue.

"We learned of a plot to sabotage this conference," he said to Irys. "However, we didn't have any details of what they planned to do, so we prepared for everything. Who gave you the cognac for the feast?"

"I bought it in Sitia. It's from my personal collection. Do you think someone snuck into my room and poisoned it?"

And risk being caught by a master magician? "No. Has it been in your possession this entire time?"

"It was in my luggage until this evening. My bag has been with me the entire journey, except for when your porters carried our suitcases to the guest suite."

No doubt Star had paid one of the porters to swap bottles— an easy thing to do.

"Find out which porter was bribed," the Commander ordered Valek.

"Yes, sir."

"Will your food taster survive?" Irys asked Valek.

"Yelena spat most of it out. She should recover in a few days, but it will depend on the concentration of the poison."

"I've some healing ability. Please let me know if I can help."

The Commander raised an eyebrow. "Magical healing?"

She glanced at Valek then set her shoulders. "Yes, magical healing." Irys drew in a deep breath. "I planned to fully introduce myself to you tomorrow. But considering the circumstances, I feel it prudent to do it now. I'm Fourth Magician, Irys Jewelrose, and a member of the Sitian Council."

"Why wait?" Valek asked.

"I wanted Commander Ambrose to decide who would be privy to this information, so I was waiting for a time when we were alone." She cocked her head. "But you're not surprised. You recognized me from the fire festival."

"I picked up that you have master-level powers, but I didn't know your name or your rank. Why did you try to kill Yelena?" He demanded.

"It was a mistake. I thought she had uncontrolled magic. Magicians who are unable to control their magic will flame out and ruin the blanket of power for the rest of us. But it wasn't her. When we met in the forest, I had more time to assess her."

Either she was lying, or Yelena had lied about their encounter. Valek was inclined to believe Yelena, as she had been properly terrified after that incident and had not been relieved. Had Irys read Yelena's mind and used Reyad as an excuse for targeting her for assassination? Why? And why would either of them lie? There was more going on here.

"Why did you think it was her in the first place?" the Commander asked.

"We felt someone with power last year in MD-5, but the surges stopped for almost a year. Then we were recently hit with another one from the castle. The timing matched when your new food taster started working, plus she arrived from MD-5 a year ago. But it's not her."

"Can you feel these…surges from Sitia?" The Commander sounded doubtful.

"I can. All the master magicians can."

"If it's not her, then who is it?"

"After investigating…" She glanced at Valek because she had just admitted to espionage. "I learned that a person died during both occurrences. When a magician dies, they create a pulse that ripples through the power blanket much like a surge, but without the destructive force. An uncontrolled magician doesn't flame out right away. It builds over time. Small surges that get stronger and stronger until they take too much power and can't control it."

In other words, she thought Reyad and Horus had been magicians. An interesting notion. Could it have been Mogkan both times? No. The man had control of his magic.

"Those people would have shown signs of having magic, which they did not," the Commander said.

"Not necessarily. Some people have what we call a 'one-trick' ability. Most of them have no idea they're using magic."

"For example?"

"A Cowan clan man always knew when someone was lying. He thought he just had good intuition, but it was really a magical ability. We tested him extensively, but that was all he could do."

"Could you tell when he used magic?" the Commander asked.

"Only when he was close to me. It's very light."

By the line of the Commander's questioning, Valek sensed he might be sent out to go door to door, looking for people with one-trick abilities. That would be pure hell.

"Is anyone else in your party a magician?" Valek asked.

"No."

"Is there anyone else investigating in Ixia?"

"No."

He wondered how many times Irys had entered Ixia to investigate.

Irys must have guessed his thoughts. "I'm the only magician who has been sanctioned by the Sitian Council to illegally cross into Ixia. Each time was due to dangerous surges that threatened the blanket of power."

Which meant, there were other magicians not sanctioned by the Council. Interesting distinction.

"Do you kill the ones you find?" the Commander asked.

"If they're too far gone, yes. If they have time to learn control, then I smuggle them into Sitia. And if they're in a position where I can't rescue them, like one of your advisers or a soldier, then I would have to…end their lives."

"All for your precious power blanket," the Commander said.

"Yes." She was unapologetic.

"Thank you for answering our questions," the Commander said.

"I wanted to be fully honest with you before going into these discussions."

"It's a promising start. We'll reconvene in the morning."

Wow. That went a hundred times better than Valek had expected. He'd hoped the Commander would only send them home and not order their arrest and Irys's execution, but to continue the talks was just another example of the Commander's personality change.

Valek grabbed the bottles of cognac and escorted Irys to her quarters. Before he left, he asked Irys, "How many magicians have you smuggled to Sitia?"

"Three. And now I'm afraid my honesty will stop me from saving more lives."

"Yes, *you* will have to stop."

Irys gave him a shrewd look as Valek bade her a good night. Kenda waited for him just outside the main entrance to the guest wing. Two of the Commanders' soldiers guarded the door.

"I've gotten a dozen reports from our agents and none of them match. What the hell happened at the feast?" she demanded.

"I'll explain on the way," he said.

"To where?"

"My suite." He increased his pace and described what happened.

"Poison, huh? You've got to admit, it would have worked," Kenda said, jogging to keep up. "The Commander would have accused the Sitians and they would have accused you."

"Me?"

"Yeah, the Commander invited them. So obviously he wanted them here. Plus, you're the magician killer."

"I thought I was the baby killer."

"That, too. You're ambitious that way." She smirked.

"Thanks," he said dryly. "I need you to interrogate all the people who carried the Sitians' bags to the guest suite. Find the person responsible and bring them to my office."

"Tonight?"

"Yes."

"Yes, sir." She saluted and headed back.

When Valek reached the entrance to his suite, he paused for a moment to banish his worry and fear into a deep dark well. Assuming a neutral expression, he strode into the living room. Janco sprang from the couch as if he'd been caught stealing. Valek set the heavy bottles on the table. The lanterns had all been lit and Yelena's door was open.

"Stop! No!" Yelena yelled.

He bolted into her room, ready to fight. But she lay on the bed with the blanket and sheets crumpled underneath her. Her uniform was twisted around her, and her boots were on the floor. Ari sat in a chair next to her bed.

"Somersault...feather...prize...," Yelena mumbled. Sweat beaded on her brow. "Barn! Barn!"

"She's been raving like this since I carried her here. Why did you order us to bring her here and not to the infirmary? Did you know she was going to be poisoned?" Ari demanded. His eyebrows were smashed together, and he clenched his fists as if he wished to punch Valek.

"She's *always* in danger of being poisoned. It's safer here, and I've a supply of poison antidotes just in case."

"There's an antidote? Why didn't you tell us?" He jumped to his feet.

"There's no antidote to My Love. Or I would have followed you right away."

"Oh." Ari's anger deflated. He gazed at Yelena. "Will she...is she..."

"...straw...fire...feathers...," Yelena muttered.

"She'll live," Valek said, moving closer. He smoothed her hair, pulling a few sweaty strands away from her face. "It'll take her a couple of days to recover from the poison. In fact, it's a good sign that she's delirious."

"What can we do for her?" Ari asked.

"Stay with her. I need to be with the Commander. You can wipe the sweat from her forehead, so it doesn't sting her eyes, and apply a cool damp cloth. You'll need a bucket because she'll empty her stomach, and clean sheets in case you're not fast enough."

"I'll send Janco for supplies. What about when she wakes?"

"Let me know right away. She'll be thirsty. Have some water nearby."

"Yes, sir."

"Somersault, somersault, cartwheel...and...fly... Fly! Fly away!"

"I'll ask the medic to come check on her just in case. She can help Yelena change into her night clothes, they'll be more comfortable."

Her eyes flew open. "Valek! My love! My love!"

Taking her hand in his, he rubbed his thumb over her knuckles. "Shhh. It's okay. You were perfect. You saved us."

Lost in another delusion, she yanked her hand away. "Fire… fly…crash…sneeze…"

"Let me know if her symptoms get worse," Valek said to Ari.

"Yes, sir."

Janco remained standing by the couch. "Did you arrest the southerners?"

"No." He grabbed the cognac bottles and headed out.

"But, they—"

Valek didn't have time to explain it to him. Obviously Janco hadn't connected the incident to Star, even though he'd been at the brainstorming session. Was it an inherent dislike for the Sitians, or were Janco's thoughts just that scattered? Valek slowed as another notion struck him. One of the other southerners could have added the poison while they were traveling. Perhaps not all the Sitians were happy about the possibility of a trade treaty. Which meant, Star could still be a threat. Janco might be on to something. Who knew?

CHAPTER 19

*A*fter checking that the Commander was well protected and confirming the schedule for tomorrow, Valek returned to his office. He set the bottles on the sideboard next to his desk. Resigned to the fact he wouldn't get much sleep over the next few days, he sat down and considered the attack.

Just because they ruined one plot to upset the conference, didn't mean there weren't others in place. If Star had poisoned the cognac, then her plan hadn't worked, and she might try again.

A knock interrupted his thoughts. "Come in."

Kenda escorted a disheveled man into his office. The man wore pajama pants, socks, and a stained shirt. He smelled like sour beer. His wide face was creased in a belligerent expression. Interesting.

Kenda pointed to the chair in front of the desk. "Sit."

The man glared at her but did as ordered.

"This here is Emmet," she said. "According to his colleagues, he's come into some money recently."

"So? I got lucky playing cards," Emmet said.

"They also said you suck at playing cards."

"Hence the *luck*," he almost growled.

"And he was one of the people who carried up the Sitians' bags."

"So? There were twelve of us. Damn southerners didn't pack light."

"But only one of you fell far behind the others on the way to the guest wing," Kenda said.

He shrugged. "The bag was heavier than it looked. I about broke my back lugging that thing up three flights of stairs."

"Your evidence is all circumstantial, Kenda," Valek said. "I think you bothered this poor man for no reason."

Kenda threw her hands up. "It's all I had. Fine. I'll go back and question the other porters again." She stormed out.

"I am *very* sorry for the inconvenience," Valek said to Emmet.

"It's all right."

"You'll never get back to sleep now."

Emmet stood. "It's okay."

"No. No. I have just the thing." Valek poured some Sitian cognac into a tumbler. "This is the expensive stuff. A few sips of this and you'll sleep like a baby." He handed the glass to Emmet.

"I…" Emmet swallowed. "I…don't drink, sir. But thank you anyway." He moved to set it down.

"You mean you don't drink hard liquor, right?" He pointed to one of the large stains on the man's shirt. "More of a beer man?"

"Uh…yeah. I don't like the strong stuff."

"You're in luck. This cognac is so smooth, you'd think you're drinking milk. Go on, try it. Just a sip."

Emmet's hand shook as he raised the glass to his lips. Then he slammed it down on the desk. "I can't."

"Why?"

"You bloody well know why."

"I do. Sit down, Emmet," Valek said in his flat tone.

He glanced at the door.

"Go on. Run. You won't get far, but if it makes you feel better, go on."

And damn, the porter did. He bolted for the door, threw it open, and stopped in his tracks.

"Innocent men don't run, Emmet," Kenda said, blocking the way. She held a dagger in each hand.

"Sit down," Valek ordered.

Defeated, Emmet returned to the chair.

"Who paid you to poison the cognac?" Valek asked.

"I didn't poison it!"

Valek waited.

"All I did was swap the bottles; I swear."

"Who gave you the bottle to swap?"

"I don't know. Some guy in a bar in Castletown. He wore a merchant uniform. That's all I know."

"Did he pay you to do anything else?" Valek asked.

"No. No. Just swap the bottles. Said it was my patriotic duty."

Valek glanced at Kenda. "What do you think? Is he telling the truth?"

"I can have my guys work on him, see what else he *coughs* up besides blood."

"Hmmm…tempting."

Emmet jumped to his feet. "That's all I did, I swear!"

"Can you describe the man?" Valek asked.

"Uh…yeah. Tall guy, thin. Really thin like all bones. One of his front teeth was broken in half. He kept running his tongue under it."

Recognizing the man as an infamous southern assassin who favored using My Love to poison people, Valek and Kenda exchanged a glance. He must now be doing jobs for Star. Lovely.

"What else did he tell you?" Valek asked.

"He warned me not to drink from his bottle. That's all."

Valek looked at Kenda. "Take him to the holding cells, we'll deal with him after the Sitians leave."

"Yes, sir. Come on, Emmet."

Kenda led the man out. Valek picked up the glass and sipped the cognac. He hadn't lied, it was smooth. He settled behind his desk and savored the liquor.

THE COMMANDER HELD the negotiations with the Sitians in the war room. Valek attended every session, acting as adviser, food taster, and magic sensor. Ambrose had invited two of his other advisers—Dema and Chelle—to the talks. They both primarily worked with commerce and natural resources. However, the Commander cross-trained all his advisers in various positions along with a required course on leadership.

Irys's companions were introduced: Gozal, an accountant; Eva, an expert in logistics; Mevin, a supply chain manager; and Pinnet, a page who would record the minutes of the meetings and draw up any forms or documents. Smart choices.

The first order of business was to establish a trade treaty.

"Ixian resources that we would be interested in purchasing are diamonds, white coal, wool, and metal ore," Irys said.

"No diamonds. As for the rest…" The Commander looked at Dema.

She had long black hair and her skin tone matched the Sitians. Dema flipped through a leather-bound book. "We've plenty of wool and ores. We're more limited on the white coal but should be able to sell you a few tons."

"Is there a reason you've taken diamonds off the table?" Irys asked the Commander.

"Yes. They're mine."

Irys looked at Valek as if trying to determine if the Commander was joking or not. He wasn't. The dead King of

Ixia had taken all the diamonds the Commander's family risked their lives to mine from the mountains, paying them barely enough to survive.

"Do you know the Sitian black market sells *your* diamonds?" she asked.

"I did not." He scowled at Valek.

"There's only so much my corps can do," he said. "Diamonds are small."

"And they cost a small fortune. If you export them to us, you get the income, we can sell affordable gemstones, and the dealers no longer get rich. Win, win, win."

"I'll think about it," the Commander said. "The Sitian resources that I'm interested in are cotton, coffee, glass, silk, and tea."

All but coffee was sold on the black market. By legally importing them, the Commander would hit the dealers hard. Not hard enough for all of them to go out of business—there would always be illegal imports—but enough to make a difference. Valek approved. The Commander might not be acting like himself, but his mind was still sharp as ever.

"What types of tea?" Irys asked.

"Anything that's not black tea. Tea is very popular in Ixia, but with our cooler climate, we can only grow black tea."

Yelena would be happy to have different teas to taste. She seemed to enjoy the beverage. Maybe he should bring some to Ari and Janco in case she woke up craving the drink, which he hoped would be soon.

The Commander, Irys, and their advisers discussed quantities, timing, and trade routes.

"Only licensed dealers in Ixia will be allowed to purchase from your vendors," the Commander said.

"How will our sellers know your merchant has a license?" Mevin asked.

"They'll have a certificate. Your people will need to be trained to spot forged documents."

"It's not hard," Valek added, seeing the concerned looks. "Most criminals don't take the time to do a proper job."

"And the ones who do?" Irys asked.

"Don't know that we treat our parchment with a special dye that will show with just a drop of water."

"Should we be telling the Sitians this?" Dema asked.

"Do you know what the dye is made from?" Valek asked.

"Uh...no." She looked at Chelle. "Do you?"

"No."

"Not many people do," he said. "All they know is the paper will turn blue when wet."

The trade discussion continued and Valek's attention waxed and waned depending on the topic. They took a break for lunch and Valek would have loved to check on Yelena, but he wouldn't leave the Commander alone with the master magician even though she hadn't tried to use her magic all morning.

After lunch, Irys brought up another topic. "I'd like to discuss magicians in Ixia."

Everyone stilled and glanced at the Commander.

"They're banned," he said. "Present company excluded for the duration of your visit."

"I'm aware of your...policies. I would like to negotiate a... trade for them as well."

Valek expected the Commander to stop all talk of magic, but he said, "I'm listening."

"I mentioned surges before and how they build. What I'd like to propose is that when we sense these new magicians, we have your permission to bring them to Sitia. You would get rid of an undesirable, and we would gain a valuable resource. We're prepared to pay a large fee for each extraction."

"What about when *we* find them?" the Commander asked Irys.

"We'll pay you an export fee for each person. You set the price for both. Sitia is willing to pay whatever is necessary to save these magicians."

What a fantastic offer. Valek loved the idea.

"Save the magicians so they can live in Sitia and propagate? Eventually you'll have an army of them, and they'll be involved in every aspect of your government, corrupting the Sitian Council. No."

Valek hid his disappointment, but Irys gave the Commander a steely glare. Valek shifted in his seat, prepared to jump to the rescue if Irys used her magic.

"*I'm* on the Council along with three other master magicians, Commander. I can assure you we would not allow that to happen."

"I believe you would do everything in your power to prevent it. However, magic corrupts and gives a person an unfair advantage. It's not a matter of *if* a magician tries to take over your Council but *when*. The answer is still no."

If Valek considered Ixian history, the Commander had a point. A century ago, the King of Ixia used to be elected, along with the dukes of each province. But a powerful magician thought he deserved to be King. He gained control of Ixia, assigning his magical friends as dukes. That had ended the elections, and the King's powerful offspring inherited the throne each generation.

Sensing it was a waste of time to argue, Irys switched topics. Everyone appeared to relax as the discussion changed to more mundane negotiations. The meeting lasted late into the night. Valek finally escorted the Commander back to his suite after midnight.

"You were tense during parts of the proceedings, Valek" the Commander said. "Did you sense magic in use?"

"No. Not at all. Although, I thought she'd blast you after your comment about magicians."

"Like you, she's good at hiding her emotions. I wanted to see if I could provoke her. However, I didn't lie. Magic corrupts."

As soon as the Commander closed his door, Valek hurried to check on Yelena. All the lanterns were lit and Janco snored on the couch. Ari sat in the chair next to Yelena's bed, looking as if he hadn't left her side. She still muttered in her sleep and thrashed, but it wasn't as frantic.

"How's she doing?" Valek asked.

"Better now." He pointed to the bucket next to her bed. "She expelled everything in her stomach this afternoon. It was a rough couple of hours, but she hasn't thrown up since."

"Did the medic stop by?"

"Yes. She said all we can do is wait it out. That, and try to get Yelena to drink some water."

Valek noticed the glass on the night table. "Any luck?"

"Some. The medic did change her clothes, making Yelena more comfortable."

"I can sit with her so you can get some sleep," Valek offered.

"No thanks, sir. I'll switch out with Janco when he wakes up." He hooked a thumb at the door. "He's exhausted from cleaning the bucket and fetching supplies. Or so he says. Besides, you look like you need the sleep more than I do." Ari smiled to soften the insult.

"I've had a tough day of sitting." Valek rubbed his back. "And I've reports to read before I can sleep. Ah, the exciting life of the Chief of Security. Are you sure you want to become my second?"

"Truthfully, I didn't want to join your corps without Janco. And I figured if I became your second, I could promote Janco. Make him my assistant. He'd *love* that."

Valek could easily picture Janco's outraged expression. He laughed.

Ari sobered and looked at Yelena. "However, I'd rather stop others from causing harm than be a scout, regardless of the drudgery." He met Valek's gaze. "Most of her ravings were nonsense words, but not all. It's a good thing Reyad is dead, or I'd have to request leave to go kill him."

Valek was tempted to ask for details, but he'd rather wait until she trusted him enough to share her story. Ari's comments confirmed Valek's guess that Ari and Janco were a package deal. "What about Janco? Would he be able to handle the grind?"

"Janco only has two speeds: in motion or asleep. But I'm working on him."

"You are the voice of reason. Why do you put up with him? He'd drive most people crazy."

"That's all part of his charm," Ari joked. "Despite his tendency to act like a distracted puppy, I wouldn't want anyone else guarding my back. Janco would do anything for a friend, and he sees the fun side of life. I tend to forget that there *is* a fun side."

"There is?" Valek asked in mock surprise.

"No offense, sir. But if anyone needs to remember there is a fun side, it's you."

"I have fun. Those challenges are fun when I have the time. And I enjoy outsmarting criminals."

"Sounds like work to me," Ari said.

"I carve statues for fun." But usually, when he carved, his thoughts were on a work problem. Ari still looked dubious. Valek gave up. "I'll be in my office if she wakes up."

"Yes, sir."

Valek considered Ari's comment as he walked through the quiet castle. He loved the late-night hours when only a few people were awake, but that wasn't exactly having fun. When was the last time he did anything, other than carving, for relaxation? The Commander took vacations and Valek always accompanied him, but as part of his security detail. Hmmm, perhaps Valek was due a few days off. Except, he'd no time. Not with Star and Brazell plotting. And that was the problem. Someone was always plotting.

When he reached his office, a stack of reports waited for him on his desk. He sighed, lit a few more candles, and read through them.

No new information on Star's plans. In fact, the recent discussions in her office provided no useful tips. Even the number of meetings she held had decreased. Valek wondered if Star had discovered their surveillance.

He read reports until the words blurred on the page. Then he pulled out his old travel mat and slept on the floor behind the conference table. The faint scent of lavender lingering on the air lulled him to sleep.

$\sim$

THE NEXT DAY mirrored the first. The only difference was, when he escorted the Commander back to his suite late that night, Ambrose stopped at the threshold. Valek had thought it was too late for a nightcap, but he'd have a drink if the Commander asked him inside.

Instead, the Commander said, "After the Sitian delegation leaves, I'm going to visit General Brazell and tour the feed factory he's been bragging about."

Completely unexpected and out of character—the Commander hated traveling in the cold season—Valek just stared at him for a long moment. "Why now?"

"Need I remind you that I don't have to justify my actions to you?"

"No, sir. I'll alert your personal guard and I'll prepare for the trip. Do you know how long we'll be away?"

"You will remain here."

"But—"

"It's an order, Valek."

"Yes, sir."

"Good." The Commander shut the door.

Valek stood in the hallway. He had never, ever disobeyed an order from the Commander, but the man that had issued the order to remain in the castle was no longer Ambrose. Valek didn't have any proof that Brazell and Criollo were the culprits, but he was determined to do whatever it took to stop them and get the Commander back.

By the time Valek entered his apartment, he'd recovered from the surprise, but his worries about the trip to MD-5 now extended to Yelena. She'd have to go with the Commander, giving Brazell plenty of opportunities to kill her.

Valek checked on her. She rested peacefully. Janco sat next to her, reading a book. Despite what Ari said, it appeared Janco did have a third speed.

"Where's Ari?" Valek asked.

"Finally in bed! He's been on a constant vigil for the last forty-eight hours. I had to threaten him at knifepoint."

"Knifepoint? Really?"

"Well…more like I sang the same song off key over and over again until he relented and left." Janco scratched the scar that cut through his right ear. "I'm not exactly known for my singing. But that doesn't sound as hard core as using a knife, so…" He shrugged.

Valek wisely refrained from asking what song Janco sang. Instead, he asked about Yelena.

"She finally calmed down a few hours ago and is doing much better."

"Let me know when she wakes up."

"Will do!"

Valek returned to his office to read more reports. A few hours later, a knock sounded and Janco poked his head in.

"Yelena's awake. She drank a bunch of water and seems to be

fine. Do you want me to go back and stay with her the rest of the night?"

"No need. She's safe there. Thanks for letting me know."

"Anytime, boss." Janco saluted and left.

Staring at the reports without really seeing them, Valek gave up and hurried back to their suite. He hoped Yelena might be still awake. When he arrived, her bed was empty, and she was nowhere to be found.

AFTER QUESTIONING THE GUARDS, he learned she'd left their suite soon after Janco. Valek considered searching for her. She knew the risks of being out this late on her own. Or did she? She left when General Brazell's men still roamed the castle. Did she not have any sense of self-preservation? But then again, she'd neutralized Nix on her own.

Valek settled on the couch to wait for her. He'd have to trust that she could protect herself, but he couldn't help being tired and grumpy when she finally returned just before dawn.

"Back so soon?" he asked her. "Too bad. I was just about to organize a search for your dead body. What happened when you knocked on the southern magician's door to sacrifice your-self? Did they kick you out, thinking you too half-witted to waste their time on?"

She plopped on the chair and listened to the rest of his sarcastic rant without interrupting him. A part of him under-stood he was being unreasonable and harsh, but he had only a few hours of sleep last night and had none tonight, and he was due to taste the Commander's breakfast in an hour. Eventually, he'd run out of energy.

"Are you done?" she asked.

"What? No rebuttal?"

She shook her head.

That was a nice surprise. "Then I'm finished."

"Good," she said. "Since you're already in a bad mood, I might as well tell you what happened while I was in the kitchen. Actually, two things: one bad, one good. Which would you like to hear first?"

"The bad," Valek answered immediately. "That allows me the hope that the good will balance things out."

She explained that she had inadvertently told Rand about Valek's undercover surveillance of Star's operation. It was the last thing he needed to hear.

"It's your fault," she said, correctly reading his expression. "I was defending you!"

He didn't quite know how to respond. Nothing like this had ever happened before. "In protecting my honor, you exposed months of work. I should be flattered?"

"You should," she said with full conviction.

Having Yelena defend him was a good sign that she no longer saw him as the enemy, but he'd hoped to learn more from Star. Suddenly exhausted, he relaxed back on the couch and kneaded his now throbbing temples. "I hadn't planned on making arrests till later this month. Better implement my cleanup plan before Rand has a chance to alert Star."

Trying to look on the bright side, Valek rubbed his eyes. "Still, this might be a benefit. I think Star's becoming suspicious. She hasn't been conducting any illicit business in her office. If I bring her in now, I might discover who hired her to poison the Sitian's bottle."

"Star? How?" Yelena asked in surprise.

"She has a southern assassin in her employ. He would be the only one with the skill and the opportunity. I'm sure the poisoning wasn't a result of Star's personal political views. Her organization would do anything for anybody for the right price. I must find out who would risk so much to compromise the delegation."

More work, but her slip wasn't as terrible as he first thought. He stood. "What's the good news?"

"The mystery beans are an ingredient in making Criollo."

Well, that explained…not as much as he'd hoped. "Then why did Brazell lie on his permit application? There's no law against manufacturing a dessert," Valek said. Even a dessert that could influence other people, but who would ever believe a ridiculous thing like that?

"Perhaps because the beans are imported from Sitia," she said. "That would be illegal; at least until the trade treaty is finalized. Maybe Brazell's been using other southern ingredients or equipment as well."

"Possible. Which is why he was so eager to have a treaty. You'll have to take a good look around when you visit the factory."

"What?"

"The Commander has scheduled a trip to MD–5 when the southerners leave. And where the Commander goes, you go."

"What about you? You're going too, aren't you?" Her voice squeaked with panic.

"No. I've been *ordered* to stay here."

She stared at him in horror, but there was nothing he could say to reassure her. He told her to get some rest and that he would taste the Commander's food while the Sitian delegation remained in Ixia.

After she returned to bed, Valek hurried to Kenda's office.

"Something wrong?" she asked.

"Yes. The undercover operation at Star's has been blown. I need you to take an extraction team and arrest Star and her people."

She put her hands on her hips. "Have we even identified all of her people yet?"

"No. But there's nothing we can do. Take Inrick and Hildred, they'll be able to recognize voices."

"Okay. When?"

"This morning."

"What about the Sitians? I'm going to need the agents assigned to watch them for the raid."

"Take them. I'll be with the Sitians all day."

Not happy, but out of arguments, Kenda rushed to round up her team as Valek headed to the war room. As he sat and listened to the discussion, he fought to stay awake. It would be a long day. He'd rather be with Kenda; the excitement of the arrests would have kept him alert.

It was only after enduring a mind-numbing day that he could meet with Kenda to learn the details about the raid. She met him in his office.

"Star wasn't in the building," she said.

He cursed. Rand must have tipped her off.

"We arrested a dozen people. They didn't resist, and they don't seem like critical personnel in her network, but I'll find out more when we interview them."

"Did you leave a couple of watchers on Star's building just in case she comes back?"

"Yeah. Although, I doubt she's that stupid."

"She's not, but maybe we can snag a few of her clients. She'll eventually settle in a new location to conduct her business and we'll find it. Next time, we'll do it right. Let me know what you learn from the interrogations."

"Yes, sir."

"And I need Inrick and Hildred for a special operation."

Kenda rubbed her forehead. "When?"

"Not until after the delegation leaves."

"Thank fate, we're stretched thin. You need to recruit more agents."

"I know, it's on my very long to-do list."

"What about those captains and the lieutenant?"

"I'm in the process of convincing them to join."

"Why don't you just *ask* them?"

"Where's the fun in that?"

She just shook her head.

THE SITIANS REQUESTED a break the next day, taking the afternoon off. After ensuring they reached the guest quarters, Valek joined the Commander in his office. He hadn't been able to update him on Star until now.

"You think Rand tipped her off?" the Commander asked.

"Unless it was just a lucky coincidence that she wasn't there. Otherwise, either he did, or he sent a message with his fetch boy. That information would have been worth a lot of money. It may have even erased his gambling debt."

"Then it's a good thing I'm sending him to MD-5."

Valek had ceased to be surprised by the Commander's uncharacteristic decisions. Instead of questioning him, Valek tried another tactic. "The food at the feast was—"

"Delicious, I know. However, I've grown tired of his schemes and Brazell is willing to take him on. We'll get his chef, Ving, in exchange."

Ah, the man responsible for making Criollo. Valek understood. "We can also arrest Rand for treason. I've more than enough evidence against him."

"No need. Brazell will keep him in check."

The insult, that Valek hadn't, was implied. Even though the Commander had agreed to the plan to use Rand to find out more information on Star.

After updating the Commander, Valek stopped by Kenda's office. She'd conducted the interviews on all of Star's people.

"Guards, muscles, and servants," Kenda said in disgust. "All very cooperative because they learned pretty quick that they were left behind to be sacrificed."

"Did they have any idea on where Star will go next?"

"Nope. These were low hanging fruit, but I've an agent searching the house. Maybe we'll get lucky and find some information."

He hated depending on luck. And he hated scrambling to prepare for the next threat. But with the Commander's decision to travel to MD-5 in the middle of the cold season, that was exactly what he had to do.

SINCE THE SOUTHERNERS were still in discussions, Valek spent the next couple of late nights getting ready for the trip to MD-5. No way was he remaining behind, but he needed to ensure Kenda could cover for him. He held meetings with Inrick and Hildred and then with Ari and Janco.

"Are we expecting trouble enroute?" Ari asked.

"No. Trouble will be at General Brazell's manor house or at his factory. Keep a sharp eye out," Valek said.

"Do you know the nature of this trouble?" Janco asked.

Valek debated. Should he trust them with the truth? Would they even believe him? He decided to confide in them his suspicions about Brazell and Criollo.

"Gah, magic," Janco spat. "Bad enough we have a castle full of Sitians, now this!"

"Can we counter it?" Ari asked.

"I can, but I haven't found anything else that will block it or stop it. The best thing to do is knock a magician unconscious or kill them. Darts filled with a sleeping potion and throwing knives are good weapons to have with you."

"Wait!" Janco leaned forward. "You have sleeping juice? Why didn't I know about this?"

"Because we don't need it working as scouts," Ari said.

"With something like that, it's more a matter of *want*. Are there any other goodies you give your spies?"

"Lots, but since you're not a spy…"

Janco groaned. His disappointment didn't last as he perked up a few seconds later. "Okay, I get keeping the magician at a distance, but what about your knife with the blood?" Janco made a stabbing motion with his hand. "The King's dead, but it didn't stop his magic."

"In those cases, the magician takes a thread of magic from the blanket of power and loops it back, so it doesn't have to be maintained by the magician. The magic flows in a continuous circle on its own."

"Blanket of power?" Janco asked.

Valek had forgotten that most Ixians knew nothing about magic. However, if Ari and Janco were going to be encountering magicians, they should be informed. "Magic surrounds the world like a blanket. Magicians have the ability to tap into the magic. They draw thin threads from this blanket and use it to light a fire, or move an object, or read a person's thoughts, or heal, or any number of different things. Some magicians can only do one thing, others two or more. The master-level magicians can do everything. Unfortunately, magic is invisible, so you might not even know a magician is targeting you."

"Oh joy. I'm really starting to *love* these guys." Janco's tone dripped with sarcasm.

"Magicians also have limits, though," Valek continued. "Some can move objects a hundred feet, while others can only move it a few feet. And they get tired when they use too much. Distance helps us as well. Some can project their magic very far, while others can't."

"You mean they can reach us here? In this very room?" Janco was aghast.

"I'm sure our guest, Master Magician Irys Jewelrose, could read your minds from quite a distance away."

"And you let her into Ixia!"

"I doubt I could have stopped her. Not unless she was within striking distance. However, she's been on her best behavior since she arrived."

"You said 'your minds.' Why can't she read yours, sir?" Ari asked.

He explained about his immunity.

"Wow. How do I get some of that?" Janco asked.

Valek laughed. "If I knew, I'd give it to all my spies, the Commander, everyone in Ixia." Then he sobered. "I've no idea why I'm immune. I discovered it when I was training to become an assassin. My goal was to kill the King of Ixia. Since he was a magician, my teacher had another student attack me with magic. It didn't work."

"Handy."

"Very. I can also feel when magic is in use. A light touch feels like a strand of spider's silk on my skin. Powerful magic is thick, like wading through invisible syrup. It can slow me down."

"Are we going to encounter magicians at General Brazell's, sir?" Ari asked.

"At least one. Adviser Mogkan is a magician. I don't know how strong he is, and he might be reluctant to use his magic in front of everyone. But don't count on it." Valek explained what they should be aware of and things to look for. They still believed he would be staying behind. Only Kenda knew his true plans.

"Magic sucks."

Trust Janco to sum things up so succinctly.

THE SITIANS FINALLY DEPARTED, and the castle staff hurried to prepare the Commander's entourage as they would leave the next morning. Valek finalized his plans. He collapsed with a groan into his bed for the first time in eight days. Bonus that a full night stretched out ahead of him. He needed a good night's rest, because he doubted he'd sleep much during the next few weeks.

Except his mind refused to settle. Worries about Yelena and the Commander kept circling in his thoughts. Brazell stood to gain power if the Commander died. But why kill him if he could control the man's actions and probably his thoughts? Yelena, though, was in the most danger. Brazell might wait a few days, but there was no way she'd leave his manor house alive. Unless Valek stopped him.

Unable to endure the dire thoughts any longer, Valek went into his carving room. The butterfly he'd carved while thinking about Yelena remained on his worktable. Picking it up, he examined the glossy black statue. Silver spots decorated the wings. It appeared so fragile, yet it was rock solid. Much like Yelena. When she'd first entered his office, he thought she wouldn't last a day let alone two and a half seasons. Not only had she survived, but thrived, transforming before his very eyes, much like the butterfly he held in his hand.

Yelena knew her life was at risk, but she didn't know he'd be close by. Making a sudden decision, he drilled a small hole in the butterfly. Then he returned to his bedroom and hunted through his personal effects from long ago, finding Vincent's silver necklace. Valek's mother had cleaned the blood off it and given it to him, thinking it would bring Valek some measure of peace. Instead, it was a constant reminder of Vincent's murder, so he had shoved it into a small box. Funny how that box stayed with him all these years.

Valek cleaned the tarnish off the silver until it glinted in the lantern light. Then he threaded it through the hole in the butterfly. Cupping the necklace in his hand, he laid down and finally fell asleep.

THE COLD GRAY morning hinted at snow. Valek intercepted Yelena before she could leave to join the entourage.

"This is a very dangerous trip for you," he said. "Maintain a low profile and keep your eyes open. Question thoughts in your mind: they might not be your own." He handed her a silver flask filled with White Fright. Valek didn't want her getting sick while in MD-5. "The Commander has your daily dose of antidote, but if he *forgets* to give it to you, here's a backup supply. Tell no one that you have it, and keep it hidden."

"Thanks," she said and turned to leave.

"Wait, Yelena, there's one more thing." Valek summoned the courage. Would she reject his gift? "I want you to have this." He showed her the butterfly pendant and necklace, then, without waiting for a response, he looped the necklace around her neck. "When I carved this statue, I was thinking about you. Delicate in appearance, but with a strength unnoticed at first glance."

His gaze met hers. *Please be safe, love.*

CHAPTER 20

*V*alek leaned against the training yard's fence. He crossed his arms and scowled at anyone who dared to look at him, acting like a petulant child who hadn't gotten his way. Or, in this case, who had to stay home while the big kids got to go. The Commander's entourage consisted of fifty soldiers from his elite guard, a handful of servants and grooms. Valek noted that Dema, Chelle, Tocara, and Felo were the four advisers chosen to accompany the Commander. It took everyone over an hour to assemble. Valek kept his vigil despite the cold air.

Yelena milled around with Rand and the rest of the servants. She had a pack strapped to her back and she carried a bo staff like it was a walking stick. He approved. She'd need every bit of protection. Occasionally, she touched her chest right below her neck. At first, he thought it was just a nervous tic, but his heart warmed when he realized she fingered his pendant. Did that mean she liked it?

Finally, the procession headed east. Major Granten led the parade, followed by twenty-five soldiers, the Commander and his advisers on their horses, the servants, and then the other twenty-five soldiers. They took the major east-west route, and it would be easy for Valek to catch up. Like he'd told Ari and Janco, he didn't expect any trouble on the way to MD-5. Besides, the captains had left hours ago, scouting the route to check for ambushes. And Hildred and Inrick would be following right behind.

Valek remained outside, frowning at the entourage until it disappeared out of sight. Then he huffed and stormed back into the castle. After meeting with Kenda, Valek made sure plenty of the castle's residents spotted him in various locations that afternoon, he returned to his suite and packed his duffle bag. He changed into his sneak suit, and then put on the uniform of the Commander's elite guard over top of it. Nights would be cold, and it would give him an extra layer of warmth. He put on a black wool hat and tucked his hair into it.

He smiled at his reflection in the mirror. That one little alteration made a huge difference in his appearance and there was no need to do anything else. However, he added his putty and makeup to his bag along with several more weapons. By the time he'd finished, it was dark.

Valek slipped out the east gate and jogged to catch up. Even with the Commander and advisers on horseback, the entourage moved at a walking pace. It would take them about five days to reach Brazell's manor house.

When he reached them, the tents had already been erected for the night. Dinner was being served and Valek snagged a bowl of stew. No one really looked at him. Yelena ducked out of the Commander's spacious tent—the one luxury the man allowed for himself—and headed to a smaller tent.

A small light blazed inside. And from the shadows cast on the fabric of the tent, Valek guessed Yelena read a book. She had borrowed a couple of them for the trip. He'd been encouraged when she grabbed the one on the old war symbols, hoping it was a sign she was still considering his offer to become part of his team.

Content all was well, Valek pitched his tent among the other soldiers.

∾

THE SECOND DAY proceeded without incident. By the third day, the animation in the Commander's face began to fade. Right after they stopped to set up for the night, Valek slowly walked in a wide arc to the east of the camp while the soldiers set up the Commander's tent. It took a few passes, but he detected a strong flow of magic. Valek positioned his body between the magic and the tent, breaking the connection, and stayed there until the magic disappeared. The strength of the power surprised him. One magician couldn't generate such power unless they were master level. Was he dealing with multiple magicians?

Tempted to stand there and block the magic all night, Valek knew it was only a temporary solution. Also, someone was bound to notice him standing there as it was still light out.

He checked for Yelena, but didn't see her, and her tent was empty. Unease stirred. Perhaps she just stepped into the woods to attend to nature. But when the time lengthened and she didn't appear, he sought Hildred.

His spies wore gray camouflage uniforms and had been guarding the camp. He stepped into the woods and whistled like a bird. Hildred stepped from her hiding place and joined him.

"Something wrong?" she asked.

"Have you seen Yelena?"

"Yes. There's a small trail just east of camp that runs north. She took it a bit ago. I figured I'd give her some privacy."

"Did she come back?"

"Not yet."

"How long ago?" he demanded.

"Uh...a while."

He cursed. "Find Inrick and provide backup. Stay hidden until needed." Valek rushed east until he found the trail. Just as he turned north a crashing sound filled the forest. He drew his sword and increased his pace. In the distance, he spotted a figure fall from the trees and land on another person. They rolled and the smaller person stood and moved as if to run away. But she—Yelena tripped! And the man straddled her, wrapping his hands around her neck.

It took only seconds to crush a person's windpipe. Valek was too far away to help. He broke into a run. Yelena fumbled in her pocket, pulling out her switchblade. Without hesitation she stabbed it into her attacker's stomach. Then a second time when he failed to release her.

Bloody hell. Valek slowed as the man collapsed on top of her. Then she pushed him off, stood, wiped her knife in the dirt and headed deeper into the forest. Bloody hell times two. Valek trailed after her, stepping over the dead man.

Yelena approached an open area where Star waited. Confused, Valek held back and scanned the area. The dying sunlight added to the macabre scene in the clearing. Rand lay unmoving on the ground with an arrow sticking out of his chest. Another man lay nearby. Considering his blank stare, blue lips, and gray skin, he was probably dead as well.

Star whipped around in surprise when Yelena entered. Her gaze focused on Yelena before searching the forest behind her. Valek froze, hoping she didn't spot him in the encroaching gloom.

"He's dead," Yelena said in a harsh, almost guttural tone, drawing Star's full attention.

The woman paled, then pleaded. "We can work this out."

"No, we can't. If I let you walk away, you'll only return with more men. If I take you to the Commander, I'd have to answer for killing your thugs. I'm out of options." Yelena stepped toward her with the clear intent to kill.

"Yelena, stop!" Valek yelled.

She spun around. He strode toward her, and she assumed a fighting stance, raising her weapon. What the hell? Then he realized she didn't recognize him. He sheathed his sword and removed his hat.

Yelena relaxed. "I thought you had orders to stay at the castle. Won't you be court martialed?"

"And I thought your killing days were over," he replied. He'd reached the thug with the blue lips and examined the man. As expected, he'd died of suffocation. Probably a bo strike to his windpipe. Damn. "Tell you what. If you don't tell, I won't. That way we can both avoid the noose. Deal?"

Yelena jerked her head toward Star. "What about her?"

"There's an arrest warrant out for her. Did you even consider taking her to the Commander?"

"No."

"Why not?" Valek couldn't hide his shock. She'd dispatched two men in self-defense. With Star, it would clearly have been premeditated murder. Was that what happened with Reyad? "Killing isn't the only solution to a problem. Or has that been your formula?"

"*My* formula! Excuse me, Mr. Assassin, while I laugh as I remember my history lessons on how to deal with a tyrannical monarch by killing him and his family."

Low blow. The King and his family needed to die. Star was no longer a threat. Valek glared at her.

"My actions were based on what I thought you would do if you were ambushed," she said.

She really thought Valek would kill everyone. That he wouldn't disarm them and arrest them first? Did she believe he was just a killing machine? If that was the case, Yelena would never trust him.

"You really don't know me at all," Valek said.

"Think about it, Valek, if I took her to the Commander and explained the details, what would happen to me?"

Yelena would be arrested for killing Star's men and executed. He hadn't considered it from her point of view. "Well, then, it was fortunate for both of you that I arrived."

Star broke for the forest. Valek signaled Inrick and Hildred as she dashed down the small trail. Yelena moved to give chase, but Valek told her to wait. His agents materialized from the dark forest and tackled Star, who yelped in surprise.

"Take her back to the castle," Valek ordered. "I'll deal with her when I get back. Oh, and send a cleanup crew. I don't want anyone stumbling onto this mess."

They pulled Star away.

"Wait," she yelled. "I have information. If you release me, I'll tell you who plotted to ruin the Sitian treaty."

"Don't worry." Valek used his flat tone. "You'll tell me." He took a step away, then paused. "However, if you want to reveal your patron now, then we can skip a painful interrogation later."

Star's expression turned shrewd.

"Lying would only worsen your predicament," Valek warned.

"Kangom," she said through clenched teeth. "He wore a basic soldier's uniform with MD–8 colors."

"General Dinno." Valek was not surprised.

"Describe Kangom," Yelena said.

"Tall. Long black hair in a soldier's braid. An arrogant bastard. I almost kicked him out, but he showed me a pile of gold I couldn't refuse," Star said.

"Anything else?" Valek asked.

Star shook her head. Valek snapped his fingers. His agents would escort Star back toward the castle.

"Could it be Mogkan?" Yelena asked.

"Mogkan?" Valek glanced at her. "No. Brazell was far too

happy about the delegation. Why would he jeopardize the treaty? That doesn't make sense. Dinno on the other hand, was furious with the Commander. He probably sent one of his men to hire Star."

Yelena wiped her blood-stained hands on her pants, which were torn. Her shirt was soaked with more blood. Was she injured? She shivered and hunted for something in the woods.

When she was about to swing her cloak over her shoulders, he said, "You better leave your clothes here. There would be quite a fuss if you showed up for dinner soaked with blood."

She found her pack and he turned his back while she changed. Then they headed back to the camp. Valek mulled over what had happened in the clearing, putting the pieces together. Star and Rand must have tricked Yelena into coming here alone, where they planned to ambush her. They probably thought it'd be easy.

But Yelena had surprised them. They had underestimated her intelligence. He'd bet that gray fabric on the inside of her cloak must have camouflaged her as she climbed through the trees to approach the clearing. She'd not only arrived armed; she'd become dangerous.

When they passed the second dead goon, Valek said, "By the way, nice work, I saw the fight. I wasn't close enough to help. You held your own. Who gave you the knife?" He was curious if she'd rat out Janco.

"I bought it with Star's money."

He laughed. Her reply had been technically correct. "Fitting."

They arrived at the camp and Yelena hurried to taste the Commander's dinner. Valek tucked his hair back into his hat and joined a group of soldiers. His mood had lightened. Yelena was still in danger. He doubted he'd ever *not* worry about her, but damn, she'd handled herself like a professional.

Fierce, determined, dangerous. No wonder her soul called to his.

OTHER THAN THE search for Rand, nothing else happened during the rest of the trip to Brazell's manor house.

Nothing, except the steady increase of magic. It grew impossibly stronger with every step closer to MD-5. Valek could no longer block the magic with his body, it flowed around him as if he stood in the middle of a fast-flowing river.

Nothing, except the Commander losing more and more of his personality. By the time they reached the manor house, his expression was devoid of all intelligence.

Nothing, except the frustration and anger over being unable to stop the attack. Valek needed to wait for the right moment to strike. He fervently hoped such a moment would present itself.

As they neared, Valek detected a faint scent floating in the air. It took him a few minutes to recognize it as Criollo. He exchanged a glance with Yelena. She had stashed her backpack and bo in the forest—a smart precaution. Her long black hair had been swept up into a knot and, on his third glance, he realized she used her lock picks to hold her hair in place. He hoped she kept her switchblade and the antidote.

By the time they arrived in Brazell's courtyard, the aroma of Criollo fogged the air. An incredible amount of magic pressed on him like a house-sized balloon. Yelena nervously fingered her pendant as she followed the Commander and his advisers into the house. The next few hours would be critical for her. Either Brazell would try to kill her at the first opportunity or wait for his grand plan to be revealed.

Valek had to stay with the soldiers who would be housed in the barracks. For now. He pulled another uniform from his bag and changed into Brazell's colors before stashing his bag under an empty bottom bunk. He folded the blanket down to mark it as taken. Ari and Janco came in and headed to an empty set of beds. Without Inrick and Hildred as backup, Valek might need them.

"Why do I always have to sleep on top?" Janco complained. "Every time you roll over the whole bunk shakes."

"I can't help that they're built out of cheap materials," Ari countered. "Imagine what would happen if I slept on top."

"Janco would be flattened like a sweet cake," Valek said.

They turned to him. Their expressions were not welcoming.

"Who the hell—oh it's—"

"Janco," Ari warned.

"You! It's you. Oh, hello, you."

"Real smooth." Ari glanced around, but no one paid them any attention. "You shouldn't be here. You're risking a court martial."

"I'm aware."

"Did you see what happened to the Commander?" Janco asked in a loud whisper. "We came back from scouting and now he's a mindless zombie! This whole place creeps me out! Is it because of the magic you warned us about?"

"Yes, and I'm going to need you two to get friendly with Brazell's soldiers. Find out what they know about Criollo and Adviser Mogkan."

"Yes, sir," they said together.

"And be ready. I might need your help."

"Yes, sir."

"What about Yelena, sir?" Ari asked.

"I'll keep an eye on her as much as I can. If things get too hot, she's smart enough to escape."

"She should have done a runner like that chef. I wouldn't have blamed her," Janco said.

Valek would fill them in later about Rand's fate. Right now, he had to hurry. Once outside the barracks, he took off his jacket and turned it inside out, transforming the basic soldier's uniform into one that the valets wore. He entered the house and strode through the magic-filled halls as if he belonged.

The manor wasn't as big as the Commander's castle nor as chaotically constructed. It was a large four-story structure with two wings, resembling a square with only three sides. All the generals' manors matched so none of them could complain of being slighted. The similar layout worked very well for Valek and his agents. He was familiar with the design, and he headed straight toward Brazell's office.

He arrived just in time to see the Commander's advisers being led out and escorted to the guest wing. The Commander and Yelena must still be inside. Not a good sign.

Ducking around a corner, Valek debated if he should charge into the office. He imagined Mogkan had trapped Yelena with his magic so Brazell could kill her. Returning to the door, he pressed as close as possible without touching it. Voices sounded, but none of them were Yelena's.

"I'll bet two silvers she doesn't last two days," a man said.

Valek glanced to his left. Two muscular soldiers headed toward him.

"I'll bet two silvers she's already dead," the other man said. "Hey, you, what are you doing? Eavesdropping?" he called to Valek.

Valek smiled. "I'll bet a gold that the general will make a big public display of her execution."

"Ho boy, that'll be fun, letting everyone watch that murderer die."

"Do you take the bet?" Valek asked.

"No way, that sounds like something the general would do."

"Too bad." Valek walked away while the guards knocked on the door and entered the office.

Once again ducking around the corner, Valek waited, listening for any cries or sounds that Yelena needed his help. The two goons reappeared, but they were too focused on Yelena to notice him. She walked between them, looking small and fragile. Boy were they in for a surprise.

He followed as they led her to the guest wing and locked her into a room. That was a good sign that Brazell planned to wait to kill her. It gave Valek some time to figure out how to stop him.

Returning to Brazell's office, he loitered nearby. Eventually, Mogkan escorted the Commander from the room to his quarters. Valek trailed behind, noting which guest room they assigned to the Commander. Valek might end up kidnapping the man in order to save his life.

VALEK LEFT the manor and followed the scent of Criollo, tracking it until he found Brazell's new factory. The long, narrow building had two silos on the northern end and a brick smokestack. The surrounding air was thick with magic. Valek hid behind a pile of black coal to assess the situation.

The Sitian beans poured from the base of the silos and were transported via conveyor into the interior. He needed to get inside, so he joined the flow of people carrying burlap bags from nearby wagons to a table. There they were cut open with a knife and their contents—beans—were dumped into a hopper.

The workers ignored him and, after noting their blank expressions, Valek figured out why. They'd been eating Criollo. Or were they? With all the magic in the air, he wondered if the magic was infused into the Criollo. Except, if that were the case, he would have sensed the magic when he touched the dessert. His knife with the King's blood always felt sticky with magic. Unless food had different properties?

Did it matter? The combination of Criollo and magic caused a person to lose their soul, for lack of a better word. The Criollo factory needed to be shut down. Valek planned to burn it down and destroy every piece of the cursed dessert. But first, he wanted to inspect it. No one in their present state of mind would bother to stop him or call out an alarm.

Inside, the beans were fed into large roasters. Heat poured from them, and the fire roared as workers shoveled coal, keeping it hot. After being roasted, the beans were dumped onto large tables where more people pounded on them with mallets. The debris was sorted either into the trash or onto steel rollers where the nibs turned to a paste.

Fascinated by the process, Valek followed the manufacturing line. The paste ended up in a steel vat where sugar, and butter were mixed with large paddles until it smoothed into a brown liquid. The end product was spooned into molds to harden. Considering the large stacks of Criollo on the tables, the factory produced quite a bit of inventory.

The workers were covered in sweat and stained with Criollo, indicating it was a labor-intensive endeavor. And expensive, as that pile of coal wasn't cheap, nor was purchasing and shipping the illegal goods from Sitia. Why would Brazell wish to manufacture it? Was it not available for sale in Sitia?

About to leave, Valek spotted his two agents mixing a vat of Criollo. They didn't recognize him, nor did they understand his hand signals. At least now he knew what had happened to them. He fervently hoped that once a person stopped eating Criollo, the magic no longer worked on them.

VALEK RETURNED to the manor house and kept a low profile during the next few days. It appeared Yelena alternated between tasting the Commander's food and being locked in her room. However, she was allowed to join the Commander and advisers during their tour of the factory.

If he needed evidence that Criollo stole a person's will, he had it by observing the advisers' expressions as they chomped down bar after bar of the dessert. The magic also swelled around Mogkan. He moved through the group of the Commanders' advisers, talking to each one, touching them on the hand. Yelena avoided eating the dessert, which was good. But now that the advisers were also under Mogkan's influence, she was in danger.

Valek followed the group to the manor house. Yelena was escorted back to her room and the tightness around Valek's chest eased. He waited until darkness, then found a hidden spot to watch Yelena's window. She'd claimed her actions with Star had been based on what she thought he would do, so he hoped Yelena recognized the danger and planned to escape tonight.

Soon after he settled into a comfortable position, her window opened, and she dropped her cloak out. Was that a sign to him that she needed help? Her room was about twenty feet above the cold hard ground. Instead of waiting for her next move, Valek climbed the wall and reached her window just as she left with her two guards.

Ah, so much for rescuing the damsel-in-distress. Janco would have been disappointed, but Valek was intrigued. He climbed inside and then followed. They stopped at the baths.

"I don't need an audience. Wait here, I won't be long," Yelena ordered.

She entered but the guards obeyed her orders. Well, the one did. The other smirked and headed off. Valek trailed him. There must be another way into the baths. Sure enough, the guard leaned on the wall across from a door.

The big man straightened at the scrape of metal. Then the snap of a tumbler sounded. The door swung open, and Yelena paused, spotting the smirking guard. Valek pulled a dart from his sleeve, but she rushed the guard, knocking him off-balance as she punched him in the groin. He crumpled in pain.

Valek silently cheered as she ran away. Once she was out of sight, he approached the moaning guard.

"Tough luck, mate." Valek jabbed the dart into his thick neck. When the guard stilled, he removed the evidence.

He considered his next move. Yelena knew this house. She didn't need him right now and would wait for him in the trees. He'd join her there right after checking in with Ari and Janco.

They played poker in the barracks with a group of MD-5 soldiers. Valek hovered at the edges of the lantern light until he caught Ari's gaze.

A few minutes later, Ari cursed and threw down his cards. "We fold."

"We?" Janco asked, glancing at his hand.

"Yes, *we*."

"Okay." He tossed his cards onto the table. "We fold."

Ari stood. "We're also tired of losing. Come on, Janco, let's get some fresh air."

Janco impressed Valek by hopping up and joining his partner without question. If Brazell's soldiers thought it odd, they didn't comment as they continued bidding on their hands.

Valek met up with the power twins outside.

"Oh," Janco said. "Well, that's good. I thought I just threw my best hand of the night because *you* were tired of losing."

"And yet you still did it," Valek said.

"Yeah, well, Ari usually has a reason and since we're in enemy territory..." He waved a hand, indicating their surroundings.

"Something happened?" Ari asked.

"Yes. All the advisers are now under Mogkan's influence and Yelena did a runner this evening."

"Good," Ari said. "Do you think we'll be tapped to aid in the search?"

"No. I think they'll keep it to a few guards. They think she can't go far."

"Why not?" Janco asked.

He explained about Butterfly's Dust and Yelena's daily need for the antidote.

"Wow. That's…" Janco cast about for a proper word.

"Smart, if you look at it from Valek's point of view," Ari said.

"Fiendish, if you look at it from her point of view."

"I'm hoping that the antidote won't be needed much longer," Valek said.

"There's a cure?" Ari asked.

Valek bit back a curse. "Sort of. I'm hoping that she'll join us as a teammate, and then I can train another food taster."

"That would be sweet," Janco said.

"Did you learn anything from your new friends?" Valek asked.

"The guards are all annoyed that they have to smell that delicious scent, but can't eat any of it," Ari reported.

"They also don't like Adviser Mogkan," Janco added. "He's acting like he's in charge instead of the general."

Valek tried to recall if Brazell had eaten the Criollo. No. Not even during the brandy meeting. But that didn't mean Mogkan hadn't been orchestrating this takeover all along.

"Anything else significant?" he asked.

"No, sir."

"I'm going to catch up with Yelena and see if she learned anything," Valek said.

"And then?" Ari asked.

"Then we rescue the Commander, take him far from all this magic, and hope he wakes up."

"We're ready when you need us, sir."

"Thank you."

~

VALEK STARTED his search for Yelena on the west side of the estate, where the trees grew close together and traveling through them would be easier. He'd been right about the hunt for Yelena consisting of only a few soldiers, but he hadn't counted on the dogs.

They strained at their leashes as they bounded west through the forest. Had they caught her scent? He cursed the moonlight. It painted the stark landscape with a silver brightness.

The dogs circled a tree, barking and yipping and appearing like they'd lost her scent. It was probably the place where Yelena had climbed into the treetops. Valek had an idea. He was far enough away from the searchers that he would look like an indistinguishable figure in the moonlight. Valek crunched some leaves under his boots.

One of the soldiers shouted and pointed toward Valek. He broke cover and ran. They chased after him. Fun.

Valek led them further west for no other reason than instinct. Brazell and Mogkan might expect her to return to the Commander's castle. To him. Yet, he sensed she'd head in the opposite direction.

The dogs, encouraged by their handlers, picked up his scent. He zigzagged, trying to throw them off. When he encountered a small stream, he ran in the water for a while before stomping through the underbrush, leaving a clear trail. Then he back stepped to the water, dashed further upstream, and used Yelena's trick, climbing a tree.

Settling on a sturdy limb high up, Valek waited. Barely a minute later, his pursuers reached the stream. The dogs lost his scent, but the search party checked the opposite bank, eventually discovering his false trail.

He waited until they were well out of sight before climbing down. Then he headed back to the manor house. It took him hours longer to find Yelena than he expected. Valek had assumed that, after she retrieved her pack and bo from where she'd hidden them, she'd stay safe in the treetops overnight. Instead, he spotted her in a large clearing. From the worn-down grass, areas of hard-packed dirt, and stakes still left in the ground, the site appeared to be where the fire festival set up their tents every year.

Yelena knelt next to a smooth area, digging in the dirt and clearly visible for all to see. Valek wondered again about her recklessness. This was another example of her being smart enough to escape, yet risking being captured.

When he neared, he slowed as she tossed her metal hook onto the ground and clawed at the dirt with her fingers. She removed something and held it reverently. Humming happily, she refilled the hole. Then she cleaned her prize and added it to Vincent's necklace. He caught sight of a flame design.

Ah. She must have been a very talented acrobat to earn an amulet at the fire festival. No wonder she risked so much to find it again. She was lucky this time, but she needed to be more careful.

He strode up to her. "Not the best hiding place. Wouldn't you agree?"

She jumped to her feet.

"They're searching for you," he said. "Why did you run?"

Yelena told him about the Commander, the advisers, Brazell, Mogkan, and the Criollo. She'd made all the same conclusions he had. Nice.

"So Mogkan is using Criollo to take control of their minds, but where's he getting the power?" Valek asked.

"I don't know. We need to search the manor."

"You mean, *I* need to?"

"No, *we*. I grew up there. I know every inch." Her shoulders stiffened with stubborn determination. "When do we start?"

Arguing would be a waste of time. "Now. We have four hours until dawn. What are we looking for?"

Yelena explained they were searching for either a circle of

diamonds or a painted wheel. Two strange and rather specific things, but he didn't want to waste time asking how she knew. Diamonds enhanced magic, but Valek couldn't imagine Brazell having enough of the gemstones to support the amount of power around the manor and factory.

He stopped in the barracks to change while Yelena waited outside. The Commander's soldiers filled the beds, and most were asleep. Valek stripped down to his black sneak suit and grabbed a bull's-eye lantern and a black tunic for Yelena. Her red shirt would be too noticeable even in the dark halls of the house. Then he paused by Ari and Janco's bunk.

Ari cracked an eye open. Valek whispered their plans to him just in case. Not that Ari and Janco could do much if something went wrong, but he wanted to keep them apprised of the situation.

Valek joined Yelena and waited as she changed into his shirt and hid her cloak. Then she directed him to an unlocked back door. They entered and he lit the lantern, sliding the metal shutter until only a thin beam of light shone.

Without any hesitation, Yelena strode to the east wing of the house. They were on the ground floor, and, as they reached the entrance to the wing, Yelena's confidence wavered. When they continued into the wing's main hallway, she glanced around nervously and bit down on her knuckle hard enough to draw blood. The area smelled of dust, stale sweat, body odor, and blood.

He picked the locks on the doors. A few of the rooms contained storage, others were guest rooms, and there were a couple of offices. Then they entered a large space that was filled with tables, various glassware, burners, jars of chemicals, and tubing, indicating a laboratory. A thick layer of dust coated everything. Valek suspected this entire level had been Reyad's domain.

As Valek explored the lab, he spotted implements of torture.

No wonder Yelena jumped at every shadow. Had she been a test subject for Reyad's experiments? If so, then the man died too easily.

He wondered why she'd brought him here. This wing had been abandoned and he doubted they'd find either diamonds or a painted design. When she halted before a room across from the lab and started trembling, Valek had a flash of insight. She either wanted to face her demons, or this was her way of trusting Valek, by showing him what she'd endured at Reyad's hands.

Yelena waited in the hall while he entered the room. It was Reyad's bedroom. This had been where she'd killed him. The sheets had been stripped from the bed, but a large brown spot stained the mattress. Valek opened a chest and peered inside. He immediately wished he hadn't. The devices stored within were used for causing pain to another person.

Valek searched the rest of the room and concluded that Reyad was one sadistic bastard, and a depraved individual that had needed to die. That should never have been born. Horrified and sickened by what he'd found, he left and joined Yelena in the hall.

He met her gaze and fervently hoped Yelena had killed Reyad before he could harm her, but from her reactions of just being here and the fact she'd been younger, he knew she'd been a victim. Questions bubbled up his throat. She must have endured so much. Yet, he swallowed them down. She'd either confide in him or not. He would not press her.

Pulling the door shut, Valek continued down the hall. He stopped at the next room and rubbed his forehead, marveling that she had the strength to return here despite the memories.

The next couple rooms revealed little. Almost at the end of the hall, he unlocked a door and stepped back as the acrid stench of excrement hit him in the face. The beam from his lantern illuminated a group of people. They had greasy hair, dirt-streaked faces, and rags hung off their emaciated frames. They flinched away from the light but didn't make a sound.

When Valek entered, he spotted the chains anchoring them to the floor. Brazell's manor was a literal house of horrors. The prisoners stared vacantly at him. More mindless victims of Criollo? Was this the Commander's fate?

He wove through them. They sat in three circles like ripples in a pond. Lines had been painted on the floor. "Who are you?" he asked a man. No reply. "Why are you here?" he asked another. Still nothing.

Yelena cried out in pain. She knelt next to a young girl, stroking her shoulder and whispering a name—Carra. Were these the children who lived in Brazell's orphanage? He scanned them, noting ages. Then he recognized a pattern. The position of the people created a wagon wheel design.

"What now?" Yelena asked Valek. Her voice shook.

"You're arrested and thrown in the dungeon," Mogkan said.

They spun. The adviser stood in the doorway. Red hot fury blazed within Valek.

Mogkan.

Needs.

To.

Die.

Now.

Valek charged. He would tear the man into tiny pieces with his bare hands. Mogkan retreated as Valek burst from the room. Eight soldiers stood in a semi-circle. Their drawn swords were pointed at Valek's chest. He stopped short and raised his hands before they decided to skewer him.

CHAPTER 21

*Y*elena rushed out and halted beside him. Valek bit back a curse. The horrific scene of those poor souls had distracted him so much, he'd let Mogkan get the drop on him—a rookie mistake. He feared for Yelena's life more than his own, but there was nothing he could do at this time. Of course, he'd jump at the first opportunity.

The soldiers took their packs, their obvious weapons, and the lantern. Then they were marched down to the holding cells. Every manor house had a small dungeon to hold prisoners temporarily. The sharp points of the swords jabbed into Valek's back whenever he lagged. Yelena kept glancing at him as if waiting for a signal.

Not yet, love.

Once in the guard room, they were stripped of their clothing and thoroughly searched. They combed their fingers through Yelena's hair and found her lock picks. The soldiers even took the time to check every inch of the material of his sneak suit, finding his weapons, darts, and lock picks. Just his bad luck to get smart guards.

They were led down a flight of stairs into the dungeon. The

fetid stench of rat droppings, moldy straw, and excrement coated the back of his throat, gagging him. There were four cells on each side. He was pushed into the first one on the left and Yelena into the second one. The doors swung closed with a loud metallic clank. A man tossed his suit at him through the bars. A small kindness, one Valek appreciated since cold damp air licked his skin, causing goosebumps.

He scanned his small cell before the light disappeared. Only one wall was constructed with floor to ceiling iron bars. The rest were made of rough stone. Dirty straw covered the floor, along with brown lumps he doubted were Criollo. No chamber pot. No mattress. Nothing to use as a weapon. The door to the guard's room shut and the blackness was instant. He dressed and considered how he could smuggle a set of lock picks on his body so they wouldn't be found during another thorough search. Perhaps if he glued them to his thigh and covered them with a flesh-colored putty. But it'd have to be expertly done or it would be spotted.

"Valek?" Yelena said.

"What?"

"Why didn't you fight the guards? I would have helped you."

That was the downside of his reputation—unrealistic expectations. "Eight men had drawn swords pointed at my chest. Any sudden movement and I would have been skewered." Still, it was nice that she had such confidence in him. "I'm flattered that you think I could win against those odds. Four armed opponents, maybe, but eight is definitely too many."

"Then we pick the locks and make our escape?"

"That would be ideal, provided we had something to pick them with." Unfortunately, they were stuck for now. With nothing to distract him, the image of those people chained to the floor rose in his mind. Yelena had recognized one of the younger victims.

Valek could no longer suppress his curiosity. "Was that your fate? If you hadn't killed Reyad, were you slated to be chained to the floor, mindless?"

There was a long silence. Would she tell him it was none of his business? Or would she continue to trust him? He wouldn't push if she didn't answer his question.

"I think Brazell and Reyad were determined to reduce me to that mental state. But I endured." Yelena explained how she thought Mogkan, Reyad, and Brazell had experimented on the children of the orphanage, children who might develop magic as they aged. Somehow, Mogkan had wiped their minds so that he could use them to enhance his power.

Yelena must have been one of those potential children. What had transpired once they figured out that she didn't have magic? "Tell me what happened to you," Valek said.

A pause, then her tale spilled out, slowly at first and then in a torrent.

"Life in Brazell's orphanage was…actually nice. We had nannies and teachers and each other. They encouraged us to enter the various Fire Festival competitions and gain skills. On our sixteenth birthday, we were required to find a job. Many of the children worked as cooks, servers, or nannies in town. Well, that's what they told us. Instead, they were turned into those soulless beings and chained to the floor." A hitch caught in her voice.

"When I turned sixteen…" She swallowed. "I was told that, since I was the smartest of the children, I would have the honor of helping Brazell in his laboratory. An honor that lasted all of five minutes. Brazell and Reyad carried out Brazell's…experiments. It was terrible, but, when it was just Reyad, he'd invite Mogkan to participate, and it went beyond horrible. Together, they'd try to outdo each other on who could create the harshest test."

As she explained the progression of Reyad's endurance tests that eventually turned into torture, Valek gripped the metal bars so hard, he expected them to bend under his fingers. Then she detailed the next two years of her life as a laboratory rat, the humiliation, the sadistic games, the torment, and the beatings.

Yelena continued, "As the sessions grew more difficult, Mogkan's voice scratched at my mind, encouraging me to flee. To find a place of peace." Yelena spared no details. She included every awful incident, trusting him completely.

Valek about ripped the bars from the concrete when she described Reyad's rape. His desire to kill fought with his need to wrap Yelena in his arms and never ever let go so no one could *ever* hurt her again.

"I killed Reyad to prevent him from harming Carra and May, my foster sisters, when they turned sixteen," she said. "Guess I should have killed Brazell and Mogkan, too." She fell silent.

Valek was outraged to learn this brutality was going on and sickened with guilt that he had no idea. "Brazell and Mogkan will be destroyed," he promised Yelena.

The door to the holding cells opened. Bright light sliced the darkness as four guards with lanterns escorted Brazell and Mogkan into the dungeon. Valek stood at the bars.

"It's good to see you back where you belong," Brazell said to Yelena. "My desire to feel your blood on my hands has tempted me, but Mogkan has kindly informed me of your fate, should you not receive your antidote." Brazell paused. "Seeing my son's killer writhing in excruciating pain will be better justice. I'll visit later to hear your screams. And if you beg me, I might put you out of your misery, just so I can breathe in the hot scent of your blood."

Valek fisted his hands. *If anyone's going to bleed, it'll be you.*

Brazell's gaze met Valek's. "Disobeying a direct order is a capital offense. Commander Ambrose has signed your death warrant. Your hanging is scheduled for noon tomorrow." Brazell cocked his head, appraising Valek. "I think I shall have your head stuffed and mounted. You'll make an effective deco-ration in my office when I become Commander."

Not a chance, you sadistic old goat.

They laughed, waved good-bye, and left. Good riddance. From the sounds emanating from Yelena's cell, he guessed she was panicking about dying from Butterfly's Dust. He debated telling her about the White Fright, but they might escape before the withdrawal symptoms started. If she knew about the ruse, then she might refuse to take the White Fright anymore. He needed her to keep ingesting it until he could slowly taper the dose until she could safely stop. Otherwise, the withdrawal was brutal on the body.

"Yelena, settle down," he said. "Get some sleep; you'll need your strength for tonight."

"Oh yeah, everyone needs to be well rested to die," she snarked. Then after a few moments of silence, "I'll try."

While she slept, Valek planned. It didn't take long. He had few options and only if certain things happened. Otherwise, they were out of luck. He took his own advice and lay down on the dirty straw.

YELENA CRIED OUT, waking Valek. There was a solid thump then the sound of a large critter scurrying away.

"Nice nap?" he asked.

"I've had better. My sleeping companion snored," Yelena said.

Valek grunted in amusement.

"How long was I out?" she asked.

"It's hard to tell without the sun. I'm guessing it's close to sunset."

"Valek, I have a confess—" She grunted.

"What's the matter?"

"Stomach cramp from hell," she said, gasping. "Is this the start?"

"Yes. They begin slowly, but soon the convulsions will be continuous." And he wouldn't be able to help her.

She groaned. "Valek, talk to me. Tell me something to distract me."

"Like what?"

"I don't care. Anything."

Time to be honest. Past time, really. "Here's something you can take some comfort from—there's no poison called Butter-fly's Dust."

"What?" Her outcry was interrupted by retching sounds.

Valek pressed against his bars, wishing he could hold her and keep her hair from her face. When the sounds of her distress stopped, he explained, "You're going to want to die, wish you were already dead, but in the end, you'll be quite alive."

"Why tell me now?"

"The mind controls the body. If you believed that you were going to die, then you might have died from that conviction alone."

"Why wait until now to tell me?" she angrily demanded.

"A tactical decision."

There was a long pause. He understood and deserved her anger and should elaborate on why he waited, but he hoped her fury would fuel her recovery.

"What about the cramps?" she asked.

"Withdrawal symptoms."

"From what?"

"Your so-called antidote," Valek said. "It's an interesting concoction. I use it to make someone sick. As the potion wears off, it produces stomach cramps worthy of a day in bed. It's perfect for putting someone temporarily out of commission without killing them. If you continue to drink it, then the symptoms are forestalled until you stop."

"What's the name?"

"White Fright."

"What about Butterfly's Dust?" she asked.

"Doesn't exist. I made it up. It sounded good. I needed some threat to keep the food tasters from running away without using guards or locked doors."

"Does the Commander know it's a ruse?" she asked with panic in her voice.

"No. He believes you've been poisoned." Thank fate.

Yelena's sigh of relief turned into another retching session. Valek stood as close to her cell as possible as she screamed and endured the excruciating cramps. One of his agents compared it to childbirth, saying White Fright withdrawal was worse. Once again, he wished for magical powers. He'd do anything to stop her suffering. It would be far easier for Valek to experience the pain than to helplessly listen to his love writhe in agony. Perhaps this was his punishment for not telling Yelena sooner about the White Fright.

Sometime during that awful night, Brazell and Mogkan arrived. They stood by her bars and gloated, taking pleasure in her condition. Valek glared at them, thinking of multiple and creative ways he would kill each. They would suffer for days. He'd slowly leak the life from their bodies.

After they left, he lay on the floor and reached through the bars. "You're not alone, love. Hold my hand," he coaxed.

She grasped his fingers, clutching hard. He squeezed back and talked to her in soothing tones. Valek had no idea what he said, but eventually she relaxed and fell asleep. Keeping hold of her hand, he dozed off.

YELENA'S FINGERS TWITCHED, waking him.

Concerned that she was having another bout of cramps, Valek asked, "Yelena, are you alright?"

"I think so," she rasped.

He sagged with relief.

The metallic clank of a door being unlocked sounded.

"Play dead," Valek whispered, reluctantly releasing her hand. "Try to get them close to my cell."

She pulled her hand away and replaced it with her left one. Valek stood, brushing the straw and dirt from his clothes as the two guards entered the prison.

"Damn! The stench down here's worse than the latrine after a brew party," said the guard holding the lantern.

"You think she's dead?" his companion asked.

The one with the lantern swung it in an arc and then reached down to touch Yelena's hand. "Cold as snow-cat piss. Let's drag her out before she starts to rot. You think it smells bad now…" The lock snapped open, and he wrenched Yelena's cell door wide. It squealed.

Valek noted which pocket he tucked the keys into as his partner grabbed Yelena's ankles and dragged her out. Lantern guard took point, lighting the way to the exit. As soon as Yelena was no longer in the lantern light, she seized Valek's bars.

"Ugh. Hold up, she's stuck."

"On what?" the lantern guard asked.

"I don't know. Come back here with that bloody light."

She released her grip and hooked an arm inside his cell. *Well done, love.*

"Back off," the lantern guard warned Valek.

He stepped back until the guard's attention switched to his partner, who tugged at Yelena's elbow. At that moment, he moved. Reaching through the bars, he latched onto the opposite sides of the man's head and twisted, snapping his neck. The guard grunted and collapsed. The lantern extinguished as it fell to the ground.

"What the hell?" the other man swore.

The sound of Yelena being dragged away filled the darkness. He hadn't let go of her ankles.

Your turn, love. Remember your self-defense lessons.

Valek checked the dead man's pocket, pulling out the keys. Then he drew the lantern closer. The other guard's surprised yelp was followed by the unmistakable crunch of bone hitting a hard surface. With luck, Yelena had killed him. Good. Valek lit the lantern and unlocked his cell.

Yelena stared at the dead man in horror. Her wild hair, freed from her ever-present braid, had pieces of straw clinging to the black strands. Her uniform was stained with filth and dirt streaked her face. Beautiful.

He checked both guards, confiscating their weapons. They each had a dagger and a short sword. He kept the knives. Depending on how many guards had been assigned this shift, the next bit could be tricky.

"Wait here," Valek said to Yelena as he unlocked the door.

He yanked it open. Three men sat around a table playing cards. They paused mid-deal to gawk. Valek charged the closest person, knocking him off his chair and stabbing him in the heart on their way to the floor. He leapt to his feet as the other two men shouted, scrambled upright, and drew their weapons. Valek parried one thrust, dodged another before stepping in close and plunging his blade into the guard's neck.

The last guard pointed his sword's tip at Valek's gut and lunged. Twisting so the blade missed his torso, Valek punched the man in the face so hard the guard dropped his weapon. The satisfaction over the sound and feel of the impact of his knuckles on flesh ignited Valek's blood-lust. He threw a left hook followed by an uppercut to the guard's jaw and finished with a knife-hand to his throat. Rendered unconscious, the guard toppled to the floor.

Giving Yelena the all-clear signal, Valek strode to the door to the manor house while she headed straight for her backpack lying on a table. He tried different keys on the ring, but none of them worked. "Damn."

"What?" Yelena asked.

"The captain has the only key to this door. He will open it when it's time to change the guards."

"Try these." She handed Valek a set of lock picks from her pack.

Nice. He grinned and set to work. Dungeon locks tended to be complex and much harder to pop. Normally he used a different type of pick, but these would work. It would just take more time.

As he eased the various pins up, Yelena headed to the wash barrel and splashed water. No surprise she wished to wash off the grime from her hands and face. Although the continued sloshing sounded as if she'd jumped into the barrel. At one point, she handed him a glass of water. Suddenly thirsty, he downed it in a few swallows.

Eventually, the tumbler turned, pulling the bolt from the jam. He eased open the door and peered into the hallway. "Perfect. No guards." He swung it wide. "Let's go." Taking Yelena's hand and a lantern, Valek returned to the dungeon. He also left that door ajar.

"Are you insane?" Yelena whispered. She dragged her feet. "Freedom's that way." She pointed to the guard's room.

He unlocked the last cell on the right and ushered her inside. "Trust me. This is the perfect hiding spot. The mess we left will soon be discovered; the open doors proof we've fled. Search parties will be sent out. When all the soldiers have left the manor, we'll make our move. Until then, we lay low."

Valek tried to make them a comfortable bed with the straw. He built it in the far-right corner. Thank fate the cells were divided by stone walls instead of bars. A guard would have to travel all the way to the end to spot them. He extinguished and hid the lantern, then pulled Yelena to lie beside him.

Shivering and soaking wet, she kept her back to him. He understood her need to wash the filth from her body, but now he also had to keep her warm so she didn't get sick. He wouldn't mind the physical contact at all, but he was uncertain of her reaction. He covered them with some extra straw for warmth and concealment, then wrapped an arm around Yelena, pulling her close to him.

She stiffened and he prepared to let her go. But she relaxed into him, and he silently rejoiced. Their shared warmth spread to his heart. Valek savored every moment that she lay in his arms, knowing it'd probably never happen again. She trusted him enough to confide in him, but that didn't mean she trusted him with her heart.

Yelena jerked when the guards discovered the open doors. They shouted and cursed and blamed each other. It would have been amusing if they'd been in a more secure location. The possibility of being discovered kept them both tense.

Eventually Brazell and Mogkan arrived. They barked orders for search parties to be organized and sent out right away, guessing the fugitives had an hour head start.

"Valek's probably retreating west to well-known territory," Brazell said.

"South *is* the logical choice," Mogkan argued. "We have the Commander; there's nothing they can do. They're running for their lives, not toward some strategic position. I'll take a horse and scan the forest with my magic."

Offended, he whispered in Yelena's ear, "They actually think I would abandon the Commander. They have no concept of loyalty." At least, it appeared they'd fallen for his ruse. The dungeon soon emptied of people, and they'd left the doors open, allowing a faint light into their cell.

Yelena grew restless after a couple hours. "Can we go now?" she asked.

"Not yet. I believe it's still daylight. We'll wait until dark." Otherwise, they'd be spotted right away.

"How did you become involved with the Commander?" she asked.

He hesitated. It was a long, complex story that he'd only shared with Ambrose. Yet, she'd trusted him with her history, it was only fair for him to reciprocate. "My family lived in Icefaren Province before it was renamed MD–1. A particularly harsh winter collapsed the building that housed my father's leather business, ruining all of his equipment. He needed to replace his equipment to stay in business, but the soldiers who came to our house to collect the tax money wouldn't listen to reason." His body tightened around her. Why had he chosen to start his story at that point in his life? Why not when he'd met the Commander?

Too late now. "I was just a skinny little kid at the time, but I had three older brothers. They were about Ari's size and had his strength. When my father told the soldiers that if he paid the full tax amount, he wouldn't have enough money left to feed his family…" Valek paused as the memory dug its icy claws deep into his heart. "They killed my brothers. They laughed and said, 'Problem solved. Now you have three less mouths to feed.'" The claws pulled and tugged, trying to rend his heart into pieces. His muscles trembled at the unexpected strength of his emotions.

"Naturally, I wanted revenge, but not on the soldiers. They were only messengers. I wanted the King. The man who had allowed his soldiers to murder my brothers in his name. So, I learned how to fight, and I studied the assassin's art until I was unbeatable. I traveled around, using my new skills to earn money. The royal upper class was so corrupt they paid me to kill each other.

"Then I was commissioned to kill a young man named

Ambrose, whose speeches called for rebellion and made the royals nervous. He'd become popular, gathering large crowds. People started to resist the King's doctrines. Then Ambrose disappeared, hiding his growing army and employing covert operations against the monarchy.

"My payment to find and kill Ambrose was significant. I ambushed him, expecting to have my knife in his heart before he could draw breath to cry out. But he blocked the blow, and I found myself fighting for my life, and losing." And he still couldn't beat Ambrose.

"Instead of killing me, though, Ambrose carved a C on my chest with my own knife. The same weapon, by the way, that I later used to kill the King." The revenge on the King had been a highlight of his life. "Then Ambrose declared himself my Commander and announced that I now worked for him and no one else. I agreed, and I promised him that if he got me close enough to kill the King, I would be loyal to him forever." And he planned to keep his oath and figure out a way to save Ambrose from Brazell and Mogkan.

"My first assignment was to kill the person who had paid me to assassinate Ambrose. Throughout these years, I've watched him achieve his goals with a single-minded determination and without excess violence and pain. He hasn't been corrupted by power or greed. He's consistent and loyal to his people. And there's been no one in this world that I care for more. Until now."

The words had just tumbled from his mouth unchecked. But the truth of that statement hit Valek like a sword thrust to his heart. It took all his courage to continue. "Yelena, you've driven me crazy. You've caused me considerable trouble and I've contemplated ending your life twice since I've known you." At least.

"But you've slipped under my skin, invaded my blood and

seized my heart." He braced for her rejection, for her horror, for her to pull away and tell him to go to hell.

"That sounds more like a poison than a person," she said instead. Her voice shook.

"Exactly," Valek said. "You have poisoned me." And only she held the antidote. No one else would ever be enough.

Desperately needing to see her expression, Valek rolled her over. She stared at him in wonder with lips parted. No longer having the strength to resist, he kissed her. Prepared to pull away the second she protested, Valek marveled when she wrapped her arms around his neck and kissed him back with equal passion.

Joy and desire burned through him, but he let Yelena set the pace, set the limits. He'd hoped for a kiss and received so much more. She gave him her trust, her soul, and her body. He would love and cherish her forever.

CHAPTER 22

*D*espite the fact they were hiding in a dank dungeon cell, Valek would have been content to remain there with Yelena in his arms. But the Commander was under Brazell and Mogkan's spell and Valek needed to rescue him.

"Let's go." He stood and pulled Yelena to her feet.

"Where?" she asked.

"The Commander's room, so we can take him back to the castle with us." Valek ran his fingers through his hair, dislodging straw. Then he brushed the dirt from his sneak suit.

"Won't work."

"Why not?"

"As soon as you touch him, Mogkan will know." She explained how the Criollo helped Mogkan become magically linked to the Commander. The dessert relaxed a person's mental defenses, opening their minds to magical influences. For someone with a strong personality like the Commander, Criollo helped Mogkan gain control of his mind.

"How do we break the bond?" Valek asked.

She gazed at him with a serious expression and took a deep

breath. Valek braced for…he wasn't sure, but it wasn't going to be good.

"There are two ways to break the bond," she said. "Kill Mogkan or block his power supply. Since we found the source of his increased magic—those poor people—that would probably be the best way. I learned all this from Fourth Magician Irys Jewelrose. She's nearby and we talked. It's how I knew to search for either the diamonds or the wagon wheel design."

Yelena held up a hand, stopping the thousand questions bubbling up his throat. "Irys came after me at the Fire Festival because she sensed my uncontrolled magic. She planned to assassinate me, but when I played the fugitive, it gave her a chance to talk to me instead of killing me. I promised to find a way to escape to Sitia before I flamed out and wrecked the blanket of power."

She gave Valek a wry smile. "When she came to the castle last week, she told me I'd stabilized my magic, and she taught me how to block my mental defenses from other magicians. She offered to help me escape, but I…didn't want to leave Ixia until we figured out what was wrong with the Commander and stopped Mogkan and Brazell. Irys said she'd help us." Yelena finished her explanation. She chewed on her knuckle while she waited for his response.

Valek's thoughts spun. He was impressed Yelena had kept her secret about her magic from him even though they shared an apartment. Irys's interest in Yelena now made sense and answered all the questions he had about their prior encounters. Happy Yelena wasn't a spy warred with a deep sadness. If she lived through the Commander's rescue, she couldn't remain in Ixia. They'd be parted unless Valek found a way to convince the Commander to allow her to stay. But that was a problem to solve later.

Right now, they needed to break Mogkan's hold on the Commander. A master magician was willing to help them. Too bad she was the same woman who promised to stay out of Ixia.

"Do you trust her?" he asked.

"Yes."

"Is there anything else you haven't told me?" He waited for more bad news.

"I love you."

Valek wrapped her in his arms as tears welled. Despite the danger waiting for them, today had been a true gift. "My love has been yours since the fire festival. If those goons had killed you, I knew then that I would never be the same. I didn't want or expect this. But I couldn't resist you."

She pressed against him, and he savored the moment. Unfortunately, time was critical.

He took her hand. "Let's go."

In the guardroom, they found MD-5 uniforms to wear. Valek had correctly calculated the time. Darkness filled the windows, and the manor house was quiet. Once outside, he headed to the barracks to grab his bag of tricks. He'd need every one.

A single lantern cast a weak glow on the empty beds. The scattered debris on the floor indicated the soldiers had left in a hurry. Good. He hoped everyone was out searching for him and Yelena.

Just as he reached his bunk, two figures jumped from the shadows. They shouted with anger and brandished their swords at Valek. He froze in confusion as he recognized Ari and Janco. Were they now under Mogkan's influence as well?

"Stop!" Yelena yelled.

Ari turned and smiled at her. The captains relaxed and sheathed their swords.

"We thought Valek had escaped without you," Ari said, giving her a big hug.

Jealousy flared until he realized he was being ridiculous.

"Aren't you supposed to be with a search party?" He pulled his black bag from under his bunk. Removing his black coverall, that had plenty of pockets and weapons stashed inside, he changed.

"We're too sick." Janco smirked.

"What?" Yelena asked.

"The charges against you were obviously fabricated, so we refused to take part in the hunt," Janco said.

"That's insubordination." Valek extracted a long knife and some darts from his bag.

"That was the point. What's a fellow have to do around here in order to get arrested and thrown in the dungeon?" Janco asked.

Valek paused as the significance of Janco's comment sunk in. That Ari and Janco were willing to be court martialed for them spoke volumes about their loyalty and friendship. Another gift.

"Which direction did the search parties go?" Valek asked, placing more weapons in his various pockets before strapping his sword and knife onto his belt.

"Mainly south and east, although a few small groups were sent west and north," Ari replied.

"Dogs?"

"Yes."

"And the manor?"

"Minimal coverage."

"Good. You're with us," Valek ordered them both.

They snapped to attention. "Yes, sir."

"Prep for covert ops but keep the swords. You're going to need them." Valek finished stashing his weapons as Ari and Janco went to their bunk.

"Wait," Yelena said. "I don't want them getting into trouble."

Valek squeezed her shoulder to reassure her. "We need their help." And he'd like a dozen of his agents for back up as well.

But Hildred and Inrick had returned to the castle and the two others had been influenced by Criollo.

"You're going to need more than that," a woman's voice said from a shadow.

He spun and drew his sword at the same time Ari and Janco pulled their weapons. Irys Jewelrose stepped into the light and Valek relaxed, but Ari and Janco brandished their swords.

"At ease," Valek ordered.

"She's a friend. She's here to help." Yelena said when they glanced at her for confirmation.

So much for being in charge.

"We discovered Mogkan's extra power source," Yelena told Irys.

"What is it?"

Yelena described finding the mindless magicians chained to the floor in a wagon wheel design. Irys's calm exterior cracked for a moment as she stared at Yelena in horror. Even the two hardened soldiers looked sick to their stomachs.

"What's this all about?" Ari finally asked.

"I'll explain it later. Right now—" Yelena stopped. "I want you to protect Irys with everything you have. It's very important."

"Yes, sir," Ari and Janco said.

Yelena stared at her friends in shock. No doubt surprised by their acknowledging her as their leader.

Her tone had been confident and commanding. Valek met her gaze. "You have a strategy?"

"Yes."

"Tell us."

VALEK AND YELENA navigated the silent halls of Brazell's manor house, heading for the Commander's guest suite. No guards stood by his door. Normally, Valek would have been outraged to find the Commander unprotected. However, in this case, it worked in their favor. They waited a few minutes longer, letting Ari, Janco, and the magician get into position. Valek had approved of Yelena's strategy. Her quick thinking was an asset to their team. And even though she trembled with fear and was on the edge of hyperventilating, she hadn't run away. Not from him. Not from the danger.

Once enough time had passed, he picked the lock and they entered. After securing the door behind them, he found a lantern and lit it. Half expecting the Commander to ambush him or yell at him for disturbing his sleep, Valek crossed to the oversized four-poster bed. Strong magic surrounded it like a giant bubble.

His heart squeezed painfully in his chest. The most powerful man in Ixia lay atop the bed still in his uniform. Wide-eyed, the Commander stared vacantly at the ceiling. The intelligence and keen cunning that had blazed from his gaze since Valek ambushed him in that dark alley was gone.

Yelena sat on the edge of the bed and took the Commander's hand. That was Valek's cue to prepare for unwelcome guests. According to Irys, Mogkan would sense Yelena's touch and come running. Valek stood against the wall next to the entrance with his sword in hand.

As expected, the rasp of a metal key unlocked the door. A pause. Then it flew open as four armed guards rushed into the suite. Valek pounced on the closest man, stabbing him in the back. The other three turned and attacked him.

He blocked one blade, dodged another, parried a third. Sidestepping, ducking, and swinging his sword, Valek fought with an intense focus. Yet he was vaguely aware of Mogkan entering the room and heading directly to Yelena. She planned to protect the Commander's mind from Mogkan with a mental shield. Since magic was still brand new to her, Valek didn't have much time to dispatch his opponents and kill Mogkan.

"A brick igloo," Mogkan said. "How nice. Come on, Yelena, give me some credit. A stone fortress or a steel wall would have been more of a challenge."

Valek increased the pace of his attack. He'd claimed he could handle four, but the fact he hadn't eaten in over twenty-four hours became apparent as the fight lengthened.

"Nice trick," Mogkan said. "Friends of yours? They're in Reyad's hallway, but unless they can fight their way through ten men, they won't make it to my children."

Oh no. If Ari, Janco, and Irys couldn't reach Mogkan's power source, then it was up to Valek and Yelena to kill the magician.

Valek poured every bit of energy into a flurry of strikes. He cut the femoral artery of one man and stabbed another in the stomach.

Just as he killed the last man, Mogkan shouted, "Stop or she dies."

Yelena had dropped the Commander's hand and stood next to the bed. Valek froze even though three more guards appeared with Brazell right behind them. Valek cursed under his breath as they disarmed him and forced him to his knees. They ordered him to put his hands on his head. Smart. That would make it harder for him to get to his darts.

"Go ahead, General. Kill her," Mogkan said, stepping back to let Brazell pass. "I should have let you slit her throat the first day she arrived."

Valek would *not* watch that sadistic old goat harm Yelena. He'd die first.

"Why listen to Mogkan?" Yelena asked Brazell. "He's not to be trusted."

"What do you mean?" Brazell demanded. He gripped his sword as he glanced between them.

Mogkan laughed. "She's only trying to delay the inevitable."

"Like when you tried to delay the Sitian treaty negotiations by poisoning the cognac? Or were you aiming to stop the delegation altogether?" she asked Mogkan.

Mogkan's shocked expression proved his guilt. Yelena had been correct that he'd hired Star. Next time, Valek wouldn't be so quick to dismiss her theories. He silently encouraged her to keep driving that wedge between them as he tensed for action.

"That doesn't make sense," Brazell said.

"Mogkan wants to avoid contact with the southerners. They would know about—" The bubble of magic swelled. Yelena clawed at her neck, unable to breathe.

Valek judged the distance between him and Mogkan.

Brazell turned on Mogkan. "What have you been up to?"

"We don't need a treaty with Sitia. We were getting our supplies without any problems. But you wouldn't listen to me. You had to be greedy. After establishing a trade treaty, it would only be a matter of time before we'd have southerners crossing the border, sniffing around, finding us." Mogkan spat the words out. "Now, do you want to kill her or should I?"

They stared at each other. Valek wondered who would back down. Then the magic in the room suddenly disappeared.

Mogkan staggered. "My children!" He roared. "Even without them, I still have more power than you!"

Yelena flew through the air and slammed into the wall. Valek dove, yanking one of his many hidden knives. He rolled and slashed at the nearest guard's Achilles tendon. Then leapt to his feet to engage the others.

At one point during the fight, Mogkan sailed through the room and hit the opposite wall with a satisfying thud. Valek had only a second to celebrate before needing to duck and parry. When Mogkan ran from the room, Valek redoubled his attack. That demon would not escape.

From the corner of his eye, Valek noticed Yelena and Brazell fighting on the Commander's bed, but there was nothing he could do. He had his hands full with the guards, who proved to be more skilled than the last three. Valek turned his full attention to ending his own fight.

"What do you think you're doing? You're a skinny nothing. I'll gut you in two moves," Brazell threatened.

Valek spared a quick glance. Yelena fought off Brazell's sword with one of the bedposts. They were no longer on the bed, but she was retreating from him and would soon hit the wall. With a surge of renewed energy, Valek lunged and stabbed, aiming for necks and thighs.

"You're dead," Brazell cried as Valek killed his last opponent.

He spun just in time to see Brazell's sword swing toward Yelena's neck. Valek scrambled over the bodies littering the floor. The room stretched toward infinity. Yelena deflected the blade down. It cut across her torso, leaving a trail of blood. Brazell relaxed and Yelena raised her weapon.

The world paused.

Then she struck that sadistic old goat across the temple with one mighty blow. They both tumbled to the floor.

Valek reached her a second later. She panted for breath, but the cut on her torso didn't look too deep. He bent over her.

"Find Mogkan." She shooed him away.

Right. He scooped up his sword as he dashed from the room. Mogkan was probably on his way to his power source. Valek raced through the corridors. Halfway to the east wing, Valek caught up to the magician.

Mogkan spun and drew his sword. "I take it Brazell is dead."

"Does it matter?"

He shrugged. "Not really. He was a means to an end. I'm sure I'll find another way."

"No, you won't. This stops now."

"I agree. Shall we?" Mogkan slid his feet into the en garde position. He held his rapier in his left hand.

Valek's arm muscles protested when he assumed a fighting

position and he wished he'd picked a lighter sword. Mogkan attacked first, lunging right at Valek's stomach. Valek parried and riposted. Then they exchanged a fast series of strikes and blocks. The swords rang with each encounter.

It didn't take long for Valek to assess Mogkan's fighting style. His technique was clean and precise with no wasted motions. Mogkan didn't block too wide or give Valek any openings. A skilled fighter, he stayed on the offensive with quick, efficient strikes. And he hadn't just fought seven opponents.

The lack of food and little sleep caught up to Valek, but he remained confident in his own abilities until Mogkan added magic to his attacks. The air thickened and clung, dragging at Valek's limbs.

"That won't work on me," Valek said, hoping Mogkan would stop.

"No. But it'll slow you down."

Valek cursed. The fight turned into one long slog of keeping Mogkan's sword from skewering him. At one point, Valek became aware of Yelena's presence. It gave him a surge of energy, which lasted all of six seconds.

Mogkan grinned and increased his speed, feinting left and lunging. The tip of his rapier slashed into Valek's arm, cutting deep into his skin, and forcing Valek to drop his sword.

"What an incredible day!" Mogkan exclaimed. "I get to kill the famous Valek and the infamous Yelena at the same time."

Yelena triggered her switchblade. Mogkan laughed, but the action drew his attention away from Valek. He palmed a couple darts as Mogkan's magic moved to Yelena. Her weapon flew from her hand.

Her face creased in panic, but then it smoothed. She pointed a finger at Mogkan and he froze. His sword clattered to the ground. Valek would have whooped with joy if he had the strength.

"You rat-spawned daughter of a demon!" Mogkan cursed at Yelena. Too bad she hadn't paralyzed his vocal cords as well.

"You're a blight on this earth. An incarnation of hell. You're just like the rest of them. The Zaltana bloodline should be burned out, erased, exterminated."

Valek tuned him out as he picked up Yelena's switchblade. Mogkan cursed and yelled in panic as he approached. Aiming at the magician's throat, Valek thought it fitting that her blade would deliver the killing blow. A quick death because Valek didn't have the energy to prolong Mogkan's agony even though he deserved it. Mogkan shrieked when the knife sliced through his carotid artery. Blood poured, staining the man's tunic. Finally silent, Mogkan's body toppled to the ground.

Good riddance.

Valek handed Yelena her knife. She'd saved his life. Bowing, he said, "My love, for you."

She solemnly took the knife. Then she gasped. "Janco!"

CHAPTER 23

*Y*elena grabbed his arm and pulled him down the
hallway. "What's wrong with Janco?" he asked.

"He's hurt. We need to get the medic," she
panted.

Valek didn't think it was possible, but he found a modicum
of energy. They roused the sleeping medic, who resisted until
Valek brandished his knife, forcing the man to grab his bag and
follow them to Reyad's wing.

The hallway in the east wing resembled a battlefield. Blood
splattered the walls and pooled on the ground. Dead soldiers
slumped on the floor along with a number of severed limbs. It
was a quick and brutal way to neutralize an opponent. After all,
they couldn't attack you without arms. Considering Ari and
Janco had been outnumbered, Valek approved.

The medic tried to stop at the first fallen man, but Valek
yanked him to his feet. The man was clearly dead, and they
didn't have time. They wove through the carnage and entered
the room with the mindless people.

Janco lay on his side with his head in Ari's lap. Good thing
the man was unconscious, as a sword's tip protruded from his

back. Looking grim with blood splashed on his face, Ari nodded at Valek. Irys sat in the middle of the wheel. Sweat beaded her brow and she gazed into the distance. He'd thank her for saving their lives later.

The medic tutted over Janco and declared there was nothing he could do for him here. Valek helped Ari pick Janco up. The big man carried his partner as they raced to the infirmary. He gently set him on an examination table as the medic gathered a bunch of supplies.

"If the sword has pierced any of his internal organs or if there is internal bleeding, he will die," the medic said.

Valek and Ari helped the medic remove the sword. Blood gushed from the wounds. The medic worked fast, cleaning and sealing them. Once he was finished bandaging Janco's torso, they carried him to a clean bed. Now they just had to wait.

The medic tended to Yelena's laceration and, when done, she immediately went to sit by Janco's bedside. Ari refused all medical attention as he claimed the other seat next to his partner. They planned to keep vigil until he woke.

When it was Valek's turn for care, he stared at the S-shaped slash along his right forearm. It throbbed but the bleeding had stopped. A minor injury considering how close he'd come to dying. How close they'd all come, and Janco's life still hung in the balance.

Exhaustion settled deep into his bones, but Valek couldn't rest. Not until he ensured the Commander's safety. Returning to the guest suite, Valek checked on him. No change in his demeanor. He'd have to ask Irys how long it would take for the magic to wear off.

Brazell remained sprawled unconscious on the floor. He'd been cuffed to the heavy bed. Yelena had resisted killing the brute. *Well done, love.* Valek considered ending the man's life, but the resulting political uproar would be a mess. Instead, he grabbed a second pair of cuffs and rearranged the general's limbs so he was more secure. Bonus that being hogtied resulted in killer cramps.

Then Valek woke up the Commander's advisers. At first, they stared at him blankly and he wondered if he should toss some cold water on their faces. However, without Mogkan's magic, and since they only recently started consuming Criollo, they regained their senses rather quick.

He explained the situation. Because this was an emergency, he outranked them all. "Collect all the Criollo you can find in the manor. Pile it in the soldiers' fire pit and burn it," he ordered Tocara and Chelle. "Guard the Commander's suite," he told Dema and Felo. "Don't let anyone in or out. Unless it's the Commander."

They hurried to carry out his orders while he searched for Brazell's other advisers. He found one. An older man with bushy gray hair that was wild and tousled from sleep.

"The general hasn't sought my advice in years," said Adviser Kirwin. "Not since Mogkan arrived."

"Where are his other advisers?"

"Reassigned. Retired. Relocated. I'm the only one left from before and that's only because I handle the budget and balance the books. The general and Mogkan couldn't be bothered."

"Did you know he planned to take control of Ixia?" Valek watched his expression closely.

"No. I wasn't privy to his plans. Although, I'm not surprised. That man was always scheming for more. More power. More wealth. More land. More control."

"He's currently under arrest for a long list of crimes."

"And Adviser Mogkan?"

"Dead."

"Oh dear."

"I need your help. The search parties will be returning soon, and I need you to run interference."

"Interference?"

"They are searching for me and the Commander's food taster. They will seek out the general and Mogkan when they return. Until I have our soldiers in position, they could decide to attack us and free the general. I also need you to send all the guards working inside the manor to the barracks."

"Oh dear. Isn't there someone else who could run...interference?"

"You're the highest authority in MD-5. I outrank you, but the soldiers believe I'm a fugitive."

"What about the Commander, surely—"

"He's indisposed at the moment."

"Oh dear."

"Do you have some loyal people to help you?" Valek asked gently.

"I..." The man straightened and smoothed his hair. "Yes. Some of the ex-advisers are still working in the manor. I'm sure they'll be happy to aid us."

"Good."

While Kirwin gathered his supporters, Valek checked on the Commander. No change. Brazell, though, was awake and started hollering as soon as he spotted Valek. He ignored him and talked with Dema.

"He's been yelling off and on for the last fifteen minutes," she said. "Threatened us with just about everything. It's nice that I no longer have the compulsion to listen to him. Do you think the Commander will recover?"

"He's a strong-willed man. I'm sure of it," Valek said in a confident tone. Was he trying to convince Dema or himself?

Valek then visited Janco—no change—before joining Kirwin and three other ex-advisers outside the manor. It was almost dawn. The search parties would be back soon to report. The units of soldiers returned at different times throughout the morning. Kirwin explained that Brazell had been arrested and Valek was no longer court martialed. Many of Brazell's soldiers appeared suspicious, but none forced the issue. Not yet.

Once the Commander's elite guard returned, Valek could breathe easier. They cheered when they spotted him. Nice to know they believed him to be innocent.

Despite being on duty for twelve hours straight, they snapped to attention, ready for action. He assigned half of them to guard the manor house, including the Commander's suite. The rest were divided up. He sent four soldiers to escort General Brazell to the dungeon and watch him. A couple were ordered to help Tocara and Chelle collect Criollo. Valek assembled a team to take all the dead bodies and Mogkan to the morgue. And the rest were assigned to help Irys free the mindless victims and find them more comfortable quarters.

By the time everything had been sorted, it was mid-afternoon. He stopped in the infirmary to see Janco. No change. Valek checked on the Commander. No change.

Beyond exhausted, and well into the realm of dead tired, Valek stumbled into one of the bedrooms in the guest wing. With his vision turning to snow and a loud buzzing in his ears, he just managed to collapse into bed before passing out.

HE WOKE...SOMETIME later. The sun shone through the windows, indicating early afternoon. He'd slept either a day or two. Moving was a massive mistake as every single muscle in his body not only ached with pain but had stiffened to immobility. Well, not quite that bad, but close. His head pounded and he thought someone had gagged him until he realized the hard dry lump wedged in his mouth was his own tongue.

Thank fate someone had left a pitcher of water and food on the night table. The fact he hadn't woken when they'd entered meant he'd gone well beyond his physical limits. It would take him a day or so to recover. Not that he'd let anyone know.

Valek drained the pitcher and ate all the food. Groaning, he rolled off the bed and stood on shaky legs. Perhaps a few days was being overly optimistic.

Once he washed up, Valek went straight to the Commander's room. Dema sat in a chair next to his bed reading aloud from a book, but she stood when he entered. Unfortunately, the Commander continued to stare blankly at the ceiling.

"We decided that one of his advisers will stay here at all times," Dema explained. She pointed to a glass of water and bowl of soup on the table. "We're also trying to get him to swallow some nourishment."

"Good idea. Do I have you to thank for supplying me with nourishment as well?"

"Yes. No offense, but you looked like death warmed over."

"None taken." That was exactly how he felt. "How long was I out?"

"Almost a day."

"What's been going on?"

"We've taken temporary control of the manor until the Commander wakes."

"Any problems with Brazell's staff or soldiers?"

"No, but Adviser Chelle has turned into quite the tyrant." She laughed. "In a good way."

"Is the master magician still here?"

"Yes, she's been in a few times to check on the Commander. She tried to wake him but was unsuccessful."

His heart sank at the bad news. "Is there a plan in place in case the Commander…" Valek couldn't even say the word.

"Two messengers were dispatched to MD-4 and MD-6 with requests for Generals Tesso and Hazal to travel to MD-5 right away."

"Good." It appeared the advisers had things well in hand.

Valek went to the infirmary. Although he looked pale and wan, Janco was awake and talking to Ari. Thank fate.

"Glad to see you pulled through," Valek said.

"That makes two of us. Ari here is still on the fence," Janco joked, but then he sobered. "I'm sorry, sir."

"For what?"

"For not doing my job."

Valek exchanged a glance with Ari. Was Janco serious?

Ari nodded. "He thinks getting almost killed was a failure."

"Isn't it?"

"No," Valek said with confidence. "It's a win. You did your job, Captain. You protected Irys with your life. If she was unsuccessful in stealing Mogkan's magic, we'd all be dead."

"Oh." Janco appeared thoughtful. "Well, when you put it like that…"

"So you believe *him*, but you didn't believe *me*?" Ari demanded.

Before they could launch into an argument, Valek asked where Yelena had gone.

"Sleeping," Ari said. "She was with Janco all night."

"I told her to go to bed, but she refused," Janco protested.

"So you could pester the nurses? I don't think so." Ari crossed his arms.

Valek wanted to see her, but he wouldn't disturb her. Instead, he headed to the prison. He had a general to interrogate. It'd be the highlight of his day.

THE FAMILIAR RANCID stench hit Valek as soon as he entered the dungeon. Funny how it no longer seemed so vile. Brazell jumped to his feet and started demanding to be let go. Valek ignored him. Instead, he enjoyed the view of the man behind bars. A man who would live the rest of his days inside a cell.

How many days would depend on the Commander. If he... No. Ambrose would pull through. And if not... Valek would take great pleasure in pulling the lever to hang the old goat.

When Brazell finally stopped posturing, Valek said in his flat killer's tone, "Your magician is dead. Your plan has failed. You now have only two choices. Cooperate. Or be forced to cooperate. What will it be?"

The general opened his mouth then pressed his lips together. Valek waited.

Finally, he said, "It wasn't my plan. It was Mogkan's."

Ah. He was going to blame it all on the dead guy. Not a surprise. "Go on."

"Mogkan had this grand scheme. He arrived with a couple dozen children, claiming they all had magical potential. He promised me I'd be the next Commander of Ixia if I gave him a place to stay. I allowed him to work with my son. They were training the children to become magicians and, I don't know, augment Mogkan's power somehow. Not all of them developed magic. Some were failures, like that murdering bitch."

Valek punched him through the bars, striking his jaw. Brazell rocked back and swore.

"She's an Ixian *hero*," Valek said. "Your sadistic bastard of a son deserved to die. It's a good thing I didn't know what he'd been doing, or I would have cut him into tiny pieces and fed him to your dogs. Call her a bitch again and I'll use my knife instead of my fist and I'll aim lower. Now tell me about Criollo."

"Mogkan brought it with him, but he waited to build the factory until he was powerful enough to reach the Commander's mind from here. He started manufacturing it last year. It was all him. He did everything. I just financed it."

Yeah, right. "Harboring and aiding a magician in Ixia is a crime."

"A stupid law that I intend to revoke when I'm Commander."

"When?" Valek was incredulous.

"Commander Ambrose is not going to recover. I'm his successor and you've disobeyed orders. Once the other generals arrive, they'll agree with me."

He laughed. "You're more deluded than I thought. If the Commander fails to wake and the envelopes are opened, the deciphered puzzle will reveal General Franis as the next Commander."

"You switched them, that's treason!"

"And you're failing to get the point. Which is, that you won't be drawing breath at that time. There's plenty of evidence of your scheme and you'll be sentenced to death. Something I'm looking forward to."

"Not my scheme. Mogkan's! He even planned to take over Sitia."

"If that's how you justify torturing and chaining children under your care, go right ahead. It won't change the facts. You'd better start hoping the Commander revives or I'll be using those lovely gallows you built just for me."

VALEK FOUND Irys with the younger children of the orphanage. They'd been too young for Brazell's experiments. She sat with one of the girls in the playroom.

"Can I interrupt you?" Valek asked.

"Of course. I've been wanting to talk to you," Irys said. Then to the girl, "May, I'll be back. I want to hear the rest of your story."

May looked at Valek and then glanced away. "Okay."

They found a quiet corner.

"I know what you want to hear," Irys said. "But I don't know when the Commander will wake. Or if he'll wake."

"Is he similar to those others you can't rouse? Mindless?"

"No. Their minds have been completely scrubbed clean. Kangom—"

"Kangom?"

"That's his Sitian name. Mogkan used his magic to erase their consciousness or souls—what makes them, them. The Commander has retreated to a white place. He's still there, but I can't reach him. I've tried."

"Can you try again?"

"Of course. But he might not want to return."

"No. Ixia is too important to him."

"It's also a ton of work. Add in the stress of being on guard all the time, dodging assassination attempts and outwitting the various schemers, his white place might be peaceful in comparison."

"I still can't accept that."

"Regardless of why he's there, you need to prepare just in case he doesn't come back."

Valek wished he could kill Mogkan again. "Why did Mogkan leave Sitia?" *And become our problem.*

"He always wanted more power. His magic was limited, which caused him much frustration. Mogkan experimented with diamonds to enhance his abilities, but they're expensive and you need a ton. He then discovered magicians could share power as long as both parties are willing. One can boost another's power for a short period of time. You can't steal magic from another magician—they would stop you. However, you can easily steal magic from a very young magician who doesn't have control yet, which is why Mogkan targeted children." Irys's scowl was impressively fierce. "He operated a kidnapping ring in Sitia, taking children from families who had strong magic in their bloodlines. It's a gamble as not all children of magicians will develop the ability to use magic when they reach puberty."

Outraged for all those families, Valek asked, "And you didn't notice when these children went missing?"

"He spaced it out over enough years and different clans that we didn't put it together until much later. By then, he had disappeared. Considering the Commander's views of magicians, no one suspected he was hiding in Ixia." She sighed. "He certainly was patient. This scheme of his has been a work in progress for the last fifteen years."

And Yelena had been caught up in it, but she'd resisted the mind scrubbing. "What would have happened to Yelena if she hadn't killed Reyad?"

Irys's fingers twitched as if she'd like to strangle someone. "When their physical torture sessions didn't work to wipe her mind, they claimed she was a failure."

"Did Yelena tell you this?" It had taken Valek three seasons to gain her trust.

"No. When I gave Yelena the magical power to stop Mogkan, I rifled through his memories before he died." She shuddered. "His methods were truly horrendous. Her rape was a form of mental torture to beat down her resistance. To convince her she was useless, and to make her want to retreat. It was a last-ditch effort to grab her power. If that didn't work, they would have had to kill her, because her uncontrolled magic would have eventually alerted the master magicians in Sitia. And, well..." She spread her arms. "Here I am, snooping around and causing trouble for Mogkan."

"And saving our lives. Thank you."

"I'm very happy you killed Mogkan. Let's call it even."

"On that note, what did you want to talk to me about?" Valek asked.

"Mmmm, maybe I was too hasty in calling it even." She smiled. "I wanted to ask you about the remaining children. I'd like permission to take them back to Sitia and find their families."

"That's an easy yes."

"Including Yelena." She held up her hand. "She's at a

dangerous point right now. She has control of her magic so she's not going to flame out, but she's still at risk for predators like Mogkan. She needs to come to Sitia and learn about her magic at the Magician's Keep."

Deep down he'd known she had to leave, but hearing it aloud sent a spike of pain right through him. "I won't stop her."

"I know, but she'll want you to come with her."

"How do you know that?" he demanded.

"I've formed a student-mentor bond with Yelena. I can't eavesdrop on her private thoughts because she has learned to shield them, so I only know what she's willing to share. Which is that she cares for you very much and it's a mutual feeling. If you're in Sitia with her, you'll not only put her in danger, but you could distract her from what she needs to learn."

In other words, don't even think about coming to Sitia to visit her. Frowning, he asked, "How long?" He hadn't bothered to keep the rough growl from his voice.

"A year at most."

Although it hit him like a slap, he knew he could wait another year. After all, he'd been waiting for her for the last thirty-three years. And she was worth every second.

IT HAD BEEN four days since Valek killed Mogkan and stopped his magic. They had halted production at the Criollo factory and destroyed all the Criollo they could find. Yet the Commander still hadn't woken.

Valek sat at Brazell's desk, trying to sort through the mess. The generals were due to arrive in a few days and would need a report. Adviser Kirwin offered to provide records of the money spent on Brazell and Mogkan's scheme.

A knock on the door was a welcome interruption. Dema burst in without waiting for a response.

"The Commander's awake!!" She danced around his desk.

It seemed too good to be true. "What happened?"

"Yelena wanted to try to wake him, so Irys brought her to his room. And it worked!"

Marveling, Valek knew he shouldn't be surprised that Yelena pulled off another heroic feat. He and Dema raced to the Commander's guest suite, but the man had already kicked everyone out and Valek was informed that he and Yelena would need to report that evening.

THE COMMANDER HAD COMMANDEERED Brazell's office. He sat behind the massive wooden desk. He'd lost weight and his cheeks were hollow. His hard expression matched his stiff posture. He didn't waste time with pleasantries. "Report."

Valek and Yelena took turns briefing the Commander on everything that transpired and all they'd learned since the general's brandy meeting.

"Brazell told me that Mogkan showed up at his manor with a group of children," Valek said. "He was looking for a place to hide and he struck a deal with Brazell to help Brazell become the next Commander. Once Mogkan achieved enough power to reach your mind from MD–5, they started feeding you Criollo, sir."

"What about the factory?" the Commander asked.

"We have halted production," Valek said.

"Good. Salvage what equipment you can, then burn the factory and any Criollo to the ground."

"Yes, sir."

"Anything else?"

"One more interesting item. Brazell said that once he and Mogkan had control of Ixia, they planned to take over Sitia."

The Commander huffed. "Brazell's trial will be tomorrow. You're dismissed."

Valek and Yelena left the office. While ecstatic that Ambrose had returned, Valek hoped the diamond hard edge to the man would soften with time. It was understandable. Ambrose hated magicians and to be enslaved by one... Valek shuddered. However, there had been a few positives to that time. The Sitian trade treaty. The delegation of work. The feast. Although, Valek suspected it would be a very long time before the Commander would allow himself to relax. If ever.

BRAZELL'S TRIAL was a quick affair. They held court in the dining room. Valek stood to the Commander's right and read a list of criminal charges, while Brazell faced them. It was a long list, and Valek presented evidence for each offense.

The Commander declared Brazell guilty of all charges, stripping him of his rank and sentencing him to life in prison.

As in every trial the Commander presided over, the accused was permitted to say a few last words.

Brazell shouted to the audience of soldiers, advisers, and officers, "You fools. Your Commander's a deceiver. You've been lied to for years! The Commander's really a woman dressed as a man!"

What the hell does that *have to do with anything? Who cares what gender he is? The Commander is the Commander.* It hadn't mattered to Valek when he found out years ago. It had changed nothing.

Valek exchanged a glance with the Commander. His expression remained neutral as the silence continued. Then the audience laughed at Brazell who had used his last chance to apologize or explain his actions to spout nonsense. They jeered at Brazell as he was escorted back to his cell.

COMMANDER AMBROSE HELD a meeting with Irys, Ari, Yelena, and Valek that evening. As he stood in front of the desk with the others, Valek wondered about the choice of attendees. A strange, unsettled feeling churned in his stomach.

The first order of business was the Commander agreeing to honor the trade treaty. Irys smiled and thanked him.

Then he turned to Yelena, and Valek held his breath.

"Yelena," he said in a formal tone, "you have saved my life, and, for that, I thank you. But you have magical abilities that are not tolerated in Ixia. I have no choice but to sign an order for your execution."

Valek grabbed Ari's shoulder, preventing the big man from doing or saying something regrettable. Or was it to prevent Valek from reacting? He waited for the Commander to add a "however." Except the man held out the assassination order to Valek.

Valek stared as comprehension dawned. There would be no "however." The Commander wanted Valek to *kill* Yelena. His stomach felt like he'd just swallowed a mouthful of glass shards and they were ripping him up from the inside out.

"Sir, I've always believed that having a magician work for us would be beneficial and could have prevented this particular situation," Valek said through clenched teeth. "We can trust her." *And I love her.*

"A valid point." The Commander drew back his arm and Valek almost fainted.

"Even though we trust her, even though she saved my life, I must follow the Code of Behavior," the Commander said. "To do otherwise would be a sign of weakness, something I can't afford right now, especially after this business with Mogkan. Plus, the generals and my advisers will not trust her." The Commander extended the execution order to Valek again.

No fucking way. "I won't take it," Valek said, keeping his emotions in check.

"You would disobey a direct order?" the Commander asked.

Yes! "No. If I don't take the order, then I won't have to disobey it."

"And if I make it a verbal order?"

The question tore his heart apart. The C-shaped scar on his chest burned with pain as if the Commander had just carved it anew. Valek had sworn his loyalty to the Commander. "I will obey. But it will be my very last task for you." Valek pulled his knife. If he was forced by his own word to kill his love, then he would do it quick and painless. And then he'd turn the knife on himself.

Ari drew his sword and stepped in front of Yelena. "You'll have to get through me first."

"No, Ari," Yelena said, pushing his weapon down.

She moved closer to Valek. Understanding and love blazed in her gaze. The sudden desire to grab her hand and run away before the Commander could issue his terrible order pulsed in his chest.

The Commander stared at them for three lifetimes. "I've signed the order, per the Code," he finally said. "I will assign someone else to carry it out. It may take a few days for me to find a suitable person." He glanced at Yelena and Irys. "This order is valid in Ixia only. You're all dismissed."

They all bolted from the office before the Commander could change his mind. Valek couldn't quite believe it. He'd gotten his "however," but the Commander had made him suffer for it. Was it a test of Valek's loyalty?

Once they were well away, Ari grabbed Yelena in a hug and whooped with joy. She grinned, but then sobered. Ari set her down and then consulted with Irys on the best way to "escape" to Sitia. There was a lot to do, and they hurried off to start the preparations, leaving Yelena and Valek alone.

He pulled her into his arms, and they kissed passionately. Now that their time together was limited, he wondered why he hadn't kissed her every day. Every hour. Every minute.

They drew apart to catch their breaths.

"Come with me." Yelena invited.

Pain sliced through him. He closed his eyes. "I can't."

Hurt, she turned away.

He pulled her back and met her gaze. "Yelena, you need to learn, you need to find your family, you need to spread your wings and see how far you can fly. You don't need me right now, but the Commander needs me."

Understanding, she hugged him tight. And he savored the touch and committed it to memory.

YELENA, Irys, and the children planned to leave that night. As they'd prepared to go, Valek visited the six soldiers who occasionally performed special operations for the Commander. Valek ordered them all back to the castle on a mission to ensure the castle was safe for the Commander's return. He might have implied that Brazell had sent a force there to prepare for his arrival.

A deep sense of satisfaction settled in his chest as he watched them gather their gear and head west. Any of those six would have taken the Commander's execution order. The rest of the company wasn't qualified.

Good luck in finding an assassin, Ambrose. And by the time he did, Yelena would be safely in Sitia.

If he hurried, he might be able to catch Yelena before she left. As he rushed through the hallways, pounding footsteps sounded behind him. He spun, grabbing the hilt of his dagger.

Dema ran up to him. "I've been looking...all over for you." She puffed.

"What's wrong?"

"The Commander wants to talk with you."

"Now?"

"No, an hour ago."

He cursed. "Do you know what he wants?"

She just stared at him.

"Yes, I know. Stupid question." Valek worried the Commander had changed his mind about Yelena's execution order. Perhaps if he waited to report to Ambrose, it would give Yelena more time to reach the Sitian border. "All right, thanks."

She didn't move. "I'm supposed to escort you."

That was interesting. Did the Commander believe Valek would disobey his summons? No use wasting any more time trying to second guess the Commander, Valek walked with Dema to his office. She chatted about the various tasks that still needed to be completed.

"I'm digging through fifteen years' worth of data. I'll probably have a massive headache when I'm done," she said.

The Commander dismissed her as soon as they entered, which didn't bode well for Valek. He stood stiffly at attention in front of the oversized desk.

"Have a seat, Valek."

"I prefer to stand."

"Sit down, you idiot."

Caught off guard, Valek stared for a moment before perching on the edge of the chair.

"That execution order needed to be signed. I cannot allow a magician to live in Ixia. You were supposed to take the order—"

He jumped to his feet. "She's an Ixian hero!"

"I'm well aware. Are you going to let me finish?"

Valek returned to his seat.

"You were supposed to take the order, read it, tuck it into your pocket, and escort Yelena to the dungeon. Where, with the help of the master magician and that set of lock picks she wears in her hair, she would escape from her cell and then flee to Sitia."

Too stunned to form coherent words, Valek gaped at the Commander. An unprecedented occurrence.

"Only one prisoner a season gets executed. I didn't want you to pull your knife and kill her right there. You would normally have remembered that important fact and not caused a scene." The Commander leaned back. "At least, I now know the depth of your love for her." He gazed at Valek. "And the depth of your loyalty to me."

"I *am* an idiot." Valek sagged in his seat.

Ambrose smiled. "Are you going with Yelena?"

"No."

"Why not?"

Was that a trick question? He had sworn an oath to the Commander. "She needs time to discover the extent of her magical powers. Discover who she is away from here. Away from me."

"And then?"

"I swore—"

"You're allowed to have a life, Valek. You're allowed to take time off. You're even allowed to retire…eventually." The Commander held up a finger. "Like in one or two," a second finger went up, "Decades."

Valek laughed.

"I'm happy you found someone. I was beginning to worry you'd never get over me."

"You'll always be my first love, Ambrose."

He shook his head. "At least, you haven't lost your sense of humor."

AFTER LEAVING the Commander's office, Valek hurried to catch up with Yelena. The party had left the manor a few hours ago, but it wasn't hard to track the group's trail. There were twelve of them and the bubble of magic in the clearing meant they had stopped for the night. Even if the Commander decided to find an assassin tonight, Irys would be a formidable opponent.

Yelena sat by the fire. She appeared to be the only person still awake. Had she been waiting for him? Valek approached and she jumped to her feet and wielded her bo staff. Hmmm, she would also be a formidable opponent. He grinned. *Sitia won't know what hit them.*

He stopped at the edge of the magical barrier and held out his hand. She grasped it with both of hers and he led her deeper into the forest. He wanted to ensure they had privacy. He found a tree with massive buttress roots creating perfect hidden hollows sized for two people.

"Why didn't you come before we left?" she asked him. Her tone indicated she'd been hurt. No wonder she was moping next to the fire.

"I was busy making sure the Commander would have a hard time locating someone to carry out his orders." Valek smiled. "It's amazing how much work there is cleaning up after Brazell." Too much.

"Who is tasting the Commander's food?" she asked.

"For now, I am. But I believe Captain Star would make an excellent candidate. Since she knows who all the assassins are, I think her help will be invaluable."

By Yelena's vicious grin, he knew she approved of her replacement.

"Enough talk," Valek said, guiding her to one of the hollows. "I need to give you a proper send-off."

They lay between the roots, and he kissed her with a passion he'd never felt for another. He cherished and loved her with his heart fully exposed, showing her the depth and extent of his love, making the night's memories last the year they would be apart.

With Yelena wrapped in his arms, Valek had a moment of sheer contentment. He held her as she slept.

This.

This is worth fighting for.

This is worth waiting for.

Unfortunately, the best night of his life ended with the sunrise. Yelena woke and smiled at him, but it soon faded. The time to part had come.

"An execution order hasn't kept us apart before. There are ways to get around it. We *will* be together," Valek said.

"Is that an order?"

"No, a promise."

THE END…AGAIN

THANK YOU!

Thank you for choosing *The Study of Poisons*!

If you like to stay updated on my books and any news, please sign up for my free email newsletter here:

http://www.mariavsnyder.com/news.php

(go all the way down to the bottom of the page)

I send my newsletter out to subscribers three to four times a year. It contains info about the books, my schedule and always something fun (like deleted scenes or a new short story or exclusive excerpts). No spam—ever!

Please feel free to spread the word about this book! Posting honest reviews are always welcome and word of mouth is the best way you can help an author keep writing the books you enjoy! And please don't be a stranger, stop on by and say hello. You can find me on the following social media sites:

- Facebook (https://www.facebook.com/mvsfans)
- Facebook Reading Group - Snyder's Soulfinders (https://www.facebook.com/groups/SnydersSoulfinders)
- Goodreads (https://www.goodreads.com/maria_v_snyder)
- Instagram (https://www.instagram.com/mariavsnyderwrites)

ACKNOWLEDGMENTS

This book wouldn't have been written without the requests, pleads, bribes, and support of my readers, especially my Soulfinders. Thank you so much for your love of Yelena, Valek, and the rest of the denizens of Ixia and Sitia. I really enjoyed writing this book and diving deep into Valek's point of view. I had a blast discovering what he was up to when not with Yelena in *Poison Study*, and loved being able to find creative ways to link the two stories together.

A gigantic thank you to my team of editors for making this book the best possible. Any typos or mistakes to be found are mine. Thanks to Nat Bejin for being my alpha editor and Chief Evil Minion—you always find those story inconsistencies and math mistakes. Thanks to my dynamic duo of beta readers, Reema Crooks and Elle Callow for hunting down those elusive typos, awkward phrases, and flagging plot logic problems. A big thanks also go to my charlie readers, Brittany Clevenger, Jenny Sampson, and Reilly Gahagan for reading through the book with a fresh perspective and highlighting those areas of confusion.

A vast thank you to my creative team!! Thanks to Joy Kenney for designing another gorgeous cover. To Martyna Kuklis for the awesome maps of Ixia/Sitia and the castle complex. And to Dema Harb, the very talent artist who drew Yelena and Valek in the forest. Thanks so much to all of you who made this book extra special!

A huge thanks to Michelle Haring and her staff at Cupboard

Maker Books. You all have been such a wonderful champion of my books and I truly appreciate all your efforts. May Cupboard Maker Books celebrate another 25 years in business!!

A massive thank you to my entire family for their love and support. I can always depend on my husband, Rodney to help me when needed. From last minute requests for sales numbers to running to the post office, he's a good man in a storm, or, in my case, in a panic. Thank you so much! Also a big thank you to my daughter, Jenna, who despite her busy schedule researching brain cancer (sorry, I couldn't resist a mom-brag), took the time to read through this book and give me helpful feedback.

ABOUT MARIA V. SNYDER

When Maria V. Snyder was younger, she aspired to be a storm chaser in the American Midwest so she attended Pennsylvania State University and earned a Bachelor of Science degree in Meteorology. Much to her chagrin, forecasting the weather wasn't in her skill set so she spent a number of years as an environmental meteorologist, which is not exciting...at all. Bored at work and needing a creative outlet, she started writing fantasy and science fiction stories. Twenty-two novels and numerous short stories later, Maria's learned a thing or three about writing. She's been on the *New York Times* bestseller list, won a dozen awards, and has earned her Masters of Arts degree in Writing from Seton Hill University, where she is now a faculty member for their MFA program.

When she's not writing, she's either playing pickleball, skiing, traveling, taking pictures, or zonked out on the couch due to all of the above. Being a writer, though is a ton of fun. Where else can you take fencing lessons, learn how to ride a horse, study marital arts, learn how to pick a lock, take glass blowing classes and attend Astronomy Camp and call it research? Maria will be the first one to tell you it's not working as a meteorologist. Maria welcomes readers to learn more about her and her books at https://www.MariaVSnyder.com